Kitty Hawk
And
The Curse Of The
Yukon Gold

Book One of the Kitty Hawk Flying Detective Agency Series

Iain Reading

This page is dedicated to all those people who like books to have a dedication page.

TABLE OF CONTENTS

PROLOGUE - PART ONE

Back Where The Entire Adventure Began

As soon as the engine began to sputter, I knew that I was in real trouble. Up until then, I had somehow managed to convince myself that there was just something wrong with the fuel gauges. After all, how could I possibly have burnt through my remaining fuel as quickly as the gauges seemed to indicate? It simply wasn't possible. But with the engine choking and gasping, clinging to life on the last fumes of aviation fuel, it was clear that when the fuel gauges read, "Empty," they weren't kidding around.

The lightning strike that took out my radio and direction-finding gear hadn't worried me all *that* much. (Okay, I admit it worried me a little bit.) It wasn't the first time that this had happened to me, and besides, I still had my compasses to direct me to where I was going. But I did get a little bit concerned when I found nothing but open ocean as far my eyes could see at precisely the location where I fully expected to find tiny Howland Island— and its supply of fuel for the next leg of my journey—waiting for me. The rapidly descending needles on my fuel gauges made me even more nervous as I continued to scout for the island, but only when the engine began to die did I realize that I really had a serious problem on my hands.

The mystery of the disappearing fuel.

The enigma of the missing island.

The conundrum of what do I do now?

"Exactly," the little voice inside my head said to me in one of those annoying 'I-told-you-so' kind of voices. "What do you do now?"

"First, I am going to stay calm," I replied. "And think this through."

"You'd better think fast," the little voice said, and I could almost hear it tapping on the face of a tiny wristwatch somewhere up there in my psyche. "If you want to make it to your twentieth birthday, that is. Don't forget that you're almost out of fuel."

"Thanks a lot," I replied. "You're a big help."

Easing forward with the control wheel I pushed my trusty De Havilland Beaver into a nosedive. Residual fuel from the custom-made fuel tanks at the back of the passenger cabin dutifully followed the laws of gravity and spilled forward, accumulating at the front and allowing the fuel pumps to transfer the last remaining drops of fuel into the main forward belly tank. This maneuver breathed life back into the engine and bought me a few more precious minutes to ponder my situation.

"Mayday, mayday, mayday," I said, keying my radio transmitter as I leveled my flight path out again. "This is aircraft Charlie Foxtrot Kilo Tango Yankee, calling any ground station or vessel hearing this message, over."

I keyed the mic off and listened intently for a reply. Any reply. Please? But there was nothing. There was barely even static. My radio was definitely fried.

It was hard to believe that it would all come down to this. After the months of preparation and training. After all the adventures that I'd had, the friends I'd made, the beauty I'd experienced, the differences and similarities I'd discovered from one culture to the next and from one human being to the next. All of this in the course of my epic flight around the entire world.

Or I should say, "my epic flight *almost* around the entire world," in light of my current situation.

And the irony of it was absolutely incredible. Three-quarters of a century earlier the most famous female pilot of them all had disappeared over this exact same endless patch of Pacific Ocean on her own quest to circle the globe. And she had disappeared while searching for precisely the same island that was also eluding me as I scanned the horizon with increasing desperation.

"Okay," I thought to myself. "Just be cool and take this one step at a time to think the situation through." I closed my eyes and focused on my breathing, slowing it down and reining in the impulse to panic. Inside my head, I quickly and methodically replayed every flight that I'd ever flown. Every emergency I'd ever faced. Every grain of experience that I had accumulated along the long road that had led me to this very moment. Somewhere in there was a detail that was the solution to my current predicament. I was sure of it. And all I had to do was find it.

Maybe the answer to my current situation lay somewhere among the ancient temples of Angkor in Cambodia? Or in the steamy jungles of east Africa? Or inside the towering pyramids of Giza? Or among the soaring minarets of Sarajevo? Or on the emerald rolling hills and cliffs of western Ireland? Or on the harsh and rocky lava fields of Iceland?

Wherever the answer was, it was going to have to materialize quickly, or another female pilot (me) would run the risk of being as well-known throughout the world as Amelia Earhart. And for exactly the same reason.

"It's been a good run at least," the little voice inside my head observed, turning oddly philosophical as the fuel supplies ran critically low. "You've had more experiences on this journey around the world than some people do in their entire lifetime."

"That's it!" I thought.

Maybe the answer to all this lies even further back in time? All the way back to the summer that had inspired me to undertake this epic journey in the first place. All the way back to where North America meets the Pacific Ocean—the islands and glaciers and whales of Alaska.

All the way back to where this entire adventure began.

PROLOGUE - PART TWO

The Arctic Trails Have Their Secret Tales

By the dancing dim light of the campfire, the group of men surrounding me looked demonic—light and shadow played off their features and made their faces seem lopsided and horrifically deformed. In such light every scene appears monochromatic, with every detail rendered in shades of only black and orange. True colors are sucked away, and objects are repainted in a hellish tint that makes every face look like a jack-o-lantern and the world look like something out of Dante's Inferno.

"There you go again," the little voice inside my head nagged. "Always making comparisons to books that you've never read."

"Shut up," I told myself. "This is hardly the time to be criticizing my choice of literary references."

Besides, Dante was writing about hell, wasn't he? And the situation that I found myself in was surely the closest thing to hell that I could possibly imagine.

The tallest one of the group walked over to get a better look at me. As he leaned in close, some dark shadows flickered hideously across his face and eyes and caused me to pull away in terror. I tried to push myself backward away from him, but it was difficult, considering that I was sitting on the ground and my hands were bound tightly behind my back. Every move that I made only pulled the binding tighter and made my wrists scream in agony as the wire cut painfully into the skin.

"I never should have come out here," I told myself as the tall one stood up again and continued pacing back and forth, trying to figure out what to do with me. How could I have been so stupid? What had I been thinking, hiking around a deserted ghost town from the Yukon Gold Rush in the middle of the night?

4

What made me even stupider was the fact that ever since I had first set off on my foolish quest, I'd felt a heavy, dark blackness filling every pore of the landscape. But instead of turning back and going home, I had stubbornly dismissed it as merely the dark shadow of the suffering and death that had occurred here so long ago, when thousands of souls had passed through on their way to the empty dreams of the Klondike gold fields. How many of those greedy fools had died chasing after those empty dreams?

"I am no better than them," I thought. I was just as stubborn and foolish as they had been, and now I was paying the price for it.

"I hate to say that I told you so," the little voice in my head said.

"Yes, you did," I agreed. "But right now, that isn't helping. Right now we have to figure out how to get out of here, because these guys are a bunch of greedy fools just like the rest of them, and who knows how far they'll go to protect the secret of their gold."

"What are we going to do with her?" the man with dark blonde hair asked the tall one, who was apparently their leader.

The tall one thought about this for a moment, and there was a long silence, broken only by the crackle of the nearby campfire. My fear of his answer made my heart pound faster and faster.

"There's only one thing we *can* do with her," he said slowly and deliberately, his voice ice cold and emotionless.

I was terrified of what that meant, and as they continued to discuss my fate among themselves, I could feel the tears welling up in my eyes and my breathing becoming shallower and faster with every passing second.

"I promise not to tell anyone," I thought, feeling completely helpless and considering the option of begging them to let me go. "I will promise not to go to the police if you just let me go free."

"Don't be crazy," the little voice in my head scolded. "They aren't stupid. You discovered their secret! You know about their stolen gold!"

I remembered a line from a poem that I'd learned back in high school—a poem about the Klondike Gold Rush and the lengths that men were driven to by their greed and lust for gold.

"*The Arctic trails have their secret tales*," the poem had said. "*That would make your blood run cold.*"

That was exactly how I felt at that moment—as though my blood was running cold. I had discovered the secret tale that these men had tried to keep hidden, and now they had no other choice. They couldn't just let me go. They couldn't trust me to keep their secret. And now they had to deal with it. And that was the part that terrified me.

The men continued their discussion, and a sudden outburst from the tall one broke my train of thought. The discussion had grown quite heated, and he'd finally put an end to it by holding up his palm and cutting off the blonde one in mid-sentence.

"There's no other way," the tall one said simply.

CHAPTER ZERO

My Favorite Adventure Clothing Company

Kitty Alexandra Hawk
P.O. Box 1971
RR1, Tofino, British Columbia
Canada V0R 2Z0

Dear Tilley Clothing Company:

First off let me say that I am a great fan of your entire clothing line, particularly your famous Tilley Hats, of which I own three in different colors. I am also a big fan of one of your latest hat models: the TWA1 Aviator Hat, which I can tell you is an excellent hat for aviators. I can tell you this from experience because I myself am an aviator and have been flying planes for as long as I can remember, which brings me to why I am writing to you today.

My name is Kitty Hawk, and I am writing to you today to ask for your assistance with a project I hope to undertake this upcoming summer. I live on the west coast of Canada in a small fishing village called Tofino, where the annual migration route to Alaska from the warmer waters farther south brings thousands of grey and humpback whales literally past the front door of my house, where I live with my parents. In addition to flying, I am also interested in studying animal behaviors and biology, and it is humpback whales that especially interest me, particularly their social interactions and feeding habits.

Unfortunately, although there are many grey whales that spend their summers near where I live in Tofino, there are only the occasional humpback whales that stop nearby to feed, and then usually only in small groups of one or two whales. As I am interested in the social activities of the humpback whale obviously this somewhat limits my ability to conduct proper research into their behaviours Fortunately for me, however, just a few hours to the north of Tofino (by air, of course) are hundreds of whales that spend their summers in the waters of southeast Alaska near the capital city of Juneau. This brings me to the point of this entire letter, specifically to ask (beg, really) for money to spend the upcoming summer in Alaska flying my photography-equipped floatplane over the feeding grounds of the humpback whales to research and gain insight into behaviours and habits of these amazing and beautiful creatures.

I believe you will find that my financial needs are quite minimal. Essentially all that I require is a modest contribution from my favorite adventure clothing company for fuel to keep flying through the summer. In return I promise to tell everyone I meet about your amazing company and its exceptional line of travel clothing. (In truth, I would have done that anyway, since I truly believe that your company makes the world's best travel and adventure clothing.)

A more detailed research proposal and information on the modest funding requirements is attached to this letter. Thank you for your time, and I hope to hear from you soon.

Most sincerely and gratefully yours, a fellow Canadian,
Kitty Hawk

CHAPTER ONE

My Father Taught Me To Fly...

My mother taught me to surf, but my father taught me how to fly. Fortunately for him, the experience of teaching me was considerably easier than it was for my mother because for my entire life—for as long as I can remember—I have been a pilot.

My mother and father and I live in a small village called Tofino on the far western coast of Canada, on Vancouver Island, where North America meets the Pacific Ocean.

Maybe you've heard of Tofino? It's quite famous, I think. At least it seems to be, judging from the hordes of tourists who invade each year and take over the town for a few months every summer. Some of those tourists even end up sticking around after the weather starts to turn colder, and eventually, after a few years, they might even be grudgingly accepted as "locals."

My mother runs her own yoga studio downtown (and by "downtown," I mean down in the center of the tiny village, between a surf store owned by her brother and an organic bakery run by her best friend), and my father is a pilot for a local airline (and by "airline," I mean he flies seaplanes that carry mail and supplies to remote islands and settlements, as well as tourists, fly-fisherman, and even the occasional Hollywood celebrity).

When I was still just a baby, my father would take me with him on his various flight runs all over Vancouver Island. My parents figured it was easier for him to take me with him in the plane as opposed to having me stay with my mom at her yoga studio. The logic was simple: In the yoga studio with my mother teaching classes and rushing around running her business, she couldn't properly keep an eye on me as I crawled off into various corners and got myself into all sorts of trouble. Up with my father in his seaplane, however, I was securely strapped into the seat next to him, atop a stack of old phonebooks and pillows and unable to go anywhere or get into any trouble.

As a child, I was always fascinated by the various dials and switches and levers in the cockpit of my father's seaplane. As my father tells the story I was always reaching out with both hands, trying to grab the control wheel in front of me in the co-pilot's seat.

"Do you want to try flying the plane, Kit?" he asked me one day when I was still very young.

I don't know what I said in reply or if I was even able to speak at that point in my life, but whatever I said or did, it was the right answer, because my father leaned over to readjust the phonebooks and pillows so I could sit closer, grasp the wheel with both hands, and fly the plane.

He was amazed, he said, by how I instantly took to it. Of course I had no idea what I was doing, but my father says that what amazed him the most was that I simply grasped the wheel and held the plane level instead of doing exactly what kids always do in such circumstances, which is to treat everything like an indestructible toy, pushing and pulling and spinning the control wheel as though there were no consequences. But I didn't do that, my father said. I held it perfectly level, and after a moment he actually took his own hands off of the controls and let me fly the plane all by myself.

Can you imagine that? There we were, the two of us thousands of feet above the surface of the Earth, with a baby flying the plane.

I was a natural, my father said. And maybe that shouldn't have surprised him all that much since I am named after the town where Orville and Wilbur Wright made the very first successful powered-aircraft flight in history: Kitty Hawk, North Carolina. From the day I was born, it seems, I was destined to fly.

In the years that followed my own first historic flight, my father gradually taught me how to fly a plane for real. Not just holding it straight and level but actually flying it, executing turns and other maneuvers. And when I was a bit older he also taught me takeoffs and landings as well. (Apparently, my father wasn't comfortable with letting a four-year-old execute these more challenging maneuvers—and I can hardly blame him.)

To my father, flying was an art form, but it was also a science, and in all of his teaching he never had any philosophical thoughts or words of ancient wisdom to share with me about the nature of flying. Those kinds of ideas were the sorts of thing my mother would have taught me, but instead my father taught me about numbers and calculations and finite, defined parameters. And one of the most important lessons he taught me was how to find the beauty and awe in numbers as well. And how to respect them.

I don't know how my mother felt about my father teaching me to fly, but she was always supportive of me in whatever I tried to do. She was always the first to cheer when I succeeded and the first to pick me up after I had fallen down. And she knew that more than anything in life I wanted to fly.

"Look, Kitty! A hawk!" she would sometimes say, grabbing my hand and pointing to the sky when she and I would take long walks together.

I would look up, and sure enough, hundreds of feet overhead, floating on the updrafts of invisible air, there would be the dark silhouette of a hawk wheeling and turning high above us. My mother knew that this was exactly how I felt when I was flying—like a hawk riding a warm rising air current, twisting and spinning free.

"A hawk," my mother would tell me. "Just like your name, Kitty. Just like you."

A hawk. Just like me.

...But My Mother Taught Me To Surf

My mother always used to tell me that courage was not the absence of fear, but the mastery of it. She was always full of wise sayings like this and always knew what to say to keep me from running away from the world and burying my head in the sand. She understood that I wanted to do amazing things in my life, and whenever doubts crept into my head she would always be there, saying the perfect thing to make me believe in myself again.

She was the grounded one in our family, she always said. When I was little I used to think that this meant she wasn't a pilot like my father and was always the one who stayed on the ground while dad and I took to the skies. But as I got older I realized that wasn't what she meant at all. She was every bit as adventurous as my father and I were. She just chose to challenge the world in completely different ways.

My mother taught me how to surf. This might sound funny, considering that I come from a small, nowhere village on the west coast of Canada, but even though there are no McDonald's or Starbucks or Wal-Mart stores in Tofino, there are mountains and islands and whales and bears and hippies, and most important of all there is surfing. Not the Hawaii or California type of surfing that you see in movies with giant waves and long, perfect rides, but in summer the waves are often worth getting out of bed for, and during the cold, wet winters when the winter storms howl in from the open Pacific, they stir up fairly respectable waves on the endless stretches of beach.

One day when I was still young I was sitting in the kitchen having breakfast, when my mother suddenly fluttered in and announced that we were going for a walk. She deposited me next to her in the front seat of her old beat-up pickup truck.

We drove a bit, singing along together, and then pulled into a small parking lot off the road from Tofino to Ucluelet.

"Are you ready, Kit?" my mother asked. "We're about to enter an enchanted forest."

"Will there be fairies?" I asked, wide-eyed and excited.

"Of course there will be," she replied. "And many other amazing creatures. But the one I really want to introduce you to is his majesty, the Cedar."

She took my hand and led me into the most amazing forest I had ever seen. Of course it wasn't my first walk in the forest, but somehow that day everything looked like I was seeing it for the first time. Everything around us was filled with vivid colors, green and gold, and little drops of water sparkled on the leaves and branches like little twinkling stars.

"Look, Mommy!" I cried out as a tiny winged creature buzzed past us. "A fairy!"

Okay, the adult me admits that it was probably just a dragonfly, but on that day it was a fairy, and no one could have ever convinced me otherwise.

"Come on, sweetheart," my mother said. "And meet the king of the forest."

She took my hand, and we approached an enormous tree trunk. I craned my neck to look up and see the top of it, but it was so high that it just seemed to disappear into the sky.

I stepped back, afraid, because to me it looked more like a giant than the king of the forest.

"Don't be scared, Kit," my mother said. "He is a wise old king who guards this entire forest. Give him a hug, and you'll see that he's not scary at all."

I approached the tree carefully and touched it first with one outstretched finger. Then two. Then three. And finally with the palm of my entire hand. His skin was rough and old, but as I drew closer I became less afraid and was convinced that I could feel him breathing. I closed my eyes and leaned forward to put my entire body next to his and gave him a hug, just as my mother said to.

Was that his heart beating, I wondered. Or was it mine?

Farther down was my mother with her eyes closed. She was also leaning forward with her arms wrapped around the tree.

My mother was a bit of a hippy, I should probably mention. Although I'll bet you've probably already guessed it by now.

"Can you feel his heart, Kitty?" my mother whispered. "It's the biggest heart I've ever felt."

My mother took my hand, and we continued down the path toward the beach, passing more majestic cedar trees as we went.

"Humans tend to only be concerned with what's best for themselves," my mother said as we made our way through the cathedral of cedar trees. "But everything in nature has to live in harmony with everything else. Nature lives and breathes in different ways that we humans do and everything in nature has an awareness of the surrounding universe that we human beings lost a long time ago."

She was right. And she was about to show me how right she was.

Leaving the forest behind we continued out onto the beach, where a duffel bag and two surfboards were leaning up against some old sun-bleached driftwood logs. Apparently, my mother had already been down there earlier that morning.

"Here, Kit," my mother said, pulling a brand-new wetsuit from the bag and handing it to me. "I bought this for you. Try it on."

Pulling on a wetsuit for the first time isn't easy, but somehow my mother helped me struggle into it and zipped me up in the back. Then she grabbed one of the surfboards under her arm and took my hand to walk with me down to the water.

It was a cold, grey day, and I remember that at first I was frightened of the dark waves crashing down behind me. I was worried that they would flip me upside down, and I would be trapped underwater.

"Don't be frightened, Kit," my mother said over the roar of the surf, smiling so brightly that her eyes lit up. "Twenty-four hours a day, seven days a week, 365 days a year, the waves are always coming here, crashing on this beach. Just as they have for a million years and will do for a million more. The waves and wind are all part of how the planet breathes."

I looked at her dubiously, then back at the crashing waves behind us.

"Just close your eyes, Kit," she said. "You are a part of this planet too. Don't you want to feel the Earth breathe? Just for an instant?"

I did want that. I did want to feel the Earth breathe. So that was that. I simply had to find the courage to get on that surfboard.

And of course my mother was right. The instant the first wave swelled up behind me and galloped forward, surging and carrying me along with it, I felt an incredible sense of power and invincibility. I was too young to understand it then and probably still don't understand it now. And maybe I never will understand it, but every surfer in the world knows what I am talking about, just as every surfer in the world is equally at a loss for words to describe it. But when that wave takes hold of you and lifts you up and carries you along, you feel for an instant like you are one with the entire universe.

Maybe my mother said it better than anyone else ever will. It is feeling the Earth breathe.

Best Friends And Great Spirits

My best friend in the entire world is Skeena Martin. I first met her all the way back in preschool, where we shared a common love of messy finger-painting and carrot sticks. Since then we've been through just about everything together. School, sleepovers, camping trips, family get-togethers, playground bullies, first crushes on boys, second crushes, high school. Just everything.

Skeena was there when I slipped on the rocks out at Chesterman Beach and chipped my tooth. She was the one who searched through the tidal pools to find the missing piece of tooth in the hope that the dentist could reattach it, finally picking it out of the grip of a hungry sea anemone while I held my bleeding mouth and cried.

Skeena was also there when I built a tent out of blankets and sheets in my bedroom, opened the windows to let the freezing winter air inside, and pretended I was a famous arctic explorer. I was dressed in my warmest winter parka, but Skeena had not expected to be exploring in subzero temperatures on that particular sleepover and had only brought a thin jacket with her. But she never complained about it and helped me to discover the North Pole.

Skeena was even there, staying up with me all night with tissues and hugs, as I cried my eyes out after Toby Richardson broke my heart in the ninth grade when he asked me to go with him to the junior high school prom and then later cancelled when Rebecca Perry agreed to go with him instead.

Need I say more? I don't need to explain. Everyone knows all the important things that make up a best friend.

Skeena is a member of a local Indian tribe known as the Tla-o-qui-aht First Nation, a fact for which I am eternally grateful, because thanks to her I have learned and experienced many aspects of their culture that I would never have been able to otherwise. And because her people have lived and worked on the lands and waters surrounding Tofino for hundreds and thousands of years, there is a lot that can be learned from them.

It was also through Skeena that I got to know her grandfather, Joseph, one of the elders in the Tla-o-qui-aht First Nation and a man who commanded great respect from his family and from the community.

Skeena's grandfather had played an important role in stopping logging companies from harvesting the trees on Meares Island back in the 1980s. The island was part of the tribe's land and home to some of the oldest trees in the world, and they owed their existence, in part, to Skeena's grandfather.

"You have to honor the land," he said as we walked slowly through the trees of Meares Island. He was already in his nineties but still delighted in taking long walks with Skeena and me, each of us holding one of his big, rough hands as he led us through the dense rainforest.

"The Great Spirit is our father, but the Earth is our mother," he said, his voice deep and slow as he carefully measured every word before he spoke it. "Kitty, when you fly up in the sky don't forget that you are sharing the sky with the birds and the clouds and the sun and moon and stars. When you are swimming in the ocean you are sharing it with the fish and the kelp and the…"

"And whales," I said, grinning.

"Yes, and whales," he agreed, grinning his toothless grin. "And you share the land with the trees and bears and wolves and every other living thing.

"Sky, water, land," he said, holding his palm flat out, high, low, middle, as he spoke. "Wherever we are in this world we are not alone. We are not the only creatures who find life in the sky and water and land. We are not the only creatures who need it. And we cannot just take and take and take. We have to give. And we have to respect."

We continued our slow hike under the enormous cedars towering above us, some as tall as office buildings. We came to an ancient spot where a mammoth cedar stood before us. Its bark was cracked and scratched and gnarled from immense age, but somehow it was still living. Still breathing.

"This tree is more than eighteen hundred years old," Skeena's grandfather told us. "It has watched the changing of the seasons here in this very spot for dozens of human lifetimes. And there are many others like it. This is what the logging companies wanted to cut down."

He sat down on a nearby log to rest for a moment before continuing his story. "We call the cedar the 'tree of life,'" he said. "Because it has brought life to my people for hundreds of generations. We believe that one day the Great Spirit looked down on the world and saw a man who was very generous. This man was always giving of himself and helping others around him. The Great Spirit smiled at this and when that man died the Great Spirit created the cedar tree in his honor and the very first one grew at the spot where he was buried and spread out across the land so that the cedar would continue to give and help my people.

"We believe that the cedar has its own spirit. And it is a generous spirit. But when man takes, he must also know when to stop taking. And when to give. But some men just take and take and take and do not know when to stop. They do not believe that they need to stop. Until they have taken everything."

He grasped Skeena and I by the hands and looked at each of us gravely. "You have to honor life. And you have to respect."

Skeena and I both nodded solemnly. "We will," we both whispered.

"I know you will," he replied. "Now help an old man up again, and we'll go into town for some ice cream."

The Rise And Fall Of Angkor Wat

Every proper story has both a protagonist and an antagonist—at least that's what we learned in Mrs Cox's English class. I suppose that makes me the protagonist—the heroine. (Aren't all of us the heroes in the stories of our own lives?)

I always liked that word 'antagonist'. I like how it is so similar to 'antagonize', which of course is exactly what an antagonist does. I also liked the word because it describes perfectly the antagonist in the story that is my life.

If every story has both a protagonist and an antagonist, then without a doubt the antagonist in my life story is Amanda Phillpott.

My antagonist.

My nemesis.

The arch-villain in the small stories that make up normal daily life.

In the complicated world of high school society, Amanda is considered one of the "smoker kids." You know the ones. The ones who hang around smoking at the edge of the woods just off school property between classes and after school. Amanda drives a beat-up, crappy pickup truck with a busted muffler and lives with her parents in a beat-up, crappy house in the middle of downtown Tofino with nasty hand-painted signs on the front lawn informing tourists that the space in front of the house is not a parking lot and warning them what will happen to their cars if they park there.

I am not sure where I fit into the high school social hierarchy. Actually, I lie. I am a nerd. I know it. Who am I kidding?

And nerds do not hang around with the smokers.

But it wasn't always that way between Amanda and me. In fact, she and I grew up together and were once even friends, long ago. (Isn't that the way it always is with heroes and villains?) We played together on the same playgrounds. We went to the same kindergarten and grade school. And we went to the same beaches.

And that's where the trouble began. On the beach.

It all happened on a beautiful summer day out at Long Beach when we were both still very small. Old enough to be in school but still young enough to enjoy it.

I remember the day with perfect clarity. It was a beautiful summer day on the west coast. One of those amazing days of blue skies and misty green forests. Hot enough to make plunging into the cold Pacific Ocean a welcome relief instead of a horrific shock that forces you to inch slowly into the water one body part at a time. A perfect summer day with forest, sky, ocean, and endless stretches of sand as far as the eye can see.

Back in those days the road from civilization out to Tofino was a lot more primitive than it is nowadays. This meant less tourists around, and the sight of summer surf schools setting up camp on the beaches was still a thing of the distant future. The only people you'd find on the beach on even the most perfect summer day were locals and a few adventuresome souls from the outside world.

One of the favorite pastimes of beachgoers on Canada's west coast is building various structures from the miles of bleached-white driftwood that lines the beaches. The driftwood comes in all shapes and sizes—from enormous logs that were once the trunks of the proud giants of the forest to tiny twigs polished perfectly smooth by the waves and sand. This abundance of easily accessible and varied building material is irresistible to amateur architects and engineers of all ages, and you always find the constructions of those who came before you on the beaches.

Some of the constructions are quite modest. A small house perfect for doll-sized inhabitants, perhaps. Some constructions are considerably more ambitious and leave most people speculating about exactly how it was that the builders got such huge pieces of wood up into such complicated positions.

Some constructions seem to be built out of necessity. Simple driftwood lean-to's to keep out the wind and rain and sun are a popular design. Or the ever-popular log cabin design, both built more for fun than actual protection from the elements.

Other constructions seem ancient. Every beach always has at least one of these. Constructions that seem as though they have stood sentinel on these sands at the edge of the world since the beginning of time. Like temples of some long-vanished civilization with primeval fire pits at their center that speak of long-forgotten rituals and glorious feasts. At least, that's how I like to think of them. The pre-historic builders of these ancient shrines are more likely a group of older teenagers who came down to the beach the previous weekend to drink beer and have a glorious feast of marshmallows and chip dip.

On the beaches I was a builder too, and of course I tried my hand at driftwood structures from time to time, but my preferred medium of architectural expression was in sand—the timeless art of sandcastle building. And it was over a sandcastle on this particular summer day that the trouble with Amanda Phillpott began.

In response to my fascination with the "ancient driftwood temples" of the beaches and my speculation as to their origins, my mother had given me a picture book of the various amazing structures of the ancient world. You know the type of book I mean. The Pyramids of Giza, Mayan temples, Stonehenge, all those kinds of things. But the one that really caught my eye and fired my imagination was in the far-off jungles of Cambodia: the temples of Angkor. And so it was on that particular summer day that I decided to reconstruct the temple of Angkor Wat on the beaches of western Canada.

My mother helped me find pictures from all different angles on the internet and maps and sketches that we printed out and took with us to the beach. She camped herself out in an abandoned driftwood lean-to with a book while I went to work farther down the beach.

I worked my way from the outside in, pacing off a square five meters to each side, then digging the moat and building the outer walls and towers first. Halfway through this first step of the project I started to question my decision to build on such a large scale, but I was determined and continued digging.

For the next phase of the construction I marked out a square for the inner walls and built up the various structures in-between: the gallery of one thousand Buddhas, the libraries, and finally the inner walls and towers.

By the time I finished this second step of the construction, I had already been on the beach for hours. I was tired and sunburned and ready to quit. But I wouldn't give up. There was only one step left. Only one building left to complete. And that was the most exciting of all. The inner temple of Angkor Wat itself with its soaring rounded towers and perfect angular symmetry.

But this final step was the most difficult of all. The towers kept crumbling as I tried to build them up. I kept falling into the already constructed inner walls as I struggled to work on the tiny details of the temple, and I was forced to patch them up time and time again. But after a long, hard day of work I finally did it. I finally finished my masterpiece.

My mother was very impressed. She made me sign my name and write the date in the sand before snapping some artsy pictures from every angle with her new digital camera.

"Amazing, Kit," she said. "You did it. You really did it."

Smiling from ear to ear, I looked up at her proudly, then back to my western Canadian Angkor again. It really *was* amazing. I couldn't believe I had actually done it and not just given up halfway through, as I had wanted to do about a hundred different times.

I was suddenly very aware of how hot and sweaty I was after having spent the entire day building. "Let's go swimming," I suggested. And so we did.

Diving into the water was heavenly, and I could feel the grit and sweat of the day washing away after just an instant in the cold ocean. Splashing out past the waves I floated on my back for a while, arms outstretched, eyes closed to the setting sun and dreamed of the tiny inhabitants of my Cambodian temple.

I floated around for a little while, then my mother and I trudged back up the beach to towel off and head home for dinner.

"I am going to take one last look at Angkor Wat before we leave," I told my mother as I raced off.

"See you back at the driftwood house," she called after me.

And that's when I saw her.

Amanda Phillpott.

She was standing in the middle of my sandcastle replica of Angkor Wat, carefully stomping on the meticulously built walls and smashing the intricately constructed towers with a plastic shovel.

"Amanda!" I shrieked. "What are you doing?"

Amanda looked up from her campaign of demolition and grinned an evil grin before running off down the beach, leaving one final splashy footprint in the moat as she did so.

Tears filled my eyes as I slowly approached the ruins. In my imagination I could see smoke rising from the collapsed towers and the bodies of a thousand tiny Cambodians littering the grounds of the temple in the wake of Amanda's destructive rampage.

"Why?" I cried to myself as I surveyed the devastation. "Why did she do this?"

And that's when I saw it. The final coup de grace. In a spidery scrawl in the sand next to my signature, Amanda had added some text of her own.

CONSTRUCTED BY
KITTY A. HAWK
27 JULY 2000

Destroyed by Amanda
27 July 2000

CHAPTER TWO
Some Postcards And A Good Meal

I t was a Thursday in June when "the letter" arrived. I had just walked in the front door after getting home from school and saw it there, propped up on the pottery vase in the center of our wooden kitchen table. A simple white envelope addressed to me with a return address that read Alex Tilley, Tilley Endurables, Toronto, Ontario, Canada.

It was the response to my letter asking for money for my crazy summer project to go to Alaska to study humpback whales. I knew it was a crazy idea, but I had tortured myself over that letter for days. Writing and rewriting it. Discarding drafts and starting over time after time. I was convinced that I sounded too desperate, and of course I was, but crazy idea or not, studying the whales was something I wanted to do more than anything. But the question was, why would some company that had no idea who I was just send me some money? Who was I, after all? I wasn't some world-famous animal researcher or something. I was just a teenager.

I walked over to the table and looked at the envelope for a moment. I was scared to pick it up. And when I finally got up the courage to do so, my heart sank down into my already heavy stomach. The letter was awfully thin. That was a bad sign.

"Oh well," the little voice inside my head told me. "It was worth a try. You knew that it was a long shot."

With a resigned sigh I tore the envelope open and pulled the letter out. With another sigh I read, my eyes darting from line to line.

My summer adventure was on.

My crazy idea wasn't so crazy after all.

Maybe I convinced them that I wasn't just a kid. Maybe it was my carefully thought-out research plans that I attached to the letter that convinced them that I was worth supporting. Maybe it was the clever diagrams and photographs of the ingenious camera mounts I had designed to mount on the outside of my floatplane that would allow me to extensively document the activities of the whales as I flew above them. Or maybe it was that I had clearly thought of every possible way to minimize the cost of the entire expedition—by arranging to stay with Skeena's relatives in Juneau and eliminating the expense of room and board, by begging and borrowing all the photographic and technical equipment that I needed, and by saving up for my own share of the cost by working part-time over the winter and picking up extra money working odd jobs whenever possible.

Or maybe it was just that I was a kid, after all. And they simply felt sorry for me.

Whatever it was, it must have worked because the thin envelope contained a brief but encouraging letter from Alex Tilley, a gift certificate from the Tilley online store (in case I needed "any additional outfitting for my expedition"), and a check! I couldn't believe it! A check covering all of my additional expenses plus "a little extra for some postcards and a good meal," Alex Tilley had written.

The ecstatic scream that I let out upon seeing that check sent the crows flying off in all directions from the fir trees surrounding my house. Exploding out of the back door, I ran and ran and ran, screaming all the while and waving the check over my head like a prized trophy. I was halfway down the beach to the ocean before it occurred to me how easily a gust of wind could tear the check from my hands and send me on a fruitless chase down the endless beach trying to recapture my prize. I shuddered at the thought of writing back to Tilley to ask for a replacement check. They would definitely realize then that I was just some stupid kid, and they would call the whole thing off.

Safely tucking the precious slip of paper into my zippered jacket pocket, I continued my crazed run down the beach, waving my arms madly and doing a little end-zone celebration dance at the edge of the water, like a football player who'd just scored a touchdown.

Somewhere behind me a dog barked, and I looked up to see our neighbor, old Mrs. McCready and her ancient yellow Labrador, Wilson, walking past.

"Hi, Mrs. McCready," I called out to her, blushing and waving sheepishly. "I'm going to Alaska."

"I never doubted it, Ms Hawk," she replied, looking at me over the lenses of her half glasses. Some of the money I'd saved up to pay for my expedition came from doing various cleaning jobs around the McCready property, just up the beach from our house. "I hope that doesn't mean you're too rich to come over this week and clear the branches from the roof and yard," she said in her endearing, stern, old-lady kind of way.

"No, Mrs. McCready," I replied. She gave me a nod and continued down the beach with Wilson walking stiffly at her heels.

For a while I just stood there, closing my eyes and turning my face to bask in the warm June sunshine and feel the cool breeze racing in off the Pacific Ocean. Without even thinking about it, the pilot inside me instinctually gauged the direction and speed of the wind, making mental adjustments as though I were preparing for takeoff.

But in a way I *was* preparing to take off, wasn't I? I was going to Alaska.

An Adventure Beyond Words

The next few weeks were a complete blur. Somehow I managed to organize all my equipment and provisions, finalize flight plans, buy new clothes, arrange my accommodations in Alaska, reassure my mother that I was going to be fine (this took a little bit of help from Dad, of course), pack and load everything aboard my floatplane, and of course write a heartfelt thank-you letter to Alex Tilley.

Oh right, and somewhere in there I also found the time to write my school exams and somehow graduate from high school.

I have no idea how I did it, but before I knew it, I was sitting in the cockpit of my trusty De Havilland Beaver out on the waters of Clayquot Sound, about to push the throttle forward to bring the engine to life and head for Alaska.

"This is it," I said to myself. "This is where my adventure begins."

And with that, I powered up and started my takeoff run across the inlet. The seaplane skipped and skimmed across the water, gaining speed as I went, but then I saw the tip of a sea kayak emerging from underneath the main pier in downtown Tofino, directly across my takeoff path.

I immediately reached forward and throttled back down again, letting the resistance of the water slow me down so I could taxi back and make another run at it. As strange as it might sound, protocol and the rules of right-of-way required me to do this. My dad always used to joke that Tofino was the only airport in the world where a tourist in a kayak can abort a takeoff or landing.

Except that this wasn't a tourist. Squinting my eyes against the bright sun to see the person who had cut me off, I recognized her. The person paddling the kayak out in front of me was Amanda Phillpott.

Hearing my cell phone chime from the seat next to me, I reached over to check it. It was a new text message from Amanda. (You might wonder why I had Amanda's telephone number saved in my phone, but if you came from a town as small as Tofino you'd understand. Everyone knows everything about everyone, including the phone numbers of their arch-enemies.)

oops sorry kitty. didn't see you there

"Whatever," I thought, shaking my head and taxiing back around to line up for takeoff again.

I waited for her to paddle out of the way, then did another final check and pushed the throttle forward again. The engine roared, and I was off for a second time, skimming across the waters of Clayquot Sound on my way to Alaska.

But then I watched in disbelief as Amanda turned her kayak around and paddled back toward the dock and across my path again.

"What the hell is she doing?" I thought angrily as I powered down again to turn around for a third attempt at takeoff.

My phone chimed again. Another message from Amanda.

sorry kitty. i forgot that i have to meet someone in town for lunch. no kayaking for me today

"Oh for God's sake," I thought as I circled back around.

I waited for her to be safely out of the way and back at the dock before I powered up yet again and started across the inlet. I had just started to gain speed again when the nose of her kayak reappeared from behind the pier and crossed in front of me yet again.

Are you kidding me?

oops again kitty. my lunch date cancelled. i get to go kayaking after all.

I was ready to scream in frustration, but somehow managed to stay cool as I turned around, yet again, to line up for another takeoff attempt. This time I waited for Amanda to paddle off far enough so that she wouldn't be able to interfere with me anymore, and I finally pushed the throttle forward and started my final takeoff run.

That third time I was successful, and as I took to the air I looked back at the beaches and trees as the earth fell quickly away behind me. It was an amazing feeling. I was finally on my way.

As I turned the wheel and banked to the right, I was surprised at how lonely I suddenly felt. I'd taken off from Tofino hundreds of times before, sometimes as many as ten or twelve times a day, and on days exactly like this one, but somehow this felt different. Maybe it was because I knew that this time I wasn't just popping over to a neighboring island to drop off some groceries or just going up to breathe and be free for a while. This time I was flying head-on into the most exciting adventure of my life.

"No time for feeling lonely, Kit," I imagined my mother saying. "There's a big mountain up there in front of you that you probably want to avoid crashing into."

I pulled back a bit more on the controls and climbed higher and higher until the islands and water were gradually replaced by snow-capped mountains and glaciers. Off to my right the rising sun was making its way up into the sky over the most beautiful landscape of craggy peaks covered with ice and snow, like a giant frosty playground.

It was going to be a beautiful day with hardly a cloud in the sky, and as I leveled out to my cruising altitude, with the blinding white rocky peaks stretching away as far as the eye could see, I relaxed and thought a bit.

"Oh my God, Kitty, I can't believe it!" Skeena had half-shrieked when I told her the news that I was really going to Alaska a few weeks earlier. "My uncle will be so happy to see you!"

Skeena's uncle and aunt were the ones living in Juneau, Alaska, who had offered to let me stay with them all summer. Free of charge of course.

"Are you sure they will be happy?" I asked uncertainly, suddenly realizing how much of my plan depended on the generosity of others. "Are you sure they won't mind?"

"Don't be stupid," Skeena replied. "Ever since their twins moved north to work on the oil rigs, my Aunt Jenny has been bored out of her head. She can't wait to see you and show you around."

"Show me around?"

"Yeah, you know, like the Wal-Mart and the cruise-ship docks. Sarah Palin's former governor's mansion. Stuff like that." Skeena replied. "And exciting downtown Juneau."

I figured Juneau, the capital of Alaska, must be a metropolis compared to Tofino. Especially if they had an actual Wal-Mart. The citizens of Tofino would never allow such a monstrosity to desecrate their town.

"Don't worry, Kit," Skeena continued, seeing the look that must have crossed my face. "It's also beautiful there. There's waterfalls and glaciers and everything. Just make sure you don't get stuck in the Wal-Mart all day with Aunt Jenny."

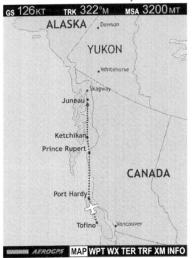

Smiling at this memory, I brought my thoughts back to the present to check my navigation. Flying to Juneau wasn't just a simple hop over the water. My De Havilland Beaver didn't have the range to fly that far, so I had to make the journey in smaller, more manageable steps to refuel along the way, as I hopped like a frog up the western coast of British Columbia and into Alaska. From Tofino to Port Hardy,

Port Hardy to Prince Rupert, Prince Rupert to Ketchikan, and finally Ketchikan to Juneau. The trip would take me most of the day, but I'd made an early start, and as I flew onward the sun continued to climb into the sky off to my right.

Continuing past the highest of the mountain tops, I was close enough to catch a glimpse of patches of brilliant blue ice hiding underneath the snow. If you've never seen it before, trust me when I say that you can't imagine a more beautiful color in the world than bright glacier blue.

"You look for the glaciers when you're in Alaska," Skeena's father had told me a few days earlier. "You won't be able to miss them. Like ragged blue highways of ice across the land for giants."

Checking my navigation again, I calculated that soon I would be approaching the first of my stops for the day, Port Hardy, British Columbia. I reached over to the drink holder to take a sip of my nearly cold coffee. I tried to remember if Port Hardy had a Starbucks. I liked Starbucks, but like Wal-Mart, the residents of Tofino would never allow such a thing anywhere near the town.

I took the final sip of coffee and squinted into the distance to see if the town coming into view just ahead of me looked anything like Port Hardy. I hoped that it was, since I had to pee fairly urgently.

Putting the coffee thermos back in its holder, I saw in the distance the bright white shape of a ferry on the water heading toward the town up ahead. It looked like I was in the right place, since Port Hardy had the only ferry terminal for miles around.

I had almost completed my first step on the way to my destination. My mother would be so relieved.

"Don't worry, Mom. I will be fine," I had told her for the thousandth time the night before, sounding more sure of this fact than I actually felt on the inside.

"I know, Kit. I know. It's just..." Her voice trailed off as she tried to think of what she meant to say. My mother always had ideas so beautiful that she sometimes struggled to find the right words for them—usually because there probably weren't any right words for them. "It's just...I would never stop you from doing this, Kit," she continued. "You have to do this. This is an adventure beyond words, and I am so amazed and proud of you. It's just that you are my little cedar tree, and I love you, and I can't help but worry sometimes."

I knew my mother would never stop me from going. And even though she sometimes struggled to find the right words, I knew exactly what she meant and how proud of me she was. If I ever doubted that she was anything but 100 percent behind me, all I needed to do was think back to a week earlier, when I had just come home after finishing the last of my school exams. I was more tired than I could ever remember being in my life, but somehow I dragged myself home. I had stayed up half the night before studying and packing, and all I could think of at that moment was a hot bath and some sleep. Skeena dropped me off at the top of our driveway, and as I made my way down toward the house I could see my mother waiting for me on the front porch.

"Come on," she said, gesturing toward her truck for us to take a ride. "I want to show you something."

"But mom, I just got here and..."

She held up her palm to shush me.

"Talk to the hand," she said. "No excuses. It isn't far, and trust me, you're gonna want to see this."

"Talk to the hand?" I asked as I reluctantly dragged myself into the passenger seat of her brightly decorated pickup truck. "Mom, I don't even know what that means." She just smiled and dropped the truck into gear and drove off with a spin of gravel.

She was right; it wasn't far. Tofino is a small town, and it wasn't difficult to figure out where she was going—she was heading down to the dock, where my father and I both kept our floatplanes moored. But even though I knew *where* she was going, I couldn't understand why.

As we turned down the road leading toward the docks, I immediately saw the familiar outline of my father's twin-engine Otter among the handful of floatplanes parked below, but I couldn't see my own plane. Mine was a slightly weathered hand-me-down silver-and-grey De Havilland Beaver that used to belong to my father, but he had bequeathed it to me on my seventeenth birthday, when I passed my pilot's license exam. It was one of the most familiar sights in the world to me, but as we drove closer to the dock I couldn't see it anywhere.

"What?!?" I said under my breath, leaning forward in my seat and scanning the dock in increasing panic. Where was my plane? Did my parents decide to not let me go and take my plane away? That wasn't possible. "Where is my...?"

"It's right there, Kit," my mother said, pointing down to an unfamiliar red-and-white plane tied up at my usual parking spot.

"I don't understand..." I said as we drove closer. I took a double and triple take at the red-and-white plane and examined its shape and outline, slowly realizing that it looked very familiar somehow. And then I saw the tail, and the answer finally dawned on me.

Painted on the tail of this gleaming beauty of a plane was the black silhouette of a hawk—the same hawk that I'd been drawing on notepads and in the margins of school books for years. My hawk. I turned to my mother, my mouth open in stunned surprise.

"You see," she explained, smiling. "Every successful adventure needs to be properly outfitted. Your father helped you take care of the technical and mechanical needs for your expedition, so I am not worried about that side of things. But I think every successful adventure also needs a sense of style as well, don't you think?"

She reached behind the seats of the truck to pull out a long, flat white box with a bright purple ribbon tied around it, and she handed it to me.

"What's this?" I asked, still in shock from realizing that this beautiful red-and-white plane floating serenely down at the dock was a freshly painted incarnation of my own De Havilland Beaver.

"Open it and see."

And so I did, pulling the knotted ribbon loose and lifting the lid off of the box. Inside was a brand-new brown leather flight jacket. Sewn into the jacket, just above the right breast, was a black-hawk insignia to match the one on the tail of my newly painted floatplane. My hawk.

"Don't you agree, Kit?" my mother asked, starting to cry a little as she leaned over to hug me. She pulled me so close and tight that I could smell her hair and feel her warmth. "Every successful adventure needs a bit of style, right?"

"A hawk," I whispered, barely able to talk. I was too choked up with emotion and tears.

"A hawk," my mother whispered back. "Just like you."

Just like me.

Funny Money, Crab Fishing And Wal-Mart

As expected, the flight north to Juneau took me most of the day, leapfrogging up the western coastline of Canada and into southeastern Alaska, a thin strip of land separating Canada from the Pacific Ocean.

Each stop along the way was familiar to me somehow. Port Hardy and Prince Rupert were familiar because I had flown there many times before with my father. But even Alaska seemed familiar as well, despite the fact that I had never been there. The rugged, beautiful coastline was comfortingly similar to back home on Vancouver Island. And even the aviation dock in Ketchikan, where I refueled for the last leg of my journey, was reassuringly identical to a hundred other such docks I'd pulled up to and docked at before.

The only difference was the money. Pulling out a small stack of colorful Canadian banknotes to pay for my fuel in Ketchikan, I couldn't figure out the amused look on the face of the grizzled attendant in overalls who had topped up my fuel tanks.

"I don't suppose you have any real money, " he said, with a grin.

For a moment I panicked. What did he mean? Did he think my money was counterfeit? What if he didn't accept my money? What if I was stuck in Ketchikan, forced to work off my debt by doing who-knows-what?

"I don't understand..." I sputtered in reply before my panicking brain rendered me speechless.

He looked at me without a word, still grinning. Then down at the money. Back at me. Then back at the money in my outstretched hand once again.

"Ohhhhhhhh," I replied, realizing my mistake. We both laughed as I stuffed my Canadian money back into the right zipper pocket of my flight jacket and pulled a stack of US bank notes from the breast pocket.

"Usually I don't mind the Canuck funny money," he said. "I can always spend it at the McD's in Prince Rupert on my way down to Seattle, but I wasn't planning to go south again until the fall."

He took the payment and gave me a pat on the back to wish me luck before pointing me toward the customs and immigration office, where I needed to check in now that I was officially on US soil.

Thankfully I was able to get through the customs formalities without any difficulty, and I was soon back up in the air again, heading for Juneau.

"We're on US money now," I thought. "I'll have to remember that."

I had converted most of my funds into US dollars before leaving Tofino, but this was yet another reminder of the adventure I was getting myself into. The ocean and islands and mountains all around me might look reassuringly similar, but I had crossed an invisible border and was now in an entirely different country.

Up ahead, the city of Juneau slowly came into view over the horizon. I made a pass over the city before coming in for a landing, just to have a look around. It was hard to miss with the huge cruise ships tied up at the docks along the waterfront, and down below, the streets were teeming with thousands of cruise-ship tourists.

Passing over the seaplane base, I saw a man and woman standing on the docks looking up at me and waving. I waved back and circled to come in for a landing. "This must be Skeena's aunt and uncle," I thought. And of course it was. They were waiting for me as I pulled up to the dock, and they guided me into my assigned parking spot for the summer.

"You made it! Welcome to Alaska!" Skeena's Aunt Jenny screamed in joy as I shut down my engine and climbed out to meet them. She was a large woman with a beautiful round face and a toothy smile. Everything about her seemed warm and friendly, and even though we'd never met before, that didn't stop her from grabbing me before I was half out of my plane and hugging me, screaming, "You made it!" over and over again as she did so.

"Me either!" I screamed in reply, infected by her overwhelming enthusiasm as we both jumped up and down and hugged again.

"I'm Joe," her partner said quietly, unhooking one thumb from his jeans and holding out a large, callused hand for me to shake. He was a tall, proud-looking man with thick glasses and long black hair tied at the back of his head in a ponytail. And even though he wasn't jumping up and down and screaming in excitement, he still gave me a warm reception. "Welcome to Juneau," he said.

Uncle Joe and I unloaded all of my gear from my plane and carried it up the dock to pack it carefully into the back of his beat-up, old pickup truck. Soon we were on our way and bouncing along the road with Uncle Joe driving, Aunt Jenny at the passenger window, and me squished in between the two of them snugly.

"Do you need anything from Wal-Mart?" Aunt Jenny asked as we drove through the streets of downtown Juneau on the way to their house.

Uncle Joe rolled his eyes. "She didn't come all the way here to go to Wal-Mart." Aunt Jenny reached over me to smack Uncle Joe on the arm.

"Don't worry about me," I said. "I brought plenty of stuff from Tofino. But what I don't understand is how you are related to Skeena and why you're living all the way up here in Alaska."

"It's simple," Aunt Jenny said. "I am Skeena's mother's sister, and I grew up in Tofino, the same as you and Skeena, but when I grew up I met a handsome young man from Juneau and ended up moving out here long before you were even born."

"And then she met me," Uncle Joe said with a smile, stroking his thin moustache with one hand and steering the truck with the other. "And in a real scandal she left this other handsome guy and shacked up with me instead."

Aunt Jenny reached over me again to smack Uncle Joe on the arm.

"He's just teasing," she continued. "Although to be honest there was a bit of a scandal after we met and decided to get married."

"A scandal?" I asked. "Is it because you are from different native tribes?"

Aunt Jenny laughed heartily at this. "Goodness, no!" she replied. "It's true that I'm part of the Tla-o-qui-aht First Nation from around Tofino, same as Skeena. And Joe here is Tlingit. But the scandal was actually because of the fact that Joe was an American, and I was Canadian, and neither of us wanted to go through the hassle of getting a green card to come live with the other one."

"Canadians are weird," Uncle Joe said under his breath, earning yet another smack from Aunt Jenny.

"Anyway," Aunt Jenny continued. "We finally decided it made more sense for me to come up here to Juneau because Joe's fishing permits were Alaskan, and it was easier for him to continue working that way."

"Oh! You're a fisherman?" I asked Uncle Joe. Growing up in a community like Tofino I had been around fishing my whole life. "What kind of fishing?"

"I *was* a crab fisherman," Uncle Joe said, looking at Aunt Jenny with a pretend look of annoyance. "Until Jenny over here started watching too much Discovery Channel and decided it was too dangerous. Stupid damn show. Deadliest Catch. So now I just take the cruise-ship tourists out on my boat and show them what crab fishing is like. The pay is still pretty good, and it's a lot easier."

"And you're home every night for dinner," Aunt Jenny added.

"And I'm home every night for dinner," Uncle Joe agreed. But a faraway look flickered in his eyes for a moment. "But it's not the same, of course." The look in his eyes flickered a moment longer before his grin returned.

"Tell her your idea," Aunt Jenny said, rubbing his shoulder lovingly and changing the topic.

Uncle Joe looked at me. "I thought maybe before you start going up flying every day looking for humpback whales that you'd like to go out on my boat one time, and I could show you the places I know where whales like to feed."

I couldn't believe the incredible generosity of these two. I was speechless and smiling like crazy. I had only been in Juneau for an hour, but Aunt Jenny and Uncle Joe's incredible hospitality already made it feel like home.

"I take it from your smile that this sounds like a pretty good idea?" he asked.

"It's a perfect idea!" I replied. "I just…I don't know what to say except thank you. Thank you so incredibly much. For doing everything for me."

"Oh, don't you worry," Aunt Jenny said. She touched my arm again, and I turned to look at her. "We're practically family already. We're from the same part of the world. Just because I moved all the way up here doesn't change that."

"It's amazing how far you've come from Tofino," I said.

Aunt Jenny snorted a laugh out through her nose in response. "I haven't gone very far at all, Kitty," she said. "But I am happy. And that is more important than anything." She reached over to touch Uncle Joe on the shoulder again. He looked over and smiled at both of us. "And I haven't gone even a tiny fraction as far as you're going to go," Aunt Jenny added.

"I haven't gone anywhere yet," I said, thinking about how Jenny had met Uncle Joe and packed up everything in her life to move all the way to Alaska. I couldn't imagine making such a monumental decision. "She must really love him," I thought.

"Where did the two of you meet, anyway?" I asked.

The two of them turned to look at each other and then broke out laughing.

"What's so funny?" I asked.

"We met in Seattle," Aunt Jenny explained. "In a Wal-Mart."

CHAPTER THREE

Brown Bears, Black Cod And Gold Of Every Color

spent my first morning in Alaska shivering on the deck of Uncle Joe's fishing boat as it cut its way through the lonely, cold maze of inlets that surround the city of Juneau and lead out toward the Pacific Ocean. The world all around us was bathed in blue early-morning light, and somewhere off to the east the sky was just beginning to catch fire in deep reds, oranges, and purples as sunrise approached.

Standing out on the deck, with my arms folded over the side railing, the cold wind cut at my face and chilled me to the bone. My hands were wrapped around a hot cup of Starbucks coffee, which I would sip occasionally and relish the feeling of heat as it flowed down my throat and warmed my insides. But as cold as I was, I refused to go inside out of the wind. I wanted to see and experience everything as intensely as possible. And with every shiver came a welcome reminder that I was living the adventure.

"See this island over here on the left?" Uncle Joe called to me, leaning out a side window of the wheelhouse. I turned my head, following his pointing fingers across the water to a massive ridge of rocky mountains and trees towering over us on the left.

I nodded my head in reply. "How could I miss it?" I said. It was hard to believe it was an island; it was so huge and stretched out into the distance along the coastline. At the edges where the water met the land, the landscape was rocky and rugged, with trees and plants clinging desperately for a foothold to avoid falling into the sea. From there the island rose up in a graceful arc, sweeping toward the heavens in a blanket of trees before tapering off in a dramatic rocky citadel that pierced the patchwork of low-lying clouds cluttering the early-morning sky.

"It's called Admiralty Island, but my people, the Tlingit, call it Xootsnoowú," Uncle Joe said, tilting his head back to look all the

way toward the summit. "That means, 'The Fortress of the Bears.'" He paused for dramatic effect, watching my facial expressions as he wove his story. "And they call it that because this island right here next to us has more brown bears per square mile than anywhere else in the entire world. There are more bears than people living on this island."

My eyes opened wide in amazement, and I turned back toward the island to scan the shoreline. I was hoping to catch a glimpse of a bear walking along the edge of the water, minding its bear business.

"The Fortress of the Bear," I repeated under my breath reverently as I scanned the shoreline up and down.

"Well, that's what my grandfather told me, anyway," Uncle Joe continued. "But I read somewhere recently that some people now think the name means something else instead." Uncle Joe looked off into the distance, quiet for a few moments, and his forehead wrinkled thoughtfully. "People always want to ruin a good story," he said.

We continued along past the island while the rising sun seeped steadily into the air and filled the world with light. It was early, but we were not alone on the water. Other fishing boats made their way past us in both directions, and occasionally Uncle Joe would raise his hand in greeting as they passed by.

We continued up the inlet, and even as the warm sun rose higher in the sky, the cold got a little bit too much for me, and I joined Uncle Joe in the wheelhouse.

"Help yourself to some coffee to warm yourself up," he said, gesturing to my empty Starbucks cup and pointing to a giant thermos in the corner, on top of the morning newspaper.

"Don't mind if I do," I said, heading for the thermos and picking up the paper to scan the morning headlines.

"Local Eagle Causes Power Outage," I read, laughing.

"What's that?" Uncle Joe asked.

I read the article to Joe.

LOCAL EAGLE CAUSES POWER OUTAGE
By Ken Lewis - JUNEAU EMPIRE

About 10,000 Juneau residents lost power Sunday after a bald eagle lugging a deer head crashed into an Alaska Electric Light & Power transmission system in Lemon Creek.

"You have to live in Alaska to have this kind of outage scenario," said Gayle Wood, an AEL&P spokeswoman. "This is the story of the overly ambitious eagle who evidently found a deer head in the landfill."

The meal was apparently too heavy. The eagle failed to clear transmission lines as it flew from the landfill toward the Lemon Creek Operation Center, she said.

Uncle Joe snorted in laughter and reached for his nose. "Oh cripes, I got coffee coming outta my nose!" he said, letting go of the wheel for a moment to grab a box of Kleenex.

"Or how about this one," I continued.

WOMAN PUNCHES BEAR TO SAVE HER DOG
By Jonathan Grass - JUNEAU EMPIRE

Black bears in residential neighborhoods aren't exactly unheard of in Juneau. While many people stay inside when bears are about, one local woman says she had a different instinct when she saw her dog was in trouble.

It started out as a typical evening for 22-year-old Brooke Collins. She let her dogs out as usual but this time, she said there was a black bear outside who took hold of her dachshund Fudge. She said she feared for her pet's life and, in an instant, ran over and punched the bear right in the face to make it let go.

"It was all so fast. All I could think about was my dog was going to die," said Collins.

"It was a stupid thing but I couldn't help it," she said. "I know you're not supposed to do that but I didn't want my dog to be killed."

Collins said when she looked outside she saw a bear was crouching down with Fudge in its paws and was biting the back of the dog's neck.

"That bear was carrying her like a salmon," she said.

She said she almost instinctively went up and did the first thing she thought of. She punched the bear's face and scooped away her dog when it let go.

By the time I was finished reading, Uncle Joe was clutching his stomach, nearly doubling over in laughter. "Oh jeez, stop, stop!" he said, wiping his nose and eyes with Kleenex.

"Ok," I replied. "Something on a more serious note, today's main headline."

FORTUNE IN GOLD STOLEN?
By Iain Reid - JUNEAU EMPIRE

Alaska State Troopers are working with their counterparts in the Royal Canadian Mounted Police to investigate the reported theft of nearly a ton of gold from a former U-Haul moving truck belonging to US citizen John Kilpatrick, better known as "Crazy Alaska Jack".

Residents of the remote gold prospecting towns of Alaska and the Canadian Yukon have been familiar with Mr Kilpatrick for more than thirty years as he prospected his way through various gold claims all over the far North. Nearly everyone was also equally familiar with the heavy duty reinforced U-Haul truck that he called home as he made his way from town to town and claim to claim for more than three decades.

"Every few years or so Crazy Jack would sell the old truck and come see us to buy another used one," said Scott Price, the regional manager of U-Haul in Anchorage. "He seemed to like the trucks somehow and was a well-known face to anyone who's been with our company for a while."

What was not well-known, however, was the incredible fortune in gold that Kilpatrick had stashed in sacks and cardboard moving boxes inside the U-Haul truck and which served as supports for the mattress he slept on.

According to the Alaska State Trooper investigation the boxes which were reported to have disappeared overnight would have contained an estimated one ton of gold valued at more than 50 million dollars. This staggering quantity of gold reported to have been stolen, combined with the unstable mental state of its owner, have left police questioning the legitimacy of the reported theft.

"For the moment we are treating this as a criminal investigation," said Detective Kevin Palin (no relation to the former Alaskan Governor, Sarah Palin). "Our analysis shows that the boxes in question did contain considerable residual gold traces. However, we cannot confirm the full quantity of gold that may have been taken other than based on Mr Kilpatrick's own claims."

"I can't believe he could have stashed away so much gold," said Patricia Summer of Fairbanks, Alaska, owner of the Quick Wash Laundromat who knows Kilpatrick well from his visits over the past ten years. "Even prospecting over thirty years like he did and living so cheap it is simply unheard of to have gotten his hands on so much gold."

The reported theft has fuelled speculation that Kilpatrick may have discovered a previously unknown motherlode of gold somewhere in the gold fields of Alaska or the Yukon and has sparked interest in exactly where Kilpatrick had staked claims over the past thirty years. Requests for the public records of his staked claims have flooded into the relevant local mining offices in Canada and the United States.

"As I said, we're treating this as a legitimate criminal investigation," says Detective Palin. "And from Juneau there are basically only two ways to get to the outside world: by boat north to Skagway and from there by road through Canada. Or south to Seattle. And we have alerted law enforcement on both sides of the border to be on the lookout for anything suspicious."

I put the newspaper down and spread out my navigation charts to see where we were going. "Imagine that," I said. "A ton of gold!"

Uncle Joe laughed a cynical laugh. "I don't believe it for a second," he said.

"Why not?" I asked.

"You remember that mountain hanging over downtown Juneau?" he replied.

"The one with the waterfalls coming down from it like they are coming from out of the sky?" I answered.

"Yeah, that one," he continued. "That's Mount Juneau. And like the city it's named after Joe Juneau, who was a gold prospector who came up here in the 1800s and found gold. He didn't just find gold but actually found a heck of a lot of gold, and for a while we had our own little gold rush around here. But even long after that died down there's *still* a heck of a lot of gold around these parts." Uncle Joe turned to look at me, raising his eyebrows dramatically.

"Still?" I replied.

"You better believe it," he said. "In fact, they say there's more gold right there in Mount Juneau than in any other place on Earth."

I couldn't believe what I was hearing. "What? Really?" I asked in disbelief. "Then why don't they go get it?"

"Simple," Uncle Joe said and shrugged, turning to steer the boat again. "Because it would cost more to take it out than you would make in profit from selling it."

It took me a moment to absorb this information. It was amazing to me that there could be so much gold buried somewhere, but that it was so expensive to mine it that it was impossible to make any money. Uncle Joe watched me working this out in my head for a while.

"But what about the gold rushes we learned about in school?" I asked. "Where prospectors with gold pans found fortunes of gold lying around on the ground waiting to be found?"

Uncle Joe nodded. "That's true," he agreed. "And after they took out as much gold as they could by hand, the mining companies moved in with machines and also took all that they could, while still making a profit, of course." He winked at me. "And then when it just wasn't profitable anymore they moved on, leaving only a small number of individual private prospectors to still search for the next big mother lode, just like the newspaper said."

"But if there's so much gold in Mount Juneau..." I started to say.

"There's a lot of gold in many places up here in Alaska," Uncle Joe said. "But the same question faces anyone who tries to get it out of the ground, regardless of whether they are some big mining company or just private individuals working their own claim."

"And what question is that?" I asked.

"It's the same question that faces gold miners all over the world," he said. "And it's the same whether that gold is golden yellow in color, or black like oil, or any other color."

"And the question?" I asked again.

"Is it profitable?" Uncle Joe said simply. "Because usually it's not. And if it is, well, that's something else we Alaskans have known very well for a hundred years or more. If something is profitable, then some people will do anything and destroy anything to get at it."

It occurred to me at that moment just how wise Uncle Joe was.

"Gold miners are lazy," he said, turning toward me again, that familiar grin on his face. "They want to find it lying around on the ground, like back in the days of the gold rushes. But nowadays all people can do is keep looking for the next mother lode. And so far no one has found it."

Spouts, Flukes And Whale Breath

By the time we spotted our first whale of the day the sun had climbed farther into the sky and had burned off the last remnants of the blue misty morning atmosphere. I was on my third cup of coffee and was standing out on deck again, leaning against the railing and alternately closing my eyes to soak up the warmth of the sun and opening them again so I wouldn't miss a second of the amazing scenery surrounding me.

Everywhere I looked revealed a view that was more stunningly beautiful than the last. Every angle was picture-postcard perfect. But the most absolutely magical thing of all to me were the glaciers. Between the soaring mountain peaks these vast rivers of ice snaked their way down toward the ocean, and I found myself completely spellbound when I caught a glimpse of the otherworldly blue of some distant glacier. I couldn't take my eyes off it. The color was so unbelievably deep and unnatural looking that my brain seemed to be unable to comprehend what it was seeing, and I would find myself holding my breath as these silent azure giants slowly drifted in and out of sight in the distance.

"Don't forget to breathe," I muttered to myself.

I suddenly heard a noise off to my left and caught a glimpse of movement out of the corner of my eye.

"Did you see?" Uncle Joe called from behind me, steering the boat slightly to the left and reducing power to the engines. I spun my head around and scanned the waters around the boat, my eyes flicking from side to side as the engine noise faded and our forward motion slowed.

"What, what?!?" I replied, pushing myself up slightly on the railing and desperately searching for anything out of the ordinary. "What is it?"

"Thar she blows!" Uncle Joe called again, putting on his best nineteenth-century whaleboat captain's voice. "See the spout just over there?"

This time I saw it. Just a short distance away from us a huge plume of mist erupted like a geyser out of the water, with a snapping, watery noise that sounded like someone blowing water out of his nose. That was exactly what the sound was, I suppose, except that the "someone" in this case was a whale the size of a bus coming to the surface to breathe just ahead of us.

A plume of mist rose several meters into the air, catching the sunlight as it expanded and sparkled before dissipating into nothing. Underneath this the back of the humpback whale rose in a graceful black arc out of the water, its dorsal fin curving at a sharp angle as the whale dove again into the deep.

"See how it arches its back?" Uncle Joe cried out. I could see it, despite my eyes nearly filling with tears at the beauty of it. "That means he's diving deep. Watch for the tail."

And there it was. As I stood there breathless, my mouth open in disbelief, the enormous tail of the humpback whale broke the surface, water pouring and dripping from it like a waterfall as it rose higher and higher, and the whale angled itself steeply downward. It continued in a graceful curve and knifed back through the surface of the water and out of sight once again.

"Oh my God," I said under my breath. "Oh my God." I looked back at Uncle Joe as he stood there grinning at me, my mouth still open in disbelief.

"Fluke," he said.

"Pardon me?"

"The tail of a whale is called a 'fluke.'"

I was still too speechless to reply. Of course, growing up on the west coast this wasn't the first whale I had ever seen. I'd seen them plenty of times from the air and even occasionally from the shoreline, but this was the first time I had ever seen one so close up. It was almost as though I could have reached out and touched it, my palm sliding over its wet, silky back as curved across the surface and dove back under again. So close that I could hear it exhale and blow that beautiful sparkling plume into the air. So close that I could...I wrinkled my nose and pursed my lips at an unpleasant smell that suddenly filled the air.

"Ugh," I said, closing my nostrils with my thumb and forefinger. "What's that smell?"

"Whale breath," Uncle Joe replied. "We're downwind from him. What you're smelling is whale breath."

I released my grip on my nose again for a moment to test the air again. A pungent odor like rotting fish and garbage still filled the air. I squeezed my nostrils tightly shut again.

"But why does it smell so bad?" I asked. "It's awful!"

Uncle Joe's forehead thought about this for a moment.

"Well," he said with a grin. "Imagine what your breath would smell like if you ate nothing but fish for your entire life and never once brushed your teeth."

I laughed and released the grip on my nostrils once again. The smell was slowly losing its power as it dissipated into the fresh ocean air, and I pushed myself up on the railing again to look out across the water.

"He took a big breath on that last one," Uncle Joe said as he scanned the horizon with a pair of binoculars. "He'll be down for a while, I'm sure."

I continued looking out across the water, hoping for another glimpse of the whale, as Uncle Joe climbed back up into the wheelhouse and slowly powered the engines up again to continue on our way. After a few minutes out on deck I followed him back inside to consult my maps.

"So where are we now?" I asked.

Keeping one hand on the wheel, Uncle Joe leaned over and ran his finger down my chart before pointing definitively at our current location.

"There," he said. "Right there."

I pulled the elastic off my Moleskin notebook and made a note of our first whale sighting, marking the location on my map at the same time.

Uncle Joe was true to his word, and throughout the day he showed me some of the humpback's favorite feeding grounds in southeast Alaska. By the end of the day my small notebook was full of notes of all the whales we had spotted and where. And by the end of the summer I would fill a dozen more notebooks and return again and again to these same locations that Uncle Joe first showed me. But from a different perspective, of course. I would return to see them from the air.

CHAPTER FOUR

Beavers, Hawks And Humpback Whales

After months of waiting and preparing, after days of worrying and nights too excited to sleep, the moment had finally arrived. I was in Alaska and about to take to the air to start my unbelievable summer adventure.

I had woken up just before dawn and shared my first cup of coffee with Aunt Jenny in her kitchen, as I organized my notebooks, maps, and charts for the hundredth time. Then she dropped me down at the floatplane dock, where I carefully went over every inch of my plane to make sure everything was working properly. I paid special attention to the camera mounts on the sides and underbelly, since it would be a waste to get up into the air over the whales and not have my cameras working.

After checking and rechecking every switch and cable, I was finally satisfied that everything was working the way it was supposed to.

Before I climbed into my plane, I stood there on the dock in the dim blue light of early morning, savoring the moment and wanting it to last forever. Fishing boats chugged past me on their way out for their day's work. On the sundeck of a nearby cruise ship the crew was busy polishing brass railings and putting out deck chairs. I closed my eyes and inhaled the salty, fishy, clean air. After a couple of deep breaths I was ready.

Pulling off the mooring lines, I pushed my floatplane off the dock and pulled myself up into the cockpit. I ran through my mental preflight checklist, checking all my controls and gauges before firing the engine into life, reassured by the familiar noise and vibration.

Powering up ever so slightly, I eased myself out into the inlet and slowly down to my takeoff position. Some early-bird

45

passengers on the nearby cruise ship waved from the railings, and I waved back. No matter where you are in the world, people on boats always feel compelled to wave at people on any other passing floating object.

Reaching my starting position, I pointed myself in the right direction for takeoff and powered down again to do one final check. Everything was okay to go.

"This is it," I said to myself. "Let's go find some whales."

And with that my adventure truly began. I pushed the throttle all the way forward, and my trusty De Havilland Beaver roared into life and cut its way through the water. Faster and faster, bouncing sharply against the small waves before finally cutting free from the surface of the water and gliding smoothly into the air. Off to my right some more cruise-ship passengers were waving and taking photos of my plane climbing up into the sky. To my left the houses lining the steep sides of Douglas Island raced by.

Slowly but surely, the cruise ships and houses slipped behind me as I climbed higher and higher, and the world opened up into a beautiful panorama of islands and inlets. It looked like a lumpy green carpet, broken up with thin fingers of water as far as the eye could see. Off in the distance snow-capped mountains and glaciers lined the horizon. It was a beautiful and perfectly clear day, and it seemed liked I could see all the way to the ends of the Earth and beyond, as though the distant mountain peaks were not even real but rather the lands of some fantasy realm.

Banking to the left I turned south and got down to the serious business that had brought me to Alaska in the first place. My plan to study the feeding habits of humpback whales called for systematic daily surveys covering a large area of southeast Alaska over the next seven weeks. For easy reference in the cockpit I had propped up a large map of my survey area, carefully divided into various zones. The long summer days made it possible for me to fly through my entire planned survey grid three times per day, with time to linger for a while over any whales that I happened to spot. (Up north in Alaska the summer days seem to last forever, with the sun rising before 4:00 a.m. and setting well after 10:00 p.m..)

Three times per day I would search every bay and inlet, every strait and sound, for humpback whales and record in photographs and video every single one that I found. The photographic record would even allow me to identify specific individual whales and where and when I spotted them. This would give me invaluable data on not only the number of whales spending the summer in this part of the world, but also their feeding and movement habits.

At the end of seven weeks all this information could be cross-referenced with observation data from various other researchers who were working from the shoreline or boats in this same area. I had already made arrangements with students from a few universities to share all our data, so we could get the best possible overview of the lives of the humpbacks spending the summer near Juneau.

All this was fantastic in theory, of course, but now it was time for me to put it into practice, and as I continued flying south along my planned survey route, I constantly scanned all around for any telltale signs of humpbacks nearby.

You might ask yourself how I planned to spot them from high up in the air since whales live in the ocean underwater. There are several answers to this, the first being that from high up in the air it is actually possible to see through the clear water and spot a submerged whale near the surface of the water where an observer on the shore might not even be able to see them. But that's a tricky thing to see from a distance, as you can imagine, so another way would be to look for what are called whale 'footprints' on the surface of the water. A 'footprint' is an area of water disturbed by the huge body of the humpback whale and it leaves a distinct area on the water that slowly dissipates. This is a lot easier to see from a distance but is still tricky to spot.

But fortunately for me whales are not fish, but mammals, and just like you and me they need to breathe air. What this means is that they have to come to the surface every once and a while to get a giant gulp of air before going back underneath again to go about their whale business. And it is that giant gulp of air that would make it a much easier for me to spot them from a distance.

Humpback whales, like all whales, breathe in and out through an opening on the top of their body called a blow hole. When they come to the surface they quickly blow out all the air in their lungs and take a big breath to refill their lungs again before sliding underneath the water again. All this happens in a matter of seconds and of course humpback whales have huge lungs so when they exhale they really blow out a lot of air. And what happens when all that wet warm air quickly hits the cool air at the surface of the water it does exactly the same thing that your breath does on a cold day and creates a misty fog, just on a much larger scale, of course. The result is a misty plume that rises several meters into the air right above the whale and on a sunny day it catches the light and makes it possible to spot the whales from even many miles away.

And that is exactly what I was on the lookout for as I continued south and pulled back on my controls to gain a bit of altitude to pass over Admiralty Island - The Fortress Of The Bears.

"Maybe I'll spot a bear," I said to myself, remembering what Uncle Joe had told me. No, no, concentrate! I scolded myself. I'm here to find whales! Maybe I could do a research project on bears next summer.

And that was when I saw it, out of the corner of my eye off to the right. A plume of mist rising into the air as the sleek black body of a humpback whale cut through the surface of the water for a moment before sliding back under again.

"Bingo!" I cheered myself under my breath as I made a smooth turn to get a closer look. Pressing a specially installed switch on my control yoke with my thumb I activated the digital voice-recorder that my dad had installed into the plane's intercom system. The "Captain's Log" he called it.

"Captain's Log, stardate two July two thousand twelve, five forty seven A.M." I recited into my headset microphone, glancing first at my watch and then the GPS to read off my position. "Fifty eight degrees, six minutes, forty point one three seconds north. One thirty four degrees, forty three minutes, ten point three seven seconds west."

Keeping an eye out for the whale to surface again I quickly glanced at my charts to see the name of the narrow finger of water where I had spotted the whale. But when I read the name I did a double take and started to grin.

"First whale sighting of the day in the area south west of Juneau near Admiralty Island." I continued my Captain's Log entry with a huge smile on my face. "Near entry to Hawk Inlet."

A Very Good Omen

Just ahead of me the humpback whale in Hawk Inlet surfaced again, taking a huge breath before submerging once again and leaving a clear 'footprint' on the surface that would allow me to guesstimate where he might surface the next time. He was swimming toward the mouth of the inlet, heading for the open water beyond, and as it had been the second breath I'd seen him take my guess was that the next time he came up for air he'd dive deep and we'd get a look at his tail. And if I could catch that on film then later on we might be able to figure out exactly which whale I was looking at.

In addition to the 'where' and 'when' information that I would be collecting that summer one of the most important parts of my survey would be to also figure out the 'who'. I would try to identify the different whales that I spotted but identifying a particular humpback whale from the air would be a tricky thing to do and this is where my special photographic equipment would come into play. By analyzing the photographs and videos that I would make over the summer I would be able to compare the markings on the head and body of each whale and hopefully be able to differentiate between various different individuals.

However, far more important than the markings on the head and body of the whale are the shape and markings on the whale's tail fin - their fluke. The markings on the fluke of a humpback whale are like a human's fingerprints - no two are exactly the same - and if I could get a photograph of that I could compare it against an internet database of known individual whales and answer the question of exactly who each whale I spotted was. Doing this would allow me to track the movements and habits of individual whales over a seven week period to see where they liked to find food or play around and just where they liked to hang out and also who they liked to hang out with.

With that in mind I slowly eased the plane into a position where I thought the whale might come up again. All my various cameras were mounted on the left side of the plane just outside the pilot's window where I could sight them properly. Once I had them lined up properly I simply pressed a button to start the pair of super high-definition video cameras rolling and kept my thumb poised over a different button to activate the digital photo cameras. All I could do now was keep my fingers crossed.

And then I saw him again, a hazy dark black shape slowly growing as he came to the surface. I couldn't believe it. I'd timed it perfectly. Pressing down with my thumb four separate digital cameras with varying levels of zoom instantly sprang into life to start taking dozens of photographs per second. Fortunately, in the age of digital photography, I could take literally thousands of photographs per day, and hopefully somewhere in all of those would be a few that I could actually use.

The whale broke the surface, spitting out another telltale plume high into the air as his dorsal fin sliced through the water. Watching the display screens from the cameras just outside my windows, I made tiny adjustments to my flight path to line the cameras up as best as I could. Taking a big breath, he began to dive again, his back arching just as I'd seen from Uncle Joe's boat the day before. He was going deep.

"Come on," I mumbled to myself. "Come on. Show us your tail."

The enormous, shiny, black body glided back underneath the surface, and for a moment it looked like he wouldn't do it after all. He wasn't going to show his tail. But then came the perfect National Geographic moment, and the fluke broke through the surface of the water and rose up, a waterfall of saltwater cascading off it. Slowly, it angled downward before slicing back through the water again and disappearing beneath the surface.

"Yesssss!" I shrieked, almost startling myself with my own enthusiasm. "I got it!" Leveling the plane out again, I did a little victory dance (which was difficult to do while strapped into the cockpit of a small airplane, as you can imagine). "I did it, I did it, I did it!" I continued shrieking as I shifted my butt from left to right in my seat, pounded my feet against the floor of the plane, and did my best dance moves with one free arm while I kept the other firmly on the controls of the plane.

After a few moments I regained my composure again, and I cleared my throat to finish my first Captain's Log entry of the summer, again noting the time and my position from the GPS coordinates. I slowly banked my plane over into a tight circle over Chatham Strait, where the whale seemed to be heading. I got a tail shot of him and had a long flight ahead of me, with lots of ground to cover and more whales to see, but before I left him, I wanted to see which direction he would go after leaving the inlet. North or south? "This is important scientific data to have a record of," I told myself. Plus, he was my first whale of the entire summer, and I just wanted to get one last look at him before I continued on my way.

I continued circling, round and round, and after a few minutes I spotted him on the surface again. He'd gone quite a distance along the shoreline to the north and seemed to be swimming with a purpose, as though he had in mind somewhere that he wanted to go.

"Captain's Log, stardate July 2, 2012, 5:59 a.m." I recited, once again activating my voice-recorder. "The first whale of the day has moved off close to the shoreline of Admiralty Island, heading toward the north, swimming a bit faster and feeding along the way."

Tipping my floatplane slightly to the right, I climbed a bit higher into the air as I passed over a rocky point jutting out from Admiralty Island.

"I will now return back to my planned flight path to continue the morning survey," I said, continuing my log entry and again stating my GPS position. I glanced at my charts to find out the name of the rocky point that I was flying over as I quickly gained altitude to pass over the summit of Admiralty Island. I smiled broadly once again. It was called Hawk Point. This was a good omen, I thought. A very good omen.

CHAPTER FIVE

Edward, Romeo, Rhett Or Mr Darcy?

IT'S A BIRD! IT'S A PLANE!
IT'S... ACTUALLY IT'S A PLANE.
By Iain Reid - JUNEAU EMPIRE

Local residents might have noticed a new addition to the regular flock of floatplanes cluttering the skies over south-east Alaska this summer. This one is the kind of plane you just can't miss. Bright red with white trim and topped off with the graceful silhouette of a bird-of-prey adorning its tail.

But unlike most of the planes whose drone in the summer skies is a constant feature in this part of the world, this particular plane is very special. Inside, instead of the normal cruise ship tourists or back-country fisherman, the only occupant of this particular aircraft is one dedicated and brave young soul on a mission.

Her name is Kitty Hawk and she has chosen to come here all the way from Canada to call Juneau her home this summer so she can soar like a bird over the waters of the panhandle in search of humpback whales. Her mission is a simple one: to find and study whales. To do this she flies her own specially modified De Havilland seaplane equipped with advanced photographic and navigational gear that allows her to study the behavior of the humpback whales of south-east Alaska.

"These beautiful and gentle creatures are simply amazing," Kitty says energetically. "To be able to spend so many hours every day with them, watching them, learning from them, is the most incredible experience of my entire life."

Her passion for her chosen field of study is clearly revealed as she enthusiastically gives inquisitive passers-by a tour of her specially outfitted aircraft, pointing out the various features that allow her to document the lives of humpback whales and gain an insight into their daily activities and habits.

"What is the greatest insight I've acquired so far?" Kitty asks herself. She ponders the question for a moment before confidently and thoughtfully providing her own answer. "I think the greatest insight so far is how similar we are - these graceful giants and us tiny humans."

"If people see me flying overhead," Kitty says. "Maybe they can remember that we are all the same. That we all have to share this planet of ours. Together. And we have to figure out how to do that."

"And buy Tilley clothing," she adds dramatically, name-dropping the company who sponsors her summertime expedition. "www.tilley.com!"

For Kitty Hawk what began as a mission of science has become a philosophical journey of growth and enlightenment. With a little harmless corporate sponsorship to boot.

"You're Kitty Hawk, aren't you?" a voice behind me said, startling me as I was making some adjustments to my outboard cameras. Lifting my head suddenly, I nearly hit it on the overhead wing, and I spun around to find myself face to face with the most gorgeous boy I'd ever seen, standing on the dock behind me.

I'd never been a fan of the Twilight books, but at that moment I felt like I instantly understood everything about them. Suddenly I was Bella, and this was my Edward Cullen standing in front of me, albeit a bit less brooding and vampirish.

"Uh," I replied, a brilliant opening line if there ever was one. I once read online somewhere about how to make a great first impression, and one of the rules was to not think too much. For some strange reason this is all I could think about over and over again as I stood there, speechless, mouth open with an adjustable wrench in my hand.

"I read about you," he said putting one foot up on the pontoons of my plane and casually putting his hand on the edge of the wing above him. "You know, in the paper."

"Yah," I said, mouth still open, crescent wrench still in hand, and still thinking about how I shouldn't be thinking too much. I was thinking too much about not thinking too much. Great move.

"I've seen you down here sometimes," he continued, apparently unfazed by my lack of participation in the conversation thus far.

"Forget Edward Cullen," I thought.

This was something more epic than that. This was like Romeo and Juliet.

Grabbing the edge of the wing with his other hand he pulled himself up onto the pontoon and stood next to me. His weight pushed the plane ever so slightly down in the water and caused it to rock gently.

"I work over there," he said, gesturing toward some fishing boats at the opposite end of the docks. "On my dad's boat."

"Cool," I replied, relieved to have finally spoken an actual word.

"Maybe Romeo and Juliet isn't sophisticated enough," I thought.

Maybe some other shockingly amazing romance. Scarlett and Rhett, maybe?

"Just for the summer though," he added. "I mean, I'm at U dub in the fall again."

"Cool," I said again. Now repeating myself. Even better.

"Forget about Scarlett and Rhett," I thought.

I've never seen Gone With The Wind, much less read the book. Maybe Elizabeth and Mr. Darcy?

"U dub, you know?" he continued, looking hopefully for a sign of understanding. "U.W.? The University of Washington? In Seattle?"

"Oh, yes, U dub," I replied. Amazing! I got four words out! Or is that only three?

"Forget Elizabeth and Mr. Darcy too," I thought. I didn't read that book either.

Taking a couple of steps closer, he leaned against the wingstrut between us in a beautiful and perfectly casual sort of way. Back to Edward Cullen, I decided. I hadn't read that book either, but at least I saw the movies. How could I not see them? They filmed parts of them back home in Tofino, after all.

"Yeah, I'm studying journalism," he said, smiling a perfect, little, crooked smile. "But to be honest, I have absolutely no idea what I want to do in life."

"Me either," I replied, trying to smile back, which was easy since I was happy to get some kind of coherent response out, even if it was only two words. From four words to two. "That's not progress," I thought. Or was it only three words?

"I think you do," he said, smiling that crooked, little smile of his again. His blue eyes sparkled like he knew something that I didn't.

"I do?" I asked, trying to speak clearly, but it came out barely above a whisper.

"Definitely," he replied, and he reached over to take a pen out of my toolbox. Fishing around in the pockets of his jeans, he found something to write on and scribbled quickly on a scrap of paper before handing it to me. "You want to fly, right?"

Jumping back on the dock, he walked away. Reaching the harbormaster's office, he looked back over his shoulder to smile one last time, and he made a bird out of his hands that he flew through the air as he turned the corner.

"I want to fly," I whispered and nodded to myself as I watched him disappear around the corner of the building. "You've got that right."

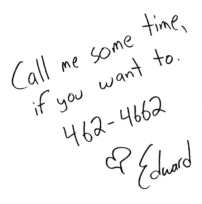

Four Six Two Four Six Six Two

Right next to the main dock in Juneau, running along the side of a long building, is a line of public telephones. When I first saw them I couldn't figure out why, in this day and age of ubiquitous cell phones and Wi-Fi, would anyone need so many public phones. My question was answered, however, the first time that I saw a cruise ship dock in the early morning. This long line of payphones was the first place that the crew headed. I guess even in this day and age of technology, where you can roam almost anywhere in the world with your cell phone and talk to your loved ones back home, it's sometimes still cheaper to just use a payphone.

For most of the summer this long line of payphones always made me smile when I saw it. It was heart-warming to see the cruise-ship crews queuing up to hear the voices of the people they love.

That was before I met Edward, however. That long line of payphones had held a silent vigil of reminder over me ever since he and I spoke on the dock—or should I say that he spoke, and I said a total of ten actual words (or nine, depending on whether "U dub" is one word or two). Ever since that day those payphones had reminded me of only one thing.

Four six two four six six two.

Edward's phone number that I hadn't called yet.

Of course I didn't need a payphone to call him. I had a cell phone of my own. Two, in fact. My iPhone from Tofino plus a cheap prepay phone from the Juneau Wal-Mart that I bought so my parents and Skeena could call me on it. Sometimes I would call them too, then hang up after two rings so they could call me back and avoid me having to pay for it—a clever system that I guess I am not the first person in the history of the world to have thought of.

A payphone would be cheaper, though. To call Edward, I mean. My carefully thought-out financial plan for the summer had not budgeted for summer romance, and using even my cheap Wal-Mart phone would cost more than a payphone. Then again, it was just a matter of a dollar or two, right? Depending how long the call would last. How long would the call last? Surely long enough to make a payphone the more fiscally responsible choice, right? I mean, I am here in Juneau for a reason, and calling Edward isn't it. I can't jeopardize my entire whale study to call some boy. As if making one phone call would endanger the entire whale study. But what if it wasn't just one phone call? What if it was one phone call, then another, and another, and text messages back and forth? Oh my God, wouldn't that be amazing?

And so went the internal dialogue in my head a dozen times every day as I stared at the long line of payphones—my constant reminder that I had not yet called him. I had to stop myself from letting my thoughts go round and round in these never-ending circles. Before I knew it, the phone calls and text messages back and forth in my imagination would spiral out of control, and the next thing I knew he'd whisk me off to some beautiful exotic island somewhere for a picnic lunch followed by—oh my God—our first kiss, his amazing lips on mine, and then he'd get down on one knee, pull a ring from the pocket of his jeans and...

I had to get a grip on myself, as you can imagine.

But of course all these financial questions weren't the real reasons that I couldn't call him. The real reason was that I had absolutely no idea what I would say. My brain was still stuck back on the dock on the day we first met, trying to get out more than just ten words. (Or nine, depending on how you count them.)

Four six two four six six two.

I sat in the cockpit after pulling up to the dock and shutting the engine down, staring at the line of payphones as I chewed nervously on my thumbnail.

Four six two four six six two.

I walked down the ramp to the seaplane docks, balancing my notebooks and early-morning coffee in my arms and telling myself not to look at the payphones but knowing they were still there.

Four six two four six six two.

I waved at the cruise-ship passengers lining the decks to watch me come in for a landing across the waters of Gastineau Channel and caught a glimpse of the payphones in the distance.

Four six two four six six two.

I glanced over my shoulder toward the long line of payphones as I tied my floatplane up to the dock at the end of the day.

"You should call him," I told myself, and the internal dialogues continued. I still didn't have a clue what I could say. It would have to be something mind-bogglingly witty, of course. Something fascinating and interesting and...all that was impossible for me. I am just not an interesting person.

"Are you kidding me?" I scolded myself. "You are a pilot! You have your own plane! You are spending the summer in Alaska studying humpback whales! Who is more interesting than that?"

I replied to myself. "But he's a university student! He's older than me and perfect and beautiful and studying journalism!"

Angry with myself for having these endless internal debates, I told myself harshly, "Studying journalism? What kind of stupid subject is that? Are there journalism degrees? There can't be, can there? Why would you want to do that with your life? Even he said he didn't know what he wanted to do with his life. What a loser! At least I know what I want to do with my life!"

Tying off the last of the lines with a final angry tug, I grabbed my backpack and jumped to my feet. Focused intently on the long line of payphones above me, I stomped along the dock and up the ramp, never once taking my eyes off them.

"At least I know what I want to do with my life," I told myself again as my courage faded slightly.

I tossed my backpack on the ground next to the building and grabbed the nearest phone, nearly pulling it off the wall. I fished around in my pockets for some coins and deposited them angrily into the payphone. Or as angrily as I could, anyway. It's not really possible to put coins into a phone angrily because you'll probably drop them, or worse yet the phone would reject them, and there's nothing worse for sustaining your anger than having to dig around in the coin reject slot and having to redeposit coins over and over again.

Dial tone—check.

Coins deposited—check.

Journalism degree, my ass. Screw you, Edward...whatever your last name is.

Four six two four six six two!

I punched the numbers angrily. Punching numbers on a payphone you can definitely do angrily.

Ring.

Tap-tap-tap-tap-tap-tap-tap-tap-tap. I tapped the edge of the payphone impatiently with a spare quarter I had in my hand.

Ring.

Tap-tap-tap-tap-tap-tap-tap-tap-tap. Oh my God, what am I going to say? What if he answers?!?? Should I hang up? Should I adopt a fake accent and pretend it's a wrong number?

Ring.

Tap-tap-tap-tap-tap-tap-tap-tap-tap. Why isn't he answering? What if he doesn't answer?

Ring.

Tap-tap-tap-tap-tap-tap-tap-tap-tap. He's not answering. He isn't going to answer.

Voicemail! Are you kidding me?

"Hey, this is Edward," the tinny-sounding recording told me at the other end of the line. In the background I could hear the sound of tinny recorded seagulls. "Leave a message."

"Interesting," I thought as I waited for the beep. His voicemail message was simple and to the point. No lame attempts at stupid humor. I liked that.

BEEEEEEP.

And that was it. It was show time. No more internal dialogues. No more vacillating.

"Hi, Edward," I said, my voice as calm and cool as the Gastineau Channel on a windless summer day. "This is Kitty."

For a second I paused to take a breath. I closed my eyes and turned my face into the wind for a moment, as though I was a plane or a bird getting ready for takeoff.

"You were right," I continued. "I want to fly. My number is 469-2813. We should do something sometime, so give me a call."

CHAPTER SIX

The Mystery Of The Century

"Commercial whale-watch vessel Fjordland, this is Charlie Foxtrot Kilo Tango Yankee," I recited into the microphone of my radio while expertly banking my trusty De Havilland Beaver into a turn. "Come in commercial vessel Fjordland, this is Kitty Hawk, over."

Don't get me wrong. I don't mean to be vain, but after a few weeks of basically living in the skies over southeast Alaska I was really getting good at this. And I don't mean, "gaining proficiency in aircraft operation and wildlife spotting techniques after extensive practical experience." That sounds too boring. What I mean is that I was really getting good at this. I was totally awesome.

Okay, maybe that starts to sound vain.

But I don't care. Because it's true.

For three weeks I'd been in the air three times a day nearly every single day over waters and islands that I was now starting to know like the back of my hand. Some days were better than others, of course, because the weather was not always cooperative. In fact, it was frequently "inclement," which is a fancy way of saying it wasn't very nice outside.

On my first day of 'inclement weather' I had called my father in Tofino to ask him what I should do. (By which I mean I called him, let it ring twice, then hung up so he could call me back and I wouldn't get charged for it.)

"I don't know what you should do," my father told me, his voice sounding too thin and far away for my taste that morning. Twelve hours earlier when the sun was shining and barely a cloud in the sky I was the queen of the universe, but the low-hanging wet clouds clinging to the mountains and hiding them from view made me uneasy. My instincts told me that this was just a bit of early morning rain and cloud like I'd seen and flown in a thousand times before back in Tofino, but somehow I started to doubt myself and felt very alone.

"I don't know either," I replied, feeling like a little girl all over again and wanting to run home where it was warm and safe and I could gather pillows around me while I read a book and drank hot chocolate while the cold rain fell on the trees outside. "My gut tells me that it's no big deal. It rains sometimes, after all. And just because it's raining here in Juneau doesn't mean it's raining everywhere. But I just don't know."

"Well, I do know this," he said, his voice still thin and far away but coming in stronger. "I know that you've flown in some pretty nasty weather before and that you can handle yourself. And I know that taking a moment to evaluate conditions before you climb into a cockpit is nothing to be ashamed of. It's how we stay safe. But the most important thing that I know is that I trust your judgement. The only question is whether you trust your judgement."

"My judgement says that this is no big deal," I replied. "That this is just a bit of cloud and it will burn off in no time once the sun comes up."

"Then there's your answer," he said.

And he was right. Or should I say that I was right. As it turned out it was just a bit of cloud and by the time the sun had climbed a bit higher in the sky it dissolved into mostly clear blue skies.

But not every day was like that one, of course. It rains a lot in southeast Alaska, and some days I only went up once or twice. Sometimes I didn't even go up at all. I trusted my judgment, and by carefully following the weather reports for the entire region, I was usually able to make observations in some areas even on an otherwise cloudy, rainy day.

"Kitty Hawk, this is the vessel Fjordland, come in, over," a voice squawked through my headphones, responding to my earlier radio call.

In addition to my becoming more and more expert in flying the skies over southeast Alaska, I was also getting better and better at spotting whales. Way up in the air, hundreds or thousands of feet, I could spot the telltale blow of a humpback out of the corner of my eye from miles away. This skill was important for my own study, but the information on where to find the whales was also valuable to the local whale-watching tour operators. Over the past weeks I'd built up a friendly working arrangement with a few of these boat crews, and I would report to them when I saw some whales near them. The Fjordland was one of the boats that operated in the area, and I'd struck up a sort of radio friendship with its captain, Glen.

"This is Kitty Hawk," I replied, again keying the microphone as I continued my turn. "How are you guys doing down there today?"

"It's gonna be a nice day," Glen replied. "We're about ready to push off here in Skagway and head south. Have you got anything for us?"

"I surely do," I said, continuing my turn and circling lower around the small group of humpback whales beneath me. "I am up over Eldred Rock Lighthouse and have a group of five humpbacks out here. A mother and two calves, maybe two mothers, and a couple of their friends. They're heading north toward you and making for the eastern shoreline of the canal."

"Beautiful," Glen radioed back enthusiastically. "As long as they stay on that track we'll bump right into them."

"That's about what I thought," I replied. "Have a nice trip south, Fjordland."

"Say, listen up, Kitty," Glen's voice squawked over my headphones again. "I was talking it over with the crew and the missus last night, and we decided that after all these whale tips you're sending us, the least we can do is buy you some dinner. What do ya say? You interested in some good home cooking one of these evenings and seeing the sights up here in Haines? We got the world's first hammer museum."

"Sounds good to me," I laughed in reply. "I am sure we can work something out."

"All right then," Glen replied. "It's a date. And when you come by, don't forget to remind me to tell you a story about that lighthouse you're looking at out there at Eldred Rock."

"A story about a lighthouse?" I asked, raising my eyebrows and turning my head to look out the window at what he was talking about. Far below me the group of humpbacks was passing by a tiny island well-deserving of the name Eldred "Rock." It was more rock than island, and perched on top of it was a cluster of small structures, white buildings with red roofs, plus a helipad and a stocky, little eight-sided building containing the lighthouse.

"You're gonna like this story," Glen replied. "That little island down there knows the answer to the mystery of the century."

"That sounds promising. We'll be in touch then. Kitty Hawk out," I radioed back, hoping that I didn't come across as rude, rushing our conversation to an end. But at that moment I must admit that my mind was a little bit elsewhere. You see, at that moment my cell phone started vibrating. It was Edward returning my call.

Nude Sea Trout Flying Dill

For three full rings, I just sat there staring stupidly at my phone and not knowing what to do. Not that the choice was that difficult. Obviously I was going to answer it, right? But what would say? "Oh for God's sake, not that discussion again," I thought, and I pressed the "accept call" button.

"Hey," I said as casually as I could, sliding my radio headset down around my neck so I could hold the phone to my ear. And for the record (and just in case my dad is reading this) let me be absolutely clear: Talking on a cell phone while flying a plane is no safer than talking and driving a car. In fact, it's probably considerably less so. But let me assure you that I leveled myself off at a safe altitude and set a clear course down the inlet where there were no mountains for me to fly into. But if you are reading this, Dad, if you'd installed that cell phone hands-free interface that I asked for, we wouldn't be having this discussion, would we?

"Dory, I could have grown nude sea trout frying dill," I heard the barely audible voice at the other end say over the roar of the aircraft engine. I think what he actually said was, "Sorry, I should have known you'd be out flying still." But who really knows? "Baby fight cow a lot stressed lime?" he continued. ("Maybe right now is not the best time?")

"No, no!" I said, cringing for answering too quickly and sounding desperate. "This is perfect. You just might have to talk a bit louder, that's all." Great. This is a romantic first phone call.

I heard him laugh at the other end of the line. "Is this better?" he said.

"Yes," I said and breathed a sigh of relief. "Much better, thank you. Sorry."

"Don't be sorry," he said. "I'm the one who called you when I knew you'd be out flying still." ("nude sea trout flying dill.")

"I'm glad you called," I replied before I could stop myself from saying it.

63

"You stupid idiot!" I yelled at myself inside my head. "You don't want him thinking you're glad he called!"

"I'm glad you answered," he responded, making me smile like a crazy lunatic, I am sure. What the hell was wrong with me? Why wouldn't I want him to think I was glad he called? I was glad. "Listen," he said. "You shouldn't be flying and talking on the phone, but I just wanted to know if you're free for lunch today. Maybe around 12:30?"

"A date!" I thought. He was asking me out on a date! Ahhhhhh! I can't believe it! I can't believe it!

"I am," I said coolly.

"Great," he replied. "Can you meet me downtown at Wasabi Willy's Sushi? I know, the name is…stupid, but it's actually really great. Do you know where it is?"

"Oh yes, I know it," I spoke again, equally coolly. Like a cucumber.

"Perfect," he said. "Fly safe, and I'll see you there, 12:30, okay?"

"Definitely," I said.

Edward was true to his word. Not only was he there on time (check!—another point in his favor), but once you got past the huge sign with a giant blob of wasabi smiling maniacally in a sumo-wrestler loincloth—presumably Wasabi Willy—the inside of the restaurant was actually really cool. Very Japanese with bamboo plants and shoji screens separating different private rooms, where you slipped your shoes off to sit on the floor around a short-legged table. A kimono-wearing waitress brought us a steaming pot of green tea and a pair of menus before bowing and backing out of the room to leave us in private.

"What do you feel like?" Edward asked me, peering over his menu across the table at me. He smiled in a way that somehow took away some of my nervousness. I smiled back.

"I don't know," I said and shrugged, looking the menu up and down. "The normal things, I guess. The tuna-roll things, the salmon-roll things, the long shrimp thing, the long tuna and salmon things?"

"Cool," he said, then paused for a moment with a puzzled expression on his face.

"What?" I asked.

"Nothing," he said and shrugged. "I was just wondering how it is that such an extraordinary person as yourself, who just spent the morning soaring between mountains chasing whales, would order just the 'normal things' at a sushi restaurant."

I thought about that for a moment, frowning at myself and wrinkling my nose as I stared at the menu. "I actually don't know," I said slowly. But maybe he was right. "I just never tried any of the other things, I guess."

"Your life is such an adventure," he said. "Why shouldn't lunch be one too?"

"You're right," I laughed. "Today I want to eat an authentic Japanese adventure. Do you know anything about sushi? Which ones do you like?"

"I know a little bit about sushi," he replied, shuffling around the table on his butt with his menu. "But I'm not like some Zen sushi master or anything." He continued shuffling over until he was right up next to me, leaning over so I could read off his menu, and I could smell his skin close to mine. He smelled like...like...Ugh, what is that smell? Fish? I wrinkled my nose again.

"You smell a bit like sushi yourself," I said before I could stop myself, nearly clasping my hand over my mouth in embarrassment after I said it.

He laughed, much to my relief. "I work on a fishing boat, remember?" he replied with a smile, totally unfazed. "But hopefully it smells like sushi wearing cologne."

I sniffed again, cautiously. He was right. It did smell like sushi wearing cologne. Or something anyway. I couldn't quite place the smell. It smelled familiar...like...like...what is that smell?

"Old Spice," he said.

I laughed hard again, straight out of my nostrils. "Old Spice? What are you, seventy years old?" I said, once again blurting out the first thing that came into my head before I could stop myself. That time I did clasp my hand over my mouth. "I am so sorry," I said, looking at him timidly. "I don't know what's wrong with me."

"Don't worry. We're having fun," he said with a grin. "Dates are supposed to be fun, right?"

Slowly I managed to return his grin. Did he just say we're on a date? "You're right. Yes, they are," I replied. And for a moment we sat there, without saying a word, a charged moment between us as we looked into each other's eyes, close enough to feel the heat of the other's breath.

Suddenly the shoji screen slid open, discharging the electricity, and the kimono-wearing waitress appeared again. "Are you ready to order?" she asked.

"A few more minutes, maybe," Edward told her, and we both giggled.

Big Macs, California Rolls And Sushi Snobs

"Okay, let's get serious," I said after the waitress withdrew and we were alone again. We were both still laughing, but the electricity of that split second between us was gone. "Show me your favorite sushis."

"Okay," he replied, turning faux serious. Leaning over me and brushing against my shoulder, he held the menu open in front of us.

"Some of my favorites are these," he said, pointing to the picture of each item on the menu and reading the Japanese names as he listed them off. "First the 'long things': Ika—squid. Saba—mackerel. Inari—fried tofu bag. Tamago—sweet egg omelet. And finally my favorite, Unagi—fresh-water eel."

"Eel?!?" I asked, making a face. "Really?"

"It's the best one, trust me," he said. "To me that's one of the 'normal ones.'"

I nodded and smiled. "Please teach me, great Zen sushi master."

He rolled his eyes and went back to the menu again. "Sometimes I like these. Oshinko—Japanese pickles."

"Pickles?"

"Trust the great sushi master," he replied.

"What about California Rolls?!?" I said. "Those are the best ones."

He looked at the picture on the menu for a moment. "I like those too," he said. "But you said you wanted an authentic Japanese adventure, and California Rolls aren't exactly traditional sushi."

"Not traditional?" I asked, confused.

"All these ones with the rice on the outside—the inside-out rolls—are all not traditional Japanese."

"Really?" I replied, surprised.

"It's kind of stupid why they were invented, in fact," he said.

"Stupid how?" I asked.

"Apparently, Americans didn't like to see or taste the seaweed," he said. "So in early sushi restaurants in California, they disguised it by rolling the maki 'inside-out' so the seaweed couldn't be seen."

"You're kidding," I said. "You're right. That is stupid."

I didn't like the idea of this for some reason. "I thought it was some ancient Japanese spiritual thing symbolizing...something important...or that it made it taste better somehow...or look pretty or something like that."

He shrugged again. "Apparently not," he said. "But I guess as different foods encounter different cultures they grow and evolve and adapt and get better. You said it yourself, the California maki are your favorite ones."

"Now I am not so sure," I replied.

"Oh, come on," he said and laughed. "Don't be a sushi snob!"

"I just don't like it," I replied with a frown. "If people didn't like the seaweed, then maybe they should have gone to eat at McDonald's instead...or something. McDonald's doesn't change when it encounters other cultures. A Big Mac is a Big Mac no matter where you go."

Edward was laughing at me harder and harder the more I kept talking. "You're crazy," he said.

"Forget the California Rolls," I said, dismissing them with a wave of my hand. "Let's get something traditional. Is that okay?"

"Of course!" he said, leaning over with the menu again. "Then how about some sashimi?"

"Sashimi?"

"Raw fish," he said, pointing to the menu at a beautiful, professionally photographed plate of various thin slices of fish.

"I thought sushi was raw fish," I said.

"It is," he replied. "I mean, it can be. But this is raw fish without the rice part."

"No rice?" I asked, wrinkling my nose at the thought of it. "Just raw fish?"

He nodded. "Exactly," he said. "You asked for something more traditional."

"You're right," I nodded in return. "Nothing modern or wrapped inside-out because people are too stupid to know what tastes good. Just traditional sushi the way the Japanese have been eating it for thousands of years."

"Okay, deal," he replied with a funny grin. "Although I should probably mention that sushi hasn't been around for thousands of years." At that moment the shoji screen slid open again, and the waitress reappeared. "But maybe that's a story for another time."

CHAPTER SEVEN
Feeling Like A Real Alaskan

"Before I tell you about the mystery of Eldred Island," Glen said, leaning back against a log and lighting his pipe (all good storytellers smoke a pipe, don't they?). "I first have to tell you the story of the last great gold rush—better known as the Klondike Gold Rush—because that story lies at the heart of nearly everything in this part of the world."

Glen had been true to his word to have me over for dinner with his family, and that is how, late on that particular summer evening, I found myself sitting around a backyard campfire with Glen, his wife, Alison, his brother Gary, and Iris, a member of his boat crew, listening to stories of the Klondike.

I had flown in a few hours earlier, arranging the route of my evening whale-survey flight to end in Haines, where Glen met me at the dock. I left my plane tied up for the night not far from where Glen's whale-watching boat was moored.

We drove to Glen's property, which was nestled among the trees out in the nearby woods.

Rather than have to fly back in the dark (or sort of dark, anyway—in Alaska the long summer days seem to last forever), Glen had arranged for me to spend the night in their guest cabin out on the edge of their property. Don't worry. I called my parents and told them where I was going just in case Glen turned out to be an axe murderer or something. Or worse yet, a hammer murderer.

Dinner made me feel like a real Alaskan—sitting outside on the back deck of Glen's house and barbecuing (what else?) wild salmon and moose steaks. With everyone talking and laughing, the outdoor table became a virtual free-for-all every time Glen served up a new batch of meat, and the meal was raucous and loud and physical.

Alison had made the most amazing potato salad I'd ever tasted and Iris had brought an equally delicious crab salad made from fresh Alaska King Crab (what else?). Add to this steaming thick slices of garlic bread fresh from the grill and a fantastic Caesar salad that we served using a pair of carved wood 'Salad Grabbers' in the shape of bear claws. But the real centre of attention were the main courses: barbecued wild salmon with a maple and brown sugar glaze that was absolutely heavenly (even that doesn't fully convey how good it was) and juicy moose steaks with a hint of teriyaki.

After eating far more than I should have Glen started a fire out in the backyard in his fire pit, and we migrated over from the deck to sit around the fire roasting marshmallows. Can you imagine a more perfect Alaskan dinner party than this? Me neither. It was perfect. And it was a good thing I didn't have to fly all the way back to Juneau that same night, because I ate so much I don't think I could have fit into the pilot seat.

As the sky finally began to darken, and glowing embers from the fire rose up to join the stars just starting to come out in the sky above, Glen pulled out his pipe, and the storytelling began. After laughing so hard that my sides hurt at tales of various kinds of difficult tourists that Glen and Gary had encountered on their wildlife-watching tours, I remembered that Glen had told me to remind him about the "mystery of the century" on Eldred Island. He nodded at that, his entire demeanor turning suddenly very solemn. He refreshed the tobacco in his pipe and launched earnestly into the story of the Klondike Gold Rush.

Over Before It Even Started

"Way back in the late 1800s," Glen began. "Alaska and the Yukon were full of all sorts of people looking to get rich. Starting with the discovery of gold down in Juneau in 1880, a lot of people started showing up around here and fanning out over the landscape in search of gold. Many were leftovers who had failed to make it big in the California Gold Rush or the subsequent silver rush in Nevada, and they just sort of wandered north in their endless quest for riches. And by the 1890s, a lot of these gold-seekers had made their way quite far inland, all the way into the Yukon up in Canada, searching, always searching, trying to find the mother lode.

"Now, if you ask me, maybe these guys just really enjoyed hunting, fishing, and camping an awful lot. I mean, why else would they wander the most desolate and inhospitable places on Earth, year after year, endlessly searching for gold that no one ever really seemed to actually find? Sure they wanted to strike it rich, who wouldn't? But to spend decades living off the land in such harsh conditions requires a certain kind of personality, I suppose. And of course it's incredible what greed drives people to do.

"So anyway, back in mid-August 1896, a few of these fellows named George Carmack, Skookum Jim, and Tagish Charlie found themselves up in the Yukon, prospecting in some small streams feeding down into the Yukon River by way of another smaller river called the Klondike. And it was there that this little group stumbled upon one of the greatest concentrations of gold that has ever been discovered in all of history.

"There are a lot of stories about exactly who made the discovery and how they did it. One version of the story has George Carmack making the discovery while panning for gold at what is now called Bonanza Creek.

"Every self-respecting kid in Alaska knows all about panning for gold. You take a flat metal pan out to a stream and scoop some dirt inside. You then fill it a bit with water and slowly tilt and swirl the water around, gradually washing out the dirt and rocks, and allowing the flakes of gold to settle to the bottom. Gold is nineteen times heavier than water, and a heck of a lot heavier than the other dirt and rocks around it, so eventually as you swirl and wash the contents of the pan, whatever gold that is in there will settle to the bottom. And once you wash enough of the worthless dirt and sand out, you'll find some shining flakes or small nuggets of gold left behind.

"George Carmack was an experienced prospector, so he would have been a lot better at gold panning than any of us, and it would have taken him only a couple of minutes to pan out a sample of dirt from along Bonanza Creek. And when he did that for the first time he could hardly believe his eyes. At the bottom of his pan was an incredible amount of gold, worth maybe four dollars at the time.

Just exactly how astonishing this was is probably best described by the Canadian writer, Pierre Berton, who said "*In a country where a ten-cent pan had always meant good prospects, this was an incredible find.*"

And yet, even after making this astounding discovery George Carmack felt drawn to look further. The discovery he'd made standing right then at Bonanza Creek could make him a millionaire, but greed is a powerful thing, I suppose, and his intuition told him to look further before staking a claim there.

"And so he and his companions went further, looking to make an even bigger discovery. A short distance upstream they came to a place where another small creek forked off and joined with Bonanza Creek. After panning a bit further up that other stream with not much result George's intuition told him to go further but he ignored that and turned around again. They explored a bit further around the area and found nothing else so they decided to return back to the original find and stake their claims there. On their way back they again stopped at this other small stream and George panned his way up it once more time, his intuition leading him farther on. Again he found nothing and under pressure from his companions he ignored his intuition and they all returned back to the location of the original discovery on Bonanza.

"The members of the group could only stake one claim each, claiming a section of land along the stream where they would return to mine for gold, so they all chose to do it at the site of the original find along Bonanza Creek. To stake a claim they posted a notice on a tree and measured off five hundred feet upstream of it as a single claim stretching up the sides of the creekbed from rimrock to rimrock. George Carmack, as the discoverer of the site - although that was later disputed by the others - was entitled to stake two claims and so, all told, the group staked out four claims along the banks of Bonanza Creek.

"And that was it. Now the only thing they needed to do was register their claims within sixty days at the closest police outpost and they would be on their way to being millionaires. But what I love about this particular version of the story is how Carmack supposedly ignored his intuition to go further upstream in deciding where to stake a claim. Because the stream he was supposedly making his way up, which is now known as Eldorado Creek, actually contained an even more incredible concentration of gold along its banks than further down on Bonanza. This fact was discovered shortly afterward by some lucky fellows who arrived on the scene to find Bonanza Creek completely staked out by some of the other people who had heard the news of Carmack's discovery. If only he'd listened to his intuition, right?

"Anyway, whatever version of the story is true, the important thing is that these fellows discovered gold, staked their claims, and then went downriver to the nearest settlement to register them. Unfortunately, the closest settlement was miles and miles away, because back then the Yukon was even less populated than it is now. Even nowadays there are twice as many moose living there than there are humans, and there's one bear for every six humans, so you can imagine that the nearest settlement wasn't much of anything, just a police post and a saloon. But it was enough for these lucky fellows to register their claim and then go drinking to shoot their mouths off to a few of the other prospectors who were also living up there in the middle of nowhere trying to strike it rich.

"At first people didn't believe them, especially George Carmack, who apparently had a bit of a reputation for exaggeration. But when he pulled out his little sack of freshly panned gold dust to show them, they were convinced. A lot of the old-timers could tell just by looking at gold dust where it had come from, and George's piles of the precious yellow metal looked like nothing they'd ever seen. Some of them set out that very night for Bonanza Creek to stake their own claims. Others quit their jobs on the spot and set out the very next morning. In no time at all the entirety of Bonanza Creek had been staked out, and some other lucky prospectors started staking claims up the even richer Eldorado Creek and other nearby creeks. Slowly but surely the word spread throughout the desolate lands of the far north, and by New Years Eve of 1896 a small town called Dawson City had popped up out of nowhere at the confluence of the Klondike and Yukon Rivers. By then all the best claims were taken. The Yukon Gold Rush was basically over. And it hadn't even started yet."

Rich Men, Poor Men And Those Pesky Mounties

"Officially, the Yukon Gold Rush and the stampede of gold seekers heading north to strike it rich wouldn't start until the following summer, in July 1897," Glen continued, his tale holding us all spellbound around the campfire. "The reason for this was simple: the cold Yukon winter. Even though gold had been discovered almost twelve months earlier and those prospectors lucky enough to have been living up in the Yukon or Alaska at the time had already staked out the best claims, the news of the discovery had only leaked out in tiny bits and pieces to the outside world, due to the fact that in the Yukon the winter comes early and lasts for more than half a year. The rivers freeze up, and easy access to the outside world freezes up with them. And so for ten long months the news of the greatest discovery of gold in history remained locked away, a secret kept by the far north, until the rivers thawed.

"But as every Alaskan knows, the thaw always comes, even though it sometimes feels like it never will. And in 1897 when it did come, some of the lucky miners who'd been working their rich claims for months already decided that they'd had enough of life in the north, so they sold their claims and made their way down the long Yukon River to board steamer ships to take them back to civilization. The whole journey south took them until about mid-July, when ships carrying dozens of these newly wealthy gold miners docked in Seattle and San Francisco. 'Gold! Gold! Gold! Gold!' the headlines read, reporting that stacks of gold were being carried ashore valued at millions of dollars by today's standards. They wrote of ships carrying as much as a ton of gold onboard and of gold nuggets up in the Yukon that were just lying around in every stream, waiting for someone to come along and pick them up. The news broke all around the world, and the real Klondike Gold Rush was finally on.

"The story burned and spread like a fever, and just as had happened nearly a year earlier, many people quit their jobs on the spot upon hearing the news and headed north. The streetcars in Seattle came to a halt after so many of their drivers dropped everything and headed for the Yukon. Even the mayor himself headed off on the spur of the moment and telegraphed his resignation back to Seattle.

"Of course getting to the Yukon wasn't exactly easy, and for the thousands of human stampeders making the journey, there were a lot of different routes to choose from that all promised to get you there. Most of these were ridiculous, some of them impossible, and many of them deathtraps. But in the end most of the people who actually made it did so by following either one or the other of the two most popular routes.

"The first of those routes was the so-called Rich Man's Route," Glen said, grabbing a marshmallow roasting stick to draw a map in the dirt. "On a steamship from Seattle or Vancouver, all the way around the tip of western Alaska to the mouth of the Yukon River at St. Michael, then by paddle-wheeler up the Yukon River to Dawson City.

"Or the Poor Man's Route, by steamship as far north as possible along the west coast of Canada and southeast Alaska to Skagway or Dyea, then up over the mountain passes into Canada and the lakes at the head of the Yukon River, and from there down river all the way to Dawson.

"Because the discovery of gold happened to be so close to the Yukon River, it's not surprising that the two most popular routes to the gold fields followed the path of that river And it is a curious twist of geological history here in this remote corner of Alaska that a drop of rain that falls up in the mountains just a few miles from the ocean must then travel through streams and lakes down into what becomes the Yukon River, past the gold fields and travelling thousands of miles, all the way down into the ocean at the far north-western edge of North America, way up in St Michael. And most of the stampeders heading for Dawson, just like that drop of rain, would follow this same route. The only question was which way you went - whether up-river or down.

"If you had money, you probably took the Rich Man's Route and made nearly the entire journey in relative comfort by boat. If you didn't have money, well, then you had some hard times ahead of you, because after taking a steamship all the way up to Skagway or Dyea, you were as likely to be robbed as you were to be cheated from the moment you stepped off the boat, because there was virtually no law enforcement down in these American towns. From there you then had to climb the brutal mountain passes up toward Canada, and you didn't just have to climb up there once, but actually dozens of times over and over again, because at the border at the summit of the passes, the Canadian Mounted Police wouldn't let you cross unless you had a year's worth of supplies to keep you alive. Unfortunately, that year's worth of supplies weighed almost a ton, which meant that you had to climb the pass over and over again until you got everything that you needed all the way to the summit.

"Once you carried all that up into Canada, you then had to camp out high up in the mountains on the shores of the headwater lakes and build yourself a boat to carry you downstream. Doing that required cutting down trees, sawing lumber from them, then putting it all together into a boat that the Mounties considered safe enough to stay afloat. If your boat wasn't seaworthy, they wouldn't let you go any farther. And then once you did all that, it was just a matter of waiting for the rivers to thaw, because it was already winter, and the rivers and lakes were long since frozen. And don't forget what I said—that so far north the winter comes early and stays long, which meant that thousands of boats and many thousands more stampeders had to build their boats in subzero temperatures, sometimes fifty below zero, and wait until the end of May 1898, when the lakes and rivers finally thawed.

"Once that happened the Mounties would check your boat to make sure it was safe and then assign it a number and register it so you could begin the five-hundred-mile journey down river to Dawson. The mighty Yukon River would just carry you along with it most of the way without you even having to paddle, but did I mention the treacherous whitewater rapids you'd encounter along the way? There were a few of those too. And the reason those pesky Mounties recorded the number of people's boats was to track them as they headed downstream, and they made sure that everyone made it to where they were going."

"Pesky Mounties?" I asked, my Canadian pride bruised slightly. "It sounds to me like they were the only sane people along this entire crazy route."

Glen laughed along with everyone else. "You're more right than you know," he said. "Down on the Alaska side of the border, the towns of Skagway and Dyea were run by cheats and thieves and were as lawless as some town out of a Wild West movie. And yet at exactly the same time, just a few miles away in Canada, the Mounted Police managed to maintain not only law and order but were also doing their best to help keep the stampeders from killing themselves as a result of their own foolishness."

"And all this more than a hundred years ago in a place no one had even heard of before," I said, nodding thoughtfully.

"Exactly," Glen agreed.

"But what's Dyea?" I asked. "Skagway I know, but I've never seen Dyea on any of my maps."

Glen smiled. "That's because it's not there anymore," he said.

"It's not there anymore?"

"It's a real Alaskan ghost town," he replied. "Once they put in the railroad at Skagway there was no point in people climbing the passes on foot anymore, so Dyea just sort of died out and rotted away. All that's left if it are some ruined and crumbling building foundations out on a remote tidal flat up a ways past Skagway."

Glen paused for a moment to fix a marshmallow on a stick before picking up the story again. "Anyway, where were we? Right, the pesky Mounties," Glen continued, winking at me. "If you made it past those pesky Mounties, after months of hardship, travelling from Seattle, climbing up over the icy mountain passes over and over again with your heavy load. After cutting down trees and building your boat and surviving the winter, the freezing cold, and the whitewater rapids, and you found yourself carried along with the mighty Yukon until you finally rounded the last bend in the river before Dawson. After all that, you had finally made it, and the bustling gold-rush city of Dawson was just ahead of you.

"You had finally made it to the gold fields! You and seven thousand other boats and their thousands of passengers who'd spent the winter along the shores of the headland lakes—not to mention the thousands of others who made it to Dawson by one of the other routes. You had finally made it to the land of gold, and as soon as you stepped off the boat the first thing you discovered is that what you'd read was absolutely not true. There weren't gold nuggets lying around in every stream just waiting to be picked up. There weren't any claims left to be found along the banks of Bonanza Creek or Eldorado Creek or any other creeks. In fact, there weren't really any claims to be found at all. They'd all been staked long before the rest of the world had even heard of a place called the Yukon."

"So what happened then?" I asked breathlessly.

Glen looked around the campfire dramatically, looking each of us in the eyes before shrugging his shoulders. "What happened then," he said simply. "Was that most people simply turned around and went back home."

The Mystery Of The Clara Nevada

"What?!??" I cried. "They went back home?!??" I couldn't believe it. After all that effort they just went back home?

"What else could they do?" Glen said and shrugged. "There was nothing for them there."

"It's just so...so..." I couldn't find the words for it. I wasn't sure if I was feeling shocked or angry, or what it was that I was feeling.

"Well, they didn't all turn around and go home," Glen clarified. "A lot of people struck it rich during the gold rush without ever setting foot on a gold mine. There were saloons and restaurants and brothels and gambling and all sorts of places for the wealthy miners to spend their gold. All along the way to the gold fields, people were making a fortune from taking other people's money."

"That's right," I commented wryly, snorting a dry laugh through my nostrils. "Down in Skagway they were robbing and cheating people."

"Any more beer for anyone?" Glen asked, looking around the campfire. "Or marshmallows? Because now we get to the point of this whole story—the Clara Nevada."

"Jeez, Glen," Gary replied with a teasing grin while tapping his watch. "If I'd known you were gonna talk for so long, I'd have brought a sleeping bag out here."

"Don't listen to him, Glen," I said, shushing Gary with a wave of my hand. "I want to hear it."

"It all began down in Seattle and San Francisco," Glen began. "Following the arrival of the first wealthy gold miners and their fortunes from the Klondike, the stampede for the gold fields started in a flash. And with just about everyone succumbing to gold fever, there was suddenly a great demand for ships that could take passengers north to Alaska. I told you about how other people managed to make a fortune from the gold rush without ever getting anywhere near the Klondike? Well, the owners of steamships were a perfect example of this. The regular steamers heading for Alaska were already overbooked far beyond their safety capacity, and the demand for passage was so great that dozens of barely seaworthy vessels were put into service to carry people north. Even ships that had already been decommissioned or even abandoned were hastily patched up and pushed back into service to meet the demand and make their owners some money.

"The Clara Nevada was one of these ships, and although she wasn't as bad off as many of the other ships pushed into service by greedy owners, she was also not very well off either. She had been built a quarter-century earlier and had served the United States Coastal Survey for most of that time under the name of the Hassler. But by the mid-1890s she was on her last legs and was decommissioned by the US government and sold to private owners.

"Her new owners renamed her the Clara Nevada, and in January 1898 she set sail from Seattle to Skagway under the command of Captain C. H. Lewis on a voyage that was doomed from the start. On her way out of harbor she collided with another ship, an accident that was hardly surprising considering the fact that the officers and crew were frequently drunk, and their seamanship even when sober was questionable at best. The voyage north wasn't much better, with the ship suffering constant mechanical failures and fighting the midwinter Alaskan weather. But somehow they safely reached Skagway a week or so later and took on some new passengers and cargo for the return trip to Seattle on February 5, 1898.

"Unfortunately for the Clara Nevada, the weather on February 5 was less than ideal. In fact, it was downright awful. It's hard to imagine when you're out on the water here on a beautiful summer day, but winter storms in this part of the world can be quite nasty, and it was during one of these storms that the Clara Nevada set sail. With waves ten to fifteen feet high and winds blowing snow at close to ninety miles an hour, one wonders why she set out at all. But she did, and what happened to her after that to make her flounder and sink is anyone's guess.

"But what we do know is that a few hours after the Clara Nevada steamed out of Skagway, residents of a small village along the Lynn Canal, south of Skagway, saw a giant orange fireball. A single body later washed ashore along with wreckage and debris from the ship, but no survivors were ever reported to be found.

"The ship appeared to have struck the rocky reefs off of Eldred Island in the middle of the Lynn Canal and had sunk. The Clara Nevada had sunk in about thirty feet of water with her bow pointing north and a large hole in her hull as the result of an explosion. The passenger list went down with the wreck and was never recovered, so the number of passengers and crew who perished that night will never be known, although it is thought to have been about sixty or so.

"Immediately following the sinking, the rumors began to circulate that the ship had gone down with a fortune in gold aboard. This obviously generated a lot of interest in what might be salvaged from the wreck in the shallow water, but no subsequent investigations of the wreck ever reported finding anything.

"Resting on the bottom in her shallow watery grave, the Clara Nevada left only questions. What happened to her on that stormy night? Did her boilers explode, or was it dynamite from her cargo hold that caused the explosion and ripped a hole in her hull? Why was the wreck pointed north when she was heading south toward Seattle? What happened to the passengers and crew? And what happened to the gold?

"Slowly the rumors started to fly. Was the sinking of the Clara Nevada really an accident? Or was she sank on purpose by criminals trying to cover their tracks after making off with a fortune in gold? Were the captain or any members of the crew involved? Could innocent passengers and crew have been killed to conceal evidence of the crime?"

"Didn't the lighthouse keeper see what happened?" I asked, interrupting Glen's narrative.

"Good point," Glen replied. "But although there is a lighthouse there today, as you have seen, there was nothing there on that particular stormy night. The lighthouse wasn't built until a few years after the disaster. So only the island itself knows the answers to the mystery of the Clara Nevada."

"But surely someone must know what happened to her," I said, feeling cheated at being left only with the lingering mystery.

"Unfortunately," Glen said, leaning back as he reached the end of his story and the evening drew to a close. "No one will ever know, because the sea left no witnesses to the fate of the Clara Nevada."

CHAPTER EIGHT
Walter The Whale

I have to admit that the next morning came far too soon for my liking. We'd stayed up pretty late listening to Glen weave his tales of the Yukon and the Clara Nevada, but I wouldn't have traded it for anything, even if it meant crawling out of bed after only a few hours of sleep and finding myself yawning and rubbing my eyes out on the dock at Haines in the cold grey-blue early Alaska morning.

I waved goodbye to Glen, who had been kind enough to drop me off at my plane so early in the morning, and he drove off with a honk of his truck horn. I headed down the ramp to my plane and popped open the cap of my traveling coffee mug to take a sip. It turned out that Glen didn't just know how to barbecue, but he also made an amazing cup of coffee as well. I took another sip to help get on the way to being fully awake, then snapped the lid back shut again.

I heard the sound of a boat floating across the water, cutting through the near complete silence of the early morning. I squinted my eyes into the dim light and saw a small private fishing boat far out on the water, heading north toward Skagway. It was white with a teal stripe down the side and was riding very low in the water, like it was weighed down. There was something very familiar about it, but I couldn't quite put my finger on it.

I sipped some more coffee and enjoyed the quiet of the morning a bit longer as I watched the boat motor along out of sight. I could see already that it was going to be yet another amazingly beautiful day in southeast Alaska, and I was looking forward to seeing my friends, the whales.

Walking back along the dock to my plane, I did my normal preflight checks of the exterior equipment before climbing inside and starting my pre-startup checklist. Everything was working perfectly, and in no time I had the engine started and untied from the dock to taxi out to the open water.

But just then the most amazing thing happened. Not more than twenty feet from me, the dark back of a humpback whale broke the surface, and a perfect plume of mist exploded out of the water as it exhaled. I couldn't believe it, and in a split second I had switched my engine off, grabbed my camera, and climbed out onto the pontoons for a better look.

Clinging to the struts under the wing, I scanned the water to see if I could catch a glimpse of the whale again. In all these weeks of watching these gentle giants from the air, I hadn't been so close to one at water level since going out with Uncle Joe at the beginning of the summer. I hoped to get another look at it before it went down deep to feed again, but I realized that I also wanted to hear it breathe. Because of the sound of the aircraft engine, in all the time that I'd spotted the whales from the sky, I also hadn't heard the watery snap of their breath since I'd been out with Uncle Joe. I had dreamed about that sound and wanted more than anything to be able to hear it again.

I waited and waited for the humpback to reappear. It had been traveling north, so I was sure it would have to surface somewhere off to my left, so I kept scanning the water as the gentle waves rocked my floatplane and slapped against the pontoons with a reassuring aluminum smack. I waited and waited, but there was no sign of the humpback whale anywhere.

But at that moment an even more amazing thing happened. Out of the corner of my eye I sensed a movement, a dark black shape moving slowly under the water right next to the pontoons. Before my mind could process what was happening, an incredibly loud snapping breath exploded in a plume of mist and spray out of the water right next to me. It was so close that it covered me in a cold fog of the most God-awful smelling whale breath as the whale came to the surface.

I shrieked in surprise and nearly lost my balance and fell in the water, but my hand clutching the wing-strut firmly saved me from a very cold early-morning swim. My heart skipped about a dozen beats, and I was in so much shock that for a few moments I completely forgot to breathe. The whale was right next to me, so close that I could have literally reached out and touched its barnacle-covered skin.

I watched as the humpback slowly rolled onto its side and hung there nearly motionless in the water. Its white-bottomed pectoral fin waved gently as he floated, and I realized that he was trying to keep his balance too, holding a position right next to the pontoon of my plane.

The slow waving of his fin so mesmerized me that I didn't immediately understand why he had turned on his side. But then it hit me. He was looking at me! I was looking down through the water into his right eye, and he was looking back at me. He had turned himself onto his side so he could get a better look at me.

"Hello, beautiful," I said, finally remembering to breathe. "Hello beautiful." My heart was pounding, and I could feel the adrenaline pouring through me like an electric charge. Never in my life had I experienced anything so sublimely beautiful as that moment. I was staring across the boundary between two species— from human to whale—and I could see that there was nothing separating us. We were the same. I didn't have time to think it through rationally, but I felt like I could understand him perfectly, this amazing and curious creature who had swum over to visit me.

We both floated there—me on my seaplane pontoon and he in the water just below—watching each other for a moment that seemed to last both a lifetime and the blink of an eye. Then he rolled slowly right-side-up again and drifted off.

For a few seconds he disappeared from view under the water, then came to the surface to breathe a short distance away. He swam away, and I saw him arch his back and go into a deep dive.

Only then did I remember my camera. I was glad that I'd forgotten it up to that point because I wouldn't have wanted anything to come between us in that special moment that we shared. Not some stupid camera. Not anything. But as he swam away and went into his deep dive, I suddenly remembered it. As his tail broke the surface and arced gracefully back into the depths again, I pulled out my camera to aim quickly and hit the shutter button over and over again in a panic. Once he disappeared again beneath the surface, I hit the playback button on the camera and scrolled through the photos, praying that I'd gotten a tail shot that I could use to ID him later on.

"Yessss!" I cried out triumphantly. "I got it! I got a shot of the tail!" The markings looked familiar, and now that I had a photo I could look him up on my whale database and track his movements, not only in the future but for the whole summer up to that point. "I think I will name you Walter," I said as I stared down at the picture of his tail on my phone. I had made a special new friend.

A Circle Of Bubbles To Blow Your Socks Off

My early-morning encounter with my new whale friend Walter must have given me good luck for the entire day, because after finishing my morning survey flight and a quick lunch on the docks in Juneau, I set off for my afternoon flight and had my second incredible experience of the day.

It all started just a little bit south of Juneau at an inlet called the Seymour Canal, where I spotted a group of humpbacks in the distance and turned toward them to get a better look. As I approached their position, I could see that it was quite a large group, consisting of maybe ten or twelve whales.

"This should be interesting," I thought. "Such a large group of whales hanging around together will make for plenty of great photographs."

Flying closer I was almost on top of them when the strangest thing happened—all of the whales seemed to almost simultaneously go into a dive. Over the span of about ten to fifteen seconds, a dozen black whale backs broke the surface as they took big breaths of air and arched their backs into a deep dive.

"There must be a school of herring down there," I thought as I put my plane into a turn to circle the group. The Seymour Canal was a rich spawning ground for herring, and in addition to eating small shrimp-like creatures called krill, the humpbacks also like to snack on some small fish like herring as well. They have to eat whatever they can, as much as a ton of food every day during the summer months up in Alaska, to prepare them for a long winter down in Baja or Hawaii, where they will go for months without food.

Circling above their position, my high-definition video cameras were already running, and my thumb was at the ready over the button that activated the digital photo cameras. As usual I would start those running as soon as I saw the whales return to the surface.

When humpback whales feed they often perform what is called a "feeding lunge," where they go into a deep dive and then swim toward the surface with their huge mouths wide open, scooping up all the krill and fish that they can before dramatically exploding out of the water. They then close their mouths and squeeze out all the excess water through a special sort of hair-like comb in their mouths called a "baleen." This allows them to filter out the water and keep all the fish and krill trapped inside for them to swallow.

These feeding lunges are almost always preceded by another dramatic spectacle, with dozens of small fish jumping at the surface of the water just before the whale breaks through. Imagine you are a little fish swimming around, and a huge humpback whale is swimming up below you. You probably will swim away in the opposite direction as fast as you can, even if that means swimming upward, where you eventually will run out of water. You reach the surface, and in one last attempt to escape you jump out into the air, hoping to avoid being trapped in the whale's giant mouth.

Those fish jumping at the surface were exactly what I was looking for as I circled the area where I'd seen the whales go down. Once I saw that, I had to make a split-second decision on whether I was at a good angle to activate the cameras, as well as make any adjustments to my flight path to get a better shot. It seems like a tricky thing to do, and it definitely is, but at that point I'd done it so many times that summer that it was second nature to me.

And so I waited and waited, and then yet another strange thing happened. I saw little pockets of air bubbles rising up one after another on the surface of the glassy smooth water beneath me. First two, then three, then four, and so on until there was a long, narrow line of bubbles. That narrow line continued to elongate and curve as the bubbles continued to rise to the surface, and soon the bent, narrow line became a graceful, arcing curve.

"What the hell?" I said, adjusting my flight path to a better viewing angle and pressing the camera button to get a few shots of the strange phenomena.

Longer and longer the line of bubbles grew until it curved all the way into a closed loop, as though some invisible finger had drawn a giant circle in bubbles on the surface of the water. It was an amazing sight, but nothing as astonishing as what happened a few seconds later.

From my viewing angle almost directly above the bubble circle, I suddenly saw dark shapes coming into view under the surface of the water. Hundreds of tiny fish started jumping out into the air, and my eyes grew as wide as dinner plates to see the giant mouths of a dozen humpback whales heading straight up to the surface toward me. I could see them in incredible detail, their huge mouths wide open and their white-bottomed pectoral fins stretched out as though they were flying through the water. The tiny jumping fish at the surface reached a frenzied boil as the humpbacks rose toward them, their mouths closing as they exploded through the surface of the water and out into the air.

There is no other word than "explode" to describe what I was seeing below me. Ten or twelve huge humpback whales, weighing forty tons each, were breaking through the middle of the bubble circle and out through the surface of the water in a great fury of white water, tiny jumping fish, and black humpback whale bodies.

"Oh my God!" I cried out in disbelief, pulling myself closer to the pilot's side window for a better look and bumping my nose hard on the glass. "Oh my God!"

It was absolute pandemonium at the water's surface. The whales closed their mouths and filtered the water out as they crashed and settled back down into the water. The frenzy of jumping fish slowly tapered off while seagulls dove and swooped, hoping to make a meal of one of the escaping herring. Slowly but surely the chaos subsided, and the humpbacks slowly sank beneath the surface again, leaving behind only a hovering flock of seagulls and a circle of bubbles.

"Don't forget the circle of bubbles," I thought. "What was that? What in the world just happened?" My thoughts were running about a hundred miles a second as I tried to understand what I had just witnessed. I could only hope to God that I'd caught all of it on film. I started to panic at the thought that I didn't, and I checked my equipment. The video was still running, and I had angled the plane perfectly to capture it. And the photo cameras? Only then did I remember that I still had my thumb pressed down firmly on the activator button. My hands were gripping the steering column tightly, and as I breathed regularly again I loosened up and finally took my thumb off the camera switch. "I just shot a couple hundred useless photos there," I thought. "But who cares as long as I got pictures of what just happened."

But what exactly did just happen? As it turned out I needn't have worried so much about whether I got pictures or not, because the spectacle I had just witnessed was about to be repeated over and over again a few more times during the next hour. Completely abandoning my regular planned survey schedule for the afternoon, I decided it was a much better idea to stay with these whales and observe this incredible feeding habit of theirs.

As I watched the group of humpbacks repeat their amazing feeding display, I understood what I was seeing. The entire group of whales would start off by taking one last breath at the surface and go into a deep dive. The entire group, that is, except for one. That one whale would then remain fairly close to the surface and blow a circle of bubbles in the water through his blow hole, which the rest of the group would then swim up through in a feeding lunge before exploding out into the air in a repeat of the chaotic scene I'd first witnessed.

By the second or third repetition of this astounding display, I understood what the purpose of the bubbles was. It was rather obvious in hindsight, actually. The entire process was an incredible demonstration of a collaborative hunting strategy.

Bubbles, you see, act like a barrier in the water to fish and other sea creatures. For some reason, don't ask me why, fish are reluctant to swim through bubbles in the water and will treat them as though they are an impenetrable wall instead of just soft pockets of air. I suppose it's because to them and their sea-creature perceptions of the world, it just appears to be a barrier.

But what this means, and clearly the humpback whales had figured out, was that if you come across a big school of fish (like herring) and blow a circle of bubbles around them, they will essentially be trapped inside that circle until the bubbles dissipate. The whales had apparently learned that with a little bit of cooperation and perfect timing, they could score much larger mouthfuls of herring and make feeding easier.

It was an absolutely incredibly, astonishingly, mind-bogglingly clever method of feeding, and it demonstrated a level of social interaction and cooperation that was astounding even for such intelligent and social creatures as humpback whales. And not only had I been lucky enough to experience it and understand its significance, I'd also captured all of it on film. And that film was going to blow people's socks off.

That Stupid Little Boat Again

When you spend as much time all alone up in a plane as I did that summer you have a lot of time to think. From the moment I woke up in the morning and all throughout the day, I had to struggle to remind myself to not let my thoughts wander to things like Edward or my family or friends or...did I mention Edward? I was proud of myself for being so disciplined and generally always keeping myself focused on what I was supposed to be doing. That is why one of my favorite times of the day was when I was flying back home to Juneau in the evening. Only then could I have some time to myself to think.

When I'd woken up that morning tired and groggy in Glen's guesthouse, I had no idea I was about to have one of the most amazing days of my life. And of course when I was flying back to Juneau that evening, I found myself replaying over and over in my mind everything I'd seen and heard. And smelled. I still could hardly believe that my early-morning face-to-face encounter with Walter the Whale had actually happened. It seemed like a dream or a movie or something that had happened to someone else, but I knew that it must have been real because I could still smell the faint scent of whale breath in my hair. "I'll have to have a shower to get rid of that," I thought, although at the same time it somehow made me sad to wash it away.

And then there was the amazing whale-feeding displays I'd seen and caught on video and in photographs. I was definitely going to write some e-mails to the university research students I was in touch with to ask them about this behavior. And of course all of that would go into my final report at the end of the summer.

I spent most of the flight thinking about these two experiences and planning what I would do to further investigate it with the limited number of days I had left for my summer project. It was already mid-September, and although it was hard to believe, the summer was coming to an end, and I had to make the best use of the few remaining flights that I had left.

But in among my reflections on my amazing experiences of the day and my mental organizing and planning for the rest of the summer, there was one other thought that kept coming back into my head. For some reason I kept thinking about the small fishing boat I'd seen that morning from the dock at Haines.

It was kind of annoying, actually. There I was dreamily trying to replay my close encounter with the whale over and over in my head, and little by little my mind would sneakily change my train of thought, and before I knew it I was thinking about that stupid boat again.

What was it about the boat that my brain was so interested in? It was just a normal little fishing boat like thousands of other little fishing boats that I'd grown up around my entire life. When I first saw it, I had thought it looked familiar, but of course it did because there are boats like it everywhere around here. What was so special about this one that my brain refused to let it go?

Again and again I tried to force my thoughts back to my beautiful early-morning whale encounter with Walter, but again and again my brain refused to cooperate with me, and I found myself flying along with a frown on my face thinking about that stupid little boat.

"Okay, fine," I thought. "Have it your way, brain. We'll think about the stupid boat. Okay…go! Think, think, think, think. See? It's just a stupid boat. Big deal. Now can we go back to dreaming about Walter again?"

But then it hit me. Apparently, my subconscious had been chewing on this all day because I suddenly remembered where I'd seen that particular boat before. It wasn't something from my childhood or the long distant past. I had seen it just weeks earlier on my first survey flight, when I spotted the first whale of the summer out near Hawk Point.

"Why would I remember that?" I wondered. But the answer to that question also suddenly occurred to me as well. It was because I was so excited and proud after my first day of flights that I'd gone over all the photographs and videos about a thousand times. That had been before everything became sort of routine, and I decided that it was better to go through the photos only once or twice at night for organizing and identification purposes so I could still get enough sleep. I would have to go through all the photos in detail once the summer was over anyway.

But on that first day the excitement was still very much in full force, and I'd ended up flipping through everything over and over and over again. And I was sure that I'd seen this little white boat with the teal stripe back on that day in the background of my first whale photos.

Fortunately, I didn't need to wonder endlessly whether or not I was remembering right. I had all the photos from the entire summer on my laptop computer right next to me in the cockpit. I always carried the entire photo archive with me at all times in case I needed to look up a certain whale sighting or any other information. (Don't worry, Dad. I backed up the entire collection every day onto an external hard drive as well, in case something happened to the laptop. Two external hard drives, in fact, which were both safely back home with Aunt Jenny.)

Reaching over, I flipped open my laptop and waited for it to start up. (Again, don't worry, Dad. I looked around to make sure I was well clear on all sides and not about to crash into anything.) After a few seconds I was at the desktop, and I went to my organized folder of photos and opened the folder for my first flight. I clicked on the first photo and flipped through them by hitting the arrow keys. (Okay, dad, you're right; it wasn't safe to be flipping through photos at four thousand feet, but I was keeping an eye on where I was going too. And besides, I had to know right then and there if I was right or it would drive me completely crazy.)

And then I found it. There it was! After flipping through a couple of dozen photos I found what I was looking for. In the background of one of the shots of that first whale was the little white fishing boat with the teal stripe down the side.

"Aha!" I said. "I knew it!"

Smiling proudly to myself, I turned back to flying once again and glanced at the laptop as I more leisurely flipped through all the photos that followed. I could see the little boat anchored close to shore along the side of the inlet, and as I flipped from photo to photo like a little movie I could see the boat disappear and reappear at the edges of the photographs as my plane circled the whale below.

It seemed crazy to remember such an ordinary boat after so much time, but as I flipped through the photos I realized that there was something else unusual about it that had apparently caught my attention. The boat in the photos I'd taken weeks earlier was riding incredibly low in the water, like it was weighed heavily down, exactly the same as it had been when I'd seen it that morning. The boat was obviously carrying something very heavy to make it float as low in the water as it was.

I flipped through a few more photos until I found one that was more or less looking straight down into the boat as I passed overhead. The boat had an open design, so from that angle I could see everything that was inside it (except, I supposed, anything that might have been stowed in the compartments underneath the seat benches). But what was strange was that there wasn't anything loaded inside the boat at all. It was completely empty except for a large beer cooler.

"Huh?" I muttered. "That's strange."

I turned my eyes away from the laptop screen and forward again to continuing flying while I thought this over. "Maybe it's just a leaky boat," I thought. "Half ready to sink?" I shook my head. That wasn't it. It looked almost brand new. I doubted very much that it was half full of water and ready to sink.

"Then what was it?" I thought.

Something about the beer cooler? It was just a normal picnic type of cooler. A big one, sure, but nothing unusual about it otherwise. Skeena's family had a few coolers that size that they used to keep groceries cold on the boat ride from the Co-Op in Tofino village out to their place on Meares Island.

"Probably has a capacity of eighty or a hundred liters," I said, talking to myself as I thought things through. I did the math in my head. A liter of water weighs one kilo, so a hundred-liter cooler would, at most, weigh a hundred kilos. That's not very heavy at all. "Whatever is in that cooler is a hell of a lot heavier than water to weigh a boat down that much," I thought. And the very next thought that came into my head made me gasp in astonishment and put my De Havilland Beaver into a steep turn, leaving Juneau behind and heading north toward Skagway.

CHAPTER NINE

It Had To Be Gold

Gold.

It had to be gold.

What else could be heavy enough to weigh that little boat down so far in the water but be small enough to fit inside a beer cooler?

Gold is nineteen times heavier than water, Glen had said the night before during his tales of the Yukon. I did some more math in my head. If a hundred-liter cooler was filled with gold, it would weigh almost two metric tons. Even if the cooler wasn't that big or wasn't completely full it could still easily hold more than a ton of gold, which was more than enough to weigh down such a small boat. And one ton of gold was also exactly what had been reported stolen more than two months earlier. I'd read about it in the newspaper out on Uncle Joe's boat, and as far as I knew the stolen gold was not yet recovered.

It all fit perfectly.

"So what if you're right?" The little voice inside my head asked.

"If I am right," I told myself. "Then...I don't know. But if I can find that little boat again I can report it to the police, and they can take care of it."

"Makes sense," the little voice replied, becoming convinced as to the wisdom of my plan.

"And it's not like it's dangerous or anything," I continued. "I am all the way up in the air in a plane."

"Exactly," the little voice agreed. "But how do you plan to find the boat?"

"Simple," I explained to myself. "When I saw it that morning it was passing Haines, heading north up the Chilkoot Inlet. That inlet only leads to a handful of other inlets, all of which are dead ends, so unless they later turned around and drove all the way out again, they must still be up there. It's just a simple matter of checking those few inlets."

"What if they docked in Skagway?" The little voice in my head was quite the skeptic.

"Fine with me if they did," I replied. "Because I'll still see the boat tied up at one of the docks there. White with a teal stripe."

"What if they put the boat on a trailer and drove away with it?" The little voice in my head was not only skeptical, but also persistent. "What then?"

Then I flew all the way up there for nothing, I guess. And lost some sleep and wasted my time. But at least I wouldn't have wasted

anyone else's time, since Uncle Joe and Aunt Jenny are down in Seattle for a few days, and Edward is at work fishing, so there is no one back in Juneau waiting for me. So there," I told the little voice, and it was finally silent.

Off to my left, the town of Haines was passing slowly behind me, revealing a short inlet just beyond. I checked my charts—Lutak Inlet, it was called. My instincts told me that the boat hadn't headed up that way. When I'd last seen it I was sure it was heading up the Taiya Inlet leading to Skagway. I quickly scanned the shorelines off to my left just in case, but I didn't see anything. I could always come back and check much closer later, but my gut feeling was that there was nothing there.

Continuing north toward Skagway, I scanned the shore on both sides for any sign of the little fishing boat. There was nothing. The shorelines were rocky and inhospitable, so I could hardly imagine anyone docking his boat there in the first place, much less pulling it up into the trees to conceal it. I was confident the boat wasn't anywhere along there either.

That made the next possibility the town of Skagway itself. I passed over a cruise ship heading south, and I could see the town coming into view up ahead. Searching for the boat here would be a bit trickier since there were quite a few places where it could be tied up, including a crowded marina, but I was convinced that this is where I would find it. There wasn't anything else up here, where the boat could have been heading when I saw it that morning.

The best way to check out Skagway, I decided, was to use a bit of technology. My plane was outfitted with a nice collection of photographic equipment, after all, and I could make like a spy plane and fly over the town to take reconnaissance photos that I could review in more detail later on.

The only problem was that my cameras for photographing whales were all mounted on the left side of my plane where I could see them from the pilot's seat. Skagway, on the other hand, was passing by on my right. I would have to make my spy-plane run on the way back once I checked out the other inlets farther north. That way it would be on my left side, and I could get the photographs I needed.

The sun would be setting soon, but I checked my charts and calculated that I could investigate farther north and still have enough time and light left to check out Skagway.

I consulted my charts as I continued north, flying past the town of Skagway and past Smuggler's Cove. Past Nahku Bay and finally to the absolute northern end of the Taiya Inlet, where a massive tidal flat stretched for miles up toward the mountains in the distance. Somewhere down there were the ruins of the ghost town of Dyea that Glen had mentioned the night before. I scanned for any sign of the town from the air, but there was nothing to be seen. It was incredible that an entire town could just rot away into nothing. Surely there must be something left to show that thousands of people had once lived and worked there.

I kept scanning for signs of the long-abandoned town, and I finally made out the remains of a long dock or pier jutting into the water. It was difficult to spot because all that was left of it were rotting stumps of the massive wooden pilings that had been driven down into the mud and sand to make up its foundation. Under normal circumstances I would have been fascinated by this amazing historical site, but at that particular moment my attention was focused on something else that I had spotted as I made my way up toward the end of the inlet.

There it was. The little white fishing boat with a teal stripe down the side.

It's Funny How Fear Works

I did a double take when I first spotted the little fishing boat. Somehow I'd convinced myself that I was going to find it back in Skagway and hadn't expected to find it all the way out there in the near wilderness. But there it was, just off to my left, tied up to a wooden post sticking out of the water.

Banking toward it, I took a few photos and slowly made a long 180-degree turn to head back down and out of the inlet again. If the bad guys were anywhere nearby, I didn't want to tip them off that they'd been spotted, so I tried to fly as nonchalantly as possible so they'd think I was just a sightseeing flight with tourists or something.

"La la la," I sang innocently and whistled a little tune as I made my turn. Playing tour guide I gave my nonexistent cruise-ship passengers onboard a flying commentary on the sights they were seeing. "Off to the right we have the beautiful...mountains with some name I don't know. And if you look below you might make out the ruins of the once busy gold-rush town of Dyea."

I shook my head and laughed at my own stupidity, all the time keeping a sharp eye on the little boat far below. "No doubt about it," I told myself as I continued my slow turn back to Skagway.

I flipped open my laptop and checked the photos from two months earlier and nodded to myself. It was the right boat. I was absolutely sure of it. But what worried me was that now it wasn't sitting low in the water anymore—it was floating normally—and that could only mean that the heavy cargo that had been weighing it down was no longer onboard. I was too late. The thieves had probably already made their escape.

Or had they? Out of the corner of my eye I caught a glimpse of a dim red-orange glow in the dense trees a short distance up the inlet. It was a campfire. "That has to be them," I thought. "Hiding out in the forest."

I resisted the urge to turn the plane around again and buzz over the fire for a closer look, because that would really have tipped them off. "I have to play it cool," I thought. So I just finished my lazy, touristy turn and headed back toward Skagway, flying as innocently as possible. But of course I wasn't going to just let them escape, so I reached down for the controls of my radio to contact the US Coast Guard.

I was about to press the transmit button when I suddenly froze. What if the thieves had radios and were monitoring the emergency channel? Wouldn't it make perfect sense for them to do that?

I took my finger off the button for a moment and tried to think it through. Of course they would be monitoring the radio. All it would take is a portable police scanner radio for them to do that, and I am sure they weren't stupid. If I broadcast to the whole world that I'd spotted them, then they would disappear long before anyone could get up here to catch them.

"Maybe I should call 911," I thought, picking up my cell phone. I doubted that they would be listening in on the cell phone frequencies as well, but it was a moot question anyway since I didn't have service all the way out here.

"Okay," I thought. "New plan. I fly back down to Skagway, land there, and find a way to contact the police in person. That way I won't have to send any radio messages or make any cell phone calls that might tip off the thieves. Good plan."

I continued my flight south toward Skagway. I would be there in no time.

"But what if you're wrong?" The little voice inside my head was back again. "What if that isn't the right boat? What if you remembered it wrong?"

No. I shook my head. Impossible. I looked at the photos on the open laptop again to be sure. That was the right boat.

"But what if there aren't any thieves?" The little voice in my head nagged. "What if there is no gold? What if it was just a heavy load of fish or beer or something else?"

No, I shook my head again. That's impossible. Fish and beer aren't that heavy. But it was too late. The skeptical little voice had done its dirty work and sown the seeds of doubt in my mind.

What if I was wrong?

As I continued flying, my mind raced with the possibilities. If I went to the police they would think I was crazy. They wouldn't even believe me. I would look like a fool! I mean, who was I? Just some girl pilot.

It's amazing how fear works, isn't it? How the worms of self-doubt can wiggle their way into your brain and convince you of the most ridiculous and impossible things? In my head the scenario played out with perfect clarity. I would arrive in Skagway and go to the police station to tell my story. At first it would be met by stares of disbelief while a few snickering police officers sat in the background laughing at me. "Okay, little girl pilot," an officer would say. "We'll check it out. You just go back to taking your whale pictures and leave the police work to us."

And just to appease me they would send officers out to check out the campfire in the woods to see what was going on. They would bust in on a perfectly normal fishing trip and scare the hell out of some poor innocent souls who were just having a few beers and sitting around the campfire. And of course a colossally embarrassing story like that wouldn't stay a secret for long. Everyone would know, and my successful summer would forever be tainted by my stupidity during my last days in Alaska.

It's funny how fear works, because right then and there my fear of looking crazy actually made me do the craziest thing anyone could possibly imagine. I decided that if I was going to the police in Skagway, then I was going to be 100 percent sure that I was right first. So I made another turn and took my plane in for a landing on a nearby inlet, so I could sneak back on foot to where I saw the campfire and check things out.

The Dark Shadow Of Greed

It didn't take long for the little voice inside my head to start telling me that this might not be such a great idea. After safely beaching my plane on a stretch of pebbles on a nearby inlet, I made my way back on foot toward where I'd spotted the campfire. I quickly realized that it was going to take a lot longer than I thought to make the hike and that nighttime would be coming on soon. I wouldn't be able to fly back tonight in the darkness.

"No problem," I told myself. I had a sleeping bag in the back of my plane that I'd used many times before when I was unexpectedly delayed.

The hike was not very difficult at first. I suppose if it had been, then my common sense would probably have overridden my stubbornness, and I would have turned back and given up the whole idea. But instead of having to hike through the woods cross-country, I could walk along a road that led back up along the side of the Taiya Inlet.

Unfortunately, that road would only take me so far, and eventually I had to climb down to the tidal flat and go overland. But that was also quite easy—just a short climb down from the roadbed to the beach below. I did wish that I'd brought my rubber boots, however, because to get to where I needed to go, I had to cross a small river delta where the Taiya River emptied into the ocean.

I walked upstream and searched for a narrow, shallow spot in the small river where I could get across relatively easily. I suppose this was the second chance for my common sense to prevail and turn me back, but I soon found a shallow spot with some stepping stones. Jumping from sandbar to sandbar, I waded and skipped and splashed my way over to the other side of the river without getting completely soaking wet all over.

Once I was safely across the stream, I made my way across the tidal flat and up the inlet. Out on the flats there was nothing for cover except short grasses and flowers growing out of the sandy soil. I felt exposed out there on that barren landscape. If anyone were looking he would see me coming from a mile away. I decided my best bet was to head for the cover of the trees on the other side as soon as possible.

As I made my way across the tidal flat I realized that I was walking through the ruins of the abandoned town of Dyea. The first clue was when I passed the rotted pilings from the pier that I'd seen earlier from the air. I assumed that many houses and shops once lined the waterfront here, but the river must have long since washed away any sign of them, because in the low grasses I couldn't make out anything that even remotely resembled building ruins or abandoned foundations. But when I finally made it to the tree line on the opposite side of the inlet and worked my way, I saw more evidence of the vanished town.

Here and there were scatterings of lumber and posts and pilings driven into the ground that must have once served as building foundations. By this time the evening twilight was coming on, and I found it difficult to see where I was going. I'd brought a flashlight, but I didn't want to announce my presence to the people around the campfire up ahead, so I gave my eyes a moment to adjust to the dim light and continued to pick my way carefully through the trees.

"This is ridiculous," I thought after I nearly tripped over the ruins of what appeared to be an old rowboat. "These people are going to hear me coming a mile away if I keep this up." I sat down on a log for a second to think things over. I'd come so far already. Would it make sense to turn back now?

"I wish I'd brought mosquito repellent with me," I thought as I waved and slapped at the little vampires flying around me. This was yet another chance for my common sense to prevail, but it was then that I saw a nearby trail leading up through the woods in the direction I needed to go.

"Well, that solves it," I muttered, and I got back on my feet again to head up the path.

Walking on the path, I moved a lot more quickly and quietly than I'd been able to through the woods, and once the darkness really began to set in I was glad to have a safe trail to follow.

Making my way through the forest, I soon came across something that made me do a double take when I saw it. Out here in the middle of the woods it looked like there was a store. And as I moved closer I could see that it was, in fact, a store.

Propped up in the trees were the remains of the front side of a building that probably had once been a store. I approached it cautiously and ran my fingers along the edges of the front window and then along the doorframe as I stepped through.

"How strange," I thought. But also how amazing. With the forest all around and trees towering above me, it felt impossible that right here on this very spot had once been a town full of life and bustle and noise. More than a hundred years ago people had stepped through this very same doorway that I just did and greeted those inside the building.

I lingered for a moment at that lonely abandoned storefront before continuing on my way again. I was filled with a sense of wonder and curiosity about the stories of the people who had lived and worked in this abandoned town.

But that sense of wonder quickly vanished as I made my way again up the path through the dark woods. I felt very uneasy about the whole idea and again thought about turning back.

Ironically, it wasn't a fear of the gold thieves around the campfire up ahead that was bothering me. It was the woods themselves and the history of this place. Something felt wrong, as though there were a dark, malicious presence hanging over the ruins of this long-forgotten town.

I thought about the scattered piles of lumber from the crumbled buildings that I'd seen when it was still light outside.

Bleached by the sun and rain, the piles of wood looked like grey bones of some ancient monsters who'd once roamed the forest in this part of the world.

Of course there were no monsters, but certainly this place had a dark shadow hanging over it. When hearing all the legends and stories of the gold rush, it's easy to think of it all as some grand, romantic adventure. And maybe in some ways it was. Maybe it did feel like a grand, romantic adventure when you were gliding down the Yukon River in the spring of 1898, the sun on your back and the current carrying you along, with the cold horrors of the winter behind you and the promise of riches just up ahead, around the next bend. But for the people landing at Dyea after days at sea aboard foul ships in even fouler weather, that sunny day was a long way ahead of them. And of course the promise of riches was all a pipedream in the first place. Maybe the only riches here in Dyea were in the pockets of those who robbed or cheated you after you came ashore. Perhaps there were monsters here after all.

As I continued farther, trying to dismiss the uneasiness washing over me, I came to a clearing in the woods and the remnants of an old cemetery. Of course seeing that did not help lift my darkening mood, and as I wandered among the crumbling wooden headstones I made out the names in the dim light. Buried there were men from all over the United States, and as I wandered farther and read the dates of their deaths, it slowly dawned on me that most of them seemed to have died on the same day: April 3, 1898. One of the next headstones that I read answered the question of what horrible tragedy had befallen these men on that day: A snow slide farther up the trail to the Yukon had swept down and snuffed the life out of these dozens of men in a flash and thunder of cold and white.

I shivered at the thought of this and really had serious doubts about the wisdom of my late-night cross-country hike. Standing there in the ruins of Dyea, I was confronted with death and greed. Despite the sugar-coated cruise-ship tourist shine put on the whole gold-rush story, there was no erasing the fact that at its heart it was a story of greed. The bottom line was that it wasn't adventure that drew tens of thousands of men and women to the Klondike. It was greed. And in the 1890s, greed had precisely the same dark effect on the human soul as it does now, more than a hundred years later, which is the same effect that it had a hundred or a thousand years earlier.

There was a shadow over the ruined town of Dyea, after all. And it was a dark and evil shadow. It was the dark shadow of greed.

CHAPTER TEN

Now We Just Listen

J ust a few moments earlier I had been feeling uneasy as I walked through the dark trees of the dense forest that had grown up and covered the ruins of the gold-rush town of Dyea. I had felt a dark presence hanging over everything that made the trees seem to close in, filling the air and making it thick and difficult to breathe. But confronting the greedy history of the town and recognizing the shallow nature of this darkness seemed to take away all of its power in an instant. The dark and claustrophobic trees retreated back to where they belonged, and the air suddenly felt fresh and clean once again.

Perhaps it is just a natural consequence of having felt afraid, but there was also a part of me that felt the stirrings of anger. Anger toward the cheats and thieves who had lived in Dyea and preyed upon the innocent dreamers getting off the boats. Anger toward the newspapers and government officials who had perpetrated and exaggerated the myths and lies that drew these innocent men and women up here to this distant land in the first place. Anger toward even the innocents themselves for being so gullible and naïve and just plain stupid for coming so unprepared for the harsh conditions, risking their lives at every turn, and all for what?

And so it was that my last chance for common sense to prevail slipped away from me on that particular night. It was driven away by the anger I was feeling toward all those people and their all-consuming greed. People just like the ones I imagined sitting around a campfire just a short distance away. And so, no longer afraid and uneasy, I gritted my teeth and continued on my mission to find them and bring them to justice.

As it turned out, I didn't have to go much farther before I caught sight of the glow of the campfire off in the distance through the trees. I noticed it out of the corner of my eye and quickly realized that I must have gone slightly off course somewhere in the dark woods, because the light of the fire was far off to my right and slightly behind me. Cursing my stupidity, I made my way toward it through the woods as carefully and quietly as I could. Thankfully, I soon came to a road and a bridge that carried me over a river.

"This is the Taiya River again," I thought. "And I am crossing over it back to the side that I started on in the first place. So I got wet boots for nothing."

After the bridge I followed another path part of the way down toward the glow of the campfire. I was getting close now, and that meant that I had to be unbelievably careful and perfectly quiet.

"This isn't a game," I told myself as I left the path and headed out through the forest again, carefully taking every step as though I were walking through a minefield. With each step I lowered my foot slowly and tested gently with my weight before stepping forward. I didn't want to break a single branch or make the tiniest bit of noise.

"What are you doing here?" The little voice in my head was back as I painstakingly made my way closer and closer through the darkness. "You're not a spy. You're just a girl. These guys are probably dangerous, and you'll get yourself killed. Are you out of your mind?"

"Don't worry," I said to myself, taking another careful step. "The last thing they would possibly expect is some teenage girl sneaking up on them in the middle of the night. If I do screw up and snap a branch or something they will just think it's an animal in the bushes."

"And what if they don't?" The voice countered.

"Then I run," I replied. "I am quite sure I know these woods better than they do after trekking through them for the last few hours."

"Didn't you get lost on the way?" the voice asked. "And get wet boots for nothing?"

I hate when the little voice in my head is right.

"Shut up," I replied. "I need to concentrate. This isn't a game, remember?"

By this point I was getting very close to the clearing where the fire was burning brightly, and I thought that somewhere in between the buzz of the insects and the rustle of the wind in the trees, I could hear voices.

"What is the plan here?" the little voice asked.

"Simple," I replied. "Get close enough to listen in on their conversation and hope that they say something that confirms that you were right and that they are the gold thieves."

"And what if they don't say anything like that?"

"Then I wait for them to go to sleep and then sneak closer to see if they still have that beer cooler with them."

"And if they do?"

"Then I sneak even closer and take a look inside."

"Oh my God, what are you doing? You are crazy."

"Don't worry. It won't come to that. And if it does, then maybe we call this whole thing off."

I heard a man's voice say, "There's no way, they...such total...passing anyway." The sound drifted through the trees toward me from the clearing ahead. I froze, and every muscle in my body was strained to stay perfectly still as I listened.

"Besides, they won't know it anyway," the same man's voice continued, followed by loud laughter that scared me nearly out of my skin. My heart was beating like a jackhammer as I stood there frozen like a statue.

"What the hell are you doing, Kitty?" The little voice in my head screamed. "This is the stupidest thing you've ever done. Just back off and get out of here. They don't know you are here yet."

"Exactly," I snapped back. "They don't know I am here! And they won't. It would be stupid to go back now!"

No response. The little voice in my head had apparently given up on me as a lost cause.

I took two more very careful steps closer to the campfire, then slowly, slowly lowered myself down to the ground into a crouching position. From there I gingerly put one knee down and let my weight settle until I was securely kneeling on the ground without any risk of accidentally making any noise.

"You see?" I told the little voice in my head. "Everything is cool."

But I wasn't sure that I believed it. My heart was hammering in my chest, and I felt absolutely terrified.

"What are you doing, Kitty? You are insane to be out here," the little voice said.

"Too late for that now," I replied. "Now we just listen."

An Extra Pair Of Hands

"Oh come on," the voice floated through the trees to where I was kneeling. "You can't tell all that after only the first two games of the season."

I had determined that there were three of them sitting around the campfire talking. I couldn't figure out any of their names, but the one who was speaking right then was the one I called, "Normal Voice." He had a normal voice, you see. The other two were "Slow Talker" (because he talked slowly and deliberately) and "Squeaky" (because he had kind of a high-pitched voice when he got excited).

I had been listening to them talk about sports for more than twenty minutes without a single syllable about gold or robberies or anything. Just sports. And they were engaged in a pretty feisty debate.

Let me summarize the debate for you:

The Seattle Seahawks, an American football team, 'suck this year', according to Squeaky. Apparently this year's team was 'the worst in the history of the universe' and that they 'couldn't score even if the other team had drunk twenty beers and was sleeping it off'.

Normal Voice disagreed. He felt that Squeaky was a 'stupid redneck idiot' who wouldn't know a good football team even if it crawled out of certain parts of his anatomy (although one might wonder why a football team would do that) and that it was too early in the season to know anyway.

Slow Talker, on the other hand, seemed unconvinced by either side of this debate and did not express much of an opinion other than to inform Squeaky and Normal Talker that they were both 'morons for liking the Seahawks in the first place'. His team was apparently the San Francisco 49'ers, a fact which drew scorn and ridicule from the other two.

And so it went. On and on for what seemed like hours. Occasionally, one of them would get up, ask the others if they wanted another beer, and then walk over to a cooler to grab one for himself. I could tell it was a beer cooler from the sound of it— like I said, I'm from the west coast, and if there's one thing I know, it's the sound of a cooler full of beer, ice, and melted water sloshing around.

So they had a beer cooler. But if that was the beer cooler, then it was certainly not full of gold. Maybe I was wrong after all. And the longer I kneeled there and listened, the more convinced I became that I was.

These guys weren't gold thieves trying to make a getaway. They were just three normal local guys on a camping trip, sitting around a campfire shooting the bull. Maybe they had spent the day fishing and were planning to go out again tomorrow in the boat I had seen earlier in the day. As I listened to them talk, I relaxed, and the feeling of fear and imminent danger slowly evaporated.

The longer I knelt there and the colder I got, the more I realized how wrong I had been. And how stupid I was. I had a hell of a long hike back to my plane and I wasn't going to get much sleep that night as it was, much less if I had hung around listening to the Seahawks debate for much longer.

My common sense finally prevailed, and I decided that before I got any colder and my teeth chattered that I'd better slowly and quietly get to my feet again and backtrack out of there. The three guys would be none the wiser as I crept off silently through the woods and back to the trail. And the road. And all the way back to my plane, where a nice warm sleeping bag was waiting for me. "I can hardly wait," I thought, and I smiled at the thought of being safe and warm again in familiar surroundings.

I had just braced myself to get on my feet again when I heard Slow Talker make an announcement.

"I need to take a leak," he said, and loudly got to his feet. Oblivious to him, the other two carried on the sports debate.

"They have no defense!" Squeaky squeaked, getting worked up a little bit by the intense discussion. "How can you be so stupid, Will?"

Aha! Normal Talker's name was Will. I felt like I had at least accomplished something.

"Yes," the little voice inside my head replied. "You came all the way out here to find out his name was Will. Good job."

"It's only been two games, Buck!" Normal Talker (Will) replied in exasperation.

Aha number two! Squeaky's name was Buck!

"Oooooh, fantastic, now we can go home," the voice in my head continued. "Or do we have to wait and find out what the third guy's name is?"

The third guy, Slow Talker, was shuffling around the campsite and seemed to be getting closer. I panicked, and every muscle in my body tensed. "What if he comes over here?" I thought. "He'll see me! Or worse yet he'll pee on me!"

But I panicked for nothing. Slow Talker shuffled off over to the opposite side of the camp from me and loudly made his way into the trees. Back at the campfire the other two had fallen silent, apparently reaching an impasse in the whole sports argument. For a long few moments there was only the crackling of the fire, and then Squeaky (Buck) spoke again.

"Charlie's going to get us all killed, you know?" he said in a low voice, as though he didn't want Slow Talker off in the bushes to hear him.

"Are you happy now?" the voice in my head asked. "Now you know all their names: Will, Buck, and Charlie. Now can we get out of here?"

"Not until Slow Talker comes back and sits down," I replied. "Then we're getting out of here, trust me."

"I know, I know," Will replied gravely. "I know the whole thing is crazy, but there's still a part of me that knows he's right."

Buck spit out a long, angry breath of air. "We'll all be dead," he scoffed. "But at least Charlie will be right."

Again they were silent, and for a few moments there was nothing but the sound of the fire and the trees.

"We should have dropped that gold to the bottom of the Lynn Canal," Buck said bitterly.

"Oh my God," I gasped.

"Don't be stupid," Will replied. "That wouldn't have solved anything."

"Oh my God, oh my God," I thought. My breath caught in my throat, and my eyes widened as they spoke. "Oh my God," I thought. "I was right. I was right!"

In an instant the sense of fear and danger came back with a vengeance. They were gold thieves! And from the sound of it they were planning a risky getaway. Finally, I had the proof I had come for, and I needed to make a risky getaway as well and get the hell out of there.

"What are you guys talking about?" I heard Slow Talker's voice again as he plodded his way back to the campsite from the bushes. "You know you're not supposed to be talking about the gold."

"Who's gonna hear us, Jay?" Buck asked. "The mosquitoes?"

"Leave Jay alone," Will snapped.

Jay? Did they call him Jay? If he was Jay, then who was Charlie? Were there four of them? And if so, then where was the other one?

"Just forget it," Buck replied angrily, pulling himself loudly to his feet. "This whole thing is completely nuts. I wish I'd never seen that stupid gold."

"We all wish that," Will said evenly, trying to calm Buck down. "But we just have to get it out of here, and everything will be fine."

"Just forget it," Buck said again, sounding almost close to tears. "Charlie's going to get us all killed. Do you know how many times we're gonna have to climb the pass to get all that gold up there?"

There was that name Charlie again. Who was Charlie?

"Don't worry, boys," a deep voice from close behind me said, sending my heart rocketing up into my throat in a startled, terrified panic. I felt a heavy weight press down on the upturned heel of my right boot, pinning it to the ground so I couldn't scurry away. "Now we have an extra pair of hands to help us."

CHAPTER ELEVEN

Three Lies And A Single Truth

C harlie, as it turned out, was the fourth member of their little gold-stealing gang, and he'd been hiding behind me out in the woods the whole time, watching me and wondering what I was up to.

Grabbing me roughly by the arm, he yanked me to my feet and dragged me kicking and screaming into the clearing, where the campfire was still burning and the sports debate had just ended. Off to the side were a couple of pitched tents, a pile of what appeared to be supplies, and the same giant beer cooler I had seen from the photos taken from the air at the beginning of the summer.

Charlie, the one who was holding my wrist in an iron-clad vise grip to keep me from running away, was in his late twenties, tall and lean and muscular with nearly black hair. Will was a bit shorter than Charlie but also muscular and in his late twenties with dark blonde hair. Buck's appearance matched his squeaky voice; he was thin and lanky, also with dark blonde hair tucked under a baseball cap, and he was awkward-looking, as though his limbs were too long for his body. Jay was more like Charlie, tall and muscular, and his dark hair was short on his head, almost shaved bald. They were all dressed in rumpled outdoorsy clothes and unshaven as though they'd been living in the wilderness for quite some time—all summer, I assumed, ever since they had stolen the gold more than two months ago—and all of them, except Charlie, had looks of absolute shock and horror on their faces upon seeing him emerge from the brush with me by his side, held in a severe death grip by the wrist.

"What the hell are you doing, Charlie?" Buck nearly shrieked. "Who the hell is this?!??"

The other two were apparently shocked speechless because they said nothing and just continued to stare wide-eyed and gape-mouthed at me as Charlie dragged me roughly across the clearing toward their tents. Reaching down with one hand, he disentangled a length of thick electrical wire from the tarps covering their pile of supplies.

"I don't know who this is," Charlie replied in a frighteningly icy, calm voice as he yanked me back toward the fire. He grabbed my other wrist, and I squealed in pain as he wrenched both of my arms painfully behind my back and bound them together with the electrical wire. When he was finished, he pushed me roughly down to the ground.

I looked around at all of their faces in terror as I tried to hold back the tears welling up in my eyes. By the orange-red light of the campfire the four of them looked like demons from another world as they gathered around me for a closer look.

"I don't understand," Will said, finally recovered enough from his shock to speak. "Who is she? Where did she come from?"

Charlie answered coldly. "All I know is that I saw her sneaking down here from up by the bridge, so I followed her to just there, outside the camp where she's been listening to the three of you for the last half hour."

"So what?" Buck asked. "We didn't say anything. Why would you grab her like this?"

"We did," Will said quietly, his voice filling with anger. "We did say something, remember? You said something, you idiot."

"Goddammit!" Buck bellowed, taking off his baseball cap and throwing it violently into the trees.

"Keep it down, Buck," both Will and Charlie hissed. Buck turned and sat down heavily on one of the logs surrounding the fire, putting his head into his hands miserably.

"Okay," Will said, gesturing with his hands as though he were trying to clear his head and think things through. "Let's just be cool about this. Who is she? Where did she come from?"

Charlie replied. "There's an easy way to find out." Charlie walked over and got down on one knee in front of me. The others gathered around him, standing behind him in a half circle. The whole thing felt unreal. In the glow of the campfire light I felt like I was sitting before some demonic tribunal, and these were the judges gathered before me. The tears welling up in my eyes were blurring my vision and making the whole scene wobble in and out of focus, adding to the surreal effect. I blinked hard a couple of times to get rid of the tears, and a couple of them rolled down my cheeks, leaving a cold, wet trail behind them.

"Don't cry, sweetheart," Charlie said, coming close and looking me directly in the eye. Like the others, he was unshaven, and I could smell that he'd been living out in the wilderness for some time. He and his clothes smelled like a bizarrely pleasant combination of campfire smoke, sweat, and aftershave—a smell I was familiar with after having been on plenty of camping trips myself. "I am just going to ask you a couple of questions."

I nodded hesitantly. "Sh...sh...Sure," I replied, stuttering.

"First off," he asked. "What's your name?"

"K...k...Kate," I replied, lying. I am not sure why I lied about something as simple as my name, but I guess the years of television and movies had taught me that this is what you are supposed to do in such situations.

"And what are you doing all the way out here in the middle of the night?" he asked.

"I...I wanted to see Dyea," I muttered in reply, lying again.

"What's that?" he said, straining to hear me.

"I wanted to see Dyea," I replied more clearly, trying to calm myself and feeling a bit stronger. "I wanted to see the ruins of Dyea. But I got lost in the woods and couldn't find my way back."

Charlie thought this over for a moment, looking unconvinced. "Then why were you sneaking around in the woods out there and spying on these guys?" he said, gesturing back over his shoulder to his companions.

"I was checking things out to see if it was safe," I replied convincingly, gritting my teeth and becoming annoyed at Charlie's icy, cool tone. As I spoke my tone grew cold and angry in return, and I became increasingly convinced by my own lies. "I am a teenage girl. And even when I am lost and scared and need help, I don't just waltz into campsites full of strange men who have been drinking and expect them to just help me!"

That seemed to get through to Charlie. For a split second I thought I saw a flicker of understanding in his eyes. He nodded and stared through me for a few moments as he rubbed the stubble on his chin and thought things over.

"One more question," he said, finally. "And this is the most important question of all."

"Okay," I replied.

"Who knows you are out here?" he asked.

In a fraction of a second my newly gained angry confidence collapsed into nothing, and I gave a truthful answer for the first time that night.

"No one," I answered, dropping my gaze and looking down at the dirt.

"Where are your parents?" he asked.

"Back in Canada," I said. "They live in Canada."

"And who are you staying with up here in Alaska?"

"With some friends of the family," I replied. "But they are away in Seattle this week."

Charlie got to his feet and continued to think things over silently for a long time while the other three watched.

"So?" Will asked hesitantly. "What are we going to do with her?"

Charlie stood silently for another long moment. "There's only one thing we *can* do with her," he said quietly, his icy, cool voice sending chills through my entire body. The other three looked as terrified as I felt at what the answer might be.

"And what's that?" Buck asked, nervously clearing his throat.

"We have to take her with us," Charlie said simply. The others stared at him in silence with dumbfounded looks on their faces.

"Are you kidding?" Will finally asked.

"Absolutely not," Charlie replied quickly. "Think about it. There's nothing else we can do now. I stood there for half an hour watching her and trying to figure out why she was sneaking around. And all that time I was hoping she wasn't on to us. But when you two opened your big mouths about the gold, I couldn't just let her get away, could I? I had to grab her."

"But Charlie," Will started to protest. "We can't take her all the way…"

"No," Charlie snapped, holding up his palm and cutting Will off in mid-sentence. "There's no other way. We either take her with us, and she can help us carry the gold. Or we…"

"Or we what?" Will snapped.

"Or we have to kill her," Charlie said coldly.

Dreaming Of An Opportune Moment

"Have you lost your mind, Charlie?!??" moaned Buck, sitting down and dropping his face into his hands again.

"Settle down!" Charlie snapped. "It's the only way!"

"Charlie's right," Will said.

Buck looked up at Will and then at Charlie again. "Then you're as crazy as he is," he said.

"Just listen," Will replied, kneeling down in front of Buck. "He's right. It's the only way now. We'll take her with us, and she can help us carry the gold over the border, and then we'll let her go."

"She can't carry the gold," Buck said. "It's too heavy."

"She can carry some," Will replied. "Not as much as the rest of us, but something at least. And the less we have to carry, the faster we'll be able to get this whole thing done."

Buck thought this over. "And then we let her go, right?" he asked.

"Yes," Will answered, looking back at Charlie. "Right, Charlie?"

Charlie nodded. "As long as she cooperates, we'll let her go," he said.

"And what if she doesn't cooperate?" asked Jay, speaking up for the first time. Surprised at hearing the sound of his voice, the others turned their heads to look at him.

"She will," Charlie said simply, walking over to their pile of supplies and bending down to rummage around for a while. When he stood up again, I saw what he'd been looking for, and my heart sank a bit further into my stomach. In his arms he was cradling a long-barreled rifle and was pulling shells from his pocket to load it. The sight of the gun seemed to make the others nervous. It made me very nervous too. Terrified, actually, and as I felt my stomach sinking deeper and deeper down, a wave of nausea crept over me. I felt like I was going to throw up.

Will walked over to Charlie and gingerly touched him on the arm as he finished loading the rifle. "Is that really necessary?" he asked quietly.

"Sure is," Charlie replied curtly, snapping the action on the rifle closed and checking the safety catch. "We need to be out of here first thing tomorrow, and one of us will have to stand watch while the rest of us get some sleep."

"First thing tomorrow?" Buck asked, getting to his feet again. "Why?"

Charlie pointed at me. "Because of her," he said. "We don't know who she is or what her story is. And we have no idea who might come looking for her tonight or tomorrow morning."

"She said she was alone!" Buck cried.

"Maybe she's telling the truth, maybe not," Charlie continued. "But we're not going to risk it. We are pulling up camp and heading upriver first thing tomorrow morning. Do we all understand that?"

Charlie looked at them sternly, one after another, and one by one they nodded in agreement.

"Good," Charlie said. "Now get some sleep. I'll take the first watch so I can figure some things out. Then Will, then Buck, then Jay. I want to be loaded up and on the water by 6:00 a.m."

Dismissed, the other three grudgingly went their separate ways and climbed into the tents that were set up nearby. After a moment Will emerged from one of them and brought a sleeping bag over to me.

"You'll need this," he said simply, draping it over me and walking away again. As he walked he glanced at Charlie, who was sitting on a log close by, where he could keep an eye on me. I felt like he wanted to say something to him, but Charlie was in his own world, focused and concentrating on something. Will climbed back into his tent and zipped the door closed. After that there was silence, broken only by the occasional cracking sound from the dwindling fire and the wind in the trees.

I looked at Charlie. In the dim orange light I could see the profile of his face staring off into the distance as he thought things through in his head, making plans. I watched him as the fire faded away, and as the darkness settled, I made some of my own plans too.

I was getting out of here, I decided. Tonight.

"But how to do that?" I thought. I had my hands tied behind my back with wire, and I was sitting on the ground leaning up against a log. Not exactly a position that worked to my advantage. The sleeping bag that Will had brought was helpful. Not only did it keep me warm, but it also hid from view what I was doing with my hands. And what I was doing was slowly working them back and forth to try to get the wire loose. Sometimes I overdid it and made too much movement, causing Charlie to glance at me. When that happened I just pretended I was shifting my weight, trying to get comfortable, and he would soon look away again and go back to his own thoughts.

"What was it that he'd said?" I asked myself. "Who was taking the shifts after him? Will, then Buck, then Jay. Makes sense," I thought. Charlie was going to be the most alert of the bunch, followed by Will. Jay I wasn't sure about. He was quieter than the rest. But Buck was the one I was wondering about. Of all of them he seemed the one who was least happy with the situation, and maybe when his turn came I could find an opportunity to escape.

"And then what?" the voice inside my head asked, actually being helpful for once. "What's the plan?"

"The plan is to get this wire off my wrists," I replied. "Then wait for an opportune moment, and run. Run like hell. Through the woods, into the darkness, and as far away from this as I can get."

"What kind of 'opportune moment'?" the little voice asked.

"Simple," I responded. "When one of them, maybe Buck, gets drowsy on his shift. Or if not that, then when he looks away for a second. Something. Some moment where I have time to get to my feet quickly and make a run for it. The trees are three meters away. I can make it."

"They will chase you," the little voice reminded me.

"I know," I replied. "And that is fine. These four guys look like they're in decent shape, but I bet I can still outrun them. I will run all the way back to my plane if I have to, and take off in the darkness."

"That's risky," the little voice said.

"Doesn't matter," I replied calmly. "It's not total darkness out here. There's moonlight and starlight, and it will be enough to get me airborne."

"If there's enough light for that," the voice asked, "then isn't there enough light for them to see you while you're running away, and for them to shoot you?"

"Let them shoot me," I replied furiously. "I bet they won't do it, but just let them try. Because I am getting out of here."

"Good plan," the little voice said and then fell silent again.

Never taking my eyes off of Charlie for one second, I continued to work my wrists back and forth, trying to get the wire loose. I don't know how he tied them, but he must have been in Boy Scouts or something, because no matter how much I wiggled and worked my wrists, the wire didn't seem to be getting any looser.

"Dammit!" I thought. "Why is this so difficult?"

Charlie looked at me, and I tried to look innocent, yawning and shifting my weight as though I were trying to sleep. He looked at me for a moment longer and then looked away again.

"That was a good idea," I thought. "Try to look innocent and as though you're going to sleep."

Wiggling myself onto my side to lean on the log, I positioned myself so I could keep an eye on Charlie and still hide what I was doing with my hands. I rested my head on the log and closed my eyes while I continued to slowly work my wrists back and forth behind me. The wire was covered in plastic, but it still cut painfully into my wrists as I constantly twisted it back and forth.

"You can do this," I told myself as I worked. "You have to do this."

And slowly, slowly, the wire seemed to be getting just the tiniest bit looser. My wrists were crying in pain, but still I continued. But slowly, slowly my closed eyes started to feel heavier and heavier. I was too terrified and determined to fall asleep. And in too much pain from the constant twisting of the wire on my wrists. But as it turned out I was wrong. And before I realized what was happening, I fell asleep.

Can you believe it? I actually fell asleep.

CHAPTER TWELVE
Going To Relive History

"Rise and shine, sweetheart," I heard a voice say, and I felt someone kicking me on the heel of my boots.

I opened my eyes slowly, unsure of what was happening. I only knew that it was freezing cold and dark, and in my waking confusion I couldn't immediately remember the events of the night before or where I was. It all came back to me in a hurry, however, and soon I was sitting bolt upright, stiff with cold and fear and pain as my wrists wrenched against the wire that held them together.

"You stupid idiot!" I screamed at myself inside my head. "I can't believe you fell asleep!! You are completely screwed now!"

Charlie was standing in front of me in the dim light. He was the one who'd been kicking my boots to wake me up. "Will, come here and help me for a sec," he called across the clearing.

"Yeah, what?" Will asked, walking over toward us.

"Are we almost good to go?" Charlie asked. "It's gonna get light out pretty quick."

"We're almost finished loading, yeah," Will answered.

"Good," Charlie replied. "Give me a hand with her and we'll get moving."

Grabbing me under my elbows, the two of them pulled me to my feet. Pulling a length of nylon climbing rope from his long jacket, Charlie handed his rifle to Will and reached over to put his arms around me and thread the rope around my back. As he leaned over, his unshaven cheek brushed next to mine, and I pulled away. I could smell that familiar scent of the outdoors again: campfire smoke, sweat, and aftershave. He tied the rope around my waist and cinched it tight, jerking me toward him violently as he pulled it.

"I am going to untie your hands now," he said, putting his hands on my shoulders to look me in the eye. "You can go to the bathroom right over there in the trees. And make it fast. Got it?"

I nodded quickly in agreement. He might as well have asked me if I would bungee jump over a glass factory at that moment, because I would have agreed to just about anything to get that wire off of my wrists. It wasn't cutting into the skin, but it was so tight and my arms were so stiff from sleeping that I was in absolute agony.

"Will here is going to be holding the other end of this rope," Charlie explained, taking his rifle back. "And I will be covering you from here. You understand?"

I nodded again, and Charlie spun me around to start untying the wire. I don't think I could possibly explain in a hundred years how good it felt when that wire came loose and I was able to stretch my arms free again. It was the most excruciatingly pleasant feeling I have ever experienced in my entire life, which I know probably sounds completely ridiculous, but it's true. I wanted to burst into tears of happiness; that is how good it felt. Maybe I wanted to cry for other reasons too, but at that moment all I cared about was that my hands were free.

As I went about my business in the bushes, I peeked around the tree I was hiding behind to survey the situation. Charlie and Will were standing a few meters away, covering me as promised, and farther beyond I could see that the tents and supplies that I'd seen the night before were already pulled down and taken away. Will had mentioned loading something, but I couldn't see what he meant. They didn't have a truck or a car or anything, so I could only assume he meant the boat. The other two must be down by the river loading the boat, I assumed.

That meant that if I could somehow untie myself, I could make a run for it in the opposite direction and not accidentally bump into any of them along the way. Reaching for the rope around my waist, I felt for the knots and looked down to see if I could untie them. No way. Not a chance. Charlie was definitely a Boy Scout with a merit badge in knot-tying, because I had no clue how I would even begin to untie the knot he'd used.

"Move it along, sweetheart," Charlie called to me from the clearing, and I felt a pair of tugs on the rope. "We haven't got all day."

With a heavy sigh, I pulled my pants up again, straightened out my clothes, and walked back out of the trees, giving my wrists a massage as I went and reveling in the exquisite pain that it caused. Will handed me a granola bar, which I unwrapped greedily and wolfed down in a matter of seconds. He handed me another one and then took the rifle back from Charlie. I wolfed that second granola bar down too. I was absolutely starving.

"Sorry, darlin'," Charlie said, spinning me around and pulling my arms painfully around behind my back again. Wrapping the wire around my wrists, he tied the wire off in another of his impossible knots and spun me forward again. I wanted to burst into tears again, this time because the wire was back on, and the stiffness and pain returned in an instant.

"Where the hell are you taking me?" I asked, trying to sound tough, but my voice was hoarse and rough from the night spent out in the cold. The sky had lightened to blue, and I was reminded of every early morning I had spent on the docks that summer getting my plane ready to fly. I would have given absolutely anything to be flight-prepping my trusty De Havilland Beaver right then.

"We're going to relive history," Charlie said simply. And with a tight grip on the end of the rope that was still tied around me, we set off through the trees and down toward the river.

The End Of The Line

My assumption had been right. While I had slept that morning they had been busy tearing down the camp and loading everything into the boat, which was now tied up down at the banks of the Taiya River. It was strange to see the boat up close. It was the same little white boat with the teal stripe that I'd seen from the air, but now I was seeing it from a much more dangerous and frightening perspective. I cursed my stupidity of the night before for coming out here to investigate. If I lived through this, I promised myself, I would never go on another adventure ever again.

Loaded onto the boat were the packed-up tents and backpacks and supplies that I'd seen the night before. Plus, of course, the beer cooler was safely onboard and weighing the boat down in the water heavily. Seeing the boat riding so low in the water on that cold morning, I surprised myself that in my treacherous situation I still managed a crooked and cynical smile in knowing that I had been right.

Lifting me again by the elbows, Will and Charlie carried me aboard the boat and deposited me on the middle bench, where they could keep an eye on me—two of them in front of me and two behind. And just to be extra sure that I wasn't going anywhere, Charlie tied my waist-rope securely to the bench.

"I hope the boat doesn't capsize," I thought. It's not like they'll stop to untie me if it does, and then I'll drown for sure."

I wasn't very convinced that the boat would stay afloat; it was loaded down so much. And yet somehow it didn't seem to be as low in the water as when I'd seen it before. It must be a trick of the viewing angle, I decided.

I watched helplessly as they finished loading the boat and untied it from a nearby tree. Buck pushed the boat off the sandy shoreline while Will and Jay pushed off from inside the boat using long steering oars. Buck grabbed the side of the boat and jumped onboard just as the current caught the boat to carry it downstream. Using their oars, Will and Jay pushed us out into the middle of the river and dug in to hold the boat in place against the strong current, while Charlie pulled on the ripcord of the outboard motor and brought it to life. The current was fairly strong, but the motor was stronger, and Charlie steered us upstream.

Even in my dangerous predicament I couldn't help but be impressed with how efficiently the four of them got us on our way. Not a single word was said among them during the entire operation. Everyone just knew what he was supposed to do and did it. From start to finish it took only a matter of seconds to get us pushed off and motoring our way up the river.

As we made our way up the river, my captors remained as silent as they had during the boat-launching operation. No one had spoken a single word since we left camp earlier that morning.

Behind me at the back of the boat, Charlie steered the boat up the channel, his face serious and focused on the river ahead. Buck sat motionless nearby, crouched down to stay warm, his baseball cap pulled down nearly over his eyes and his hands stuffed into his pockets. Up at the front of the boat, Will was standing with his knees braced against the bench, and he would periodically test the depth of the water with his long oar or help steer the boat from the bow. Jay sat nearby with his oar at the ready in case Will needed some help pushing us off an unexpected sandbar or a sudden shallow patch. As we made our way farther and farther upstream, Jay's help was needed more frequently as the river got increasingly narrow and shallow.

And so it went for what seemed like an eternity. No one saying a word, just the low drone of the outboard motor, as the distance between the river banks gradually decreased, and the dawn slowly poured light into the sky.

As daylight broke across the world, it revealed a beautiful fairytale landscape in front of our eyes. Under different circumstances I would have found this early-morning boat trip to be rather pleasant. It was freezing cold outside, but it was really a lovely morning. I always had a fondness for the early morning, and this particular day was especially beautiful. The sky was getting lighter and bluer with every passing second. Up ahead in the distance and on all sides the snow-capped mountain peaks were wreathed with fragments of mist and beautiful ice-blue glaciers. High in the trees lining the river, bald eagles were perched, silently standing watch like majestic sentinels as we made our way past them on the river below.

But of course I was unable to enjoy any of this, being in fear for my life and sitting with my arms twisted painfully behind my back. My fingers were getting more and more frozen the longer they were exposed to the cold morning air. I wiggled my fingers to keep the blood flowing and managed to pull my sleeves as far over my fingers as possible, but it didn't help much.

On and on we rode, and after what must have been hours I wondered how far up the river they were planning to go. It seemed to me like we weren't going to be able to go much farther at the rate that we were scraping the bottom, and Will and Jay had to keep pushing us along with their oars.

Finally, we reached the end of our river journey. A short muddy beach on the right bank came into view, and Charlie steered us toward it.

"That's it," he said, his voice cutting through the wordless morning and startling me a little. "This is where we put in yesterday."

"So they were up here yesterday," I thought. "Doing what?"

Will surveyed the river for a moment. "The river's a lot higher today," he said. "Should we try to load the rest of the gold and go a bit farther?"

"So I was right," I thought. The boat wasn't riding as low as it had been before. They'd taken some of the gold upriver yesterday and dropped it off somewhere.

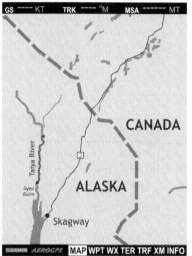

Charlie shook his head. "We won't get much farther," he said. "And we'd waste as much time loading up again as we'd gain getting farther upriver." He shut the engine down, and the constant throbbing buzz was replaced with just the sound of the river and the incredible perfect stillness of the early morning.

Will nodded as he and Jay used their oars to guide the boat to the shore and run it aground. Will planted his oar in the mud and held it secure as Jay jumped off and pulled the boat even farther up, tying it securely to a tree.

"End of the line," I heard Charlie say from behind me as he clapped me on the shoulder. "It's all on foot from here on in."

Thank God For Small Favors

After securely beaching the boat on the shoreline, the four of them unloaded all of their equipment and supplies—and of course the beer cooler containing the gold. I hadn't realized it while we made the trip upriver, but as it turned out, not all the gold was in the cooler. While they were unloading and I was sitting in the boat still tied up, Charlie swatted my feet out of his way and strained to pull up a flat package wrapped in plastic from the floor of the boat. After seeing the amount of effort it took to lift it, I didn't have to be Sherlock Holmes to figure out what the contents of that relatively small package could be. It could only be one thing. Gold. And some of it had been under my feet the whole time.

As they continued unloading, I saw that they had laid similar small packages along the entire length of the boat. That was to distribute the weight, I realized, and to keep everything balanced. They weren't stupid, these four. Or maybe it was just Charlie who was the smart one.

I continued to sit there, helplessly tied to the boat as I watched them unload. They worked with the same military efficiency that they had when we'd pushed off downriver earlier that morning. Again, no one saying a word and everyone knowing exactly what to do and just doing it.

As I sat there watching them, my mind numb and blank and my wrists killing me, my thoughts began to wander a little bit. I remember that I was thinking about something completely stupid—popcorn, I think—when I realized that I was all alone. I sat bolt upright and looked around me, straining my ears to listen to the sounds of them carrying their supplies up through the trees.

"Am I really all alone?" I thought. "Are all four of them really up there in the woods without leaving someone to watch over me?"

They were being awfully cavalier about keeping an eye on their hostage. But I didn't care. That was to my benefit.

I had to act fast. With my right foot I stretched over to see if I could reach the cleat where the mooring rope was tied up to the boat. If I leaned back I could easily reach it.

Charlie might have been a Boy Scout, but this knot I knew well: a cleat hitch. I used the exact same knot when tying up to docks with my De Havilland Beaver. And I was betting I could untie it with my foot.

Kicking at the knot with my boots the little voice in my head started up again. "I don't mean to be a naysayer," it said. "But even if you can get it untied...then what?"

"Then we escape," I replied, continuing to work the knot with the tip of my boots.

"But the boat isn't just tied up," the little voice said. "It's also half-beached on the shore. How do you plan to push it off into the water? And even if you could do that, what's the plan then? Float downriver while your hands are tied so you can't steer? And don't forget that you're still tied to the boat. If the boat flips over, you're dead."

I clearly hadn't thought my escape plan all the way through, and I stopped kicking at the knot. With a deep sigh, I returned to just sitting helplessly on the boat.

Eventually, the four of them emerged from the trees once again, and without a word they untied me from the boat, grabbed me by the elbows, and lifted me onto dry land. (Or should I say partly dry land—the mud squished beneath my feet as they set me down on the shoreline.)

Buck kept an eye on me while the other three struggled to drag the boat completely out of the water and up into some bushes along the side of the river. They secured a green tarp over it and threw some tree branches on top to camouflage it.

We headed up through a path in the woods to where they had stashed their supplies. A similar green tarp was in the process of being secured over the top of their cache, and nearby there were five backpacks laid out on the ground. There were four large ones for them and one small one for me.

"Okay," Charlie said, finally breaking the silence. "Let's divide up the gold for the first trip so each of us is carrying as much as possible. Me and Will as much as we can, Jay and Buck a bit less, and maybe twenty-five pounds for her."

"Why does she get to carry so little?" Buck asked. "She's not carrying anything else."

The other three looked at him like he was an idiot.

"Don't be stupid, Buck," Will said. "She's a girl. And besides, we don't want her slowing us down."

Charlie nodded and thought this over. "You're right," he said. "We don't want to be slowed down. Only give her twenty pounds."

"Well thank God for small favors," I thought, sounding like my grandmother. This was the first good news I'd had all day.

They loaded up the backpacks with some more of those curious flat plastic packages and tested the weight of the packs on their backs. The rest of the plastic packages went inside the beer cooler until it was quite full, and then they filled it the rest of the way with bottles of beer and cans of food to disguise it.

When they were all finished, they pulled the tarp over the rest of the supplies and secured it. Wherever we were going, apparently they were planning to come back here to make additional trips. But were they planning to leave all that gold unguarded while we were away?

"Is that going to be okay here alone?" Will asked, apparently thinking the exact same thing I was.

Charlie nodded. "There's hardly anyone on the trail this time of year," he said. "Maybe no one at all. And even if there was, they aren't going to be sidetracking into the forest on the off chance that someone stored a pile of gold out here."

"Did you see anyone on your way back last night?" Will asked.

Somewhere in my frightened and numb brain something clicked. I'd already figured that they made a trip upriver with half of the gold the day before—it was too heavy to take in one go on the shallow river—but now I realized that when they did that, they must have left Charlie to walk back on his own. Maybe to finish camouflaging their gear or something.

"That explains why he was walking around in the forest at the same time I was," I thought. "Just my luck."

"Not a soul," Charlie replied.

Will seemed convinced by this and pulled his backpack up over his shoulders. The other three followed suit and secured their shoulder straps and waist straps until they were comfortable.

"Your turn," Charlie said, walking over to me with the smaller backpack and his rifle. Reaching around behind my back, he fumbled with the wire around my wrists and quickly untied it.

Oh my God, what an amazing feeling it was when that wire came off. I almost groaned in pleasure as my arms swung free, and I brought my hands to the front to massage my wrists.

"No funny business," Charlie said, shaking a finger at me and yanking on the rope tied around my waist to remind me that it was still there. He handed me the small backpack and gestured for me to put it on. When I was done we were ready to go, and he turned to the other three. "Okay," he said, getting serious. "Will in the lead, then her, then me, then Jay. And Buck brings up the rear. Got it?"

Everyone nodded, including me, my instinct to be polite kicking in before I could stop myself. Charlie nodded back, and with that we were on our way.

CHAPTER THIRTEEN
Walking In The Footsteps Of History

For almost the entire day we walked in silence, wordlessly picking our way through the rocks and trees. The path we were on was obviously a well-used and marked one, but it was still rough going in some places, and I was glad to have my hands free so I could steady myself as I clambered over the rocks and tree roots that covered most of the trail.

The path through the trees was clearly worn, and the occasional well-built suspension bridge or wooden walkway over beautiful mountain streams reminded me of the government-maintained nature-hike trails that we had back home in Tofino. There were even signs pointing the way, and we passed a government campground complete with wooden outhouses and a log cabin shelter off in the trees. All of this was evidence that a lot of people used this trail. But where were they? Charlie had said that it was "late in the season," and there probably wouldn't be many people on the trail—maybe no one—but what did they plan to do with me if they did run across someone?

"What they plan to do doesn't matter," I thought. "What matters is what you plan to do."

I didn't know. Should I scream for help? Try to make a run for it? Or would Charlie kill all of us then?

I snorted air out of my nose and laughed cynically to myself. "It won't come to that," I thought. "They'll see or hear the others a mile away and not get anywhere near them with me."

"Is she okay like that?" Will asked, turning around from in front of me to speak to Charlie. "With her hands untied? What if she drops her pack and makes a run for it?"

"Damn right that is what I will do if I get the chance," I thought, laughing cynically to myself again.

"Don't worry," Charlie said, tugging on the rope around my waist. "I've got her."

"Yes," I thought. "That stupid rope tied around me is a problem."

There was no way that I could surreptitiously untie it with Charlie directly behind and undoubtedly keeping a very close eye on me. "But if you loosen your grip on that rope for even one second, I am out of here," I thought.

"Okay," Will replied, and he turned forward again.

"Besides," Charlie continued. "She's a smart girl. She knows that if she made a run for it out here with no tent and no supplies, she'd be a goner."

"Don't count on it," I thought, clenching my teeth. "I'd rather die out here in the wilderness than stick around with you four."

In my head I talked tough, but I wasn't 100 percent convinced. Charlie was right. I would probably die out here, even if I could follow the well-marked trail back.

"There are supplies back at the river," Will reminded Charlie.

I'd forgotten about those. And there was a boat there. Maybe there was hope for my plan after all.

"She'd never find them," Charlie responded. "They're too deep in the woods off a trail she's not familiar with."

"That's true," I thought, my hopes dimming again.

"And I'll bet she didn't make a mental note of where the stash is either," Charlie concluded. "Did ya, darlin'?"

I could hear in Charlie's voice that he was grinning behind me.

"No," I muttered under my breath as I continued along the trail. I didn't.

Behind Charlie I could hear Buck and Jay talking about something between themselves. Sports again, it sounded like. Why was everyone suddenly so talkative?

I realized that ever since we left the river, the nervous tension that had been hanging over everyone seemed to have gradually evaporated. You could almost feel the pressure lifting with each step forward. Maybe the four of them were just more comfortable out here in the wilderness than they were back in the civilized world? Or maybe it was just the comfort of finally being on their way, working toward a goal? I could understand that.

"Do you realize that you're walking in the footsteps of history?" Charlie said behind me. It took me a moment to realize that he was talking to me. "How many thousands of people have gone before us down this very same path and have taken the very same steps that you're now taking?"

I turned to look back at him. He was smiling. He was actually smiling. "There really must be something in the air up here," I thought. It made Charlie so chatty and smiling.

"No," I replied, my voice full of gravel. It felt like I hadn't spoken in days.

"This is no place for the weak of heart," Will said cryptically, apparently quoting something that I wasn't familiar with. "*The North wants strong men. Strong of soul, not body. The body does not count.*"

Charlie laughed at this. "Do you know Jack London?" he asked, again speaking to me.

"Not really," I answered after clearing my throat.

"Doesn't matter," Charlie replied. "He's not for everyone. But Will up there adores him."

"He was a writer, right?" I asked timidly.

"Exactly," Charlie said. "A kind of nineteenth-century Ernest Hemingway. You know Hemingway, right?"

"We read him in school," I answered.

"Hemingway, I love," Charlie said. "Jack London, I don't."

From in front of me Will made a booing sound.

Why was Charlie suddenly so chatty? I thought again. It really must be the air. Maybe there was some truth to that because I'd never breathed such air before in my life - and I come from a place where the air is already clean and beautiful. Every breath I took was cool and clear and wonderful and seemed to fill my lungs much more than normal air ever did. Like the air had substance to it somehow. And filled you with spiritual energy.

"Why don't you love Jack London?" I asked. Maybe if I was friendly with them they would relax and let down their guard long enough for me to get away.

Charlie was quiet for a few moments. "He's too confusing," he finally said. "I find myself constantly rereading entire sections, struggling to understand what he's trying to tell you."

"Oh boo!" Will said from up at the front of our little hiking party.

"Not to mention," Charlie said. "I want to read a book once. Not three or four times over because the writer didn't write it clearly enough."

I surprised myself by laughing a bit at the conversation that the two of them were having back and forth. In the circumstances that I was in at that particular point, laughing was the farthest thing from my mind.

"Okay, okay," I said before I could stop myself. "But what does Jack London or Hemingway or anyone else have to do with hiking through the woods and walking 'in the footsteps of history'?" I surprised myself by raising my hands in the air and making air-quotes and using a playfully sarcastic tone of voice. For a split-second I forgot where I was and who I was with. Maybe because the pain in my wrists had subsided considerably. Maybe because the unbearable tension had been lifted. I don't know. I guess for a split-second I forgot all of that and got caught up in the moment.

I think I must have surprised them too, because for a long few seconds all conversation ceased, and we walked along in silence.

"What all this has to do with Jack London," Charlie finally said, "is the fact that if Jack London had not once walked the exact same trail on which you are now walking, then none of us would ever have heard of Jack London."

An Unlikely Good-Luck Charm

"Way back before anyone ever heard of Jack London," Charlie said as we continued our hike through wilderness, "he was living with his parents down in California, going to university but dreaming of making it big as a writer.

"Around the time that he runs out of money and has to drop out of school, he reads in the papers about this gold rush that is happening way up in Canada at some place called the Klondike. The whole world eventually joins the rush to get rich, but Jack London was one of the first to drop everything and jump on a steamship north.

"So he jumps on a ship and sails all the way up here to Dyea, where you were wandering around last night. He goes ashore and partners up with some people he's met on the voyage, and they get themselves a boat and head upriver toward Canada with all their stuff—the very same river that we came up this morning. They went as far as they could on water, then pulled over and continued along on foot, just like we're doing now.

"So Jack London," Charlie concluded dramatically, "walked this same path that we're walking on right now, headed in the same direction that we are, up toward Canada. That is like I said—we are reliving history."

"Good story, Charlie," Will said, turning to look over his shoulder back at us. "Except you left out the most important part."

"And what's that?"

"That Jack took all his experiences from the way through here and later weaved them into stories that made him a millionaire," Will replied.

"Then drank himself to death and died at forty," Charlie finished.

"Sad but true," Will agreed and we walked on in silence for a little while.

As we continued along the trail, I tried to imagine what it had been like more than a hundred years earlier when Jack London had been there. It wasn't difficult, because throughout the day we had passed various reminders of that bygone era—small bits of rusty metal hiding in the bushes here and there or larger rusting derelicts like a huge iron stove and what looked like a giant steam engine. All of these relics were clues to unraveling the story of what had taken place here in the not-so-distant past.

Of course, when Jack London had passed through, he and his group were just a handful among thousands climbing through the forest and clinging to the distant dream of striking it rich up the Yukon. Our small group, on the other hand, seemed to have the entire trail to ourselves. The good condition of the trail and the well-maintained amenities along the way made it clear that even in the twenty-first century there was still a human presence here, but that human presence had clearly packed up for the winter and headed south to warmer climates.

As we continued up the trail, I noticed that it was getting dark. The sun was getting low in the sky far behind us and projecting long shadows on the mountain peaks ahead. I tried to remember when we had last stopped for a break and a granola bar by the side of the trail. It felt like a hundred years.

"We have to stop soon," I thought. But we just kept going, climbing the trail up the long mountain valley with no end in sight. Occasionally, we would break out of the trees for a moment, and amazing views of the long mountain valley would reveal themselves. I watched as the shadows on the distant mountain peaks climbed higher and higher toward the summits, turning redder as they advanced and as the sun began to set behind us.

Finally, there came a break in the monotonous routine of that seemingly endless hike. As Will reached the top of a small climb, he held up his hand to signal for the rest of us to stop. "We're there," he said quietly, nervously keeping his eyes forward and focused on whatever lay beyond this small incline.

"Drop your pack and check it out, Jay," Charlie hissed over his shoulder to Jay, a tense expression on his face. I heard Jay's pack hit the ground behind us and watched as he scrambled up the incline to disappear past Will down the other side.

"What the hell is it?" I thought. "Where are we? And why is everyone so nervous?"

For a minute or two we all just stood there, tense and silent, until we heard Jay's voice calling to us from far ahead. "All clear," he yelled, breaking the silence and the tension in one go, and everyone relaxed again.

"Let's go, sweetheart," Charlie said, clapping me on the back as he stepped up next to me, smiling once again. I climbed the rest of the way up the small incline and stopped for a moment at the top to see what it was that was making everyone so nervous. It was a building with a flagpole and some kind of official-looking wooden sign tacked on the side. Beyond that in the distance was another one of those well-maintained government-looking campgrounds like the ones we'd passed earlier in the day.

"That's it?" I thought. "What's so scary about that?"

And then I realized what it was. I'd forgotten that we weren't just on some pleasant afternoon hike out in the woods. I was a hostage, the four of them were criminals, and this was a park ranger station. Jay had been sent up ahead of us to check things out and make sure that no one was there.

"It's totally deserted," Jay said, jogging back toward us to recover his pack. "Everyone's packed up for the year and left, just as you thought."

"Told you so," Charlie said to the others. He turned to me, smiling. "Sorry, darlin'. You're stuck with us a bit longer."

I couldn't help but give him a little smile in return. His smile was a bit infectious, I guess. Or maybe I was actually glad that there wasn't a park ranger there. Who knows what that would have meant? It could have been an ugly scene at worst, and at best it probably would have meant we'd have to take a long detour around the camp. At least now we could stop for the day and take our packs off. I don't know how the rest of them felt, but my back was killing me. Actually, everything was killing me. I was hurting all over.

Will was also smiling and shaking his head in disbelief as we wandered down toward the campground. "You were right, Charlie," he said. "Everyone has packed up and left the trail for the year."

"Sheep Camp," a sign told us. "Next camping area, Happy Camp, eight miles, allow ten hours."

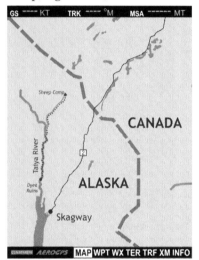

Was that where we were headed? Happy Camp? Ten hours? Are you kidding me?

"It happens every year," Charlie said. "There's nothing but the grizzlies between us and Canada until next spring."

"Was this why they were hiding out all summer?" I wondered. I wrinkled my nose and forehead as I thought this over. I'd first spotted their overloaded little boat back at the beginning of July on my first whale flight. That was more than two and a half months ago. During the long boat trip and hike that day my mind had sometimes wandered, and I found myself wondering why they'd picked yesterday as the day to make their move with the gold instead of weeks earlier. Because if they'd picked a different day I would be back at home, blissfully unaware of any of this and getting ready for bed.

I pondered this riddle as we continued the short hike down into the deserted campground. Along the sides of the trail the brilliant purple blossoms on the ubiquitous fireweed had nearly reached the top of the plant, a sure sign to any native Alaskan that winter was almost upon them. And of course, with the onset of winter, the tourist season—not to mention the hiking season—had come to an end, leaving trails and campgrounds like these completely empty.

"You were waiting for the trail to be clear," I heard myself say as I worked things out in my head, speaking the words before I could stop myself. "You knew the police would be watching all the ferries and border crossings, so you were waiting for this trail to be clear so you could escape up into Canada."

The four of them stopped cold in their tracks. For a few long seconds they looked back and forth among one another with surprised expressions on their faces.

Charlie's face broke into a wide smile, and he erupted into a robust laugh. The sound of it cut through the trees and echoed off of the nearby mountains.

"I told you she wasn't stupid," he said to the others after laughing heartily for a few seconds. "Kate here is going to be our good-luck charm."

Oh right. My name is Kate. I'd forgotten about that.

The Brotherhood Of Wolverine

The four of them impressed me again with their military efficiency. In just a matter of minutes they finished setting up camp for the night. It wasn't much to do, I suppose, just put up a couple of tents and sleeping bags while warming some water on a small camping stove, but I was still impressed with the way they worked together so effectively.

Charlie kept an eye on me, holding tightly onto the rope tied around my waist, while the other three did most of the work. He had given me a plastic water bottle earlier in the day, and as we watched the others working, he refilled it with some freshly purified water that tasted like sour tin and chlorine.

After they finished, we all sat down at one of the campground's picnic tables to a dinner of hot tea and energy bars. The sun was long gone from the sky at this point, so we ate in darkness and silence.

It was cold. And damp. But Alaskan mosquitoes must be tough because that didn't stop them from buzzing around us and diving in for their own dinner. There weren't too many, thank God, so it was relatively easy to brush them away.

All the time Charlie stood off to the side behind me, keeping an eye on the rest of us sitting at the heavy wooden table. Just as I wondered about the sleeping arrangements and whether I was going to have to spend another night sleeping on a log, he answered the question for me.

"Buck and Jay, you guys store the food and take the smaller tent," Charlie said. "Will and me and her will take the larger one. I want to be on the way tomorrow before 4:00 a.m."

Everyone nodded, and just like that, without another word, dinner was over. Flashlights were switched on, and Jay stashed the food supplies in some special bear-proof lockers nearby while Buck cleared the rest of the gear from the table.

Everyone took turns visiting the wooden outhouses before heading for the tents. Charlie stood watch outside with a firm hand on the rope that was still around my waist while I went inside. It was freezing cold, and the smell was foul and horrific—you know, standard outhouse aroma—but it was a luxury compared to crawling out in the bushes as I had done earlier in the day. It was a luxury, but a very smelly one, so of course I got out of there as fast as I could.

Jay and Buck disappeared inside their tent while the rest of us made our way back over to our own with Will leading the way by flashlight.

"Sorry, darlin'," Charlie said when we reached the tent, holding up the wrist wire in front of his face. My heart sank.

"Not that again," I thought. But at least he didn't tie me up with my arms behind my back. Instead, he lashed my wrists together out in front of my body, which was a lot less painful.

He held the tent flap open and gestured me inside. Ducking my head, I stepped into the tent and paused while Will pulled my boots off, leaving them outside of the tent. The pain of having the wire back on my wrists was made up for by the sheer intense satisfaction of finally being able to take my boots off. My feet hurt like you wouldn't believe, and when he slid my boots up off my toes, it was the most amazing feeling. The blood rushed back into my feet and brought with it the most exquisite pain. I didn't know whether to cry or laugh or both.

"A foot massage maybe?" I thought, sarcastically. "Anyone want to do that? No?"

I am not sure I could have withstood it even if they had. I think if anyone would have even breathed on my feet at that moment it would have made me scream in pain. But oh my god what an amazing beautiful pain that would have been.

I wormed my way into the tent awkwardly, using my bound hands to steady myself. Charlie came next and checked the knots on the rope around my waist before zipping me into a sleeping bag and stuffing a balled-up fleece under my head as a pillow. He tied the other end around his own waist and then crawled into his own sleeping bag next to mine at the head of the tent. Will came in last and closed the text flaps behind him.

"Lash my wrist to hers," Charlie said, holding out his left arm. Will nodded and quickly tied Charlie and me together while holding the flashlight with his armpit. Finishing off the knots, Will switched off the flashlight and plunged the tent into a darkness that was blacker than anything I had ever experienced in my life. An inky, velvety, cold blackness.

In the dark I could hear Will crawling into his sleeping bag and stretching out at our feet by the door of the tent. They weren't taking any chances. To get out of there I would have to somehow untie my wrists without anyone waking up and noticing. Then I would have to do the same with the rope around my waist. Then wiggle out of my sleeping bag and somehow crawl over Will. Then unzip the tent flap. Then get outside. Then put my boots back on. All without waking anyone up.

"And then what?" the little voice inside my head asked.

"I know," I replied to myself. "It's pitch dark outside, and I wouldn't dare switch on a flashlight."

Although I could probably get to the food supplies and disappear into the darkness.

I thought my escape plan through a bit further.

After I got the food supplies I could continue forward on the trail instead of turning back, I thought. They would never expect that. And I would have their food.

I felt more hopeful about my plan.

"But do you know how long the trail is ahead of you?" the little voice asked.

"No," I thought. "No, I don't. But surely it eventually has to reach civilization again at some point."

"Are you sure?" the little voice responded. "If it does, then why would these guys be following it?"

I didn't know the answer to that. I was too busy trying not to fall asleep again.

"It has to meet up with a road or something," I thought. "And then I can flag a passing vehicle down and get to safety."

"I suppose so," the little voice replied. "But you wouldn't have a tent or a sleeping bag or anything. You'll probably freeze to death."

I thought about that for a second. "Maybe," I thought. "But maybe not."

"Not to mention," the little voice continued, "that to do any of these things, you'd still have to get out of this tent in the first place. If you can do that, then maybe you can run off into the dark wilderness where the bears are and freeze yourself to death."

"The little voice is right. I'm screwed, aren't I?" I asked myself.

"Not entirely," the little voice responded reassuringly. "Right now you're warm and relatively safe with four guys who seem to know what they are doing out here in the wilderness."

"Ironic," I thought. "I'm safer with these four criminals than I would be if I were on my own."

"Just get some sleep," the little voice advised me. "Tomorrow we'll figure out what to do."

"Okay," I replied.

I didn't need much convincing, to be honest. I was so exhausted and broken from all the hiking that day that all I wanted to do was sleep. A daring escape, even if successful, did not really sound as appealing at that particular moment.

I abandoned the thoughts of plotting my escape and let my mind wander instead.

"I wonder what Edward is doing right now," I thought, smiling to myself in the darkness and my heart warming at the thought of him. "Maybe when he's back from fishing we can go for sushi again?"

"You'll have to get out of this mess first," the voice inside my head helpfully reminded me.

I frowned. "Helpful, thanks," I told myself.

In the darkness I could hear both Will and Charlie breathing heavily. My eyes had adjusted to the darkness a bit, and I thought that maybe I could make out the vague, dark outline of Charlie's face against the rest of the blackness. Maybe or maybe not, I wasn't sure. It didn't matter. After the events of the past twenty-four hours, I had his face burned permanently into my memory.

"Actually," I thought, smiling to myself in the darkness as I picture Charlie's chiseled jaw and infectious grin in my head, "he's a pretty good-looking guy. He reminds me of that actor, you know, the Wolverine?"

"Hugh Jackman," the little voice in my head said helpfully.

"Yah, right," I replied. "Hugh Jackman. He reminds me of him."

I wrinkled my nose and forehead, thinking.

"Actually," my mind continued, "they all kind of remind me of Wolverine somehow. All four of them have a bit of a Hugh Jackman thing going on."

As my eyelids became increasingly saturated and heavy with sleep, I muttered, "You are brothers."

"That's right, sweetheart," I heard Charlie answer, his voice close in the darkness. "Why do you think we're doing all this?"

"I don't understand," I remember thinking and wanting to ask in reply. "What does that mean?"

But that was it. I couldn't say another word, and my mind went as black as the world around me as I fell asleep.

CHAPTER FOURTEEN
Some Idiot Has Always Been There Before You

"The four of them are brothers," I said to myself as I sat in the darkness, chewing on an energy bar and watching them tear down the tents the next morning. I couldn't believe that I didn't see it before.

As usual Charlie was keeping an eye on me while the others did most of the work. He leaned over and offered me another energy bar.

"No thanks," I muttered, shaking my head. I don't know how they lived off those things. It was only a day for me so far, and I'd already had enough energy bars for a lifetime.

"Eat it," he said, sliding it down the picnic table toward me, bouncing it off of my elbow. "We have a serious climb ahead of us today. All uphill."

"It was all uphill yesterday," I replied, grabbing the bar off the picnic table.

"Not like today," he replied cryptically and went back to finishing his own energy bar and washing it down with some purified water.

I did as I was told and scarfed down my third energy bar of the morning, eating it as fast as I could so I didn't puke it up again. I looked at the wrapper. "Energy Plus," it read. I am sure it had lots of energy. I just wish it was "Taste Plus."

The other three finished tearing down the camp and made their way back over to Charlie and me, the beams of their flashlights bouncing eerily off the trees in the early-morning light.

"Time to go," Charlie said, giving me a gentle tap on the leg with his boot. He pulled his backpack on and adjusted it while I did the same. "Okay, boys," he said to the others as they got closer.

"Same as before. Will in the lead, then Kate, then me, then Jay, then Buck."

And without another word we were off again, hiking up the trail through the early-morning darkness. Everyone had a flashlight except me, but Charlie kept enough light on the path directly in front of me so that I could see where I was stepping.

Before long I could tell that we had left the cover of the forest and were more out in the open. The path became much rockier than it had been before, and I found myself scrambling to keep my balance and footing as we climbed.

Somewhere nearby the resonating sound of a mountain stream came steadily closer and stayed with us as we climbed endlessly upward. The sound of running water had been an almost constant companion on this entire trip thus far, but this was somehow different. The roar of this stream was fresher somehow. Cleaner. And cold.

As the light crept into the sky I made out more of the landscape surrounding us. We were hiking steadily up a narrow mountain valley, with walls of rock patched with green and snow towering high above us on both sides. Glancing back from time to time, I could see the valley zigzagging back and forth down toward the ocean behind us. Somewhere back there was the Taiya River, leading all the way to Dyea. In fact, I realized, this mountain stream that we were following up the valley was probably where some of the waters of the Taiya River came from.

"Hold up," Charlie called out from behind me. "Let's take a break here."

"Thank God," Buck said with a groan, releasing his pack and setting it on the ground with a dull thud.

"My thoughts exactly," I said as I pulled off my pack as well. "This is brutal."

"You know that it gets much worse," Will said, somehow finding the energy to smile.

"Worse than this?" I thought. My calves were burning like they were on fire. Yesterday it had been my feet that had hurt the most by the end of the day, but I could guess that tonight it was going to be my legs when we set up camp. Wherever that might be. Somewhere farther up, I guessed.

Everyone sat in silence, taking occasional sips from water bottles. We all tried to catch our breath. We had stopped at what looked like a natural stopping point, with plenty of flat rocks to sit on and a commanding view of the valley stretching out behind us. People had stopped there before, I could tell, thanks to the collection of various stone piles that people had constructed around the perimeter.

"Inukshuks," I muttered under my breath. 'Inuksuk' (the proper spelling) was the Inuit word for a small stone cairn that travelers in the far north would build as markers for themselves or fellow travelers and hunters.

The favorite version of the Inuksuk was stones piled up into the shape of a human form, although these had a different name - I forget what, but anyway we just call them all Inukshuks.

Whatever they are called they are getting out of hand, I thought. When I was a kid no one had ever heard of them. Nowadays they were everywhere. I couldn't leave the house without seeing an Inukshuk piled up out of stones somewhere and ruining the beauty of nature at every turn. It didn't matter where I was, they were always there. Outside of the Tofino Co-Op store standing on the edge of the parking lot wall, along the side of the road at my favorite secret spot on the drive out to Port Alberni, and now here, far out in the godforsaken wilderness. Wherever I went some idiot had already been there and ruined the view by building an Inukshuk—a constant reminder in our modern world that no matter where you go, some idiot has always been there before you.

"I wonder what the Inuit think of that," I wondered as I took another sip of strange tinny-tasting water.

"Inunnguaq," Charlie said, looking at me.

I shook my head. I didn't understand.

"The man-shaped ones are called 'Inunnguaq,'" he said, gesturing at the human-shaped Inukshuk closest to me.

"Ee-non-wok?" I repeated, mimicking his pronunciation.

"Close enough," he said, capping his bottle and standing up again. He walked over to the human-shaped Inukshuk (the Inunnguaq) and dismantled it stone by stone, catapulting each stone off into the distance down the valley. When he finished he looked over to see me staring at him. "People need to stop building those and just let nature be nature," he explained simply, then called over to the others as he walked back to his pack. "Let's go, break's over!"

We all pulled on our packs once again and fell into line, and just like that we were back on our way.

Our Own Ton Of Goods

"Do you know the Alaskan license plate?" Charlie asked from behind me as we continued our climb higher and higher up the mountain valley.

We had reached a relatively flat stretch of ground, where the trail seemed to dissolve into an enormous field littered with giant boulders. Far off in the distance the valley tapered off into a lopsided v-shaped depression filled with dull, grey stones and patches of snow. With the valley and the trail coming to an end, I didn't understand where we were supposed to go from there.

"Are you talking to me?" I asked, looking back over my shoulder.

"Yeah, you," he said. "Have you ever looked closely at an Alaskan license plate? The white, yellow, and blue ones. Have you ever noticed what's pictured on them?"

I thought about this for a second, picturing the license plate of Uncle Joe's truck in my mind. "EDE 989," it read. But there was something else between the letters, printed directly on the original plate as part of the design. After a few seconds it came to me.

"A line of men!" I answered excitedly. "Climbing up toward some mountains in the distance."

"Hey!" Will cheered from up in front. "Good memory."

"Nice one," Charlie congratulated me. "And do you know where that image comes from?"

"Ummmmm, no, sorry," I said. "Something to do with the gold rush?"

"You're halfway right," Charlie replied. "It comes from a series of very famous photographs that were taken back in the 1890s showing men headed for the gold rush in Canada and climbing in an endless human line up and over an icy mountain pass."

That description sounded familiar. Somewhere in my memory I could remember a photograph like that. Maybe I'd seen something like it back in Juneau. A colorless photograph showing a long thin line of men climbing like a trail of ants on a stark white background of snow and ice, up and up and up, disappearing in the distance over the summit of the mountains.

"I think I've seen that," I said.

"I'm sure you have," Will said from in front of me. "They are hanging everywhere."

"But do you know where those pictures was taken?" Charlie asked.

I shook my head. "No idea," I answered.

Charlie tugged gently on the rope around my waist and stepped up behind me, clapping a hand on my left shoulder to bring me to a halt as he moved up next to me.

"Right there," he said, leaning in close so I could see as he pointed off into the distance up the v-shaped, stone-filled valley ahead of us. "The Chilkoot Pass."

I stared off into the distance and tried to overlay the memory of the photograph in my head with what I was seeing in front of me. It didn't look right somehow.

"How can this be the same place?" I asked. "There's hardly any snow up there, and in the photo it's all snow."

Buck and Jay had caught up to us by this time, and we all took off our packs and took a moment to catch our breath.

"It was winter then," Buck said, gesturing to the distant mountains with his water bottle. "When they took the photo, I mean."

Charlie nodded. "Right," he said. "And because it was the middle of winter some enterprising young businessman had the idea to cut a primitive staircase directly into the ice and charged people to use it. Fifteen hundred steps all the way to the top."

"Oh my God, " I gasped. "In the middle of winter?" I shuddered to think what the temperature was up there in the middle of winter.

The four of them nodded almost in unison. Just like four brothers. I smiled to myself.

"The lucky ones only had to climb it once," Will said. "But if you didn't have enough money to pay someone to help carry your stuff to the top, then you had to climb it over and over again to get your ton of goods up there."

That sounded familiar somehow. Glen had mentioned something about that during his tales of the Yukon at the barbecue three days ago.

"Oh God," I thought. "Was that only three days ago?"

It felt like an eternity.

"What ton of goods?" I asked, wrinkling my forehead, trying to remember. "What does that mean?"

Charlie pointed again up into the distance to the top of the mountain pass. "Up there," he said. "Is Canada. And back in the gold rush days there were Mounties stationed up there who wouldn't let you into Canada unless you had enough gear with you to survive."

"Flour, sugar, bacon," Will said, counting the items on his fingers.

"Ropes, canvas, whipsaws, nails," Charlie continued the list.

"Socks, boots, picks, shovels," Will took over again.

"Tent, tools, stove, tea kettle," Charlie said, pointing off to the side of the trail on the last two items. I looked over to where he was pointing to see an old iron stove top rusting away complete with a half disintegrated kettle sitting on top. The whole landscape around us was littered with rusting remnants and twisted bits of metal.

"Blankets, medicines, frying pans," Will kept going. "And so on."

"And until you had it all," Charlie said. "They wouldn't let you in. So up and down you went until you'd carted all that stuff all the way up there."

"Unbelievable," I said.

"Of course, if you were lucky," Will commented. "You could negotiate with the local Indians and hire them to carry your stuff to the top for you."

"And that's where we're standing right now," Charlie said, gesturing to the rocky landscape around us. "This is where the Indians would weigh your packs of gear and tell you what it was going to cost you to get them to the top."

Will nodded in agreement. "The Scales," he said. "That's what it's called."

Charlie took another sip from his water bottle, then snapped the lid closed and reached into his pack. Pulling out a pair of gloves and a pair of wool mittens, he handed the mittens to me and put the gloves on himself.

"Enough chit chat," he said. He pulled on his pack again, and all of us followed his example. It was amazing how everyone, including me, just fell instantly back into climbing mode once Charlie gave the word. He was our leader, that was for sure. "We don't have native packers to help us," he said. "We'll have to carry our own ton of goods all the way to the top by ourselves."

CHAPTER FIFTEEN
A Waterfall Of Rock

The scope of what lay ahead of us slowly became clear to me as we continued our hike farther up the valley. The v-shaped gorge tapered off into nothing far up ahead, and from a distance it appeared as though the sides of the valley floor were covered in gravel and small rocks that had slid off the mountain sides. However, as we hiked closer I realized that these small rocks weren't actually small at all. They were huge boulders. And this altered the entire scale by which I viewed the scene ahead of me. The distance from where we were to the summit was much farther than I had estimated, and the vertical distance that we had to climb was a lot greater too—and a lot steeper. It had to be a forty-five-degree-angle climb, straight up to the summit.

The well-worn trail was long gone by this point, and the path was marked instead by long orange poles sticking up through the stones at periodic intervals. The poles were long enough to stick out through a thick layer of snow, and I could imagine that earlier in the summer, there had probably been a lot more snow up here than the relatively small patches of snow that were scattered randomly on the valley floor. These poles were clearly designed to keep the trail clearly marked even in the event of heavy snowfall.

"Or fog," I thought. The weather was relatively clear up to the summit. Overcast, but without rain and a high cloud ceiling, far above the highest peaks. But even in the middle of summer the weather up here could just as easily be a dense, soupy fog, and these poles would certainly be a lifeline to any hikers out in such conditions.

Of course, the men and women who hiked this trail more than a century ago didn't have such helpful conveniences. Looking around and imagining the scene around me as it would have looked back during the gold rush, I suddenly remembered the graves I had seen back in the ruins of Dyea two days earlier.

Maybe I was being too hard. Maybe it was too easy to dismiss them all as greedy fools, including the four greedy fools who held me captive. But I could not imagine anything other than greed that would drive someone to come all this way, risking his or her life at every turn to make this horrific climb over and over and over again. Were they really such fools that they truly believed that up in the Yukon an endless supply of gold was just lying around on the ground waiting to be picked up? Even if they did believe it, hundreds must have turned back when they saw that final climb to the summit ahead of them. Maybe even thousands.

I stopped to catch my breath for a moment. My calves felt like they were about to tear wide open, the muscles and tendons snapping and giving way from all the strain. With every breath the cold air burned in my throat and continued to burn all the way down deep into my lungs. I wasn't sure I could do it. I wasn't sure I could survive the climb all the way to the top.

Every step I took had to be planned in excruciating detail. First balancing myself with my hands and fingers on a couple of nearby rocks, then lifting one foot carefully as I steadied myself uneasily on the other leg. Next, I had to decide where I was going to put the foot down. This decision should have been made *before* lifting my foot off the ground, but in my numb mental state more often than not I forgot to do this. That foot then had to be set down gingerly somewhere that looked solid. This was more difficult than you can believe in the incredible jumble of sharp-edged stones that made up the entire route to the summit. Once that foot was down, I carefully tested the stability before transferring my weight (and the horrible weight of the gold on my back) onto that forward foot to pull myself upward. With that done I started the process all over again to take the next step.

The others weren't doing much better than I was, even though they were clearly all experienced climbers. We all climbed without a word, and I could hear them breathing heavily, the cold air catching just as hoarsely in their lungs as it was in mine. Every single step was for them just as intricate a procedure as it was for me. And I couldn't forget that their packs were considerably heavier than mine was. Heavier by a long shot.

And so we climbed. One agonizing step after another. Pausing every few steps to catch our breath before continuing the painful climb once again. This cycle repeating endlessly as we crept our way higher and higher, one small step at a time.

Stopping for what felt like the hundredth time, I leaned over, face down on all fours, to inhale and exhale raggedly. Stretching my neck forward, I looked up toward the summit. The line of orange poles seemed to stretch on forever, winding back and forth across the waterfall of rocks and stones and boulders that cascaded down between the two small peaks up above me.

That is exactly what it looked like—a waterfall of rock. There could not possibly be better words to describe it than that. It was as though some immense pair of hands had poured a gigantic bucket of rocks and boulders down the slope toward where I was catching my breath.

"Why did the stampeders do it?" I asked myself, my inner voice screaming to be heard over the whirlwind of emotions swirling inside my head as I climbed on. What possessed those people to do it? To climb all this way. To suffer all this. For nothing! My contempt for those naïve and greedy fools of the gold rush grew with every step I took in their footsteps. With every scorching breath my anger bubbled closer and closer to the boiling point.

"And who the hell built an Inukshuk all the way up here?!??" I shrieked internally as I reached over with my mittened hands to push a carefully constructed pile of stones off its foundation and into the crevices of the chaos of rocks below. What was I doing here?

I stopped to compose myself. "Just be cool," the little voice in my head told me.

"Yes," I replied. "You're right. Just breathe."

I took a deep breath. Then another. And another. And slowly my heart rate began to slow, and my anger subsided.

"We're almost there, sweetheart," I heard Charlie say from behind me. Taking a few more steps he climbed up to my level and put his hand on my pack. "You see that gap on the left up there?" he asked, pointing up ahead with one gloved finger. "That's the summit."

I followed his finger to see what he was talking about. Not more than a few meters ahead was a small gap through which a tumble of rocks seemed to be pouring.

"That's it?" I asked breathlessly.

"That's it," he answered. "Can you make it?"

I nodded. I wasn't about to allow the trail or anyone who had ever climbed it to get the best of me. And somehow I found the strength to pull myself forward and clamber over the remaining rocks between me and the summit.

The Mummies Of The Chilkoot

Stepping up onto the summit of the Chilkoot Pass was one of the greatest moments of my entire life. With just one very long, painful, burning step I felt like I had stepped out onto the top of the universe. A few small mountain peaks littered the large plateau at the top of the pass, but it was clear that there was nowhere left to go except down. Up ahead I could make out lakes and mountain ranges stretching out flat into the distance. Behind me the rock fall cascaded down to the floor of the valley, which twisted and wound its way all the way back down to Dyea and the ocean. I had done it! I had climbed the Chilkoot Pass!

"Hold up here," Charlie said, holding up the palm of his hand in a "stop" motion. He gestured to Will, who had reached the summit a few minutes before us. "Go check things out up ahead," he said to Will. "Make sure we're alone up here."

Will nodded and dropped his pack on the ground. Scrambling over the summit plateau, he made his way over to a group of small buildings nearly hidden behind the rocks up ahead. The Canadian border park ranger station, I assumed. I watched him disappear behind the rocks in the distance, then I doubled over to breathe in and out as deeply as I could.

Jay and Buck soon joined us at the summit and likewise leaned up against the rocks to catch their breath. Charlie tilted his head toward where Will had disappeared, and they nodded back in understanding.

After what seemed like forever Will finally reemerged from behind the rocks in the distance in front of us. He yelled something, but I couldn't quite make out what it was. Judging from his body language, however, it was all clear up ahead.

"Okay," Charlie said, tugging on the rope around my waist and gesturing to everyone to keep going. "Just a bit farther."

I had expected that we would head for the group of buildings and the Canadian border, but instead we traversed along the edge of the summit ridge until we came to a small grassy depression between the rocky peaks of the summit. Scattered along the bottom of the depression was various debris from the gold-rush days and strange, long packages rolled up in a reddish canvas. These strange canvas packages were lined up in rows and piled in an orderly fashion that made me uneasy.

"What are those?" I asked nervously as Will scrambled over rocks down into the depression. The packages looked a lot like cloth-wrapped corpses. Mummified remains of those who did not survive the Chilkoot Pass.

"Those?" Charlie said, jerking his thumb down toward the piles below. "Those are do-it-yourself boat kits."

"Do-it-yourself what?" I asked.

"Boat kits," he said. "Back in the gold rush some fellow had the brilliant idea to ship a couple hundred boat kits all the way up the Chilkoot and sell them to new arrivals over on the other side in Canada, so people could use them to float downriver to Dawson."

"Boat kits," I nodded, relieved that they weren't the Mummies of the Chilkoot.

"The only problem was that the boats weren't very seaworthy," Charlie continued. "And the Mounties wouldn't let them into Canada. So the guy just left them up here."

I nodded, and as I climbed down into the depression out of the wind, I got a better look at what Charlie was talking about. The rolled packages were obviously not corpses—just piles of lumber and rusting metal with red canvas wrapped around them—but they were still kind of creepy looking. The lumber was bleached white from a hundred years of sun and snow and rain, and they looked like the bones of some ancient supernatural beings. I shuddered at the thought of it. Or maybe it was just the cold wind.

Everyone stripped off their packs and found somewhere to sit while Jay broke out the energy bars.

"We'll have lunch here and take a breather," Charlie said. "Then we'll unload the gold and stash it here before we head back down."

"What did he say?!?" I asked myself. "Unload the gold? Head back down? What?!?"

Looking at Charlie sternly, I asked, "What do you mean?"

Charlie glanced at me. "What?" he asked, confused.

"What do you mean, head back down?" I said.

Charlie laughed. "Back down to get the rest of the gold," he replied.

I'd forgotten about the rest of the gold down there back at the river. Somehow I thought that once we made it to the top of the pass and into Canada that they'd go their own way and finally let me go. "We couldn't carry all that gold in one trip," he said.

I thought about this. "So you have to go all the way back to the river, then all the way back up here again?" I asked.

Charlie nodded. "And then again and again and again," he said.

"Again and again?" I replied in disbelief. "How many times?"

"Eight or ten trips," Charlie said. "Give or take."

"Eight or ten trips?" I responded. "Are you kidding me? That will take days!"

"A couple weeks, probably," Will said.

I looked at him and then back at Charlie again.

"And then what?" I asked, growing increasingly frustrated.

"Then down into Canada," Charlie replied calmly, his mouth full of energy bar.

"Maybe it will have snowed by then," Will said. "And we can pull the gear on a ice sled. Otherwise it'll be more trips back and forth into Canada."

"But that will take forever," I protested.

Charlie shrugged. "We got time," he said simply, finishing off his energy bar and stuffing the wrapper into the pocket of his jacket.

I looked at him in disbelief and then at the other three, one by one. They were all sitting quietly and eating their energy bars— perfectly calm in the face of this unbelievable revelation. Although I suppose for them it wasn't a revelation. This had been their plan all along. But it wasn't my plan. I couldn't stay out here in the wilderness for the next two months with these guys, hiking back and forth all day.

I put my head in my hands in disbelief. I was nearly in tears, but I wasn't going to let these guys see me cry. My pride wouldn't let me. So I bit my lip, hard, and kept the tears inside.

"This is ridiculous," I said. I didn't care how far out in the wilderness we were or how risky it was for me to try to make it on my own. I had to get away from these guys, even if it killed me. "In twenty minutes I could have flown everything up here in my plane instead of going through all this craziness," I said.

The thought of my safe, warm plane was just too much for me. All the way up there at the summit of the Chilkoot Pass I did what many of the stampeders must have done a hundred years ago, no matter how tough they were. I sat there and cried—hot, wet tears streaming down my face.

"Wait a minute!" Charlie bellowed, startling me out of my tears. I looked up to see the others, who had surprised expressions on their faces. They were looking at Charlie, who was standing there was a huge maniacal grin on his face. "Change of plans," he said.

CHAPTER SIXTEEN
A Change Of Plans

"Do you know who this is?" Charlie asked as he strode over toward me. The other three sat there with surprised and confused looks on their faces, startled by Charlie's sudden outburst. Buck had just stuffed an entire energy bar into his face and was sitting there with his cheeks swollen out from the half-chewed bar in his mouth. It would have been funny if we weren't all so terrified of Charlie at that moment. He was grinning like a crazy man.

Will and Jay and Buck slowly shook their heads.

"Her name isn't Kate," Charlie explained. "This is Kitty Hawk." This information brought only more head shaking and confused looks from the others. "Didn't you guys read the newspapers I brought out from town every couple of days?" he asked.

"I read the sports section," Buck said, still as confused as the rest of them.

Charlie rolled his eyes and dismissed them with a wave of his hand. He turned his attention to me, walking over and kneeling down in front of me.

"How did you get to Dyea?" he asked.

I shook my head. I didn't understand.

"Dyea," he repeated. "How did you get there?"

"I told you," I answered, confused. "I walked there."

"Before that," he said. "How did you get there before you started walking?"

I looked a him for a moment and then at the others, my eyes going from man to man to look each of them in the eye. I looked back at Charlie again.

"I flew there," I said, and on hearing that, a flicker of recognition flashed across Charlie's face, and his eyes widened. His smile grew until he looked like the Cheshire Cat, which I suppose made me Alice, but the Chilkoot Pass summit was definitely not Wonderland.

"What did she say?" Will asked breathlessly.

"Did she say she flew there?" Buck said, looking at Jay for confirmation. Jay shrugged his shoulders.

Charlie nodded, his grin still widening.

"She has a plane?" Will said, grinning and putting a hand on Charlie's shoulder as he kneeled down next to him.

"She has a plane?!?" Buck repeated, bouncing with excitement, shifting his weight back and forth from one foot to another.

"Yes, she does," Charlie replied, nodding. "Don't ya, darlin'?"

I nodded hesitantly, and Buck exploded with delight, putting his hands on top of his head to let out a deafening whoop that echoed off the mountain tops.

"Settle down, Buck," Charlie said, turning serious. He looked me in the eyes again. "Remind me, Kitty," he said, speaking softly. "Who knows that you went out to Dyea?"

"No one," I replied truthfully.

"And who is there back in Juneau who might have reported you missing?" Charlie asked. "Tell me the truth. No more lies."

I wrinkled my nose and thought about that for a second. Uncle Joe and Aunt Jenny were in Seattle, Edward was out fishing, and not even my parents would have noticed I was missing because they had gone to Banff for the week.

I shook my head. "I don't think anyone," I said slowly. "Everyone I know is out of town for at least a couple more days."

"And where is your plane?"

"Just off Taiya Inlet," I replied.

Charlie bit his thumbnail, thinking this new information through very carefully while the other three waited for him to speak.

"It's worth the risk," Charlie said finally, nodding to himself.

"What's worth the risk?" Will asked, hopeful.

Charlie rose to his feet again. "If no one's reported her missing," he said slowly, thinking it through as he spoke. "We can be done with this whole thing in a matter of days, instead of months."

The thought of this made everyone smile, including me. Apparently, the rest of them also weren't keen on the idea of trekking back and forth out here in the wilderness for the coming weeks and months. For my part, as long as I could go home soon I would be happy to play along with their little schemes and fly them wherever they wanted to go. In fact, I laughed to myself. I was happy to fly them anywhere just to avoid having to make the climb to the summit up that cascading waterfall of rocks again.

"So how do we do this?" Buck asked. He could hardly contain his excitement at this possible change in plans. I was excited too, I have to admit. In my head I was already home, warm and safe and stopping at a McDonald's drive-thru for a cheeseburger happy meal. Two cheeseburgers, actually, I decided.

Charlie silently paced back and forth and he thought things over. Minute after long minute he continued to walk and think. Five minutes. Then ten.

While we waited for him to finish, the weather on the summit gradually changed. One moment we were all sitting there under a bright but overcast sky, the next moment a cloud descended on the summit, and we found ourselves in a deepening fog. With the air turning much colder, I zipped my jacket up and sank my neck down into the collar.

"Will the gold be too heavy for the plane?" Charlie asked. "Do we have to make two trips?"

I said, "We're definitely going to be over maximum weight. But with a good headwind I think we can do it in one go."

Charlie turned to Will and said, "Worst case is we lose this one trip to the summit, and it sets us back a couple of days."

"Right," Will agreed.

"Best case," Charlie continued. "We're in Canada by tomorrow."

Charlie looked at Will, who nodded his agreement. "We'll have to be careful," Will said cautiously.

"We will be," Charlie assured him as he leaned over his pack and reached inside. Pulling out a small black case, he stood up again and turned to address the rest of us. "Here's what we're gonna do," he said. "We'll head back down with all the gold we have on us right now and check things out down there. If the coast is clear and everything looks kosher, then we'll have young Ms. Hawk here fly us to freedom."

Everyone nodded in understanding. "Okay, Charlie," Buck said.

Charlie looked at his watch. "Let's be ready to go in five minutes," he said, zipping open the black case that he still had in his hands. "But first I have to make a phone call."

Following A Different Kind Of Footsteps

"Who's he calling?" Buck said to Will after Charlie had walked away to make his phone call in private.

Will shrugged. "Probably Eddie," he replied. "Probably telling him to get his butt on a ferry to Skagway to grab the truck since none of us can do it now."

Buck nodded and went back to stuffing an energy bar into his mouth. I tried to finish mine, but I couldn't make myself do it. I wrapped it up again and stuffed it in my jacket pocket.

The wind had picked up a bit by this point and was blowing the fog and cloud across the summit. My legs were aching like never before in my life, but I would still be glad to get on our way again if for no other reason than to just get warmed up a little.

I couldn't believe we were going to climb all the way back down the pass again. I should have opened my big mouth six hours ago, I thought, and saved us having to climb all the way up here. Although I was glad I did it. I felt like I had really accomplished something amazing. I was only sorry that it had to be under these circumstances.

"Under what other circumstances would you have otherwise climbed all the way up here?" the little voice in my head asked.

"Yah right," I replied. "When I get out of this alive and am sitting in Uncle Joe's truck in the parking lot of McDonald's with my cheeseburgers—I am pretty sure I burned off enough calories on the climb up to justify having a couple of cheeseburgers—then I will be glad I did it and proud of myself."

Charlie emerged from the fog a short distance away. "Let's go," he said. "I wanna get down out of this cloud as soon as we can."

We all got to our feet and put on our packs, but for a moment I wasn't sure that I could do it. My legs were hurting so badly that I wasn't sure if I could even stand up again. Jay was next to me and held out a hand to pull me onto my feet.

"Thanks," I said, and he nodded in reply.

And so, simple as that, we started our long climb back down the Chilkoot Pass. I'd like to tell you that the climb down the chaos of rocks was easier than the climb up, but I am not entirely sure that it was. It was down instead of up, of course, but in a lot of ways that just made it much worse. Each step was still a delicate process of gently testing your footing before putting down all your weight and bringing the other foot forward. And because we were now going down instead of up it meant that all the tendons in my legs that hadn't already been strained on the climb up were now burning just as much as their counterparts had been earlier in the day.

The fog was also a problem on the downward climb. We could hardly see ten feet in front of us as we scrambled from one rock to the next. Thank God for those long orange poles to mark the way, or who knows where we might have ended up.

Up ahead of me, Will disappeared and reappeared as the fog shifted and moved around us. Back over my shoulder Charlie was close by, keeping a firm hand on the rope around my waist, but behind him I could only catch occasional flickering glimpses of Jay climbing down farther behind. Beyond him Buck was a complete ghost. He was so far back in the fog that the only way I knew he was still there was from the occasional swearing and cursing that floated down to me on the wind.

Oh yeah, and I forgot one other thing. It also started to rain. Hard. And as if being cold and soaking wet wasn't bad enough, I am sure you can imagine the effect that rain had on the slippery stones of the infamous rock waterfall. Did I mention that they were fairly slippery already when they were still dry? Now imagine them wet. Needless to say, I slipped more times on the way down than I would like to remember, and I bounced my knees and elbows and butt off the hard stones until I was bruised all over.

But eventually, we made it down to the valley floor once again, and the worst of it was over. The fog lifted as we descended, and it rained even harder, but at that point it hardly mattered since we were all soaking wet anyway. At least we were back on semi-normal ground with a trail to follow down through the winding valley.

The path was a lot better here, and I was thankful for all the rocks and stones, because in the rain they made a lot better hiking surface than the mud did. They were slippery, for sure, but I was much happier taking my chances with slipping than I was stepping into the mud with every step. And so we went. Down, down, down—following the mountain stream whose roar now had to compete with the sound of the heavy pouring rain, following the valley down and back into the forest again.

Under the trees I'd hoped for a bit of cover from the rain, but actually the exact opposite was true. Trees only provide cover from the rain up to a certain point, and once they get totally saturated, they become their own little rain clouds, pouring giant heavy drops of rain down onto the forest floor and any unfortunate hikers below. But this was coastal rainforest just like we had back in Tofino, and I'd walked through that in the rain a thousand times before in my life. It felt familiar to me and cheered me up a little.

There was also another reason why I felt cheery once we were back in the woods again. I remembered from the hike out that morning that we would soon be back at the campground where we'd slept the night before—Sheep Camp. I can't tell you how happy I was to see the main cabin of that campground appearing up ahead of us through the trees.

The cabin had a porch with an overhanging roof that we all scrambled under to finally get out of the rain. Through the windows, I could see a wood stove on the inside and bunks to sleep on. Even if the door was locked, I planned on breaking it open myself if I had to, just to get inside and get dry again.

"Let's take a breather and stay out of the rain for a second," Charlie said once Buck and Jay joined us under the cover of the cabin's porch. "Five minutes, okay?"

"Five minutes?!?" I thought. "What does that mean? Are we not stopping here?!?"

"Are you sure we should keep on in this weather?" Will asked.

Charlie nodded. "We can still make the river by nightfall," he said. "It will be wet, but then we can make an early start tomorrow morning. The sooner we get this over with, the better."

"The sooner, the better," I thought. That much I could agree with. I didn't like the idea of going back out into the rain again, but Charlie did have a point. I supposed that this was their plan all along, to get back to the river tonight. Why else had we left camp so early in the morning and climbed in darkness? And it made sense. There was no point taking two days to carry a load of gold from the river to the summit and back when you could do it in one.

Will leaned out and looked up to examine the sky. "If this keeps up, the water level on the river will be nice and high," he said.

Charlie nodded again. "I was thinking the same," he replied, also leaning out from under the cover of the cabin roof to check the sky. "I hope it does. I'd sure like to take the entire load with us downriver when we go instead of making two trips."

"The river will be higher if it keeps raining?" I asked myself. Of course it would be. But I wasn't sure I liked the sound of that—boating down a raging, flooding river on an overloaded little boat full of gold.

"Okay, boys and girls," Charlie said, looking at his watch. "Back out into the rain."

Will stepped out first, leading the way as usual. Then me and Charlie, while Jay and Buck stayed under the cover of the cabin as long as they could before falling in line behind us.

The rain hadn't let up at all, as we started down the trail through the forest once again. And all this mud wasn't helping either. The longer the rain kept falling, the worse it got.

Looking down at the path in front of me to plan my next step, I noticed something that made my heart skip a beat. Imprinted in the mud just ahead of me were the tracks of a very large animal—a grizzly bear, to be exact. I'd seen plenty of bear tracks in my life, usually black bears, but I was also perfectly familiar with grizzly bear tracks as well, and that was definitely what these were. The print of the front paws sank deep into the mud, and the marks made by the bear's claws were spread in an arc far out from the toe-prints. Only a grizzly bear's long front claws would leave a mark that far out.

But what worried me about that particular bear's prints was how fresh they were. They were so fresh, in fact, that the depressions in the mud were just starting to fill with water from the rain. Whatever bear made these tracks was close. Very close.

"Uhhh, guys," I started to say when I was jerked backward by a hard tug on the rope around my waist. Charlie splashed up behind me and pulled me close in to his body. He'd seen the tracks too. But it was already too late.

CHAPTER SEVENTEEN

What To Do When You Meet A Grizzly

The grizzly stepped out onto the path just in front of Will. In the dim light of the rainy forest, Will didn't see him at first and just kept walking toward him with his head down for three or four more steps before realizing it was there. Finally, he saw it and froze in his tracks just a few feet away from the enormous bear.

In a fraction of a second Charlie had slung his rifle off and brought it up to his shoulder to take aim. But he didn't fire. I waited and waited and braced myself for the report of the gun, but nothing happened.

"Why don't you shoot?" I whispered.

"I'm waiting," Charlie said calmly, his right eye focused tightly down the rifle's telescopic sight.

"Don't shoot, Charlie," Will said calmly, raising his arms over his head and moving them around in the air. "It's too big, and that gun of yours will barely scratch it."

"What the hell is he doing?" I asked myself.

Slowly, slowly Will began to step backward away from the bear. The huge grizzly stepped forward on all fours and raised its head up to sniff the air.

"Just be cool, Charlie and Buck and Jay and Kitty," Will continued in an amazingly calm tone as he kept waving his arms in the air and slowly backing away. "It's going to be fine."

Now I understood what he was doing. It was textbook bear etiquette. He was raising his arms to make himself look bigger and talking as much and as calmly as he could while he backed off so the bear didn't feel threatened and charge. Growing up in Tofino, I'd read about this a hundred times before but never actually saw anyone put it into action so flawlessly.

"Slowly," Charlie said, keeping his eye pointed down the rifle sight.

"Don't worry," Will said calmly, still backing away. He was a good fifteen feet away from the bear already and still backing up. "That's a good little bear," he said. "Just be cool."

But the bear wasn't cool. Apparently, he didn't appreciate Will's peaceful tone of voice, or maybe he was just angry because he was out in the rain, soaking wet. Whatever it was, he grunted once, then twice, and launched into a full-on charge straight at Will.

Every muscle in my body tensed, and my instincts told me to run for my life, but I stayed frozen in place, mesmerized by the charging bear.

Will didn't move a muscle. He just stood there, like a frozen statue with his hands over his head, as the giant grizzly charged directly at him. I have no idea how he did it, but he did, and at the last possible moment the bear turned and veered off into the bushes.

I couldn't believe it. He'd actually called the bear's bluff and stood his ground. And if I didn't believe it the first time I saw it, I still had another chance because the bear circled back around, crashing through the bushes to take another run at Will. Again my muscles tensed, but again Will stood his ground, and the bear veered off at the last second, circling back onto the path in front of him.

It was absolutely unbelievable. My mouth was hanging open in absolute astonishment at what I had just seen.

Will resumed backing away from the bear as it raised its head again to sniff the air intently. "What does it smell?" I wondered. And then I had a thought. The half-eaten energy bar in my pocket!

"Oh my God," the little voice in my head said. "Are you so stupid?!?"

Twenty feet away the bear sniffed the air a bit more, then raised itself up onto its hind legs and let out a deafening roar. I was absolutely terrified. I'd never seen a bear act this way before, and it was certainly the first time I ever saw a fifteen-hundred-pound grizzly bear rear up on its back legs. It was absolutely huge, towering unsteadily and continuing to sniff the air.

"That's it," I thought. I had to get rid of that stupid energy bar. I unzipped the side pocket of my jacket and grabbed it out as quickly as I could. Pulling my arm back, I threw it as hard as I could at the bear.

Charlie pulled back, startled by my sudden movement, and for an instant we both stood there in dumb silence, watching the shiny foil package arc gracefully through the air over Will's head and hit the ground a few feet from the grizzly bear. It bounced twice and landed in the mud next to the bear's left back foot.

Curious, the bear lowered itself back onto all fours and inspected the gift of food that had just landed at its feet. Pulling the package apart with his paws and teeth, he swallowed the bar in a single gulp and licked the foil clean.

"Nice shot," Will said. He had finished backing up to where Charlie and I were standing, and the three of us stood there watching the bear lick the empty wrapper of the energy bar.

"He likes those as much as Buck does," Charlie said.

"They're disgusting," I said, my voice shaky and frightened.

The three of us continued to watch the bear lick the wrapper until he lost interest and sniffed the air again. I wondered what we were going to do next, when the deafening crack of Charlie's rifle went off right next to me.

The bear went tense but didn't seem hurt. Had Charlie shot it? I looked over to see Charlie with his rifle pointed safely up into the air. He fired again, and that time the bear got the message, dashing off into the bushes, frightened by the ear-splitting noise. We listened as the he ran off loudly through the trees, breaking branches and snapping twigs as he went. After a few moments the sounds faded off into the distance, and we relaxed again.

"Dammit, Charlie," I heard Buck say from behind us. I spun around to see Buck kneeling on the ground on one knee and massaging his left buttock with his hand. Jay was doubled-over with his hands on his knees, laughing.

"What happened?" Will asked, walking over and offering Buck his hand to help him to his feet.

"Your shooting scared the crap out of me, that's what happened," Buck said. "And I slipped in the mud and fell on that log." He pointed over to a log lying nearby with a sharp, spike-shaped branch sticking out of it.

"Turn around," Will said, spinning Buck around and leaning over to inspect his buttock. There was an inch-long tear in the green fabric of his cargo pants and a little bit of blood, but it didn't look life-threatening. "Don't be a baby," Will said soothingly. "You'll be fine. It's barely a scratch."

"It hurts like hell," Buck said.

"It's just bruised more than anything," Will assured him and gave him a playful swat on the butt.

"Owww!" Buck yelled. "Are you crazy?"

We were all laughing by this point, even Buck. I laughed so hard that before long I could feel myself turning red, and the tears rolled down my cheeks, mixing with the raindrops that continued to run down my hair onto my face. And I just kept laughing and laughing until long after the four of them had already stopped and were just standing there watching me bent over at the waist, turning blue from lack of oxygen.

"I don't know how you did it, Will," I said, still laughing uncontrollably. "You stood your ground, and that grizzly totally backed off."

"Get a hold of yourself," the voice inside my head told me. "You look like a crazy maniac."

"Shut up, stupid voice," I said, continuing to laugh. All the tension and fear and uncertainty that I'd kept bottled up inside me for the past few days just seemed to come out all at once. Laughing had opened the floodgates, and once I got started I was finding it difficult to stop.

To their credit the four of them simply stood there patiently, waiting for me to laugh and cry myself back to sanity again. Eventually, I did slowly get a grip on myself again, and when I finished, I wiped the tears from my eyes with my wet, muddy hands and stood upright again.

Charlie waited a few moments to see if I would start up again, and when he was sure I was done, he took charge once again. "Okay then," he said. "It's getting dark, and we still have a ways to go."

Will walked past me, patting me on the shoulder and smiling as he took up the lead once again. Charlie just stood there, smiling and looking down at the ground. It took me a moment to realize what he was looking at. He was looking down at the opposite end of the rope that was tied around my waist. When the bear had appeared and he'd pulled out his rifle, he'd dropped it to the ground, and there it had stayed ever since. I could have made a run for it if I had wanted.

He laughed as he bent over to pick it up again, pulling it from the mud and coiling it around his hand. Standing up again, he smiled and gestured for me to head down the trail after Will. "After you, sweetheart," he said. "Let's get out of this rain, shall we?"

Out Like A Light

After the encounter with the grizzly bear, I am happy to say that the rest of the hike back to the river was uneventful. It was wet and raining hard, that's for sure, but at least we didn't run into any more bears. Or any other animals or people for that matter.

The hike back seemed to take a lot less time than I expected. I guess that's a normal thing—when you are going somewhere for the first time it seems to take a lot longer to get there than it does when you return. Or maybe my mind was just simply occupied during the rest of the hike back, replaying the bear encounter over and over again in my head.

I still couldn't believe what Will had done. He had been so calm, doing all the right things that you're supposed to do when you meet a bear, as though we were filming a public service announcement on proper bear-challenging techniques. And then standing his ground against the bear charge. That was unbelievable, but it had worked. The bear was totally bluffing. I could never have done that. I would have run for my life for sure and been mowed down by the grizzly's claws as a result. But not Will. He just stood his ground like a weird funny statue with its hands over its head. I wished that I'd had my cell phone on me to make a video of it. That would have definitely gone onto YouTube. Not that I would have been cool enough to actually try to film anything. I had been terrified.

Charlie had been no less amazing during the whole encounter. He'd probably seen the bear prints even before I did and had his gun out and aimed at the bear before I even figured out what was going on. And then, even more amazingly, he'd held his fire. I would have started shooting for sure, I was so scared. But not Charlie. He knew that shooting the bear would probably not have much effect and that to resolve the situation there were a lot of options that had to be exhausted before he resorted to that.

I could learn a lot from these guys, I realized. Not just about outdoorsy wilderness kinds of things, but more like lessons on how to stay cool in tense or dangerous situations, so I could think my way out of them, and to think fast, instead of just acting on instinct. These guys looked like dumb wilderness men, but they certainly knew how to use their heads.

That's about as far as I'd gotten in my thinking before we reached the end of our hike and arrived at the spot where their stash of supplies was hidden down by the river. It was still raining, unfortunately, but I knew from experience that Buck and Jay would have the tents up in no time flat, so Charlie stood with me while I sat on a nearby log, as much out of the way and out of the rain as I could, eating an energy bar and waiting patiently.

True to form, those two had the tents up and sleeping bags laid out in record time, and Charlie and Will and I walked over to the big one. The tent had a kind of covered "front porch" area where people could hang their jackets and clothes, and I was surprised when I took off my jacket that my clothes underneath were still reasonably dry. It certainly hadn't felt that way, with the wet outer skin of the jacket glued to me for the past few hours, but at that moment I certainly had a newfound appreciation for the Viking clothing company in Vancouver. I would have to send them a letter when this was all over and tell them how much their jacket saved me.

The top half of my body was dry, but my pants and boots were most certainly not. For a moment the three of us looked awkwardly at each other as we decided what to do next.

"Don't worry, sweetheart," Charlie said, gesturing for me to crawl inside the tent. "We won't watch."

"Thank you," I said simply and crawled inside, Will pulling off my boots outside the tent just as he had done the night before. My socks were soaking wet, and I pulled those off too.

"But make it fast," Charlie said, switching off their flashlight and plunging us into complete blackness so I could have some extra privacy. "And don't mess around with the rope around you."

He didn't have to worry about that. I was so cold that I ripped off my pants in a flash and nearly jumped into my assigned sleeping bag. But I still couldn't resist feeling the knot at my waist to see if I could maybe untie it. The rope was soaked and the knot tighter than ever. I doubt I could have untied it even if I'd had all the time in the world to do so.

"You done?" Will asked from outside the door.

"Yes," I replied, zipping the sleeping bag up around me and trying to shiver myself warm.

The two of them crawled inside, one after another, in a repeat of the procedure from the night before. Once again Charlie had Will tie the two of us together at the wrist so I couldn't escape, but I noticed that he gave me a little more slack than he had the night before. That was progress, I supposed.

I think Will crawled inside his own sleeping bag and closed the tent door after switching off the flashlight, but I can't be sure. I was out like a light. I think maybe that night was the first time I fully understood that expression, because once Will switched off the light and I found myself in that complete and total blackness once again, with the reassuring patter of rain on the tent's roof (reassuring not only in its calming natural rhythm, but also in the fact that it was outside, and I was inside), once all that happened I was definitely out like a light.

CHAPTER EIGHTEEN

This Isn't The Zambezi River

When I awoke the next morning, it was already getting light outside, and I could hear the others moving around in the bushes, presumably uncovering the boat and loading it down by the river. It was the sound of them moving through the trees that woke me up, but I was more interested in the sound that I *wasn't* hearing, specifically the sound of rain on the roof of the tent. It had stopped raining, thank God.

"But wait a minute," I suddenly thought, and I sat upright. "Did they leave me in here all by myself? That was nice of them to let me sleep, but are they crazy? I could so easily have made a run for it."

"How, exactly?" the little voice in my head asked. "You're in a tent."

"Give me a break; it's not a high-security prison cell," I snapped.

Crawling over to the door, I peeked out through the mosquito-net window. I couldn't see much, just the legs of some of the others working nearby, grabbing bags and packs from their cache of supplies and carrying them off out of sight.

I unzipped the tent flap and snatched my pants and socks off the clothesline strung up under the tent's covered 'front porch." My pants weren't dry by any stretch of the imagination, but they were certainly not as wet as they'd been the night before.

The zipping sound from the tent flap attracted the attention of someone nearby, and he walked over, so I lay on my back and quickly pulled on my pants before he got there.

"You see?" the little voice in my head said. "How were you supposed to escape unnoticed? You're in a tent."

"Good morning," I heard Will say. His hand appeared under the front flap of the tent with an energy bar. "It's not bacon and eggs," he said. "But it's healthier."

I quickly pulled on my boots and jacket and crawled out of the tent. Standing up, I could see that they were very nearly finished with their boat-loading operation. Efficient as always, nearly all the supplies had been carried down to the boat, and almost nothing was left but the tents.

Will handed me the energy bar and leaned over to grab the other end of the rope around my waist, which was dragging in the mud.

"Do you want some coffee?" he asked, holding up a thermos bottle.

I nodded enthusiastically, and he poured some into a metal mug for me.

"Has to be black," he said. "No cream."

I waved my hand to say that I didn't care as I grabbed the mug and wrapped my cold hands around it. Feeling that heat was such an amazing feeling, and I eagerly sipped the hot coffee, relishing the feeling of warmth pouring down through my body.

It was actually amazingly good coffee considering we were in the middle of the wilderness. There was no cream but sugar and…something else I could taste that I felt warming me from the inside out.

"Irish," Will said simply, and I smiled.

Buck and Jay had already started collapsing the tents by this point—there was no messing around with these guys—and Charlie emerged from the bushes in the direction of the river. He surveyed the scene and walked over toward us.

"How's the weight?" Will asked, referring to the weight of all the supplies and gold in the boat.

"The river's high enough," Charlie replied. "We'll scrape bottom a lot at first, but the current will carry us off."

I couldn't decide if this was good news or bad news. Good news in that we wouldn't have to make two trips down the river and I would be on my way home sooner, but bad news in that I still didn't like the sound of the combination of a flooded river and a heavily overloaded little boat. But if I had learned anything from my couple of days with these guys, it was that they knew what they were doing.

"Okay, let's go," Charlie said as Buck and Jay finished packing away the last bits of the tents and slung them over their backs. I finished off the last of my coffee, and Will took back the mug, screwing it back on top of the thermos container.

Buck and Jay led the way down to the river while Charlie and Will and I followed. I could see through the trees as we headed down that the river was definitely much higher and faster than it had been two days before.

"Was it only two days?" I asked myself.

It was. Less than forty-eight hours, in fact. Unbelievable.

We stood on the riverbank while Buck and Jay secured the last of the supplies into the boat. I noticed that once again they had distributed the weight of the gold over the whole length of the boat by laying the flat plastic packages along the floor. But this time they were taking no chances and had securely strapped them down with bungee cords, presumably so that in case the boat capsized, they wouldn't lose the gold.

"That's all fine and well," I thought. "But what happens to us if the boat capsizes?"

With everything secure, Will and Jay gently slid the boat down off the riverbank and almost completely into the water. The current caught it and rocked it back and forth uneasily.

"Same configuration as before," Charlie ordered, and we climbed into the boat one at a time, all of us except Buck, who remained on shore to push the boat into the river with the help of Will and Jay and their long oars.

Leaning over with his hands on the edge of the boat, Buck waited for the signal to push off. All eyes were on Charlie, who had just finished tying my waist-rope loosely to the bench next to him. He made eye contact with me to make sure I could see how loose it was in case the boat went over.

"Okay," he said as he locked a pair of oars into place on each side of the back of the boat. "The river is running fast, so I'm not going to use the engine unless we have to. The current will just carry us, and we'll have enough to worry about dealing with that. This isn't the Zambezi River here, so it's going to be reasonably flat and calm most of the way, but we're riding heavy, so just stay focused. Got it?"

Everyone nodded in agreement, and we braced ourselves to push out into the river.

"Okay," Charlie said, giving Buck a nod. "Let's go."

Time Travel Down The Taiya River

With a grunting heave, Buck pushed us off the riverbank and into the river. In one single fluid motion, he hurdled himself into the boat, grabbed an oar, and took up a position on the bench to the right of me to help Will and Jay push us the rest of the way into the current.

"Here we go," Charlie said as he used the rear oars to steer the boat nose-first down the river.

Slowly but surely the swift-running current grabbed us, and we hurtled downstream. I clutched the bench underneath me with my hands as the river caught hold, and we accelerated to keep up with it. It was definitely running fast, but Charlie was right; for the most part it was flat and calm. Or maybe "calm" isn't the right word— there was too much kinetic energy at work for it to be "calm"—but we certainly weren't passing through giant waves and whitewater rapids along the way.

Charlie used his oars to deftly guide us along the safest route downriver. As expected, at first we frequently scraped bottom with a frightening screech of gravel on aluminum as the boat passed through shallow patches. But using the current and their oars, Will and Jay would always somehow push us off, and soon we would break free and continue downstream.

I was a little too nervous to fully enjoy myself, but I have to admit that once we got going and stopped scraping bottom so much, the ride was actually a lot of fun. The heavy rain overnight had given way to a beautiful Alaska morning, with plenty of sun and blue skies spotted with puffy white clouds. On either side of the river the mountains rose up high above us, piercing the sky with their jagged rocky peaks, and nestled into the high mountain valleys were beautiful blue hanging glaciers. I never tired of seeing these blue giants that always seemed to lurk around every corner up here in Alaska. Their color was the most beautiful blue I had ever seen - a cool ancient ethereal blue that seemed impossible to exist in nature, looking so out of place surrounded by familiar natural greens and grays and sky-blues. These massive brilliant jewels of ice had watched over this valley for thousands of years, oblivious to the passage of time and the drama of human greed that played out below.

The Irish coffee had done the trick and had warmed me up from the inside. Now, as we continued to race downriver, I closed my eyes and turned my face into the sun to get warm from the outside as well. It was a beautiful day, and it felt good to be out in the fresh air. Every breath I took seemed to heal me from the inside out, like breaking open the windows of a dusty room and letting a cleansing wind blow straight through. Gone were the memories of all the fear and discomfort I had experienced for the last two and a half days. Only my aching muscles and bruises reminded me of the pain I had suffered, but somehow I didn't mind that so much, because to me those aches and bruises were a badge of honor, reminding me that I had climbed the Chilkoot Pass all the way to its summit. They reminded me that I had done something remarkable and special.

I smiled at the memory of that climb as we continued down the river back to Dyea. It was as though the river were some kind of time machine transporting us from the era of the Klondike Gold Rush back to the twenty-first century. Every passing mile seemed to bring us closer and closer to the modern world, and a part of me felt sad to be leaving the rough, hard world of the wilderness behind.

And then in the blink of an eye it was over—we were back in the twenty-first century again. Coming around a bend in the river, I saw a bridge. The same bridge I'd crossed over three nights ago on my stupid quest to prove I was right about gold thieves and their overloaded little fishing boat. "I guess I proved myself right," I thought cynically. "They were gold thieves, all right, and they're sitting all around me in their overloaded little fishing boat at this very moment."

We passed under the bridge and floated past the campground where I'd snuck up on the gang sitting around the campfire.

Correction. I snuck up on everyone *except* Charlie, who was busy sneaking up on me at that exact moment. Somehow I found the strength to laugh about this tragic comedy of errors as we floated past the spot where we'd loaded up the boat two days earlier and set off upriver. It seemed like a different lifetime to me.

"Keep a sharp eye out," Charlie called up to Will and Jay, breaking me out of my daydreaming. I could sense that the four of them were nervous about being back in the civilized world again. The tension among all of us had seemed to be increasing ever since the bridge first came into view a few minutes earlier. "The river gets narrow and shallow here," Charlie said. "We'll have to find a way through."

We reached a point where the river flattened out and emptied into the ocean at Taiya Inlet. Somewhere along here three nights ago, I had found a spot where I was able to splash across to Dyea. It was hard to believe that I'd actually done that, because right then the river was so high and moving so fast that I couldn't believe I hadn't been swept out to sea.

"Dammit," Will cursed as the boat scraped the bottom hard and rattled its way across a shallow spot in the river. Pushing on his oar with all his weight, he freed us, and we floated a short distance downstream again before running aground again on Jay's side of the boat.

"Sorry, Charlie," Jay said as he pushed us off back in the other direction again.

Back and forth we went, and again and again we scraped bottom as we inched our way toward the ocean. "We are so close," I thought. "What if we have to unload the boat to get past this last bit out to the inlet?"

"I think we're clear," Will said as he pushed us off what turned out to be the final sandbar. He tested the bottom with his oar, pushing it down farther and farther on each successive attempt before he hit bottom. Finally, he drove his oar down as deep as he could and couldn't touch anything. "That's it," he said, turning around with a grin. "We're clear."

"Okay, boys, hold on tight," Charlie called out to everyone as he pulled his oars out of the water and handed them up to Jay. "I'm gonna fire the engine up." Will and Jay took a seat on the front bench and strapped all the oars to the side of the boat as Charlie pulled the rip cord on the outboard engine. The motor sputtered reluctantly into life, and soon we were motoring our way down the inlet and leaving Dyea, Taiya, and the Chilkoot Pass behind us.

"Okay, darlin'," Charlie said, leaning toward me and putting a hand on my shoulder. "Now where's your plane?"

Charlie Foxtrot Kilo Tango Yankee

"Up around that headland," I told Charlie, pointing ahead of us, and curving my fingers around to the left. "And then up the next inlet over."

Charlie nodded and continued nervously scanning the horizon and shoreline. "Keep an eye out for anything suspicious," he called up to the others.

"How far down the inlet are you?" Charlie asked, leaning close to me again.

I shrugged. "Maybe halfway down the inlet on the left," I guessed. It was a long time since I'd beached the plane. Or at least

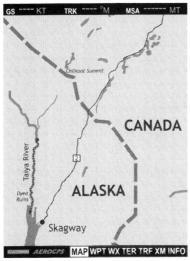

it felt that way. Charlie nodded again and continued steering down the inlet, staying close to the shoreline on our left.

"United States Coast Guard Sector Juneau," a tinny voice filled with static squawked loudly from beside me, startling me. "UNITED STATES COAST GUARD SECTOR JUNEAU, ON CHANNEL ONE-SIX, BREAK." It was the boat's radio, tuned to the emergency frequency. Charlie must have switched it on at some point.

Will turned around on his bench at the front of the boat. "Do you want one of us to go cross-country over the peninsula and check things out?" he asked Charlie.

Charlie reached over to turn down the volume on the radio so he could hear what Will was saying. "What did you say?" he asked.

"REPORT... OVERDUE AIRCRAFT INBOUND... JUNEAU," the voice on the radio continued, barely audible now.

Will repeated what he had said.

"ZERO-ONE PERSONS... RED AND WHITE... CHARLIE... TANGO... YANKEE," the Coast Guard transmission continued in the background while Will and Charlie talked.

"I thought about it," Charlie said. "But let's just scope it out from the water first."

"That's me!" I cried. "I think."

Everyone turned to look at me, confused.

"What are you saying?" Charlie asked suspiciously.

"I am saying you guys need to shut up for a second," I said, pointing impatiently at the radio. "I think they're talking about me!"

It took everyone a few seconds to understand what I was talking about. but when they did, their jaws almost dropped to the floor of the boat. Charlie leapt forward, letting go of the engine throttle as he did so, and the boat instantly slowed down and glided to a stop. He twisted the volume knob on the radio so hard that it almost came off.

"What did she say?!?" Buck asked anxiously.

"Shhhhhhhhhhhhh!" we all hissed in unison and turned our attention to the radio to listen.

"REPEAT, UNITED STATES COAST GUARD SECTOR JUNEAU, ON CHANNEL ONE-SIX, BREAK." As usual the US Coast Guard repeated the entire message a second time.

"AT ONE-SIX-FOUR-TWO GREENWICH MEAN TIME, ZERO-EIGHT-FOUR-TWO LOCAL TIME, THE COAST GUARD RECEIVED A REPORT OF AN OVERDUE AIRCRAFT INBOUND TO JUNEAU WITH ZERO-ONE PERSONS ONBOARD, RED AND WHITE, TAIL NUMBER CHARLIE FOXTROT KILO TANGO YANKEE. UNITED STATES COAST GUARD REQUESTS VESSELS IN VICINITY SOUTHEAST ALASKA TO KEEP A SHARP LOOKOUT, ASSIST IF POSSIBLE, AND REPORT ALL SIGHTINGS, BREAK. UNITED STATES COAST GUARD, OUT."

With a final burst of static the radio went silent again and left the five of us speechless and staring blankly back and forth from one to another for what seemed like an eternity.

"Wait a minute," Will said, finally breaking the silence. "What does that mean?"

Charlie grabbed me by the shoulder. "That's your plane?" he asked. "You're sure?"

I nodded. "Tail number Foxtrot Kilo Tango Yankee," I said, nodding some more. "That's me."

"I thought you said there was no one who would have noticed you were missing," Charlie said sternly, frightening me a little bit.

"There wasn't," I said nervously. "I don't know what happened."

Charlie thought this over for a moment.

"What does that mean?" Buck said frantically, turning around to face Charlie. "We have to go back upriver again, quick."

"Cool it, Buck," Charlie snapped. "Let me think for a minute!"

Buck opened his mouth to say something else but thought better of it and closed it again. We all sat around watching Charlie's facial expression very carefully as he stared off in the distance and thought things over. Finally, he sat upright again and looked at his watch. He nodded in satisfaction and looked at all of us.

"I think we're okay," he said.

Buck opened his mouth again. "How..." he said, but Charlie cut him off.

"The message said they received the report of the missing aircraft at 8:42 a.m.," Charlie said, thinking aloud. "That was barely five minutes ago. That means that was the first broadcast they made to try to find her. Which means they only noticed she was missing this morning."

"So?" Buck said. "What difference does that make?"

"That means," Charlie continued, ignoring Buck and continuing to think aloud, "that if we hurry, we still have time to get to the plane and get out of here."

Charlie grabbed the throttle of the idling outboard motor, and with a roar he powered up, and we were on our way again.

"I don't want to lose time," he explained, raising his voice to be heard over the engine. "Because we're fifteen minutes from her plane, tops. Which means we still have time."

"But they're looking for her!" Buck cried.

"Yes," Charlie replied. "But they don't know she's been kidnapped."

"They'll still come looking for her," Will said, crawling farther back in the boat and kneeling in front of me to join the conversation.

Charlie nodded in agreement. "Of course they will," he said. "But they will be looking for her all over southeast Alaska. The last place they'll be looking for her is up in Canada. They won't even broadcast the emergency message up there."

Will shook his head, not understanding.

"They don't think she's been kidnapped. They think she's crashed somewhere," Charlie said. "They think she's dead."

CHAPTER NINETEEN

Where Do You Wanna Go?

"Dead?" I thought, stunned. "They think I'm dead?"

But Charlie was right. In this part of the world, when the US Coast Guard sends an emergency message about a missing plane, it almost always means the worst has already happened.

"Do we still have time?" I asked Charlie. By now every boat with a working radio in southeast Alaska would be keeping an eye out for me.

He looked at me strangely for a second. "I think so," he replied. "But we'll have to be quick."

I nodded and looked up to see that we were almost finished rounding the end of the inlet. Any second now we would see my trusty De Havilland Beaver, safely beached off to the left side. Or at least I hoped so.

I sat forward on the bench, nervously craning my neck to catch a glimpse of the red-and-white tail of my plane. "Where is it?" I thought anxiously. "Shouldn't we see it already?"

And then there it was, creeping into view from behind the shoreline and trees at the end of the inlet. It was perfectly safe, and what a beautiful sight it was. I felt my eyes well up with tears as I saw the full body come into view.

Charlie saw it too, and he adjusted the direction of the boat to steer toward it. Just a few more minutes, and we would be there.

"Okay, guys," Charlie called out. "This is serious now. I want everything on this boat unloaded and loaded on that plane in record time. No fooling around."

He didn't have to remind them. They were all sitting nervously on the edges of their seats and waiting to spring into action.

"I don't think anyone's spotted it," Will said, scanning the water and sky for any boats or aircraft that might have reported my missing plane.

Charlie nodded. "I was thinking the same," he said. "There's no one around anywhere."

By that point we were just seconds away from beaching the boat right next to the pontoons of my plane. Charlie reduced power to the engine, and Will and Jay crouched at the front of the boat, ready to jump out the second we ran aground.

With another terrible screech of stone against metal, the nose of the boat ran up onto the rocky beach, and Will and Jay catapulted over the side and grabbed the sides to pull it farther up. Charlie cut the engine and untied me, and within seconds we were all climbing off onto dry land again.

"Make me proud, boys," Charlie said as the other three sprang into action, pulling packs and bundles out of the boat and stacking them on the shore.

"How long before you can be airborne?" Charlie asked, leading me over to the plane.

"A few minutes," I replied. "But we can start my preflight now."

He nodded and called Will over to keep an eye on me while he climbed inside the plane to check things out. I watched as he confiscated my iPhone and packed away my laptop, which had been lying on the seat next to me in the cockpit. He then climbed into the co-pilot's seat and gestured for Will to let me come aboard.

Stepping onto the pontoon I climbed up into the cockpit. Everything was exactly as I'd left it, but oh my God, it felt like forever since I'd last sat behind the wheel of my beloved plane. Climbing inside and sliding into the pilot's seat felt like being reborn. All the fears and discomforts of the past three days seemed to disappear even farther away.

I started my preflight checklist, checking all the instruments and controls. Behind me, Buck was already loading things into the back of the cabin while Will and Jay pulled the empty boat up into the trees and tried to conceal it as best they could.

"No funny business," Charlie said, putting a hand on my arm as I pulled on my headset. His rifle was leaning propped up between his legs as a chilling reminder in case I'd forgotten about it.

I shook my head and pulled my arm away. "You'll want to put those on," I said, gesturing to a headset on his side of the cockpit. "Or else you won't be able to hear me once I start the engine."

He looked over and nodded, taking the headset off its hook and pulling it over his head.

"We're done," I heard Will say from behind me. Charlie and I both turned around to see the back of the plane loaded with gear in a haphazard but reasonably well-organized fashion. Impressive, considering how quickly they'd done it. The beer cooler of gold was there too, of course. Quickly loaded up with the flat plastic packages off of the bottom of the boat.

"Okay, then let's get..." Charlie said, but I interrupted him.

"Tell Jay to climb inside and get strapped in," I said, taking charge. "Then you and Buck untie us from that tree and slowly— and I mean slowly—push the pontoons back off the beach until we're floating free. We're gonna be heavy in the water with all this weight so take it slow."

Up in the mountains, Charlie might be the boss, and maybe he still was and I was still their prisoner, but this was my turf now.

"Charlie?" Will asked, looking from me to him uncertainly.

"She's the boss," Charlie said, shrugging his shoulders.

"Damn right I am," I thought.

"Once we're floating free," I continued, "grab a paddle off the inside of the pontoons and paddle us out a little way and turn us around so we're facing out toward the water."

Will nodded and climbed down off the plane to get started. Jay climbed aboard, quiet as usual, and slid into the seat directly behind me. Outside, Will was barking my orders to Buck, and he ran over to untie us from the tree I'd tied up to three days earlier.

"UNITED STATES COAST GUARD SECTOR JUNEAU." A scratchy voice filled the headsets, making both Charlie and me jump.

Charlie and I looked at each other nervously as we waited for what the voice would say next.

"AT ONE SIX FOUR TWO GREENWICH MEAN TIME, ZERO EIGHT FOUR TWO LOCAL TIME, THE COAST GUARD RECEIVED A REPORT OF AN OVERDUE AIRCRAFT INBOUND TO JUNEAU WITH ZERO ONE PERSONS ON BOARD..." the Coast Guard radio operator repeated robotically. Charlie breathed a sigh of relief. They were repeating But they repeated the same message as before, which meant that no one had spotted us. Charlie breathed a sigh of relief.

"Let's get moving!" he yelled impatiently out the open door to Will and Buck, who were getting ready to push us off.

Will nodded, and he and Buck leaned up against the noses of the pontoons to push us off the beach. After a few seconds of screeching metal on gravel, we were already floating free, and the two of them stepped up onto the pontoons as we continued to float slowly backward. I looked out of the window to see the pontoons and judge how badly weighed down we were. If it was too heavy, we would have to make two trips.

I grimaced to see how low in the water the pontoons were, but I was still confident we would get airborne. The inlet was long, and we would have plenty of room to pick up enough speed.

"How is it?" Charlie asked, a worried expression on his face. "Should we make two trips?"

I shook my head. "I think we're okay," I said. "Let's give it a go and see how it goes. If we can't do it, we'll circle back on the water and make two trips."

Buck was on my side of the plane and out of my window. I could see him as he climbed aboard, steadying himself by grabbing a stationary propeller blade. I couldn't help but laugh when he looked up to see what he was grabbing onto, and he quickly pulled his hand away with a terrified expression on his face. Hearing my burst of laughter, Charlie looked at me quizzically. I gestured, "Never mind" with a wave of my hand.

Will and Buck wiggled their way farther back on the pontoons and grabbed the paddles. Slowly but surely they paddled us out into the inlet and spun the nose of the plane around.

"Okay," I yelled out the cabin door. "That's enough. Make sure you put those paddles away properly and then climb inside."

Will climbed in first and slid into the seat across from Jay, wrapping the seatbelt around himself and snapping it closed. Buck was on the other side of the plane and had no way to get over to the open door. He knocked on the glass window of the opposite door, which was closed and locked.

"Let me in," he said, and I couldn't help but laugh again. I don't know what was wrong with me. Even with everyone around me being so tense and nervous I just felt loose and relaxed now that I was back where I belonged—at the controls of my own plane. I felt at home, I guess. There's no other way to explain it. Nor any other need to explain it. Everyone knows what feeling at home means.

"Sorry, Buck," Jay said, releasing the catch on the door and opening it so his brother could climb over him.

"Where do I sit?" Buck asked.

We all turned around to see what he meant, and I realized that of course there was no seat for him. My plane was configured with only two seats in the back.

"For God's sake, Buck," Charlie snapped. "Just close the door and sit somewhere! Sit on the beer cooler if you have to!"

"It doesn't have a seatbelt," Buck said, slamming the door closed behind him.

Charlie turned around angrily and was about to say something to Buck (actually he was probably going to yell at him), but I cut him off.

"Speaking of the cooler," I said. "Can you slide it as far forward as possible, between Will and Jay?"

I didn't like how the weight of it was pulling down on the tail of the plane.

Buck did as he was told, and with a series of deep grunts he somehow managed to jerk and slide the cooler a centimeter at a time forward to just behind the passenger seats.

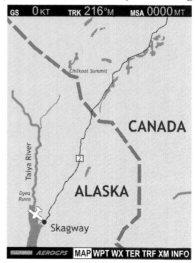

"It won't go any farther. It's too heavy," he said nervously. "Is it enough?"

"Perfect," I replied, giving him a thumbs up. He climbed over the cooler and used it as a chair, positioning himself between Will and Jay so he could hold onto the backs of their seats.

"That's it," I thought, checking the plane and my instruments one last time to make sure everything was okay. We were ready to go.

"So," I said, turning to Charlie. "Where do you wanna go?"

The Legend Of The Orca Whale

Charlie looked at me, confused, as though he hadn't understood the question. I reached down into my collection of maps and found an appropriate one showing our current location and extending up into Canada as well.

"Sorry," he replied, taking the map and examining it closely. As he oriented himself he slid his index finger across the map from our current position near the Taiya Inlet, up over the Chilkoot Pass and to the lakes beyond. "There," he said, pointing and holding the map up for me to see. "Right there is where we want to go."

I looked over to see what he was pointing at. It was a large lake up above the Chilkoot Pass called Lake Lindeman. From what I could tell it was just a few miles up past the summit where we had turned around the day before. "Was this where they had been headed all along?" I wondered.

I took the map from him and examined it, calculating in my head the route we would have to follow. It was almost a repeat of what we'd already done by boat and on foot. Northwest up the Taiya Inlet, over Dyea, up the Taiya River, then up over the Chilkoot Pass to the lakes beyond. It was the only option we had. The only other route up into Canada from here would take us right over the town of Skagway and to the border stations, where we'd surely get spotted.

Having chosen a route on the map, I leaned over to switch on my aviation GPS, and I quickly went over the route for a second time on it as well until I was completely satisfied that I knew where we were going and how to get there.

"Okay, I've got it," I said, putting the map away.

"Will it be a problem to land up there?" Charlie asked.

I looked out the window. It was still a beautiful, clear day outside. "The weather should be fine," I replied. "But we'll make a final decision once we're there."

"Just as long as we get out of Alaska and into Canada as soon as possible," Charlie said. "And away from anyone who might be looking for your plane."

"Don't worry," I said, checking all my instruments one final time. "I'll stay low and out of sight, and no one will even know we're there."

"Good," Charlie said. "Thank you."

"You don't have to thank me," I said curtly. "I'm your prisoner, remember?" After I said this I thought for a second that I saw a pained look flicker across Charlie's face, but then it was gone, and he was just as stone-faced as ever.

I reached down to pump the engine primer and pushed the mixture lever all the way forward. Flipping the master switch to on, I was about to start the engine when I suddenly heard a familiar sound out of the window off to my left—a snapping, watery noise that sounded exactly like someone blowing water out of his nose.

As I spun my head to see what it was, I heard the sound again. And again and again and again, like soft, watery firecrackers going off just outside my window. I turned, expecting to see the familiar arched backs of humpback whales, but I was surprised to see something completely different.

It was a small pod of killer whales that had surfaced right beside us. Seven or eight of them were all coming up for air at once, their black dorsal fins slicing through the water like obsidian knives and their heads breaking through the surface to reveal their white eye-patches.

"Would you look at that?" Buck said in amazement. "Where did they come from?"

"Unbelievable," Will said.

I glanced back at the passenger cabin and saw that everyone was leaning over to the left side of the plane to get a look at the orcas as they swam by, all of us with our mouths and eyes wide open in amazement. And then, just as suddenly as they had appeared, the whales disappeared again like ghosts, silently cutting through the water down out of sight.

For a few moments everyone was silent, and we settled back into our seats again. I tried to remember what Skeena's grandfather had taught me about the legend of the orca whale—that the orcas had once been magical white wolves who transformed themselves into wolves of the ocean.

But there was something else too. I tried to remember what it was, but it wouldn't come to me.

Jay leaned forward and interrupted my thoughts by tapping me on the shoulder. "Don't scare them when you take off," he said quietly.

"Don't worry," I replied, smiling. "I won't." They were swimming off toward the south, so I would make sure to give them plenty of room when I took off.

Checking my controls again to make sure everything was still okay, I hit the engine starter switch, and my trusty De Havilland Beaver came to life. He grumbled and complained a little bit at first, but soon the engine caught, and I powered down to a rough and rumbling idle to let it warm up for a few minutes. Instinctually, I scanned all around me for any other boats or planes that might get in the way, but of course we had the entire inlet to ourselves. I pointed us into the wind (and away from the orcas) and looked around one last time to be sure.

"You can really fly this thing, right?" I heard Buck ask from the passenger cabin behind me.

"You better believe it," I said, pushing the throttle forward to wake the engine from its low, sputtering idle and making it smooth out into a wonderful, loud, and throaty roar.

Slowly but surely we gathered speed, the pontoons cutting through the water as we raced faster and faster across the glassy surface of the inlet. I could feel the plane was really heavy, and for a few moments I wondered if it would even get off the water, but after a very long takeoff run I finally felt the plane slowly starting to tug at the controls in my hands like an excited animal eager to take to the air.

As we ploughed across the inlet, I finally remembered what it was that Skeena's grandfather had told me about the orcas. He said that sometimes when you saw an orca swim close to you or come near your boat that it was a spirit trying to communicate with you, trying to warn you of some impending danger.

"That doesn't bode well," I thought. "Maybe he was trying to warn me that the plane was too heavy to get into the air."

But it was too late. The plane groaned forward heavily on the pontoons and finally broke away from the surface of the water. The vibration of the pontoons cutting through the dense water disappeared in an instant, and we glided smoothly up into the air. We were airborne and on our way to Canada.

CHAPTER TWENTY
How I Climbed The Chilkoot Pass For A Second Time

Sweeping off the surface of the water, I put the plane into a steep, banking right turn, screaming past the headland we'd motored around in the boat less than an hour before and heading up the Taiya Inlet. The plane was flying sluggishly with all the extra weight, and it took me a few moments to get used to it.

Glancing out the right-hand window as we made the turn, I looked down and saw the group of orcas surfacing once more. As I leveled off and headed up the inlet toward Dyea, they disappeared beneath the surface again as mysteriously as they had appeared, and a very strong feeling of the presence of Skeena's grandfather came to me again. I tried to remember what else he had told me about the legend of the orcas.

"Sometimes men would go out on the canoes to work and fish," he had said, the powerful memory of his face and voice filling my mind. "And they would not return because the orca had taken them and carried them deep underneath the sea to transform them into whales. They would take them because they were skilled hunters like the orca themselves, and they needed many hunters. So when we see an orca near the shoreline or swimming near our boats, we know that it is the spirit of a friend or loved one trying to communicate with us."

I wondered if he was trying to tell me something now. I asked him, "Is that you down there right now, trying to communicate with me? Is that why I feel your presence so powerfully? Who are the other whales with you? Are you as much a leader to your clan now as you were in life?"

There was no answer.

The only answer came from the radio on the emergency channel.

"UNITED STATES COAST GUARD SECTOR JUNEAU, UNITED STATES COAST GUARD SECTOR JUNEAU, ON CHANNEL ONE SIX, BREAK," the coast guard radio operated said again and again Charlie and I looked at each other nervously as we waited to hear the rest of it.

"AT ONE SIX FOUR TWO GREENWICH MEAN TIME, ZERO EIGHT FOUR TWO LOCAL TIME, THE COAST GUARD RECEIVED A REPORT OF AN OVERDUE AIRCRAFT INBOUND TO JUNEAU WITH ZERO ONE PERSONS ON BOARD..."

The Coast Guard was still transmitting the same emergency message. No one had reported spotting my plane yet.

"And they won't ever spot it," I thought, keeping my flight path so low off the water that I was almost skimming the surface.

"Maybe we should fly a little higher," Buck suggested as he looked out the window at the water close underneath us.

"Kitty is doing just fine," Charlie said. "We don't want anyone to see us."

"Yeah," Buck said sarcastically. "It would be a shame if anyone were to see us crash and burn because we were flying too low."

I laughed at this, and to my surprise so did Charlie. He was a strange one. Heading toward Canada always seemed to put him in a better mood somehow. And he had reason to be happy because we were making good progress. We passed over the rotted wooden pilings of the Dyea town pier that I'd seen on my hike three days earlier, and we continued over the tidal flats, following the Taiya River upstream.

Looking down at the Dyea townsite it was hard to believe that there had once been an entire town down there. I looked for signs of the street grids and building foundations that once made up the town, but there was nothing except a few bits of lumber here and there. The trees and grassland had completely taken back the town.

God, I was so scared down there." I thought, remembering the brilliant idea I'd had of sneaking up on these guys out in the woods. But I didn't feel so scared anymore. Probably because I was back in familiar surroundings behind the controls of my own plane, but maybe it was also thanks to having faced down the dangers and fears that I'd encountered over the last three days. "I've done a lot of growing up this summer," I thought. "Mom and Dad will hardly recognize me."

185

The thought of my mom and dad and of being back in Tofino made my eyes well up with tears. As hard as I tried I couldn't make them stop, but I hid it well by pulling on a pair of sunglasses and surreptitiously wiping the tears away with the sleeve of my jacket. No one seemed to notice. Or maybe Charlie did, but he didn't say anything.

By the time we reached the forest, I had pulled up quite a bit and was now flying a little higher off the ground than I had been earlier. "I am sure Buck is happy about that," I thought as I checked my GPS and made a slight turn to the right to continue up the valley toward the pass.

Down below was the area that we'd been hiking through for the past two days, but I couldn't make out any sign of the infamous Chilkoot Trail down below. I saw what I thought were a couple of cabins or buildings down in the trees, but it was impossible to tell whether they were the ones that we'd passed or not.

I continued climbing steadily as the earth came up underneath us. We were gaining altitude fairly quickly, and the forest was thinning out as we neared the end of the valley. Up ahead I could make out the familiar lopsided, v-shaped depression full of grey stone, and as the rock waterfall slowly came into view I was astounded at how steep it looked from there.

"Unbelievable," I thought, staring in amazement. "I actually climbed that."

"We're coming up on the Canadian border," I announced to everyone.

"Do you think there's radar coverage up here?" Charlie asked. Apparently, he was worried that the Canadians might have radar stations or something that would see us crossing the border illegally.

"I have no idea," I replied. "But I don't plan to take any chances. I'm going to keep it really close."

Charlie nodded. "Good," he said.

"You won't think it's so good five minutes from now," I thought to myself. I intended to keep it really close.

Down below, the giant grey boulders raced past us in a blur, and as I approached the face of the pass I pulled back sharply and went into a steeper climb. Out of the corner of my eye I saw everyone grab his seat nervously, and I smiled to myself. I was showing off. I admit it. But I wanted them to see how tough I was after everything I'd been through the past few days down below in the wilderness.

Besides, they'd scared me enough over the past few days, and it was my turn to scare the crap out of them for a change.

"Maybe you should take it up a bit," Will suggested from behind me.

"We can't risk it," I replied. "What if someone spots us?"

"I think we can risk it," Buck said, gripping the backs of the passenger seats.

"No we can't," Charlie said sternly.

"Still not scared, Charlie?" I thought. "How about this?"

Leveling the plane out, I made for the top of the pass. I planned to make it with inches to spare if I could.

I don't know where this newfound bravado came from, but at that moment I felt like I was the absolute master of the universe. I remembered how I felt when I reached the summit of the pass the day before. I had felt invincible. And that was exactly how I felt right then as I approached the summit for a second time.

Closer and closer we flew.

"Uhhhh, Charlie?" I heard Buck say as we bulleted toward the top of the pass. "Are you sure about this?" But Charlie didn't have time to respond. We were already there, blowing through the wisps of cloud lingering around the summit and passing over the jagged rocks and boulders so closely that I am not sure that we didn't scrape a pontoon going over.

I climbed up a little bit higher as the summit fell behind us, and as we flew over the buildings of the Canadian ranger station I started the gradual descent down to the lakes, which I could see ahead of us.

As I pulled up to a slightly comfortable altitude, I could feel everyone in the plane relaxing again, including Charlie. I looked over to see if I could read his expression, but as always his stone face was difficult to read. The white-knuckle grip of his hands on the sides of his seat was not, however. It was a dead giveaway. Even Charlie had been scared.

"Don't worry, darlin'," I thought. "Your secret's safe with me."

And that's how I climbed over the Chilkoot Pass for the second time in my life—screaming over the summit in my trusty De Havilland Beaver with only inches to spare and four big, strong men clinging on for dear life.

Now We Wait

With the Chilkoot Summit falling rapidly behind us, I checked with the GPS to make sure I stayed on course. Up ahead of us I could see a handful of small lakes and what I thought was probably Lake Lindeman. Scrolling around the area a bit with the GPS's electronic map and comparing it with what I could see looking out the window, I was satisfied that we were on the right track, and I leaned back in my chair once again.

"Buck, for God's sake will you stop moving around?" I heard Will say from back in the passenger cabin. Buck was wiggling and moving around loudly on top of the beer cooler.

"I can't get comfortable!" Buck snapped. "I didn't get a proper seat like the rest of you." He continued shifting his weight around, trying to get comfortable, but he couldn't seem to find the right position. "And don't forget," he said, finally settling down. "I was the only one who was injured in the grizzly attack."

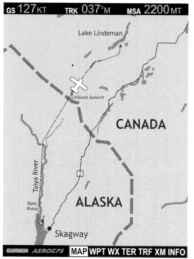

The four of us turned around in unison to look back at him.

"Oh please," Will said, expressing what everyone was already thinking.

"Give me a break," Buck said. "My butt hurts."

Charlie turned forward again, shaking his head in mock sadness. "I apologize for my brother," he said. "Being such an idiot."

I smiled. And as I glanced around the cabin, I noticed that everyone else was smiling too. The mood had been gradually improving for the entire flight, but now that we were past the summit and safely into Canada, it felt like an enormous weight had been lifted off of everyone (except my poor plane, of course. The plane was still heavy with gold and flying sluggishly).

I continued smiling to myself as I looked down at the barren landscape. Leading down from the summit and farther into Canada was a small, narrow valley that pointed all the way down to Lake

Lindeman. The grassy floor of the valley was speckled with white boulders and snow patches, and it looked pretty inhospitable, but I thought I could make out some deserted campgrounds below and a trail winding down past a series of small lakes to the end of the valley and Lake Lindeman beyond.

This made me think about where we would have gone if we had continued carrying the gold up to the summit over and over again.

I looked at Charlie.

"After we'd gotten all the gold to the summit," I asked. "Would we have had to carry it all the way down here as well?"

"Yup," he said. "There's nowhere else to go."

I nodded and continued flying down the steep-sided valley. Nearing the end, I pulled up to climb a little higher so I could get a bit of a look around. We were safely inside Canada by then, and with all the tall mountains around us no one was going to see us anyway.

I banked to the right a bit and followed a small river down out of the valley. A rocky ridge stretched out in front of us and hid Lake Lindeman from view for a moment. I pulled back to fly over the ridge, and the lake was revealed again, stretched out below us and curving along the base of a steep mountain range to the left while low flatlands spotted with lakes led off to the right.

"Okay," I said, turning toward Charlie and pointing to the lake below. "That's Lake Lindeman. Where are we going now?"

Charlie pulled himself forward and craned his neck to take a look around. "Down there," he replied after a few moments, pointing to a spot where the small river emptied into the lake. "Can you beach the plane there?"

"Sure," I replied, starting my descent and checking my different approach options.

Lake Lindeman was nice and long and flat, and it was actually a perfect place for landing a seaplane. I banked over and doubled back to bring us down over a nice long stretch of calm open water. We skimmed over the treetops and out over the lake as I slowly brought us in for a landing.

"When we're down," I said, glancing back at Will. "I'll taxi us over there toward the beach and shut the engine down. When I do, can you get outside to paddle us in and tie us up?"

"Will do," he replied with nod.

I took us down lower and lower until we were hovering just a few feet off of the water. For a few seconds I just hung there, racing over the surface and taking a moment to focus myself and make sure that everything was okay before I set us down. It was a habit of mine, to just take a moment to center myself, take a deep breath, and find a bit of peace before I touched down.

Once I was ready, I gently powered back and floated us down onto the water. I am proud to say that even with my plane being loaded well past its weight limit, I made the most amazingly soft and incredible landing that I had ever made in my entire life.

"I wish Dad had been here to see that," I thought as I powered the engine down and let the speed slowly bled away. "That was classy."

Deploying the water rudders, I steered us off to the place that Charlie had indicated earlier, where a small river poured out into the enormous lake. It was probably the most beautiful spot on the lake and would be a nice place to beach the plane.

"Are you ready, Will?" I asked, quickly turning my head toward the passenger cabin.

He clicked his seatbelt off. "Ready," he said.

I shut the engine down and gave Will a nod. He opened the cargo door and stepped outside onto the pontoon. Grabbing a paddle from its storage place, he slowly paddled us to the shore. With a hollow metallic bang, we collided softly with the rocky beach, and Will jumped off to tie the mooring rope.

"Tie us off to a tree upwind of us," I yelled out the window to Will. He needed to tie us to an upwind tree; otherwise, the wind would catch the plane and spin it around on the shoreline.

"I know," he called back.

"Of course he does," I thought as I watched him expertly secure the rope and then wait as the plane settled on the shore and the rope pulled taut. Once that was done, he walked back to join us onboard.

"So what now?" I asked, unbuckling myself and turning to face the others as Will crawled back inside through the cargo door.

"Now we wait," Charlie said.

CHAPTER TWENTY-ONE

Waiting For The Spring To Come

"Now we wait for what?" I asked as Charlie took a cell phone out of his pocket and switched it on to check if there was any reception.

"Because of our sudden change of plans our half-brother is meeting up with us today," Charlie replied, waving the phone around in a vain attempt to get a signal. "But he won't get to the rendezvous point until much later in the day, so until then we'll just have to wait here."

"Oh," I replied, absorbing this new information. "Where is the rendezvous point?"

Charlie switched off the phone and put it back in his pocket. "Just a bit farther on," he said. "Up on Lake Tagish."

I pulled out a chart book and flipped through the pages until I found the lake. "It's huge," I said. "Where exactly?"

"Up around here," he said, pointing to the area of the crossbar of the enormous H-shaped lake.

I nodded and instinctually began calculating the best route to get us there. In the back of the plane Buck was loudly digging around through their gear and supplies, trying to find something. After a few minutes he pulled out a sleeping bag and a handful of energy bars.

"What are we doing all sitting around in here?" he said. "It's a beautiful day outside."

We all looked at Charlie, who shrugged his shoulders in approval, and one by one we all climbed out onto the shore. Buck waited onboard until everyone else had crawled out, then handed the energy bars to Jay and laid his sleeping bag out on the floor to make himself comfortable.

"I have to give my ass a rest," he said, pulling the door closed behind us. "Now get the hell out of here. I can't get any sleep with you four yakking all the time."

I laughed, and Charlie shook his head sternly, but I don't think he minded very much at being kicked out. Buck was right; it was a beautiful day outside. The sun was shining, and the sky was clear, and we were on the shores of a beautiful mountain lake surrounded by a peaceful silence that was only broken by the sound of the birds and the wind in the trees.

Jay offered me one of the energy bars, and I was about to decline the awful thing when I saw that the packaging didn't look right. It was red, not green, and the shape and size were wrong. Tilting my head to the side so I could read the text on the package, I realized that it wasn't an energy bar at all. "Kit Kat Chunky," it read.

"Where did you get that?" I asked, greedily snatching the chocolate bar out of Jay's hand and ripping it open.

"What do you mean?" Jay asked. "I always had these."

I rolled my eyes. I could have used one of those up on the Chilkoot Summit instead of the disgusting energy bars.

Biting into that Kit Kat Chunky was the most amazing sensation that you can possibly imagine. The way my teeth had to struggle to cut through the thick, heavy chocolate, the crunch of the wafers inside and the dancing swirl of chocolate and sugar on my tongue. And it was also deliciously cold, the way a good chocolate bar always should be. As I ate I spilled crumbs all over myself but I didn't care. It was heaven.

With my chocolate bar in hand, I looked out across the lake to the mountains rising beyond. "What a breathtakingly beautiful place," I thought. "I should do things like this more often."

Like flying out into the wilderness to just spend a few hours alone. Of course I could do that any time I wanted to. All I had to do was just hop into my plane and head up to some remote mountain lake to just sit there, meditate, and get far away from everything. "I will definitely do that," I promised myself. If I ever get out of this.

"I suppose there are worse places to spend a day," I said as I stood there watching the lazy clouds race across the deep blue sky overhead. "It's so peaceful here."

"It wasn't always peaceful here," Charlie said.

I raised my eyebrows and looked at him. "What do you mean?" I asked.

"A hundred odd years ago all of this was completely different," Charlie said, making a sweeping gesture with his hand across the entire landscape. "There were tents as far as the eye could see, and all this forest wasn't there because it had all been cut down for firewood or lumber for building. You can see a couple of the old cabins up there in the trees, in fact. There's a cemetery too."

I looked up to where he was pointing, and I saw an old log cabin with some rickety picnic tables out in front.

"Nowadays they use this place as a campground along the hiking trail," Charlie continued. "But back in the gold-rush days it was an enormous city of logs and canvas with a population of thousands. And the tents ran all along the shores of this lake and down the shores of the lake farther north as well, Lake Bennett. And all these people out here in the middle of nowhere were doing the same thing we are doing now—they were waiting. Except they were waiting for the spring to come and for all the lakes and rivers to melt so they could get out of here."

Charlie and I wandered farther along the shoreline as he spoke.

"Even though these lakes are in the middle of nowhere, they actually have something very special about them that was very valuable to these stampeders—they all form the headwaters of the Yukon River."

Charlie sat down on a log, and I sat next to him, enjoying the sunshine and the fresh mountain air.

"The Yukon River is one of the great rivers of the world," Charlie continued again. "In fact, the name itself means 'great river,' but it also happens to flow right past Dawson City, where the gold was and where everybody so desperately wanted to go. And since this lake right here is where the Yukon River starts, naturally this is where everyone wanted to go."

I nodded as Charlie spoke. This sounded familiar. Glen had mentioned some of this during his tales of the Yukon around the campfire a few days earlier.

"The only problem," Charlie carried on, "was that it was the middle of winter, and the lakes and rivers up here were frozen solid and wouldn't melt again for another seven months. So they set up camp. Thousands of people cutting down every tree in sight to build boats that would take them to Dawson and make all their dreams come true once the spring thaw came. And once it finally did come, and the lakes finally melted, more than seven thousand boats set out, the tent cities disappeared almost overnight, and thousands of people headed downriver to Dawson."

"Where they just turned around and went home," I said distantly, remembering Glen's story. "Because all the claims were long since staked, and there was nothing left."

Charlie looked at me. "You know this story?" he asked.

"A little bit," I replied dreamily, remembering what Glen had said and trying to imagine everything around me as it would have looked more than a hundred years earlier—the lake frozen solid and an icy, cold wind blowing across it, chilling everything to its very core. I imagined how it would have been with all the trees cut down and the white roofs of tents spread all across the landscape. The smell of campfires and wood stoves in the air and everything a sea of frenetic activity, chopping, sawing and hammering everywhere as people who'd never built a boat before struggled by trial and error to cobble together something seaworthy enough that the Mounties would let them take it downstream.

"I just can't believe the stupidity and greed of it all," I said. "All that for what? Some gold? Who cares?"

"I couldn't agree more," Charlie said as he stared vacantly off into the distance, which I thought was a funny thing for a gold thief to say, as he was making his way over the very same mountain passes and lakes in search of his own dreams of gold.

Are We Looking For Anything In Particular?

After standing around the lake for a while, Charlie and I wandered back to the plane and climbed onboard. I pulled myself up into the pilot's seat, and Charlie slid into the seat next to me. Jay grabbed a sleeping bag for himself and stretched out on the floor of the cabin between the passenger seats, while Will grabbed a book and sat on the pontoon outside in the sunshine reading.

Buck's plan of shutting himself up in the plane to take a nap was a pretty good idea. Yawning and with nothing better to do to pass the time, I balled up my jacket to use as a pillow to prop my head up against the window. I closed my eyes, and the combination of the gentle rocking of the plane on the water and the perfect, beautiful silence of the wilderness outside put me to sleep in no time (probably the brutally exhausting activity of the past days and a lack of sleep also helped).

By the time I awoke again, the sun had traveled far across the sky and was already well on its way to going down behind the mountains off to the west. Charlie's voice woke me up, and as I rubbed my eyes and sat straight up, I could see that he had climbed outside onto the pontoon to make a telephone call.

"What time will you be there?" Charlie asked, speaking to the person on the other end of the line. As he listened to the answer, he nodded along and looked down at his watch. "Good, see you then," he said and ended the call.

Putting the satellite phone away, Charlie kneeled down on the pontoon next to Will and spoke quietly with him for a moment before opening the door and poking his head inside the cockpit. Seeing that I was already awake, he gave me a simple nod of his head that said everything.

"Rise and shine, kids," Will said, climbing in through the rear door and using Buck's baseball cap to swat him and Jay on the heads to wake them up. The two of them grumbled like I used to on school days when my mom would come in to wake me, but they eventually pulled themselves off the floor and threw their sleeping bags into the back of the cabin, out of the way.

Charlie pulled himself up into the co-pilot's seat and grabbed the chart book we had looked at earlier. He examined it for a moment, then leaned toward me. "This is where we're going," he said, holding his finger on the map as he held it up toward me.

"Got it," I replied, and I took the book from him. I studied it for a few moments, the same as I had earlier in the day, and I decided on the best way to get to where we were going. Satisfied with that, I switched on the GPS to go over the whole route there again, just to be sure.

The others waited patiently for me to finish, and when I was 100 percent confident in my flight path, I looked up and turned around to give Will a nod.

"Let's go, Buck," Will said, and the two of them climbed out to push us off the beach. I was impressed to see that they took to this with the same military efficiency that they had demonstrated during our trek up the Chilkoot Pass. They had us untied and out onto the water in no time.

"Take my seat, Buck," Jay said as Buck and Will climbed back up into the cabin. "It has seatbelts."

"Thanks, buddy," Buck replied, sliding into the seat behind me and carefully strapping himself in.

With everyone inside and the doors secured, I went through my start-up procedures and soon had the engine idling nicely. I let it warm up for a while, then leaned forward and eased the throttle up a bit to taxi farther out onto the lake to line myself up for takeoff.

"Here we go," I said and pushed the throttle forward. The seaplane sprang into life, and as the rumbling of the engine settled down into a nice even roar, we charged down the lake.

Even with a stiff headwind and a lot of lake ahead of us as a runway, I once again wondered if we were going to make it into the air with all the gold onboard.

"Come on, Bucky, you can do it," I muttered as we slowly picked up speed. "Bucky" was the nickname I'd given to my good old, trusty De Havilland Beaver many years before. Bucky the Beaver. A bit silly, perhaps, but I usually only used it in particularly difficult situations and this was most definitely one of those.

It took a while, but eventually we managed to pull up off the surface of the water. I took it easy and made a slow climb as I flew along the length of Lake Lindeman and out over Lake Bennett. Seeing the lakes from the air, I again tried to imagine what it must have been like back in the gold-rush days, when the shorelines were packed with tents and people and activity.

As we climbed higher, I saw a railway line below us and a highway far off to the right. I had to remember that we weren't out in the wilderness anymore and to watch out for power lines and other low-lying obstacles as I tried to stay out of sight on the way to our destination on Lake Tagish. I had seen a nice long valley on the charts that I was planning to duck into as soon as we'd gained enough altitude.

We continued our climb and came out from behind the shadow of the mountains lining the lakeshore. As we flew farther the sun continued getting lower and lower in the sky, and I suddenly realized that by the time we landed at Charlie's rendezvous point it would already be nearly dark. I had assumed that once I dropped them off that they would let me go, but now I began to panic at the thought that this might not be the case.

"What if they don't let me go?" I thought.

"Just be cool," the little voice in my head said. "They will. After you drop them off, they won't need you any more."

"But what if..."

"No!" the voice told me sternly. "Just be cool."

I forced myself to take deep breaths, one after the other, until I calmed down.

"Okay," I told myself. "Everything is going to be fine. We will land the plane, and they will let me go."

"Exactly," the little voice told me. "Just make sure you have an escape plan in mind in case they..."

"In case they what?!?"

"You know," the little voice said. "In case they have to...dispose of you."

"Forget this. I am just going to ask them."

I asked as innocuously as possible. "What happens after we get to Lake Tagish? Because it's going to be dark soon, and once it is, we won't be able to fly any farther today."

"Don't worry, " Charlie said, with a laugh. "Once we get there and get everything unloaded, we'll be out of your hair, and you'll never see us again."

"Okay," I replied, my voice quivering slightly.

"You'll have to sleep in your plane though," Charlie said, turning to look at me. "Sorry."

I opened my mouth to respond, but I felt the tears rushing into my eyes and decided I'd better not risk bursting into tears. I took a couple more deep breaths and then cleared my throat. "Just be professional," I told myself.

"We're almost there," I said simply.

Charlie nodded. "It's just up there," he said, pointing. "Do you see that truck down there at the shoreline?"

I pulled myself forward to get a better look.

"Yes," I replied. "I see it."

"That's where we need to land," Charlie said. "But first I want to make a pass overhead to check things out."

"Okay," I replied, keeping my sentences short so I didn't start to tear up again. "Are we looking for anything in particular?"

Charlie looked at me with a confused look on his face. "Isn't it obvious?" he replied. "I wanna make sure there aren't any gold thieves around."

CHAPTER TWENTY-TWO

The Bonds Of Brotherly Love

I brought us down a bit so Charlie could get a better look as we flew over the truck on the shoreline and the trees beyond it. Everyone leaned over to look out the window as we passed overhead and circled back again, but there wasn't much to see. Just a brand-new shiny SUV parked on a little rocky beach at the end of a very old and abandoned-looking dirt road that led up from the lake and through the trees. The truck was a strange color that I couldn't quite place, and from what I could see there was a solitary person sitting in the driver's seat.

"I think Eddie scratched up your truck, Will," Buck said, teasing. "I am pretty sure I saw a scratch on the passenger-side door."

We finished our second pass and headed back over the lake to circle in for a landing.

"Uh-oh," Jay said, laughing. "You're gonna have to buy some brown paint."

"Mocha," Will corrected.

Mocha! That's it. That's a good name for the color of the truck.

"Oh, that's right!" Buck cried, also laughing. "Mocha!"

"It's a unique color," Will replied, defensively. "And at a huge grocery store parking lot, it makes it easier to find."

"Mocha," Buck continued laughing. "That's sweet."

"Cool it, you guys," Charlie said, always the serious one. "Let Kitty concentrate."

"Why are you always so serious, Charlie?" I asked myself. "You're the big brother, I guess. The oldest of the bunch."

Or *was* he the oldest? I hadn't met their brother Eddie yet.

"Is this Eddie older or younger than you?" I asked Charlie.

He looked at me with a completely baffled look on his face that almost made me laugh.

"Half-brother," Charlie replied, confused. "And he's younger."

"So you *are* the oldest," I thought. I knew it. Their leader.

"Half-brother?" I asked.

"Same mother, different fathers," Charlie responded. "Our dad died when Will was still a baby, and our mother later remarried."

"So Will is the youngest of the four," I thought.

And their father died when they were all quite young. I'd watched enough daytime television and movies to be familiar with the conventional pop-culture psychoanalysis for situations like this. After their dad died, poor Charlie had to grow up quick and be the man of the house. Their natural leader, big brother Charlie.

"Don't be stupid," the little voice in my head snapped at me.

"Why?" Charlie asked, interrupting my thoughts.

I shrugged. "Just curious," I said.

Charlie looked like he wanted to say something else, but didn't. I think he knew I was psychoanalyzing him.

"What he doesn't know," the little voice said, "is that you're psychoanalyzing him on the basis of a lifetime of trashy television shows and fictional movies."

"Whatever," I replied. "I am just trying to fill in a few missing pieces about what makes these guys tick before they leave, and I never see them again."

I refocused my concentration on flying, and after making a tight turn over the lake I circled back over the water almost parallel to the shore, and I slowly brought us down. Lower and lower, powering back a tiny bit as we got close to the water and finally touching down. Another perfect landing. Maybe even better then my last one had been. This whole experience was good for my skills as a pilot.

Will and Jay unbuckled themselves as I approached the shore, and the moment I shut down the engine they were out the door and paddling us in to get the plane secured. As Will jumped ashore with the mooring rope, he raised a hand in greeting to the driver of the truck. The setting sun reflected off the glass windows of the truck, so I couldn't see if the driver returned the wave, but the driver's door swung open as Will finished tying us up.

"Let's go," Charlie said, talking to me and Buck, and the three of us climbed out onto the pontoon on the far side of the plane.

We could hear muffled voices from the other side as Will and Jay greeted their half-brother.

"You better not have scratched my truck, Eddie!" I heard Will say, only half-jokingly.

I didn't hear the reply because Charlie talked as he examined the pile of gear they were going to unload from my plane.

"I don't want to hang around here any longer than we have to," Charlie said. "How long will it take to load everything?"

Buck shrugged. "It'll be pretty fast," he replied. "There's lots of hands to lift things, so we can make a kind of human conveyor belt and transfer the stuff pretty quick."

"What about the cooler?" Charlie asked, referring to the gold.

"We still can't put all the gold in it and carry it around, if that's what you mean," Buck replied. "It weighs too much. We'll have to transfer it like we always do, a bit at a time."

"But in the truck, I meant," Charlie said.

"Yeah," Buck replied. "In the truck we can fit it all in and cover it later with ice and beer and bacon and whatever else to hide it. No one will ever know it's there."

That was the answer Charlie was looking for, and he nodded.

"Let's get the others and get started with this," Charlie said, starting down the pontoon to the shore. "I don't want to waste any time."

I followed the two of them along the pontoon toward the beach and looked to see where their brothers were. I was thinking again about the family dynamic among them. As an only child, I couldn't really understand from experience the relationships they had with each other. My parents were also both still (thankfully) alive, and I also couldn't fully understand how the early death of a parent could affect a family. All I knew is that these four guys with whom I had just spent three days in the wilderness shared an incredibly close bond with each other.

Yes, yes, I know they were thieves and criminals and hostage-takers and that I was terrified and in fear for my life for most of the time that I had spent with them, but that didn't change the fact that by watching them and seeing how they interacted with each other I also got to know them a bit. And from what I could tell they were a close-knit and loving family—loving, in that kind of tough-guy, never-talk-about-anything, never-discuss-your-feelings kind of way that boys have and that I will also never understand. But no matter what, they always had each other's backs. And while I was with them I felt as though they'd had my back too, even if I was their prisoner, and even if I wasn't one of their little clan.

I thought about Charlie telling me about the history of the Chilkoot Trail as we climbed. And Will helping me take my boots off as I crawled into the tents at night. And Jay silently reaching out with his hand to help me to my feet at the summit of the pass. And Buck complaining that my load of gold to carry up the trail was so much lighter than everyone else's. After spending so much time in their company, I couldn't help but feel like I was a part of their family too. Somehow in little ways here and there over the previous three days they had treated me like a little sister. And as an only child, this felt completely new to me.

Of course I wasn't their sister. I was still their hostage. And in case I'd forgotten it, I still had that stupid rope tied around my waist to remind me—my leash. But would you think I am crazy if I told you how much I was going to miss those guys once they got in their truck and drove away forever?

Because of all this, I was naturally curious about this fifth brother of theirs. He was a half-brother, and a lifetime of daytime television and movies told me that he wasn't as close with the other four as they were with each other. But I was still curious to see how he fit in their little brotherly circle, so as we climbed down onto the beach I craned my neck to see past Charlie and Buck to get a look at him.

"You will never believe this," Will called over as we headed up toward the truck. "Eddie knows her."

"What do you mean he 'knows her'?" Charlie asked, not understanding what Will meant.

I didn't have time to think about the question, because at that instant their brother Eddie stepped out from behind Will as they both walked toward us.

"Edward?" I said in complete and utter astonishment.

"Hey, Kitty," Edward replied, waving sheepishly.

Their half-brother "Eddie" was Edward.

I Guess This Is Goodbye

Charlie stopped dead in his tracks with a look of shock on his face that must have been similar to the look of shock that I had on mine.

202

"He knows her?" Charlie asked. "How the hell does he know her?"

"He works down on the dock in Juneau where she parks her plane," Will explained.

Charlie seemed to be struggling to comprehend this new turn of events. I could see him trying to figure out what implications it might have for their plans, but he was too shocked to come up with anything.

Will said, "And they've been out on a date."

"Wasabi Willy's," Jay added helpfully.

"Of course Wasabi Willy's," Buck replied sarcastically. "Fancy schmancy Eddie wanted to impress her."

"Oh yeah," Will said. "Where would you take her?"

"The Douglas Café," both Buck and Jay said in unison.

"Where else?" Buck asked, laughing. He turned and put his arm around my shoulders to give me a rough hug—just like he might have done to a younger sister of his. "You like burgers, don't you?" he asked.

"Just shut up a second, all of you," Charlie snapped, holding up the palm of his hand to silence them. "I need to think."

Everyone quieted down and gave Charlie a moment to figure things out.

"Can you give us a second, Eddie?" Charlie said after a moment. "Alone?"

Edward nodded obediently and walked back toward the truck. Charlie huddled the rest of us into a close circle around him so he could speak without Edward hearing. "This doesn't matter," he said in a low voice. "It doesn't change our plans."

Everyone breathed a sigh of relief at this news, including me. I was having trouble with the difficult mix of emotions swirling inside my head. On one hand (the crazy hand, I suppose) the thought of these guys leaving me behind made me very sad. I would miss them, I was sure of it. On the other hand, the thought of spending another night dragged along on this crazy escape of theirs made me desperate to find any way possible to avoid it.

"Eddie doesn't know about the gold," Charlie continued, whispering. "He only knows that I asked him to get to Skagway to pick up Will's truck and drive it up here to meet us. That's all."

"And neither of them knows where we're planning to go from here," Will said, referring to both Edward and me.

Charlie nodded. "Exactly," he said. "So the plan is to just load up the truck and get the hell out of here. And we leave Eddie behind. Kitty can fly him back to Juneau."

Charlie looked at me for confirmation. "Yes," I said and nodded. Of course I could do that.

"And then they can tell the police whatever they want," Charlie finished. "Because by then it won't matter anymore anyway."

I hadn't thought about that, I realized. What would I tell everyone when I got back? I would have to explain myself somehow, since I was reported missing and presumably dead. But for some reason it hadn't occurred to me that I would have to report them to the police as soon they let me go. Not that it mattered. The police would never find them. Now that they were in Canada, they had half the North American continent laid out before them, where they could drive without having to pass through any border controls. They could drive all the way east to Toronto or Montreal and pass back into America, where the border agents wouldn't even be looking for them. Or maybe just slip unnoticed across the border somewhere along the thousands of miles between here and there. It wasn't called the "longest undefended border in the world" for nothing, after all. They could get just about anywhere from here.

"What will you tell the police?" Will asked me.

I shook my head. "I have no idea," I replied honestly. "I hadn't even thought about it."

"It doesn't matter," Charlie repeated. "By then it won't matter. Are we agreed?"

The others thought about the plan for a second and nodded in agreement.

"Whatever you say, Charlie. You're the boss," Buck said, expressing what everyone, including me, was thinking. He was their big brother, and at that moment he was my big brother too.

"Okay," Charlie replied. "Then let's get that stuff unloaded as fast as possible."

The other three jumped into action and waved for Edward to come over and help them while Charlie took me aside. I watched Edward as he walked past us, and we made eye-contact. He shrugged apologetically as he walked by and continued down to help the others. I wanted to talk to him, but I knew it wasn't a good time. I would have the chance to talk to him soon enough anyway.

"Will you be okay here with him?" Charlie asked.

"Of course," I replied, nodding.

"We'll leave a tent and sleeping bag for him," Charlie said. "So the two of you don't have to share the plane together."

"Thank you," I said.

"And we'll leave you plenty of water purifier and food," Charlie said like a nervous parent sending his kids off to camp.

"Charlie," I said, putting my hand on his arm. "Don't worry. We'll be fine." He nodded and smiled reluctantly but said nothing more.

We watched the others quickly unloading everything from the plane in the fading light of the evening, and we walked to the back of the SUV to help load it. It was funny to watch everyone carrying these small flat packages of gold. They were small but so heavy that we struggled to lift them up into the beer cooler in the back of Will's shiny new SUV. Charlie tried to distract Edward a little bit by chatting to him while the transfer of the gold took place, but I am sure he had to notice that something strange was going on.

"Put a few of those on the floor in the front and backseats," Will whispered to everyone when Edward was out of earshot. "So we don't have all the weight over just the back axle."

As usual I was impressed with how fast and efficient they were, but even from watching this simple exercise it was clear that Edward was somehow a little bit of an outsider to the group. By then I was used to seeing the others work together seamlessly, everyone simply knowing wordlessly what their job was and knowing whatever everyone else's was too. But with Edward thrown into the mix there was a lot more discussion about what he should do or what he should carry. But in no time at all the truck was loaded up, and they were ready to go.

"That's it, Charlie," Will said. "We're ready."

And just like that it was over. They were leaving me.

Buck came over to say goodbye first while Edward stood awkwardly off to the side. I could feel the tears welling heavily up in my eyes, and I was sure I was going to cry.

"You're a good kid," Buck said, roughly clapping me on the shoulder. "And you probably didn't notice, but I am a little afraid of flying. But not with you. You're a hell of a good pilot."

I laughed and sniffled as the first teardrop ran down my cheek. It was pretty dark outside by now, but in the light of the truck's headlights I am sure Buck still noticed it. He gave me a playful punch on the shoulder and walked off toward the truck.

"These are for you," Jay said, handing me the rest of his Kit Kat Chunky bars. "I know you like them."

I took the handful of chocolate bars from him and clutched them to my chest as another pair of tears rolled down my cheeks, leaving cold, wet trails behind them in the cool evening air.

"This is also for you," Will said, stepping over and handing me a thin, weathered, little paperback book. I quickly stuffed Jay's candy bars into my jacket pockets and took the book from him. I turned it over to read the cover. Daughter of the Snows by Jack London.

"I can't take this," I protested, but Will cut me off.

"Just take it," Will said. "It's a story about a tough young lady who climbs the Chilkoot Pass. Just like you did."

I nodded and fought back the tears as I held the book close to me. Will and Jay walked up toward the truck as well, and finally it was Charlie's turn. He would be the last one to say goodbye.

He walked over and slowly unfolded a jackknife that he had pulled out of his pocket. He gestured at the rope around my waist, and I lifted my jacket up so he could cut the rope away.

"You won't need that anymore," he said slowly. "Although I am not sure we needed it at all the past day or so."

I lowered my head, afraid that if I said anything I would cry.

"Take care of yourself, sweetheart," Charlie said as he stepped closer and gave me a big hug.

That was it. That was the last straw. It was all too much for me, and I burst completely into tears, wrapping my arms around Charlie and returning the hug. He was warm and tall and still smelled of that familiar outdoor smell—campfire smoke, sweat, and aftershave. It was a smell that I was sure I would remember for the rest of my life.

"This is completely crazy," the little voice in my head yelled at me. "Why are you crying? These are your kidnappers!"

"Not anymore," I told myself and went back to crying and hugging.

Charlie slowly let me go and stepped back once again.

"Buck is right," he said. "You're really a hell of a good pilot."

He smiled at me and lowered his eyes, and without another word he walked the short distance up to the others, who were leaning against the front of the truck waiting for him.

"So this is it," I thought. This is the end of this crazy, amazing, terrifying, unbelievable, exhausting, exhilarating, agonizingly extraordinary adventure.

But it wasn't the end. Because at that exact moment we all heard the sound of something rustling through the bushes, and we turned our heads to see a lanky, thin, old man emerge from the trees and step out into the light of the truck's headlamps. In his hands was a large double-barreled shotgun, which he leveled squarely at Charlie and the others as they stood over by the truck.

"Reach for the sky, pardners!" he shrieked at the top of his lungs, laughing maniacally. His voice was as creaky and wobbly and crazy-sounding as he looked. "I've always wanted to say that," he said, taking a few steps closer and aiming the shotgun menacingly from one person to the next.

"You all better do as he says," I heard a voice say from behind me, and I spun around to see Edward standing there with a revolver in his hand. And it was pointed straight at Charlie.

CHAPTER TWENTY-THREE
We Have To Steal It Back

I don't know what shocked me more. Was it the crazy old dude with a shotgun emerging from the bushes and shrieking maniacally at the top of his lungs? Or was it turning to see Edward pull out a gun and point it at Charlie?

Actually, I take that back. I do know which one shocked me more. And it was Edward.

"What are you doing, Eddie?" Charlie asked calmly, raising his palms halfway up from his waist. Edward was acting nervous and agitated, and Charlie clearly seemed to think that made him dangerous. He had the same look and tone as he'd had back in the forest when we were all staring down the enormous grizzly bear.

The rest of us were too surprised to be calm. Our jaws were nearly dropped to the ground as we held our hands up and nervously stared back and forth between Edward and the crazy old guy.

"What do you *think* we're doing, Charles?" the old guy said, his voice still creaky and wobbly. "We're coming to get our gold."

"It's not your gold," Buck yelled, and Charlie held up his palm to tell him to stay cool.

"Buck's right," Charlie said. "It's not your gold, Jack."

Jack? Jack? Where did I know that name from? Of course! It was completely obvious. This was Crazy Alaska Jack, the guy whom I'd read about in the newspaper weeks earlier who'd had his gold stolen—the guy whom Charlie and the others had stolen the gold from in the first place.

"It sure as hell *is* mine," Jack replied threateningly, squinting his eyes down to narrow slits as he stared Charlie down. He took a couple more steps closer and waved his shotgun, gesturing for them to move closer to me. "And I'm gonna get into this fancy truck of yours and drive it out of here," he said. "Unless one of you wants to try to stop me."

I was terrified. Even more terrified than I had been three days earlier when Charlie had first grabbed me out in the woods outside of their campsite. I was absolutely 100 percent terrified then—Charlie had scared the crap out of me—but not even Charlie's frightening calm at that time could compare to this. Somehow the combination of an obviously mentally deranged old man and a nervous half-brother, both waving firearms around, made me feel very uneasy and frightened. At least Charlie had never actually pointed his rifle at me.

True, Charlie had threatened to kill me, but in hindsight I knew that was just a bluff to scare me into cooperating with them. But it felt like these two were truly dangerous. I was sure that crazy old Jack would think nothing of letting someone have it with a blast from his shotgun if he tried anything, and Edward was so tense and nervous that I was afraid that he would just shoot one of us by accident.

It was almost funny, really. That week I was learning a lot about the various ways that people can threaten you with a gun.

I looked at Edward. "Actually, this week I am learning a lot about a lot of things," I thought.

"Why, Eddie?" Will asked as Edward and the old man used their guns to round us up together a short distance away from the truck. "Why would you do this?"

"How did he even know about the gold?" Buck asked, turning to Jay and Charlie. "Who told him?"

"Clearly I underestimated our half-brother," Charlie said with a disturbingly calm fury. "And overestimated how much he could be trusted."

"We never should have gotten him involved," Buck said.

"We didn't have a choice," Will replied. "Once we decided to fly over the pass instead of walking we needed someone to go back for the truck and meet us up here."

"Then one of us should have done it," Buck argued. "Like we originally planned."

"There wasn't time, and you know it," Will said.

"Shut up, all of you," Jack shouted. "You ladies are all givin' me a headache! Now lie face down on the ground with your hands behind your heads."

All of us looked at Charlie in panic. "Just do as he says," Charlie said calmly. "They aren't going to hurt us if we don't interfere."

"That's right," Jack said as we all kneeled down and planted our faces on the cold rocks of the gravel beach, our hands on the backs of our heads. He waved his shotgun at Edward, gesturing up toward the truck. "Go get in behind the wheel," he said. "We're getting out of here."

"Okay," Edward replied weakly and headed up the beach, his footsteps crunching on the stones as he went.

Jack slowly followed him, walking backward while keeping his shotgun trained on us as he went.

"Don't none of you try nothing," he said as he crunched up the beach behind Edward. "And no one will get himself killed."

We heard the sound of the truck doors opening and closing and the engine starting up. I peeked up with one eye to see Crazy Jack leaning out of the open window on the passenger side of the truck, pointing his gun at us and grinning as the truck rolled and ground over the stones. Then suddenly the truck sprung forward as someone stepped hard on the gas, and off it went, spitting rocks and fishtailing up the dirt road.

Slowly we all sat up and climbed back to our feet as the red taillights of the truck disappeared up the road into the trees. They were driving fast and were gone in no time, leaving us with nothing but the heavy silence of the wilderness that was broken only by the occasional buzz and chirp of the nighttime insects. Far above us the stars were coming out in full force as the bluish glow in the sky to the west slowly faded.

"Dammit!" Buck screamed, throwing his baseball cap to the ground. "That's the second time he's stolen our gold!"

Charlie was still sitting on the ground looking dejected. He sighed heavily and leaned back on his hands like a boxer who'd just lost a prize fight.

"What do we do now, Charlie?" Will asked quietly.

"I don't know," Charlie replied weakly. The others fell silent. They must have felt the same way that I did seeing Charlie look so defeated. "I honestly don't know what to do," he said.

"Can we follow them in the plane?" Will suggested.

Both Charlie and I shook our heads. It was too dark outside. It would be too dangerous.

"But we have to steal it back again," Will said. "Right, Charlie?"

My ears perked up. Steal it back again? Buck had said something similar. He said this was the second time that Jack had stolen their gold from them. And he'd also called it, "their gold."

"What do you mean by 'again'?" I asked, looking back at the four of them. "What do you mean that he stole it from you '*again*'?"

Just Go Back To The Beginning

Charlie looked at Will, then at me and back to Will again. Will shrugged.

"You might as well tell her," Will said. "She's kind of one of us now after all this... stuff we've been through."

"I don't know, Will," Charlie said.

"Just tell her, Charlie," Buck interrupted. "Or I'll do it, and it will be the crappiest version of the story you ever heard."

Charlie sighed and crawled slowly up onto his feet. "Okay," he agreed, dusting off his hands. "But first we show her how to start a campfire. It's going to be cold out here overnight."

"I know how to start a campfire," I said. "You just throw gasoline on some logs and then throw a match on it."

The four of them stared at me in disbelief.

"Oh, you silly, macho wilderness boys," I thought.

"What?" I asked, grinning. "That's how the kids back in high school always do it."

Charlie looked at me and shook his head sadly. "First we show her how to start a fire *properly*," he said. "Then story time."

Everyone laughed, and we broke up to make ourselves a comfortable little campsite for the night. Buck went back to grab the tent and supplies they had left behind for me and Edward, while Will and Jay collected wood to start a fire.

Charlie and I walked down the beach a short distance to where a couple of fallen trees made an obvious place to have a campfire—it was so obvious, in fact, that there was already a cold, burned-out circle of stones there from previous campfires that other people had built. Like the ruins of an ancient civilization.

"At least no one had constructed an Inukshuk," I thought cynically.

Charlie grabbed some of the wood that Will and Jay delivered, and he constructed his campfire foundation.

"Some people like the teepee method," Charlie said as he piled up the wood. "But I've always been a log-cabin kind of guy."

I watched while Charlie stacked the wood into a loose log cabin stacked with heavier pieces of wood at the bottom, suspended over a small pile of kindling, and tapering off to smaller pieces of wood and kindling again at the top. Finishing the job, he leaned down to light the kindling on both the bottom and top and watched as everything slowly ignited and burned.

I sat watching, mesmerized as the fire spread and ignited the larger pieces of wood, crawling from one to the other like a living being. Will sat down on the log next to me and handed me an energy bar and a bottle of freshly purified water.

"Quit stalling, Charlie," Buck said, tearing open his energy bar and sitting down on the other log. Charlie and Jay joined him there, sitting across from me to my left.

"Fine," Charlie said and looked at me solemnly. "What Buck said was right. This was the second time that Crazy Jack has stolen our gold from us. And it's "our" gold because it belongs to us. To our family.

"The first time he stole our gold from us was a few months back. He had been working for us the last couple of years up at our claim in Dawson City, but we suddenly stopped hearing from him. Usually he'd call us from a pay phone down in Dawson at least once every couple of weeks or so because he needed something. Some petty cash or a piece of equipment or something. But because he would sort of randomly call either one or the other of us from one time to the next, it took us a while to figure out that none of us had heard from him in a while. And of course he doesn't have a phone himself, so to find out what was going on, Will had to drive all the way up to Dawson to investigate.

"We figured he must have finally keeled over and died or something and was lying around rotting in the mobile home we keep out at the claim. But when Will got up there he wasn't anywhere to be found, and after talking to some of the locals it seemed like he'd skipped town some weeks before without any explanation or warning. This obviously sounded some alarms for us, so I hopped on the first ferry to Skagway and headed up to Dawson as well. While I was still on my way up, Will went digging under the house to see if our gold was still there, and it didn't take him long to realize that Crazy Jack had taken off with all of it.

"Will called me to tell me the news, and we tried to figure where the heck Crazy Jack had taken off to with all our gold, not to mention trying to figure out how the hell he had known that we'd buried under the house in the first place. We got lucky because a friend of ours who runs the gas station up in Chicken, Alaska, just happened to see him and his big U-Haul trailer go barreling by one day, so at least we knew where he was headed. After that we picked up his trail and followed him all the way down through Haines and Juneau, where we got lucky again, and he stopped at a rest stop to go to the bathroom. And we locked him inside the toilet long enough to get our gold back.

"But then he did something we didn't expect, and he called the police to report that the gold was his and that it had been stolen. I don't think the cops really believed him, but they sure as hell were taking it seriously enough to watch the ferry terminals and border crossings closely. Since there's no way out of Juneau except by boat or plane, we've just been hiding out in the wilderness ever since, waiting for the end of the season to come so we could trek the gold back up into Canada unnoticed. And that was when we met you."

There was a moment of silence.

"That was terrible, Charlie," Buck said. "That was the worst story I ever heard."

"What are you talking about?" Charlie asked. "Isn't that exactly what happened?"

"I have to agree with Buck," I said, my mind filled with a hundred different questions. "That story doesn't tell me, duh, why millions of dollars in gold was buried under a mobile home up in the Yukon, unguarded."

"Or how about the curse?" Buck suggested.

"What curse?" I asked, turning to Buck.

"Or how Eddie knew about the gold," Will said.

"You know I don't know the answer to that!" Charlie snapped.

"And why didn't you call the police when he first stole it?" I asked.

"Stop it!" Jay shouted, and everyone went instantly silent, surprised at this sudden outburst from the quietest member of the group. It was like one of those moments in a movie when the jukebox in a bar suddenly stops playing when someone says something shocking. "Just go back and tell it from the beginning, Charlie," Jay said, his voice quiet once again. "The *very* beginning."

CHAPTER TWENTY-FOUR

A Nice Warm Cabin To Sit In

Charlie leaned back with a sigh and looked around at each of us. We were all sitting around the campfire and were bathed in its orange-red glow. I remembered the first time I had seen these guys by the light of a campfire—they had looked like devils, and I was terrified. Now I could hardly imagine a campfire without them, and the glow on their faces looked warm and comforting instead of frightening. It's funny how our perceptions can change in life, and we can see the exact same thing again with brand-new eyes.

"Okay, sweetheart," Charlie said after a moment, leaning forward and looking me in the eyes. I smiled at this. Even Charlie calling me "sweetheart" had taken on a new meaning since the first time he'd said it. It no longer felt like an annoying, cynical nickname but rather a term of endearment, and I wouldn't want him calling me anything else. "The very beginning of this story goes back more than a hundred years, to the late 1890s and the time of the Klondike Gold Rush."

"It starts with a group of grizzled prospectors showing up in Skagway one day in early February 1898. By that time, as you know, the stampede to the gold fields was already well into its first winter, and thousands of people were climbing up Chilkoot Pass or heading up the nearby White Pass leading out of Skagway, all of them heading to the same place, Lake Lindeman and Lake Bennett, where we were a couple hours ago.

"By the time this group of gold miners showed up in Skagway, most of the people who were trying to get to the Klondike were already crossing the passes and spending the winter of 1897 to 1898 half frozen and building boats over at Lakes Lindeman or Bennett.

"But these guys weren't trying to get to the Klondike. In fact, they'd just come from there and were actually heading in completely the opposite direction, back down to Seattle. And the reason they were doing this was because unlike all those other unfortunate stampeders, who would soon get to Dawson to find all the best claims already taken, these guys had actually just sold their claims—good, rich claims, actually—because they'd already struck it rich and were heading home.

"These guys were *real* prospectors, you see. Not these wide-eyed dreamers from the outside world who dropped everything and headed for the Yukon at the drop of a hat, thinking they were going to strike it rich. When George Carmack and his friends first discovered gold up on Bonanza Creek in August 1896 these guys were already there and had been for years, doing exactly the same thing that George Carmack had been doing—looking for gold. And that meant that once word of Carmack's discovery got around, they were among the first to head over to the Klondike River and stake claims along the very same creeks where Carmack had done so—Bonanza and Eldorado.

"And so each of them had worked their separate claims throughout the entire winter of 1896 to 1897 and then again all through the summer of 1897, accumulating piles of gold dust while the rest of the world was just hearing the news and starting the stampede north. By the time winter started to loom on the horizon in late 1897, these guys had already pulled a fortune out of the ground and were facing another long, cold winter in the Yukon. It was a daunting prospect, but they stuck with it until one day around Christmas 1897, when they each happened by chance to take a break and head in to Dawson City.

"Sitting around drinking Christmas drinks together in one of the saloons, they got to talking about how they were sick of the darkness and cold and loneliness and how things weren't like they used to be, thanks to the many outsiders who'd made it north before the rivers froze. They were talking about quitting the far north and getting out with the gold that they already had. It was enough to last a lifetime, after all. What more did they need?

"So they headed back to the civilized world. Not even waiting for spring but just selling their claims right away, hiring some dogsled teams and heading south for the passes down into Skagway. And that's exactly what they did. They sold their claims for an added fortune to some wealthy newcomers or locals and packed up their gold and whatever belongings they had and got out of Dawson.

"It wasn't an easy trip, of course. You can imagine the conditions up here in the middle of winter. But it probably wasn't any more difficult for them than staying and working their mine all winter. Working a mine meant waking up each morning in the freezing cold and crawling down into a tiny little hole in the ground. Overnight they would have left fires burning underground to melt the earth because up here the ground is frozen as hard as rock. Without lighting fires they could never hope to dig up anything.

"The fires worked pretty good for thawing the earth but it also meant that their hole in the ground wasn't just cramped and tiny, it was also smoke-filled and nasty. Half choking in the smoke they would then dig out the thawed dirt and muck and haul it all the way up to the outside and pile it up outside in a big heap because they couldn't extract the gold from it yet. That would have to wait until spring when the creeks thawed and they again had access to running water to separate the gold dust and nuggets from the rocks and dirt.

"And once they were done digging and carting all that frozen mud all the way out they would have to repeat the process, over and over again endlessly, chopping down every tree in sight to build their fires.

"It was a harsh existence and it's not a surprise that these men had grown sick of it and decided to take their riches to go somewhere else to live a more comfortable life. And so they made their way south, all the way down to the top of the White Pass, where they hired porters to help carry their loads all the way down the pass. They had plenty of gold dust with which to pay, after all, and there were plenty of backs for hire.

"It was a grueling trip, but once they made it to Skagway it was easy going from there, because all they had to do was buy a ticket on the next steamer ship heading south, and they'd be on their way with a nice warm cabin to sit in while the ship did all the work. Their days of hardship and backbreaking labor were over.

"And that's exactly what they did," Charlie said. "Except unfortunately for this particular group of fellas, the next ship heading south to Seattle was a ship that's infamous up in these parts. The ship they booked passage on was the Clara Nevada."

The Mystery Of Eldred Island

"The Clara Nevada!" I cried. "I know this story!" Glen had, of course, told me the story of the Clara Nevada a few days earlier as I had sat with a different group of people around a different campfire that felt about a million miles away at that moment.

"I'm not surprised," Charlie said. "You've been in Alaska long enough to hear all the stories. But what you're going to hear tonight is the real story of the Clara Nevada. And it's a story that very few people know. And most of those people are sitting here right now around this very campfire."

I grinned and looked at the others, but their faces were grim and drawn, the flickering firelight casting long shadows across their faces and making them appear desperate and sad. "Maybe it isn't just a trick of the light," I thought. "Maybe that's exactly how they are feeling right now."

"This is where our family enters the story," Charlie continued. "Because our great-grandfather, Captain Charles H. Lewis, was the captain of the Clara Nevada.

Charlie paused and looked around at his brothers for a moment before going on.

"The Clara Nevada was a real piece of crap of a ship," he continued. "It had just about everything wrong with it that you can possibly imagine. It was old and falling apart. The boilers were failing. Even the lifeboats were in poor shape. But the stampede was on, and there was a huge demand for ships to take people north, so the owners put her into service despite all her flaws.

"To make things worse the crew of the ship also left a lot to be desired. Most boats around that time were having trouble keeping good crews, because every time they sailed north to Skagway or Dyea their crewmen would jump ship and head for the gold fields instead of staying onboard. The only ones left available were often hopeless drunks or just poor seamen.

"But not many other ships were in any better condition that particular winter, so these wealthy gold miners who'd just arrived in Skagway from the gold fields didn't have much choice. And besides, they wanted to get home as soon as possible, and the Clara

Nevada was the first ship they could get passage on that would take them to Seattle.

"So that's how these men found themselves climbing the gangplank to board the Clara Nevada on the morning of February 5, 1898. Along with them, of course, came their combined fortunes in gold, weighing almost two tons, which was locked securely away into the purser's safe.

"The rest of the story you probably already know. That afternoon the Clara Nevada set sail south from Skagway down the Lynn Canal into some particularly nasty Alaskan winter weather. A few hours later the ship was burning and on fire. It ran aground on a rocky reef, where it exploded and quickly sank, apparently taking everyone with her except for the body of the purser, which later washed ashore.

"Rumors flew that the ship had gone down with a fortune in gold aboard, but despite repeated attempts over the years to recover that gold, it has never been found. Which was strange, because the ship sank in only a few dozen feet of water, where it was easily accessible.

"But what no one knew was all that gold wasn't even on board the Clara Nevada when she sank. It had been secretly taken off hours earlier without the knowledge of its owners by a group of four men, who had conspired to steal it.

"The first of those men was the purser of the Clara Nevada, George Foster Beck. He was the one who controlled access to the safe, and along with a second man, George Rogers, the freight clerk, they surreptitiously arranged for the removal of the freight boxes containing the gold dust before the ship left port. Rogers then remained behind in Skagway with the gold, awaiting the return of the other men, when they would split the loot four ways.

"The third man in on the conspiracy was the ship's fireman, Seamus MacDonald. He was a Scotsman, but because of his Irish first name everyone just called him 'Paddy.' And I am sure you have guessed who the fourth and final man in the conspiracy was. Our great-grandfather, Captain Charles H. Lewis, the Clara Nevada's captain.

"Except for MacDonald, none of these men were real criminals. MacDonald, however, was a bit of an unsavory character, but he was exactly what the others needed to pull off the heist—

someone who was familiar with the seedier elements of life and society.

"And so the ship set out for Seattle while the gold remained safely behind in Skagway with George Rogers. The gold's true owners were none the wiser for the moment, but when they reached Seattle there would be questions to answer. That wasn't a problem, however, because the conspirators had a plan that would allow them to escape with the gold without anyone knowing that a robbery had even taken place. Their plan was to sink the Clara Nevada.

"As I said, other than MacDonald, these men were not criminals. Nor were they murderers. But the plan didn't require them to be. Their plan was a simple one: Set fire to the ship to create a panic that would send everyone running for the lifeboats, and once the passengers and crew were safely off, they would sink the ship into the vast depths of the Lynn Canal, where it would never be found, and their secret would be hidden forever.

"It was a good plan. A perfect one, actually. The only problem with perfect plans is that they almost never turn out perfectly. And this one certainly didn't.

"As they steamed south, the conspirators put their plan into action, and MacDonald set fire to the ship—witnesses would later report seeing the flaming hulk steaming down the Lynn Canal. But something was wrong. The fire spread too quickly, and before anyone could get to the lifeboats, it was already far out of control. Down in the boiler room, explosives had been set to go off to sink the ship, and the conspirators knew there wasn't enough time to get everyone off.

"But there was still a chance. Nearby was a small island called Eldred Island where, if they could run the ship aground on the reef, there was still a chance that the passengers and crew could swim to safety, even in the icy waters.

"The ship's pilot swung the ship around and steamed north to try to beach the Clara Nevada on the rocks of Eldred Island. With a horrible screech of metal she ran aground and stuck there. There was still a chance for everyone, but the weather was against them. Battered and beaten the ship floundered helplessly on the rocks, with all souls still on board.

"The conspirators had to make a decision. The explosives would go off at any moment, and once they did there would no longer be any chance of anyone escaping. So they decided to abandon the ship and everyone on board.

"Quickly putting a lifeboat into the water, MacDonald and our great-grandfather climbed in. Beck was about to climb in as well when the ship finally exploded, and Beck's body was thrown like a ragdoll across the water, where he landed some distance away, already dead. Somehow the lifeboat was miraculously thrown clear, and without even as much as a scratch on their heads, MacDonald and our great-grandfather got to shore and made their escape. As they rowed for their lives, they watched the helpless Clara Nevada go to the bottom, along with dozens and dozens of her passengers and crew.

"The nearest shoreline was miles away from anywhere, and after making it safely ashore, the two men lit a fire to keep from freezing to death while they waited out the night and the storm. The next morning they started the long hike cross-country back to Skagway. Their campfire and the lifeboat, complete with a life-preserver from the Clara Nevada, would later be found.

"Once they got back to Skagway they expected to find the ship's clerk, George Waters, still there guarding the stash of gold, but when they showed up at the prearranged meeting place, there was no one there. Waters had decided to keep all the gold for himself, it seemed. MacDonald was enraged and vowed that he would kill him for double-crossing them. Our great-grandfather agreed, and the next day they set off to find George Waters.

"He wasn't difficult to find, it turned out. Like I said, he wasn't a criminal, and they soon caught up with him hiding out in a cabin he had rented halfway between Skagway and Dyea. Kicking in his door late one night, they confronted him about his theft of the gold. He hadn't stolen it, he said. After he'd heard of the ship's demise, he had assumed that everyone was dead and had logically kept all the gold for himself.

"He may have been telling the truth. Or maybe not. Either way, MacDonald didn't buy the story and shot him dead on the spot. Now the gold was all theirs, to be split two ways instead of four. And so they split it and went their separate ways, assuming disguises in case anyone recognized them and taking separate steamer ships back down to Seattle."

CHAPTER TWENTY-FIVE

A Ghost Of The Clara Nevada

*C*harlie paused for a moment to take a drink of water, then continued with the story. "They successfully made their escape, each with his fortune," he said. "Both men now had to decide what they would do next. They could do almost anything they wanted. They could live a life of luxury for the rest of their lives with the money they had. But greed is a powerful thing, and even though they already had a fortune in gold, they wanted more. They needed more.

"MacDonald had acquired a taste for life in the far north, and he set out for Dawson City that spring. He wanted more gold, and whether he planned to get it by legitimate or criminal means was not certain. The only thing that was certain was that he'd caught Klondike Fever the same as everyone else had, and he headed north.

"Our great-grandfather had a different idea of how he was going to add to his fortune. He was always a sailor at heart and realized that there was a fortune to be made running riverboats from the mouth of the Yukon River up to Dawson City and back. So he bought himself a share of a flat-bottomed paddle-wheeler riverboat and joined a scheme to tow these riverboats all the way to Alaska and the Yukon River. But the project was doomed from the start and encountered disaster after disaster—the ship running aground, violent storms, near sinkings, and passenger mutinies. But despite everything seeming to be against them, they somehow finally made it to the Yukon River and headed for Dawson.

"The final disaster in the venture came when the boat ran aground on a sandbar halfway up the Yukon River and was left stranded there until the river froze. Of course, once the river froze, there was no escape for the passengers and crew, and they had to spend the entire long winter stuck there out in the middle of nowhere on the frozen river. And you can imagine how horrible that must have been, spending month after month on a frozen riverboat up in the arctic.

"The entire enterprise had been plagued with bad luck from start to finish, but being stuck that whole long and cold winter gave our great-grandfather a lot of time to think. And he was slowly starting to think that the stolen gold was cursed.

"The passengers and crew that he'd left behind to die that night on the Clara Nevada haunted him. They would come to him in his daydreams as he stood on the bridge of his frozen ship as he looked out across the never-ending snow and ice of the arctic winter. He could see them walking and floating like ghosts across the endless wastes, taunting him and pointing their fingers in accusation. Even in his sleep he wasn't safe. Nightmares of the sinking filled his sleep. He would dream of dark, fiery infernos like the one that had consumed the Clara Nevada and taken those dozens of souls down with her. He would awaken, sitting bolt upright and screaming, only to see the faces of the dead pressed up against the frosty glass windows of his cabin. He had killed them. His greed had killed them.

"By the time the breakup of the river ice finally came in the spring, our great-grandfather had decided that he must continue on to Dawson City to find his coconspirator MacDonald. He was the only man left alive with whom he could discuss the tragedy. And the curse.

"And so he did. Leaving his own grounded riverboat behind, he transferred to another passing boat that was heading upriver for Dawson. And along with him came his share of the stolen gold, which he'd kept close to him ever since leaving Skagway.

"Arriving in Dawson City, it didn't take long for him to track down MacDonald, who was a well-known local con man and suspected criminal who lived out at the gold creeks on a claim that he'd bought, or more likely conned, from its previous owner. Knocking on MacDonald's door one night, our great-grandfather was welcomed warmly and ushered inside to sit beside a hot stove to share a night of drinking and talking.

"Our great-grandfather told MacDonald about the visions and nightmares that he'd been having and of his theory that the stolen gold must be cursed. Nonsense, MacDonald told him. Ever since the robbery MacDonald hadn't had such a run of good luck in his entire life. Within hours of arriving in Dawson, he purchased a rich claim on Bonanza Creek for a pittance from a miner who'd suddenly grown tired and wanted to head back home. Then he quickly obtained a parcel of land with a building in the middle of town that he'd since made into a thriving restaurant and saloon. Half the town assumed he'd done all this by some deceitful or criminal means, but in reality he had just been in the right place at the right time. But of course it didn't hurt to have such a daunting reputation, he said, especially out in this wild frontier town. But the truth was that for the first time in his life, he was living honestly and making far more money than he ever had as a criminal.

"After their pleasant evening together, MacDonald could see that our great-grandfather had nowhere to go, and he let our great-grandfather move into a vacant cabin on his claim.

"That night, as our great-grandfather tried to fall asleep in his warm new cabin, he thought a lot about his sudden good fortune, and suddenly he made a life-changing decision. The curse of the gold had been lifted, he decided, because he'd finally returned it to the place where it came from in the first place—Bonanza Creek. He'd brought the gold home.

"This theory fit perfectly, and it also explained why MacDonald hadn't experienced any bad luck. MacDonald had already brought his share of the gold back home in the first place. With this realization our relieved great-grandfather fell into the first undisturbed sleep he'd had in many months.

"Night after night our great-grandfather slept soundly in his new home, and the visions of the dead from the Clara Nevada never returned. He came to an agreement with MacDonald to work the claim in exchange for using the cabin. MacDonald readily agreed because he had discovered that he disliked gold mining, but in order to retain his rights to the claim, someone had to work it. MacDonald had also decided to head downriver, along with most of the city of Dawson, to Nome, Alaska, where the latest gold rush was already in full swing. He'd already bought some land and a building there, where he planned to open another saloon and make another fortune. It was a win-win situation.

"So the two of them parted ways. MacDonald and his share of the gold headed down the Yukon River to Nome, and our great-grandfather stayed behind to live an uneventful life on Bonanza

Creek. And that's how things went, day after day, our great-grandfather filling his days with honest work and sleeping the nights free of haunting nightmares. This continued, month after month and season after season, until one night during a sudden winter snowstorm, he was on his way back from town and saw lights burning in both his cabin and MacDonald's old cabin. Standing between the two was a terrifying white figure standing like a statue. He was convinced that it was a ghost from the Clara Nevada who was finally going to extract revenge for being left behind to die.

"Drawing closer to the figure, he did discover a terrifying white ghost from the Clara Nevada, but not the kind that he'd expected. It was MacDonald, half frozen and bleeding. He collapsed in the snow, and our great-grandfather carried him in to bed to get him warm and tend to his wounds."

The Curse Is Real

"The curse is real, MacDonald told our great-grandfather as he lay there dying. Even before he'd reached Nome he'd already suffered the first in a long string of misfortunes. On the voyage downriver he had contracted some kind of fever and had nearly died. Once in Nome he had arrived to find the building he had bought and planned to convert into a saloon had mysteriously burned to the ground. He then discovered that the Mounted Police had sent word ahead to the local authorities in Nome that the notorious criminal, Paddy MacDonald, was on his way there with a gang of thugs. The local police were on the lookout for him, and 'Paddy' wasn't even his proper name, MacDonald complained. It was Seamus.

"On the run from the law, MacDonald had escaped on a steamship heading south to Seattle. And on arriving in Seattle he finally found sanctuary with his family, but the bad luck continued to follow him. First his young son suffered an attack of tuberculosis and died. His distraught wife had then tried to kill herself by cutting open her wrists using a shard of broken glass. By this time he also started seeing familiar faces on the streets of Seattle that he became convinced were spirits of the dead passengers and crew of the Clara Nevada. When the nightmares began, he finally decided that to save himself and his family he had to get the gold back to Dawson as quickly as possible. He booked passage and set out on the next steamship north.

"The passage north was uneventful, but MacDonald spent most of the voyage holed up in his cabin, too frightened to venture outside in case the ghosts of the Clara Nevada returned. But even inside his cabin he wasn't safe. The nightmares continued. The worst was yet to come, however, because on the day when they were to reach their destination at Dyea, the ship passed by Eldred Island and the final resting place of the Clara Nevada.

"MacDonald had managed to doze off into a restful sleep in his cabin that morning. But some time around midday, at the exact moment that the ship was steaming past Eldred Rock, the deafening and horrifying ghoulish shrieking of a hundred different voices woke MacDonald. He clasped his hands over his ears to block out the sound, but it made no difference. The screams cut right through his head, and he felt himself spiraling farther and farther down into complete madness with every passing second. Hearing a screeching sound at his window, he looked over to see the waterlogged and rotting faces of the dead squished up against the glass, blocking out the sunlight.

"And then in an instant it was gone again, as quickly as it had started. In the blink of an eye, the faces at the window disappeared, the deranged shrieking ceased, and MacDonald spent the rest of the voyage curled up in his bunk, sweating and cold and terrified.

"Disembarking at Dyea, MacDonald hired a boat and plenty of porters to carry him and the gold upriver and over the Chilkoot Pass. From there he floated downriver to Whitehorse before the river froze. Stuck there, still hundreds of miles from Dawson City, he tried to wait out the winter, but the bad luck continued to plague him. His reputation as a notorious criminal had followed him, and the local Mounties had been alerted that he was in town. He couldn't wait for spring after all, and he quickly hired dogsleds to carry him and his gold back to Dawson. After arriving at his claim, he had stashed the gold and went to find our great-grandfather in town. But before he got there, some local Mounties recognized him, and a terrible gunfight ensued, and MacDonald had been shot. Wounded but still able to walk, MacDonald had somehow managed to escape from the police into the snowstorm and stumbled back to the two cabins on his claim on Bonanza Creek, where our great-grandfather had found him.

"The curse is real, MacDonald told our grandfather a second time as the last remnants of life were slipping from his body, but he had beaten it. Moments later, just before he died, MacDonald handed our great-grandfather a picture of himself that was taken in more prosperous times and that showed him sitting contentedly in front of his cabin. On the back of the photo, he had written where he had hidden the gold."

I hid the gold in the secret hollowed-out logs behind the stove in my cabin.

You have been a good friend, S. M.

"And with that MacDonald's body went limp, and he passed from this world into the next. Our great-grandfather sat there for some time, saying a silent prayer for God to take mercy on MacDonald's soul and to forgive his evil deeds. He had good reason for such a prayer, after all. There would also come a day when he himself would stand before the all-mighty and account for his own evil deeds.

"The next day he loaded the body onto a sled and dragged MacDonald into town. Turning him over to the local Mounties, he wasted no time transferring the registration of MacDonald's claim into his own name.

"That claim on Bonanza Creek," Charlie said. "Would be passed down from generation to generation and stay in our family for more than a hundred years. It's the same claim that we still have today just outside of Dawson City.

"Our great-grandfather could now relax. The remaining stolen gold was now safely back in the Klondike, where it came from, and the curse was lifted. And he knew it would stay that way as long as the gold stayed where it was. Eventually, he would leave the Klondike and make his way back to his family in the outside world, but he was always careful. With all the gold safely hidden up at the claim just outside of Dawson, the only thing he had to worry about was making sure that someone continued actively working the claim so it would remain in the hands of our family. Sometimes he himself would return to the Yukon and work the claim for a time, and sometimes his sons would make the journey, often staying for years to enjoy the adventure of the far north. A couple of those sons, like our own grandfather, loved the adventure so much that they actually moved north to put down roots. That also made it a lot easier to keep an eye on the claim as well, of course.

"And so it went until our great-grandfather finally died, and the claim was passed on to his eldest son, who in turn passed it down to his own sons. The true story of the Clara Nevada was also passed down this way, from father to son, as a dangerous family secret to be held close and unspoken, and under no circumstances to ever be shared with anyone."

CHAPTER TWENTY-SIX
One Final Twist

Charlie paused to take another sip of water, then inhaled deeply. "There is one final twist to the story," he said.

"Another twist?" I thought. It was already a story with more twists and turns than a rollercoaster.

"It happened shortly before our grandfather died," Charlie continued. "And before the claim was passed to his eldest son, our father, who would, in turn, pass it down to me.

"Grandpa was really a tough one. A real Alaskan man. And he lived to be exactly one hundred years old, so when this happened it was already the late 1970s or early 1980s.

"At that time the two original cabins up at the claim were more than eighty years old, and Grandpa put a mobile home on the site to serve as a more comfortable place for anyone who was up working the claim. But a nicer place to stay wasn't Grandpa's only reason for installing a mobile home there. He also had another motive. His plan was to gather all the gold together in one place from all the various hiding places and bury it deep under whatever house he put in. Grandpa was tired of the family having to endlessly work the claim up in the Yukon, and by burying the gold and hiding it safely away, he knew we could then lease our claim out or even hire people to work the claim for us. With the gold all gathered together and buried deep enough, we would never have to worry about it being accidentally discovered by whoever might be working the claim.

"It was a good plan since Grandpa's family roots were solidly set down in Juneau, and although the trips to the Yukon sometimes made for fun family camping adventures, it did get a bit tired and repetitive after a while. There was only one problem, which they discovered after gathering the nearly one ton of gold that made up

228

great-grandfather's original share from the robbery. They turned their attention to MacDonald's share of the gold and cut into the logs behind the stove in his cabin, where the note had said it was hidden. But there was nothing there. No hollowed-out logs. No secret hiding place. And certainly no gold. All those years everyone just assumed it was there and left it safely hidden. What no one realized was that it was never there in the first place."

"What?" I cried. "Then where was it?"

Charlie shrugged. "No one has any idea," he said.

"But the note said it was in his cabin, in the logs behind the stove," I protested. "Why wasn't it there?"

Charlie shrugged again. "I know," he said. "But it wasn't. Trust me, I've even looked myself."

"What about the other cabin?" I asked.

"They also looked in the other cabin as well," Charlie replied. "But with no luck. And in desperation they even checked every single log on both cabins just to be sure. But they found nothing."

"But what happened to the gold?" I asked in frustration.

"We will never know," Charlie said. "Maybe whoever demolished the cabin found the gold and never reported it. If that is true, then the curse is his problem to deal with, not my family's.

"Whatever happened to it, they couldn't figure it out, so they just buried great-grandfather's share of the gold under the house and left it at that. The curse was lifted, and there the gold remained, hidden away for years, while either our family worked the claim or we hired other people to do it for us. That's where Crazy Jack comes in, because he was one of the people we hired to work the claim for us. Until he stole the gold, that is. I guess we'll have to fire him for that."

Everyone laughed, but Charlie turned serious again.

"But what really bugs me," Charlie said, "and bugged me for all those weeks we were hiding out in the wilderness, was how Jack had found the gold. We just couldn't figure it out."

Everyone fell silent, thinking of Edward's betrayal of the family's secret.

"But I guess now we know," Charlie said sadly, ending the story. His brothers nodded in agreement, with dark expressions on their faces.

"So what do we do now?" I asked after a few uncomfortable moments of silence.

Charlie shrugged. "We do nothing," he said. "There's nothing we can do."

"What are you talking about?" I cried. "We have to get the gold back!"

Charlie shook his head. "I've had enough of this whole thing," he said angrily. "I'm tired of living in a tent. I haven't had a shower in weeks. And I sure as hell am tired of eating energy bars!" He crumpled up the empty wrapper of an energy bar and hurled it into the campfire.

"But you can't just give up!" I replied.

Charlie looked at me. "Sure I can," he said. "Besides, even if we wanted to go chasing after them again, we still couldn't do it."

"Why not?" I asked stubbornly.

"Because we don't know where they're headed," Charlie replied, just as stubbornly. "They could be headed almost anywhere by now."

"You found Jack once before," I protested.

"We got lucky," Charlie said.

"You could get lucky again," I replied. "You can't just give up!"

"Actually, we *do* know where they are headed," Jay said quietly.

Charlie had opened his mouth to say something clever to me, but Jay's comment caught him off guard, and he immediately looked at Jay in confusion.

"What did you say?" Charlie asked.

"I said," Jay repeated, "that we *do* know where they are going. They are going to Dawson."

Charlie didn't understand. "Why the hell would they go to Dawson?" he asked. "Everyone would recognize them there. It would be crazy."

"They'll go there to get the rest of the gold," Jay said simply. "To get MacDonald's share."

"What rest of the gold?" Charlie asked in frustration. "You know there isn't any, and you just heard me tell her how no one ever found it."

"I know that," Jay said calmly. "And you know that. And Buck and Will know that. And now even Kitty knows too."

"But?" Charlie asked.

"But Jack doesn't," Jay said with finality. "And neither does Eddie."

A Symphony Of Pale Green Fire

We all sat there in stunned silence, looking back and forth at each other with our mouths hanging open, then back at Jay again.

"Wait a minute," Charlie finally said, shaking his head. "You're wrong. How would they even know about MacDonald's share of the gold? Crazy Jack can't possibly know about that because Eddie doesn't know the story either."

"Because of the photograph," Jay said patiently. "Remember we packed it in with the gold way back in Juneau two months ago when we decided to dump the gold in the river?"

"Dump the gold in the river?" I asked. "I think I missed that part of the story."

Charlie didn't hear me. He was too stunned by what Jay had just said and sat there quietly, deep in thought.

"Oh my God," Buck said after a moment. "We did!"

"Jay's right," Will said in disbelief, clapping Jay on the back.

Charlie nodded, still thinking everything through carefully. "He sure is," he said. "And as soon as Jack finds that photo you can be sure he's gonna hightail it up to Dawson to get the rest of the gold. He won't be able to resist it."

"But what if he's found the photo already?" Buck asked. "And he drives all the way up to Dawson overnight and gets there before we can?"

Charlie shook his head. "Even if he did find it tonight," he said, "he still won't get there before we can." Charlie turned and gestured toward the plane. "We have a plane, remember?" he said.

"You mean, Kitty has a plane, right?" Will said defiantly. "She's not our prisoner anymore." His last sentence wasn't a question.

Charlie's face blushed red. "Yes, of course," he said sheepishly and turned to face me. Putting a hand over his heart he addressed me in his most sincere tone of voice. "Ms. Hawk," he said. "You would do me a great service if you could fly my four brothers and me to Dawson City at first light tomorrow. And if you do, we would be forever in your debt."

"It would be my honor, sir," I replied, bowing my head in return.

Charlie rose to his feet. "We'd better get some sleep, then," he said, dumping the rest of his water bottle over the fire and kicking sand over the smoking, steaming logs.

The rest of us got to our feet as well to help Charlie put out the fire. As the flames were extinguished, our little camp was plunged into thick darkness, and it took a moment for our eyes to adjust.

"Oh look," Will said. "The aurora."

I looked at him blankly, not understanding what he was talking about. My head was so filled with stories of the gold rush and curses and gold that the first thought that popped into my head was that he meant some old-time gold-rush boat called the Aurora or something like that.

"The aurora," he repeated, pointing his finger toward the sky. "The Northern Lights."

I leaned my head back to look up and nearly fell over backward when I finally saw what he was talking about. It was the most beautiful thing that I have ever seen in my entire life.

Coursing down from the northern tip of the sky like a celestial river were bright-green streamers of light that danced and trembled and flickered like great flames across the sky. I gasped at the beauty of it, my breath and voice caught in my throat.

I watched in awe as the rivers of light moved and changed like supernatural apparitions up in the heavens. It felt like they were the ghosts of all the animals and people who had lived here in the north and had passed on to the other world. For a moment it would almost be frightening and I felt as though I could feel each of their individual spirits then the patterns would change and shift and the eerie feeling would pass, leaving only the beauty of it behind.

The patterns were constantly shifting and changing—chimerical green fingers of radiance flaring across the sky, their tips and edges coursing with tinges of red and purple. The fingers swayed and stirred until they reached across almost the entire sky, covering the dome of our little world, protecting us. And then the fingers dissolved and stirred across the sky, the heavenly flames growing calm again and continuing their ever-changing and ethereal dance.

"It's so beautiful," I whispered so quietly that it was almost to myself. The magnificence of what I saw weakened my legs, and I worried that I might actually faint, so I slowly sat down to lean back against one of the campfire logs to watch the spectacle.

The other four watched for a while, then returned to setting up camp for the night. I wanted to help and get ready for sleep too, but I absolutely couldn't take my eyes off the dance of light I was witnessing in the sky.

"The natives here believe that the aurora are the dancing spirits of their ancestors," Will said, walking over and kneeling next to me. "The spirits of the animals and people who walked this land before them."

"I could feel that too," I said breathlessly. "Exactly that same thing."

"Some other tribes farther south think they are an omen of war," I heard Charlie say from somewhere nearby.

Will nodded. "I think tonight they might be both," he said simply, then rose to his feet and left me to watch the sky.

Time and again I tried to make myself get up and help the others, but I just couldn't pull myself away from the symphony of pale-green fire in the sky. I felt my eyelids getting heavier and heavier, but I still couldn't pull myself away. Eventually, I just nodded off to sleep without even realizing it, passing seamlessly from the waking world into the dreaming one.

But the dance continued even in my dreams. The fiery streamers of light danced across my eyelids, morphing and changing, first taking the form of a wolf, then a bear, then an orca whale.

"Come on, sweetheart," I heard a distant voice say, echoing into my dreams as if from across a great chasm.

I felt myself lifted up into the air. I was flying and joining the dance with the spirits. I could feel the wisps of otherworldly green fire surrounding me. Was it Skeena's grandfather again? Visiting me and protecting me? I could feel his presence again and almost hear his voice. And the smell of smoke and sweat and aftershave filled my nostrils.

But then I set down once again, my flight over, and I settled deep into the warmth of the earth while the fiery dance continued without me far above.

CHAPTER TWENTY-SEVEN

No Time To Be Scared

I awoke early the next morning wrapped in my warm sleeping bag and lying comfortably on a thick yoga mat in the back of my plane. In the darkness it took me a moment to realize where I was and that Will was shaking my leg to wake me up.

It was time to go.

I was reluctant to leave the warmth of my sleeping bag, but somehow I managed to get out and shake myself out of my slumber. The cold early-morning air certainly helped to wake me up, and I stood on the pontoon on the pilot's side of the plane waiting for the others to quickly load everything inside.

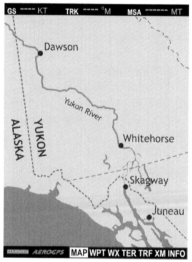

It was still quite dark outside, and I was a bit nervous about taking off in such darkness. Off to the southeast, the sky was brightening, but it was still dark enough that I couldn't see properly. What if there were power lines over the lake somewhere or strung between the low-lying hills? I couldn't see any indication of such obstacles on the GPS, and I didn't remember seeing any the night before when we came in to land, but I still worried. I couldn't help it. What if there was a log in the water or something?

"When will we go?" Charlie asked, pulling himself into the co-pilot's seat and buckling himself in. Will and Buck had pushed us off the shoreline and were climbing in through the back door on the other side.

I didn't want to be pressured into taking off when I wasn't comfortable.

"I'd like to have a bit more light in the sky before we leave," I said.

"Agreed," Charlie said. "I trust your judgment."

I looked at him, his face illuminated by the waving beam of a flashlight that Buck was using to get himself settled in the passenger cabin.

"He trusts my judgment," I thought, proud of this somehow.

"But do you trust your own judgment?" the little voice in my head asked me.

"Of course I do," I replied.

"Do you really?" it asked again.

"Yes I do, and my judgment tells me that this is an adventure and that there's no time to be scared."

I pulled myself up into the cockpit confidently.

"My judgment also tells me that it's light enough, and I see that there are no power lines or logs out there anywhere," I thought and slammed the door closed behind me.

And with that I started the engine and let it warm up while more and more light poured into the sky with every passing second. I poured on the gas, and with all the extra weight gone from the plane we were up and away in no time, turning north to head for Dawson City, with me feeling excited and frightened and exhilarated all at the same time.

As we made our way north, the day got brighter and brighter, and soon we saw everything below us bathed in that familiar blue-tinged light that is unique to the early morning. There was a bit of cloud in the sky, mostly lingering around the mountain peaks, cloaking them in mysterious veils, but it was otherwise a fairly clear day.

"Do we have enough fuel to get to Dawson?" Charlie asked as I leveled us off from our takeoff climb.

I squinted at my fuel gauges for the tenth time that morning. I did the calculations again in my head as I leaned over and tapped the glass to make the needles settle. "It will be close," I replied. "We've already used the reserve fuel in the wingtip tanks, but I think we're okay."

"Maybe we should stop somewhere along the way," Buck suggested. "Like Whitehorse?"

Charlie vetoed the idea. "We're still wanted fugitives, remember?" he answered. "And she is a missing person. We can't risk it."

"If Kitty says we can make it," Will said. "Then we can make it. Don't worry."

"Actually I believe her exact words were, '*I think*' we have enough fuel," Buck protested, but he let the matter drop.

Charlie was right. I was still a missing person. And I had to call my parents.

"Where did you guys put my backpack?" I asked.

"It's back here," Will said, grabbing it from Buck, who had pulled it out and handed it forward.

"I need to call my parents," I said to Charlie. "They will be worried about me."

He nodded in understanding. I knew he was worried that somehow this would give us away and ruin our plans, but he also trusted me and knew that I wouldn't tell them more than I needed to.

"Don't worry," I told him and held the phone up to my ear to make the call. Luckily, by that time we were more or less back in what passes for civilization up in the Yukon, and I got a signal.

My parents were overjoyed and relieved to hear from me. My mom cried a lot, and my father insisted that he'd known all along that I was okay, but of course he had been worried sick too. I told them I was completely fine and that the whole thing was just a big misunderstanding. I would explain it later, I said, and because both of my parents were familiar with the near impossibility of holding a phone conversation in a loud cockpit, they accepted this but wanted to hear from me as soon as possible. I promised I would call again as soon as I could, and they promised to call Uncle Joe and Aunt Jenny and alert the US Coast Guard that I was not missing after all.

After I hung up, I handed the phone back to Will to put away in my bag, and we flew on in silence. After a long while with no one saying a word, I had the feeling that hearing me talk to my parents made the other four feel guilty for kidnapping me. But that was in the past as far as I was concerned, and I didn't blame them.

There was no reason for them to feel bad, so I tried to break the ice and make a bit of conversation.

"Yesterday Jay mentioned something about throwing the gold into the river," I said. "What was that about?"

There was a short pause, but then Charlie spoke. "It was Will's idea," he said. "Maybe he should explain?"

Will cleared his throat and leaned forward. "I thought of it when we were hiding out in the wilderness during the summer," he said slowly. "And we were discussing what to do with the gold. We knew we had to take it back to Dawson, and the obvious thing was to just bury it again, but I knew if we did that, we would never be free of it for the rest of our lives. Even if we took it back and hid it somewhere else, Crazy Jack would still be out there, and he would never give up looking for it. And if Jack knew about the gold, then probably even more people outside of our family would know about it, and we'd waste the rest of our lives taking care of it and keeping it safe. So we decided to take the gold back to the Klondike as we needed to, but instead of burying it we'd instead dump it into the Yukon River. And not just the gold, but also everything that ever had anything to do with it, including MacDonald's photograph with the writing on the back that he'd given our great-grandfather. That way the gold dust would be returned to where it came from, and the curse would never return."

I nodded. "That makes sense," I said as I wrinkled my nose and thought through the plan a bit more. "But then wouldn't the gold just eventually run downstream?" I asked. "Flake by flake, nugget by nugget, until it washed up somewhere, and someone found it and started a whole new gold rush all over again?"

Charlie shrugged. "Maybe eventually, yes," he said. "But it would probably take hundreds or even thousands of years for that to happen."

"Fair enough," I said.

I guess. I suppose. I understood that they needed to do something to get rid of the gold forever and to free themselves of the curse once and for all, but I wasn't sure that I liked this idea of dumping the gold in the river.

What Striking It Rich Really Means

I thought about Will's gold-dumping idea some more, and the more I thought about it, the less I liked it.

"What about giving it to charity?" I suggested. "That would also work, wouldn't it?"

The four of them stared at me with blank faces, thinking this over.

"I'm not sure," Will said, shaking his head hesitantly and looking to Charlie.

Charlie thought it over. "What kind of charity?" he asked.

I shrugged. "Some Yukon gold miner's charity?" I suggested.

Will shook his head again. "No," he said. "If there was anything our great-grandfather was against, it was the never-ending greed and searches for gold up in the Yukon."

"But you have your own gold mine claim," I replied.

"Yes, we do," Charlie said. "But the family has never worked it very seriously. Only enough to retain our rights to it and nothing more."

I thought about this some more. "You definitely can't throw it in the river then," I said. "Because eventually it will wash downstream and be discovered. And it will set off another mini gold rush and another cycle of greed."

This observation hit home with them, and I glanced back to the passenger cabin to see that they were all nodding in agreement as they thought this over.

"I think she's right," Jay said.

"Surely there must be some charity we could give it to," Will said.

"Or more than one charity," Buck suggested.

"What do you think, Charlie?" Will asked.

Charlie kept nodding his head slightly as he thought the idea through.

"I think that sounds exactly right," he finally said. "This gold has been a curse for long enough. Maybe it's time to do some good with it."

"Maybe all the gold in the Yukon carries a curse with it?" I suggested as some interior wall inside me broke, and all my anger toward all the fools who had ever chased gold came suddenly spilling out. "From what I've learned and seen so far, it brings nothing but greed and suffering. With foolish people climbing freezing mountain passes in the middle of winter to get it. Lying and stealing and cheating for it. And killing."

This last remark was directed at them. At their great-grandfather. And I felt bad for saying it, but the four of them simply looked at me in stunned silence, waiting for me to finish with my outburst.

I turned to face Will, turning my fury unfairly onto him. "I flipped through your Jack London book a bit this morning while I was waiting for you guys to get finished," I said. "You quoted from it one day when we were on the Chilkoot Trail. I recognized the quote as I flipped through the pages. In the book the main character tells a man that he is weak of heart and that the north doesn't want him, remember?"

Will nodded. "The country has no use for you," Will quoted. "The north wants strong men. Strong of soul, not body."

"The north can go to hell," I said, continuing my rant. "Only those who are weak in their soul would come up here and go through all of this for some stupid, shiny yellow metal. People who are strong of soul would know better and stay at home. People who are strong in their soul wouldn't lie and steal and cheat and do everything else possible just for some stupid gold. They wouldn't irresponsibly drop everything and run off chasing fool's dreams. They would know better than to believe that there was actually an endless supply of gold nuggets sitting around on the ground for just anyone to come along and pick them up. And they wouldn't come into a place as beautiful as all this and cut down every tree in sight to fuel their foolish obsessive quest for riches. And striking it rich—really, truly striking it rich—never, ever has anything to do with money."

The four of them continued to sit in silence as I finished my rant.

"I am sorry," I said, after I calmed down a bit and realized all the things that I had said. "I wasn't trying to attack you guys, and I certainly didn't mean to hurt you, so I am sorry if I did. I know that you guys are not greedy or evil or anything like that."

"Don't worry," Charlie said, reaching over to gently put his hand on my arm. "We know what you mean, and I think we all agree with you. Because we are all strong of soul. Every one of us. Especially you."

"I know you are," I replied quietly. I started to say something else but didn't. I wanted to tell them what I thought striking it rich really meant. That it was everything that had happened to me that summer and every experience that I'd had. From the beautiful humpback whales I'd seen all the way to climbing the Chilkoot Pass. And all the amazing new friends that I had made. But I didn't have to tell them this. Of course they already knew.

"I should have given you a different book, maybe," Will said, breaking the silence.

We all turned to look at him.

"I should have given her The Lorax," he explained.

No one had any idea what he was talking about. Will sighed as he looked around at his brothers in frustration.

"Doctor Seuss? Our mother used to read this to us, don't you remember?" he asked. "In the book the people cut down every tree in sight just to make their stupid Thneeds."

I nodded. Now I understood, and I did know the book.

"Yes!" I replied. "In the book they cut down every tree in sight. Just like the men in their tent cities on the shores of Lake Lindeman and Lake Bennett did."

"And just like the men on the gold creeks of the Klondike did," Jay added. He shook his head thoughtfully. "You're not going to like Dawson City," he said.

A Perfect Runway Right In Front Of Us

Down below us the mighty Yukon River flowed north toward Dawson City and meandered across a changing landscape.

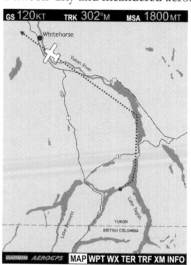

"This is the route that the stampeders followed during the gold rush," Charlie said, looking out his window to the river far below. "After building their boats up on the headland lakes and waiting for the river to thaw, they just floated easily downriver all the way to the Klondike."

"It doesn't look that easy to me," I replied, also looking out my window to where the river churned and boiled its way through a narrow canyon.

"That's Miles Canyon," he

said. "And you're right; it wasn't that easy to get through there. In fact, there were so many accidents that the Mounted Police started controlling the entry to the canyon and required the boats to hire a local river pilot to guide them safely through. Except that was too expensive for most people, so many just pushed their boats off, said a prayer, and hoped for the best while they walked down on foot to hopefully find their boats down at the other end of the canyon."

"That's crazy," I said, laughing.

Charlie shrugged. "There are a couple of rapids along the river on the way to Dawson," he said. "But most of the way it's smooth sailing."

It was also a pretty smooth morning for flying as we continued making our way over the nearly deserted landscape below. Back in the passenger cabin, Buck was busy sleeping, while Jay looked out the window with a smile on his face, and Will read a book. It almost felt like we were on a family outing.

Up front in the cockpit, Charlie was looking out of his window too, but instead of a smile on his face he was wearing a frown, and his forehead was wrinkled into a concerned expression.

"What's the matter?" I asked.

He continued to stare intently out of the window. "Nothing," he said. "I am just keeping an eye out for Will's truck down there on the highway."

"Any luck?" Will asked.

Charlie shook his head. "No," he replied. "Not yet anyway. But it should be easy to spot because of it's color."

"Aha! Now you're glad I got it in mocha," Will said with a grin and returned to his book.

Mile after mile we flew, and the sun rose higher and higher in the sky. There was a bit of cloud, but it was turning out to be a perfect, peaceful September day—perfect except for the fact that we were getting dangerously low on fuel. I'd already transferred the fuel from the wingtip tanks the day before, but I gave it another try to make sure I got every last drop.

"We have to transfer whatever fuel might be left in the wingtip tanks," I said, watching the needles on the fuel gauges dropping.

"Okay," Charlie said, cool as always. "What do I do?"

"Just watch me," I said as I reached up over my head and opened the valve above the cockpit door and activated the fuel pump. I banked the plane into a right turn in the hopes that it would drain every last bit of fuel out, then I closed the valve again. "Now your turn," I said to Charlie, and I made a turn back to the left as we did the same thing on the other side.

The needle on the forward fuel tank bobbed a tiny bit higher but not much. Better than nothing, I guess.

"What's wrong?" Buck asked, waking up instantly when he felt the plane turn and heard us talking about fuel.

"Nothing," I said, leaning over to check the fuel gauges. "We're okay for now."

"Are we going to make it?" Charlie asked, also leaning over to check the gauges along with everyone else back in the passenger cabin.

"It's going to be close," I said, pointing to the gauge for the forward tank. "We're running on only this tank now."

Jay was no longer smiling, and Will had put his book away. Everyone's eyes were glued on the needle of the forward fuel tank as it slowly fell lower and lower as we flew on.

"How much longer?" Charlie asked, a hint of tension creeping into his voice.

"Not much," I replied, trying to sound calm, but I was getting nervous. Of course I'd never flown on so little fuel before, and it was just like driving a car—you didn't know how far below empty you could go unless you actually tried it. Except in a car when you ran out of gas, you just pulled off to the side of the road. In a plane you didn't have that option.

"I can see Dawson up ahead," Charlie said, and everyone back in the passenger cabin breathed a heavy sigh of relief as I started to take the plane down. Their relief didn't last for long, however, because just then the engine popped and gasped for a split second.

"What was that?!?" Buck asked as the engine gasped for fuel.

"That," I replied, "is us finding out just how far below empty we can go."

I was filled with a sudden wave of calm serenity as the engine really wheezed and sputtered, burning off the last of the available fuel. There was nothing I could do to keep the engine running, and I knew it. So I just planned around it.

"We have to find somewhere to land, fast!" Buck cried, clinging to the backs of the passenger seats. Will and Jay were clinging on too as the engine stuttered and coughed even more frequently.

"We already have a place to land," I said, banking left, then right, and taking us down even lower. "We have a perfect runway right in front of us that will take us all the way into downtown Dawson.

Charlie leaned forward and immediately knew what I was planning to do, but it took the others a few more seconds to figure it out.

As the last fumes of fuel fired the engine for the last time, it sputtered abruptly to a stop and quit. With the roar of the engine gone, all that was left was an eerie silence and the whistling of wind over the wings outside of the windows. Normally, this is not a sound you want to hear when you're flying an airplane, but I didn't mind because as far as I was concerned I didn't need the engine anymore. Stretched out in front of us was a big, wide-open stretch of water that had followed us all the way from Lake Tagish, and when the engine finally quit, I glided down and coasted in for a near-perfect landing right down the middle of the mighty Yukon River.

CHAPTER TWENTY-EIGHT

Always Have Friends In Every Port

With the trees on the banks of the river rushing past us, we touched down on the river and gradually slowed as the pontoons settled into the water. I turned to face the others with a big, wide grin on my face.

"Piece of cake," I said calmly, feeling invincible. "You can let go of the seats now."

Everyone was looking quite pale, even Charlie, but I was surging with adrenaline and confidence.

"That was too close," Buck said.

"No time to dwell on it now," I said, taking charge of the situation. "I need Will and Jay out on the pontoons on either side right now with the paddles to make sure we don't run aground going through this curve in the river up ahead."

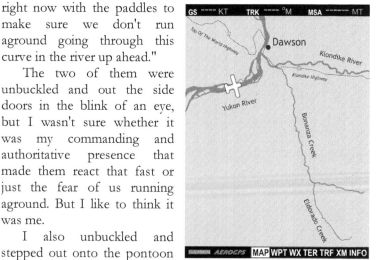

The two of them were unbuckled and out the side doors in the blink of an eye, but I wasn't sure whether it was my commanding and authoritative presence that made them react that fast or just the fear of us running aground. But I like to think it was me.

I also unbuckled and stepped out onto the pontoon to just stand in the sun and enjoy the feeling of being carried along by the powerful river. The current was moving fast, and soon

Dawson City came into view as we were carried into the final bend in the river.

"This must be what it was like for the stampeders," I thought. "Making this last turn and finally reaching their destination after months of backbreaking work and suffering."

"Careful," Charlie called to Will and Jay. "The river makes a wide turn up here. Let's make sure we don't get stuck up on a sandbar or anything. Keep us heading straight up the middle of the channel."

I was glad for Charlie's help. Up in the air I might be the boss, but when it came to paddling things down rivers, I was afraid that I wasn't of much use.

The town disappeared for a moment as the river carried us through the turn, but as the river straightened out again, it came back into view. It wasn't much of a city, though, just a small town located on a flat stretch of land nestled into the base of a short mountain at the right side of the river. In the distance straight ahead, a rock slide had left a patch of white on the hillside where the river suddenly veered left and the town came to an end. Lining the riverside was a wide street filled with interesting storefronts and restaurants, all painted in a rainbow of bright colors. I couldn't figure out why Jay had said I wouldn't like Dawson. It looked like a charming and colorful little town.

At the right, just before we reached the edge of town, another river flowed perpendicularly into the Yukon, joining it and making it stronger. According to my GPS, this was the infamous Klondike River, and farther up beyond it and out of sight would be Bonanza and Eldorado Creeks, where the first claim had been staked and the gold rush was born.

"Where are we headed?" Charlie asked, gesturing toward the town's waterfront, which was rapidly approaching. I scanned the side of the river for somewhere to put in, and I saw a dock with a seaplane and a couple of other boats tied up to it. "That must be the seaplane base," I thought. It was where we were headed before we ran out of gas.

"Right there," I said, pointing. "Just past that big paddlewheel riverboat."

Charlie nodded and took command again. "Steady, boys," he said. "We only get one chance at this. Paddle hard when I say."

With the expertise of a seasoned sea captain, Charlie guided us perfectly into the dock, and soon Will was scrambling ashore with the mooring lines to get us secured.

We had done it. We'd made it to Dawson City. But there was no time to relax just yet, because Charlie was already pulling out his cell phone to make a call.

"I'm going to call in a few favors," he said. "And get us a truck and some aviation fuel for the plane." It was a valuable lesson for me. Always have friends and outstanding favors in every port, because less than half an hour later a friend of Charlie's from the Dawson airport (who was also named Charlie) had refueled my plane and was handing the keys to his truck to Will.

We covered my plane with some tarps that the other Charlie had brought with him. We needed to disguise it, because with my bright red-and-white paint job it stuck out like a sore thumb. If Crazy Jack happened to drive by, he couldn't possibly miss it, and he'd know for sure we were in town.

"Okay," Charlie said after saying goodbye to his friend, and it was just the five of us again. "I know that every single one of us wants more than anything to have a shower and get into some clean clothes, but we have to keep moving. We have no idea where Crazy Jack is or if he's already found that photograph, and for all we know he could be out at the claim already. So we have to get into position to stake the place out as soon as possible."

"It might also take him weeks to show up," Buck observed. "What do we do then?"

"We keep waiting," Charlie replied. "And keeping watch 24/7."

"What if he never shows up?" Buck asked.

"Then we'll be waiting a long time," Charlie snapped. "Now shut up and listen. If we're clever about it, we can get men posted on stakeout duty and still allow one of us at a time to go grab a shower."

"Who gets to go first?" Buck asked.

"We draw straws," Charlie answered, grabbing stems of dry grass from the shore, breaking one of them in half, and holding them in his fist.

"In your face, suckas," Jay taunted as he drew first and drew the short straw. "Short straw wins!"

"Okay, listen," Charlie said, turning first to Jay. "You get us three rooms at the Westmark Inn—a single for our young guest

Kitty and a pair of double rooms for the rest of us. Also stop in somewhere and get us some clean clothes, including for her, and some fresh razors and soap and everything else. Kitty will wait here with the plane while I drive Buck out and put him on top of the hill overlooking our claim, where he can keep an eye on things. Then I'll drive Will up to the top of Midnight Dome overlooking the creeks and the city, so we can see anyone who goes in or out of there. Then Kitty and I will get a shower, and we'll switch up so the rest of you can get a shower too. Is that cool with everyone?"

Everyone nodded. "Whatever you say, Charlie," I said.

"And don't forget," Charlie said. "Keep a low profile and don't get spotted. And everyone keep your phones on. We have no idea when or if Crazy Jack is going to show."

Only Men Would Put On Something Called "Icy Blast"

After dropping Will and Jay off at their stakeout spots, Charlie came back for me, and we drove through the town to a brightly colored series of buildings that was the hotel. Jay was waiting upstairs with a room key for me and a brand-new set of clothes. Somehow he had managed to find the exact same clothes that I was already wearing—a pair of jeans, some black socks, and a purple t-shirt.

"That's imaginative," I said sarcastically. "I'm already wearing this outfit."

"Ha-ha," Jay replied. "You're hi-larious."

"And where's some clean underwear?" I asked. "There's none for me, but I notice there's a couple packages of Fruit-of-the-Loom boxer shorts in your bag."

"I think I liked you better when you were our prisoner," Jay said, grinning. "You were a lot quieter." He handed me one of the plastic packages of boxer shorts. It wasn't ideal, but better than nothing. "But I forgot to buy bras for Buck," he said. "So I think you're out of luck on that score."

I laughed. I didn't care. I couldn't wait to get into my room and finally get clean and get these disgusting clothes off.

"Take this too," Charlie said, reaching into Jay's shopping bag. He pulled out some men's deodorant and a jacket and handed those to me as well.

"Perfect," I thought. "I can burn everything that I am wearing right now."

"Let's get going," Charlie said to Jay. "Head out and switch with Will up at Midnight Dome and tell him to get showered and switch with Buck. Then we'll all be squeaky clean. I'll get a shower of my own right now, and Kitty and I will stay in town near the plane."

Jay nodded and headed out, and I let myself into the room next door. It was unbelievable. An actual hotel room! Of course it was nothing fancy, but it was heavenly all the same. I threw my backpack on the desk and flopped onto the bed. An actual bed!

"You'd better get up or you'll fall asleep," the little voice in my head told me. And for once I listened and got back up again.

Taking my phone out of my bag, I switched it on. One hundred and eighty-seven missed calls and ninety-two text messages.

"Ugh," I thought, putting the phone away again. "I can't even begin to deal with that right now."

I walked to the bathroom and looked at myself in the mirror. I looked terrible. I had never looked so awful in my entire life. And I know girls always say that, but trust me, this time it was definitely true.

I turned on the shower and let it run for a while until it was good and hot. "This better not be one of those low-flow shower heads," I thought as I peeled off the sweaty, dirty clothes that I'd been wearing for days and slept in.

What incredible bliss that shower was. I turned the temperature up as high as I could stand it and then turned it another quarter rotation higher still. As the scalding-hot water blasted my skin, I felt the layer of grime that covered my entire body slowly dissolving. Unwrapping a soap and grabbing a washcloth, I scrubbed everywhere until all the dirt and my first three layers of skin had gone down the drain. Then I changed to a clean washcloth and repeated the entire process.

My hair was also a mess, and ignoring the instructions to simply "wash, rinse, and repeat," I washed, rinsed, and repeated at least three times before I felt fully human again. Only then did I step out of the shower and towel down until I was completely dry.

In my bag I had a hairbrush, and I combed my hair for the first time in days. It hurt like hell, and I must have pulled out half the hair on my head in the process, but eventually it was straight and smooth again.

The final touch was to put on some of the deodorant that Charlie had given me. Irish Spring Icy Blast, it was called. I smelled it and pulled my nose quickly away again in distaste. "Definitely something for men," I thought. What about "Enchanted Cherry Blossom" or "Rain-kissed Waterlilly," like the ones I had back in Juneau? Only men would put on something called "Ice Blast." I put it on, half expecting to get an "ice blast" when I did, but there was nothing.

"What kind of icy blast is that?" I thought. It doesn't even smell icy. I am not even sure what icy smells like."

"Oh right," the little voice in my head said. "Like you feel rain-kissed by a waterlilly when you put yours on."

But blast or no blast it was still better than nothing.

Next I put on the clothes that Jay had bought for me. He was going to make some lucky lady very happy some day, I thought as I pulled on the jeans and t-shirt. He picked my sizes perfectly.

Finishing off the job, I pulled on my new clean socks and used a washcloth to clean my boots a bit before putting them on. After that I was finished, and I stood up to look in the mirror.

"Pretty good," I said, turning from side to side to see how I looked. I even kind of liked how these boxer shorts felt.

That was it. I felt completely reborn. Like a phoenix rising from the ashes, I was ready to face the world again.

And perfect timing too, because at that very second there was a knock on the door. I opened it to find Charlie standing there, looking completely reborn as well—clean-shaven with his wet hair combed back, wearing jeans and a black workman's shirt.

"Did they see him?" I asked. "Is Crazy Jack here?"

Charlie shook his head. "Will's having a shower right now, and then he'll go switch up with Buck," he said. "After that, all we can do is wait."

"Oh," I said.

"You and I have to stay close to the plane," Charlie said. "So I thought you might want to get something to eat."

Dawson City Walking Tour

With our borrowed truck in use shuttling the others back and forth for their showers, Charlie and I had to walk. But Dawson City was not a city at all—hardly even a town—so it was easy to get anywhere that we wanted to go on foot.

"How about a little walking tour?" Charlie asked.

"Sure," I replied, and we set off together to explore the town.

It was a strange place. Big, wide streets but no pavement or asphalt—everything was dirt roads. The buildings were also strange. Modern schools and houses mixed in with creaky, old, sun-bleached wooden buildings that were leaning dangerously and half falling into the ground.

"It's the permafrost," Charlie explained, pointing at the crooked buildings. "All the ground around here just under the top layer of soil is permanently frozen, all year round. So what happens is that when you put up a building on top with heating stoves to keep it warm, it melts the permafrost, and eventually the building sinks into the ground."

We walked away from the river to where the back edge of the town met the woods and the slope leading up the small mountain behind it.

"This is Eighth Avenue," Charlie said grandiosely. "Where you can find the homes of the three writers who made the Yukon famous, and which made them famous in return."

We were standing in front of a cute little property with a white picket fence around it. Charlie pointed to an old-looking log cabin at the back of the yard.

"Jack London's cabin," he said.

I stepped up to the picket fence to get a better look. It was a simple little square log cabin with a peaked roof and tiny windows along the sides. "Amazing," I said. "This is where Jack London lived?"

"Actually," Charlie said. "This isn't where the cabin was originally located. When Jack London lived in the Yukon, it was standing a hundred miles from here on the creek where he had tried in vain to strike it rich mining for gold."

"He was a gold miner?" I asked.

Charlie nodded. "He was," Charlie replied. "And long after he left, some fur trappers in the 1930s came across this cabin one day and found his signature inside on one of the logs. "*Jack London. Miner, author, 1898*," it read, which is interesting because even when he was a gold miner he still thought of himself as an author."

"So they brought the cabin here," I said.

"Actually," Charlie replied. "They dismantled the cabin, log by log, and sent half the logs to his hometown in California and half of them up here. They replaced the missing logs on each version of the cabin and reconstructed two complete replicas in two different places."

"Weird," I said, and we continued our stroll down Eighth Avenue.

We walked a short distance, then stopped in front of a yard with a rustic-looking old cabin with a small porch in front of it, sitting back in the trees just a few steps up a small hill.

"The second of our three famous Yukon writers is Robert Service," Charlie said. "Like Jack London, he was made famous by writing poems and stories about life in the Yukon."

I nodded. "I've heard of him," I said. "I studied him in school. 'The Cremation of Sam McGee.' I know that one."

"*The Northern lights have seen queer sights,*" Charlie recited. "*But the queerest they ever did see, was that night on the marge of Lake Lebarge that I cremated Sam McGee.*"

I laughed, remembering the poem. Across the street was the next stop on our little walking tour, a long white-and-green wooden house that wasn't an old log cabin like the others, but something a bit newer.

"Our last Eighth Avenue writer is Pierre Berton," Charlie said as we approached the house's fence. "Who you may not have heard of but who also helped tell the stories of the gold rush, although much later on than London and Service did."

"I'm not sure if I know him," I said. "Maybe?"

"Doesn't matter," Charlie said. "But anyway, it was here in this house that Berton grew up with his family in the 1920s. They eventually moved away when he was eleven or twelve, but he never forgot the Yukon and later wrote several books about it, which were quite popular. Nowadays, they use the house as a writer's retreat, and writers come up here to live rent free and work on their books."

I looked at Charlie in surprise. "Really?" I asked. "Rent free?"

He nodded. "Really," he said. "Although if you're a writer from some warm country somewhere, and you come up here in the middle of winter, I can imagine that it is a bit of a shock."

"No kidding," I replied, and we continued walking.

Charlie had a place in mind for lunch, so we headed back through town toward the river, crossing the dirt-paved streets, walking on wooden sidewalks, and passing strangely named businesses like Klondike Kate's Restaurant or Diamond-Toothed Gertie's Gambling Hall. Most of the buildings were from the gold-rush era with colorfully painted storefronts. Behind the shiny façades, however, the buildings were dilapidated and looked like they'd been patched together from whatever anyone could find lying around.

"*Don't laugh at me!*" a sign next to one such building declared and made me laugh. "*I am over 100 years old. I'm rusty and crude-looking but during the time of the gold rush builders didn't have a lot of choices for materials. So they used old flattened barrels for siding, and here I am. Signed, The Wall.*"

We walked down Front Street—the street directly next to the river—and past more colorfully painted buildings until we came to a restaurant called Sourdough Joe's.

"Here we are," Charlie said, gesturing for me to step inside. "I hope you like seafood."

"Are you kidding?" I replied. "I'm from the west coast. I love seafood."

Mocha Bear Has Arrived

After stepping inside the restaurant and smelling the warm and delicious smells of food, my stomach immediately growled ferociously. I was incredibly hungry. I hadn't noticed it before, but it would be correct to say that at that moment I was hungrier than I had ever been in my entire life.

We grabbed a table and sat down to read the menus. "What are you having?" Charlie asked.

I skimmed the menu. Dawson's best fish and chips, it claimed. Yukon salmon. Alaskan halibut. Seafood chowder. Homemade burgers and fries. My stomach growled ever more ferociously by the second.

"Fish and chips for me," Charlie said, closing his menu with a snap.

"Chowder for me," I said. "And… ummmmmm… I'd like some salmon, but…"

"One fish and chips, a cup of chowder, and a salmon," Charlie told the waitress.

"It might be too much," I protested.

"Don't worry, we'll share," Charlie replied and ordered coffee for both of us as well.

Charlie took out his phone to check if there was any messages from his brothers. There was nothing yet so he put it down on the table between us.

I decided it was time to ambush Charlie and finally find out about him and his family.

"So," I said. "Tell me about yourself. We've been up and down rivers, hiked up and down mountains, and flown hundreds of miles together, and yet I have no idea what you or your brothers do with yourselves back in the real world."

Charlie smiled and took a sip of his coffee. "We're fisherman," he said. "Crab mostly, although my dream is to get a sablefish license."

"Crab fishing?" I replied. "Like Deadliest Catch?"

Charlie laughed. "Not quite," he said.

"The uncle of my best friend used to be a crab fisherman, " I said. "I'm staying with them back in Juneau."

"Oh yah?" Charlie asked, leaning forward in his chair. "What's his name? I might know him."

"Joe Thomas," I replied.

Charlie's face lit up at the mention of Uncle Joe's name. "Joe Thomas!" he cried. "I know Joe. I mean, I don't know him well, but I bought one of his non-native fishing licenses off him when he gave up fishing to go do that... whatever he does now. Take tourists out to show them how to fish."

"Oh yah?" I said. "What an incredibly small world."

"Either that or Juneau's just not a very big place," Charlie replied.

"What about wives? Girlfriends? Family?" I asked.

"Buck's been married once," Charlie said. "It didn't last. But he has a girlfriend. So does Jay. Or at least they used to have girlfriends. I'm not sure if they still do now after this summer. And our father passed away, as you know, so the only family we've got is our mom, and you already know our brother Eddie."

Charlie paused for a moment, both of us uncomfortable at the mention of Eddie's name.

"Our half-brother Eddie, I mean," Charlie added. "Who we now have to rescue from that idiot Jack."

"Rescue him?" I asked, confused. "Didn't he betray you and steal from you? Why would you rescue him?"

"Because he's family," Charlie said. "And he's young and doesn't know what he's got himself into. Once Jack doesn't need him anymore, who knows what he'll do. But he certainly won't want to split the gold fifty-fifty with him, that's for sure."

"Do you think he's in danger?" I asked.

Charlie nodded. "I think so," he said.

"I hadn't thought of that," I replied. "I just thought you were going to kick his ass when we caught him."

"Oh, I'm definitely going to kick his ass," Charlie said. "No doubt about it. But first I have to save his ass before I can kick it."

"Because he's your brother," I said, always amazed by the brotherhood bond that these guys had.

"Half-brother," Charlie corrected. "He was never in on the family's secrets. No one ever told him about the gold. But in hindsight after everything that's happened, I figure he must have just put it together by himself over the years. Just by listening and paying attention to certain details. He's a smart kid."

"Great for him," I thought cynically and looking forward to Charlie kicking his ass.

Our food arrived, and the waitress set down a steaming cup of creamy seafood chowder and a plate of grilled salmon in front of me, while Charlie got a basket of fried fish and chips. Mine was too much food—I would never finish it—but I was eyeing Charlie's fish and chips as well.

"Good thing we're sharing," I said as I reached over to grab a French fry.

"Yoink," Charlie said.

"What?" I asked.

"Yoink," Charlie repeated, hoping for a flicker of recognition. "That's what you say when you snatch someone's food like that. And as long as you say it, there's nothing anyone can do to stop you. You have carte blanche to steal whatever you want."

"Ohhh, I get it," I replied, nodding. I leaned over to take another fry. "Yoink!" I said.

We both laughed, and I opened my mouth to fan some cold air inside with the palm of my hand. The fries were really hot. But they were so good. Although to be fair, at that point in time, after so many energy bars, just about anything would have tasted amazing.

I tried some of my soup, blowing carefully on the spoon to cool it down. It was magnificent to feel the heat of it filling my entire body, warming me from the inside out. Then I tried the salmon, which was also amazing, tasting meaty and smoky with a hint of cedar.

"You're eating too fast," the little voice in my head told me.

"I don't care," I replied. "I am so hungry."

Of course that little voice was right, but fortunately for my stomach and me, I didn't have a chance to finish eating, because right then Charlie's phone vibrated and chimed. He had an incoming text message.

For several long seconds the two of us just sat there with our mouths half full of food and staring at the phone. Then Charlie finally grabbed it and checked the message.

His face turned instantly serious as he read it, and he nodded to me as he turned around the phone so I could read it. It was from Jay.

mocha bear has arrived

CHAPTER TWENTY-NINE

Another Favor

ocha Bear? I thought to myself. What does that mean? Is that some kind of code or something. Apparently even in deadly serious situations boys simply can't resist the urge to play like they are secret agents or something.

Charlie was already getting to his feet and counting off some dollar bills onto the table. "I need to call Buck," he said. "I'll be outside."

"I'm coming with you, Agent 007," I said with a grin, grabbing my jacket and following him out.

We crossed the street to a park running along the edge of the river, and Charlie put the phone to his ear.

"Buck," he said. "You saw Jay's message. They're on their way to you right now." Charlie paused as he listened to Buck's response. "Okay, keep us posted," Charlie said and ended the call.

Charlie looked at me. "Buck talked to Jay," Charlie said. "He spotted Will's truck headed up the Bonanza Creek Road toward our claim. Buck will let all of us know what happens when they get there."

"Okay," I said, sitting down on a park bench overlooking the river while Charlie paced nervously.

"I didn't expect them so soon," Charlie said, stopping to look at his watch nervously. "I thought we would have to wait up here for days and would have time to plan a proper ambush."

"Where do you think they came from?" I asked.

Charlie shrugged. "There's not much between here and Whitehorse," he said and returned to pacing back and forth.

"Charlie!" I said, raising my voice slightly. Charlie stopped and looked at me. "Just sit down," I said. "We just have to wait it out and see what happens."

Charlie blushed and smiled half-heartedly. "You're right," he said and slid onto the bench next to me.

For a while we sat there in silence, watching the river flow past us as it had done for an eternity and would continue to do for an eternity more. This mighty river that had brought those thousands of foolish souls right here to this very spot, where they finally realized that their dreams were nothing but empty promises, and they turned around again and went home. I could almost feel their heartbreak even more than a hundred years later.

"What charity would you give the gold to?" Charlie asked, out of the blue.

I didn't realize what he meant at first. "What do you mean?" I said.

"On the plane you suggested that we give the money to charity," he said. "What charity would you give it to if it was you?"

I thought about that for a moment.

"Different ones, I suppose," I said. "But if it was mine, I would definitely give some money for humpback whale research."

Charlie nodded.

"That's what I was working on before all of this," I said.

Charlie nodded again. "I know," he said. "I read about you in the newspaper, remember?"

"Oh, right," I replied.

"I think what you were doing is really amazing," Charlie said. "And seeing you behind the wheel of your plane and how you handle yourself is something really impressive."

Now it was my turn to blush.

"Thank you," I replied.

Charlie's phone vibrated and chimed again. Another text message. He slid next to me so I could read over his shoulder. It was from Buck.

mocha bear has landed. ps how was your shower? i still didn't get a shower

"Now we'll see what they do," Charlie said.

"And then what?" I asked.

"Then we see which way they leave town, and we go after them," Charlie answered. "There aren't many roads out of here, and once we see what direction they're headed, Will is going to follow in the truck, and we're going to track them from the air."

"Sounds good," I said.

Charlie chewed on his thumbnail for a moment. "It's not the best plan," he admitted. "But it will do."

The phone vibrated and chimed again. It had only been a couple of minutes, but there was another text message from Buck.

mocha bear is leaving the nest. ps still no shower

"What the hell?" Charlie said, dialing his brother's number and putting the phone to his ear.

"Hey, Charlie," I heard Buck say at the other end of the line.

"Why is he leaving so quickly?" Charlie asked. "Is something wrong?"

"I don't think so," Buck said, his voice crackling loudly through the phone. "I think he just could tell that there was nothing there. There are holes cut in the logs behind the stove, remember?"

Charlie nodded. "And he's headed back to town?" he asked.

"Definitely," Buck replied. "There's nowhere else to go."

"Okay," Charlie said. "Once we pick him up again at this end, you start hiking back into town, okay?"

"Will do," Buck said. "I'll get that shower, finally."

Charlie ended the call and immediately called Jay.

"Jay?" he said. "Do you still have a clear view from up there?"

"I sure do," Jay replied, his voice coming through the phone even louder than Buck's. "In fact, from up here I can even see a couple of goofy-looking people standing down by the river."

Somehow he could see us. Charlie and I both spun around. I wasn't sure where to look, but Charlie pointed up the small mountain, where a lone figure was standing and waving his arms. We waved back.

"Okay, keep us posted, Jay," Charlie said and hung up.

Immediately he called Will.

"Will, where are you?" Charlie asked.

"I was about to head out to trade places with Buck," he said. "But I guess that's off now."

"Stick near the hotel in the truck until we know which way he's going," Charlie said. "And then be ready to move fast."

"Got it," Will said.

Charlie hung up and turned to look at me.

"Now we wait again," he said, leaning back on the bench and trying to stay relaxed. We watched for a little while longer, and then he spoke again. "I think you're right about the charity idea," he said, a faraway look in his eye as he watched the river flow by. "Humpback whale research for sure. And cancer research too."

I turned to look at him, not sure what I should say. His eyes were looking somewhere else very far away, and I sensed something was going through his head, but I didn't want to intrude.

Just then his phone rang, and the moment was broken.

"Tell me," he said, answering the call.

"I can see him," I heard Jay say.

"Where's he headed?" Charlie asked.

"Just wait a second," Jay said as he watched. The seconds ticked by painfully, and Charlie was biting his thumbnail again. "He's heading for town," Jay finally said.

"Okay, I'll call you back," Charlie said and quickly hung up. Within seconds he had Will on the phone again.

"Stand by, Will," Charlie said. "He's headed for town."

Charlie hung up again and called Jay back. It was almost comical, all these phone calls.

"Charlie?" Jay said as soon as the call connected. "You guys better get out of sight. He's heading your way."

Charlie grabbed me and pulled me to the edge of the dike running along the side of the river. We crouched down in some tall grasses and watched the street nervously.

"Where is he, Jay?" Charlie asked, his eyes scanning the road leading into town.

"You should just about see him... right... about... now," Jay replied as Will's strangely colored mocha SUV came into view.

Charlie pulled us both down farther into the grass, and we watched silently as Crazy Jack and Edward drove right past us. I was terrified that they would spot us, but they drove right on by and continued down Front Street, driving out of sight off to our left.

"He has to be heading for the ferry, Charlie," Jay said. "That's the only place he can be going."

"Okay, Jay, you keep your eyes on him, and I'm gonna call Will," Charlie said. He was about hang up the phone when Jay spoke again.

"Uh-oh, Charlie, we have a problem," Jay said.

"What?" Charlie cried. "What is it?"

"He's backing up now and getting out of the truck."

"What is it, Jay?" Charlie shouted into the phone. "What is he doing?"

Jay's voice was cold and distant at the other end of the line. "He spotted Kitty's plane."

"Dammit!" Charlie said, standing up and stepping out onto the grass to see down the street, where Will's SUV was stopped. "What's he doing now?"

I raced after Charlie onto the grass. "I'm not sure," Jay said, and there was a long pause. Charlie walked quickly down the riverbank, trying to see what Jay was seeing. "Uh-oh, Charlie," Jay said. "He's got a knife, and he's cutting some wires or hoses or something around the engine at the front."

"What the hell is he doing to my plane?" I said angrily.

Charlie looked at me. I shook my head. Whatever he was doing, it was bad, and the plane was going to be out of commission for a while.

"He's driving off again now, Charlie," Jay said. "And heading for the ferry."

"How long until the ferry goes across?" Charlie asked. "What if I run down there after him?"

"They're loading now," Jay said. "He'll make it across on this trip. You'll never make it."

"Keep an eye on him for as long as you can after he goes across," Charlie ordered. "Then get back down into town as fast as you can."

Charlie hung up the phone and immediately dialed Will.

"Get down to the park in front of Sourdough Joe's right away," Charlie said, then hung up again. Flipping through the address book on his phone, he looked up a number and hit dial. "Time to call in another favor," he said, looking at me.

At the other end of the line I could hear the phone ringing. Once. Twice. Three times. Finally, someone answered.

Charlie's voice was calm again as he spoke into the phone. "Hey, Charlie," he said. "It's me again. I need to ask another favor. A big one."

Raiders Of The Lost Gold

No more than twenty minutes later, Charlie and I were climbing into the cockpit of another De Havilland Beaver out at Dawson City airport. The speed and efficiency of Charlie and his brothers, especially in crisis situations, would never cease to amaze me. Will had roared through town in the borrowed truck to pick Charlie and me up at the river, and together we continued down the road out to the airport. Charlie's friend, the other Charlie, was waiting for us, and walked us over to a shiny yellow-and-green De Havilland Beaver that was parked at the end of a line of planes.

"Do not get even so much as a scratch on this plane," the other Charlie warned us. "It belongs to some Hollywood actor who's up here for a week on a fishing trip. He won't be back for a couple of days yet, but I am sure he'll notice if his plane is all banged up."

"An actor?" I replied. "Who is it? Someone famous?"

"Harrison Ford," the other Charlie said, pulling open the cockpit door for me.

"Harrison Ford?" I cried, climbing inside. "Are you serious? Like Indiana Jones?"

"Yeah, that one," the other Charlie answered.

"I owe you one, buddy," Charlie said as he climbed in next to me, and we slammed the doors shut.

"You do," the other Charlie agreed as he backed away so we could start the plane. "Big time."

I quickly checked over the controls and instruments on the plane to orient myself as I prepared to get the engine started.

"Can you fly it?" Charlie asked as he pulled his cell phone out again.

"Of course," I replied. "It's the same as mine. More or less."

Charlie gave me a funny look as he dialed the phone.

"Will," Charlie said. "Where are you now?"

Charlie paused and waited for the answer.

"Okay, good," Charlie continued. "Now pick up Jay and get over to the ferry and across the river. Then head out on Highway 9 as fast as you can to catch up with Jack. If you do catch up, just back off and don't let him see you. He's got nowhere to go up there, and we'll be airborne in a few minutes."

With a reassuring growl, the engine spun to life, and I let it warm up a bit before we took off.

"Have you flown a plane with wheels before?" Charlie asked. Harrison Ford's De Havilland Beaver was quite similar to my own except for one big difference. Instead of floating pontoons like mine had, his had wheels for taking off and landing on normal runways.

"A few times," I told Charlie, patting him roughly on the arm for reassurance. "But don't worry. Wheels are easier."

Charlie blushed. "I was just wondering if you knew how to, that's all," he replied.

We taxied down to the end of the runway and checked everything one last time before pushing the throttles forward and sending the plane galloping down the runway.

"Daa da duh daa, daa da daa," I sang at the top of my lungs as we barreled down the runway. Charlie looked at me like I was insane. "Come on!" I yelled over the roar of the engine. "It's Indiana Jones's plane! We have to sing the song!"

But Charlie wasn't in the mood for singing, so I had to sing it all myself.

"Daa da duh daa, daa da da daa daa," I continued singing as we lifted off the runway and into the air. I made a slight turn and headed in the direction of Dawson City.

I looked out of the window off to my left and noticed a series of huge wormlike piles of rock and gravel weaving their way almost randomly back and forth through the valleys. We had driven right through them as we raced to the airport, but from ground level they had only looked like normal gravel piles lining the road. From the air, however, they were completely bizarre, weaving and curving like long, giant maggots all over the valley floor.

"What are those?" I asked, pointing out of the window.

Charlie craned his neck to see. "Dredge tailings," he replied. "They're normal up here. After the original gold miners sold or abandoned their claims, the big mining companies came in to scoop up whatever gold they had left behind. With huge dredging machines they extracted a lot more gold from the creeks than the miners ever could have working by hand. The dredges were as big as warehouse buildings, and they just slowly ate their way up and down the creeks, moving only a few feet a day, and digging up everything in their path, extracting the gold from it, then spitting out the leftover rock and gravel behind them." Charlie leaned over and pointed out the window. "And those long piles of rock and gravel are the trails they left behind them as they went."

"They're creepy and ugly," I said, and Charlie shrugged again.

"Head out this way," Charlie said, pointing with his finger as we passed over Dawson City.

"What's the plan?" I asked as I adjusted my course a bit to the left and followed his lead.

"We just follow this highway down here on the opposite side of the river," Charlie said, pointing down at a narrow stretch of road that I would hardly call a "highway."

"Jay kept an eye on Crazy Jack and watched them cross the river on the ferry," Charlie said. "There's only one road over there, and that is it. That means he's headed for Alaska. So all we have to do is follow the road until we find him."

"What if he turns off onto a side road or something?" I asked.

Charlie shook his head. "There aren't any side roads," he said. "This road is called the Top of the World Highway, and for good reason. It just winds its way across the tops of this mountain range all the way to the US border, then down into Chicken, Alaska. And we're going to stop them before they get anywhere near the border."

"And how are we going to do that?" I asked, nervously looking down at the rifle that Charlie had propped up between his legs. "Stop them, I mean."

"With this, of course," Charlie replied, lifting up the rifle for a moment while keeping his eyes focused intently ahead.

I'm Going Outside

"Don't worry, darlin'," Charlie said as we passed over the Yukon River, and Dawson City slowly disappeared behind us. "I'm not going to kill them or anything like that."

I was relieved to hear it, because I had wondered if that was exactly what he did mean to do.

"I'm just going to shoot out the tires on the truck," Charlie continued. "And strand them up there on the road where there's no one else around. Will and Jay are following so they won't be far behind. They will take care of things on the ground, while we keep an eye on everything from the air."

"But they have guns," I said, referring to Jack and Edward. "How are Will and Jay supposed to 'take care of things'?"

"Will and Jay have guns too," Charlie replied, glancing at me. "It wasn't just a truck and a plane that we borrowed from my buddy Charlie. They've got a couple of hunting rifles as well. But I pray to God it doesn't come to that."

"What else could it possibly come to?" I asked anxiously. I was imagining a shootout like from an old Western movie.

Charlie looked at me and smiled reassuringly. "Don't worry," he said again. "I don't think it's going to come to that. None of us are killers, especially Eddie. It's only Jack who I am worried about. He's not called Crazy Jack for nothing."

"But what do you expect him to do if you shoot out his tires and back him into a corner?" I asked. "He's gonna fight back, isn't he?"

Charlie shook his head. "I don't think he will," he said. "It's one thing to ambush us like he did back on the beach, where they definitely had the element of surprise, but it's a whole different thing when he no longer has the upper hand and there's three rifle barrels pointed back at him."

I was still worried, but Charlie's confidence was very comforting.

Down below us the Top of the World Highway weaved back and forth across the mountain tops, but there was still nothing in sight. Not even any other cars. "That's not surprising," I thought, since the road appeared to alternate between paved asphalt with big potholes and dirt road with even bigger potholes. But despite the condition of the road, it was beautiful up there. The mountains seemed to stretch away until the end of the world—mountain ridges and peaks repeating endlessly into the distance without a single sign of human habitation, except for the single long, twisting road below us.

The land itself was also desolate with hardly any trees anywhere. Just dull brown grasses covering the peaks as far as the eye could see, sparsely dotted here and there with evergreen trees but not enough of them to constitute a forest. I now understood why Charlie was so confident that we would find them up here. There was nowhere to hide.

"There might be nowhere for them to hide, but there's nowhere for us to hide either," I thought.

"They're going to see us coming from miles away," I said.

Charlie nodded. "They will," he agreed. "But I don't think it matters much. Will and Jay will stay far enough back from them and stay out of sight."

"And what about us?" I asked.

"What about us?" Charlie repeated. "I think they did us a favor by forcing us to switch planes. They'll probably never think we managed to get another one so quickly."

"Good point," I thought. They'd be looking for a big red-and-white plane coming after them, not a bright yellow-and-green one belonging to Harrison Ford. (I admit it, at the thought of his name, the Indiana Jones musical theme played in my head again. It was the perfect music for such an adventure, after all.)

Mile after mile the road passed below us. It seemed to go on forever. And Charlie was right—there were no side roads at all. There was nowhere for them to go except back to Dawson or ahead to Chicken.

"Why do they call it 'Chicken'?" I asked as we continued skimming the mountaintops at the top of the world.

Charlie chuckled. "It was originally supposed to be called Ptarmigan," he said. "Which is a bird they have up here that sort of looks like a chicken. But no one could agree on how to spell that, so they just called the town Chicken instead."

I laughed. "You're kidding me," I said.

"True story," Charlie replied. "It's a funny little town. No electricity. No phones. No internet. No water. No plumbing."

"And how many people?" I asked.

Charlie rubbed his chin to think. "Ummmmmm, maybe twenty?" he guessed.

I laughed again. The farther north we went, the crazier it got. But I stopped myself in mid-laugh when I spotted a vehicle on the road ahead of us.

"There's Will and Jay," I said, turning serious in an instant when I saw the beat-up, old truck.

Charlie nodded. "I see them," he said.

Will and Jay were bouncing along the rough highway in the truck that we'd borrowed, winding back and forth with a roar as it crossed the mountains.

"And there's Mocha Bear," I said as Will's strangely colored SUV came into view just a few kilometers farther up the road.

"Got it," Charlie confirmed. "And Will is staying a good distance behind them, so they probably don't even see him."

"What do we do now?" I asked, suddenly feeling very nervous again. I could feel a cold heaviness building in the pit of my stomach now that we had finally caught up with them. There was no more fooling around now. No more Indiana Jones theme songs. This was serious.

"Just bring us down nice and slow," Charlie said, taking off his headset to grab his rifle and unbuckle his seatbelt. "As slow as you can go."

"What are you doing?!?" I asked as he reached for the door handle. "Are you insane?"

"You didn't expect me to shoot from in here, did you?" Charlie replied. "I'm going outside."

CHAPTER THIRTY

Too Bad You Studied Journalism Instead Of Physics

"Don't worry, darlin'," Charlie said for the tenth time that day so far, his hand on the handle of the cockpit door.

"No, no, no, no, no," I said, grabbing him by the arm. "There's a window vent. Shoot through that."

"It's too small," Charlie protested.

"Just deal with it," I said. "Because there's no way I am letting you go outside."

Charlie looked at me in frustration. "It will be fine," he said. "I promise."

I shook my head emphatically. "No way, Charlie," I said. "How do you even expect to shoot from out there anyway? It's not like my float plane where there's a pontoon to stand on. There's only a tiny step to stand on, and you'll be too busy hanging on for dear life to aim your rifle. You only have two arms. Plus it will be windy, and you will get blown around all over the place. How are you going to shoot like that?"

Charlie looked out of his window down to the landing gear and the tiny stairs welded onto them. "You might be right," he said after a few seconds. "It might not be as easy as I thought."

"Thank God he isn't a complete idiot," I thought.

"We'll compromise," he said. "I'll open the door and shoot through the gap between it and the airframe."

I thought about this for a second. "Okay, but you stay buckled in," I agreed. "And don't shoot the propeller!"

Charlie nodded in agreement and buckled himself back into his seat. He pulled on the door handle to open it, and instantly the cockpit was flooded with a hurricane of noise and wind. Forcing the door open against the headwind, he jammed his foot into the gap to hold it open as he contorted his body and twisted himself into position so he could aim the rifle out of the window.

"Okay," Charlie said, his arms and legs bent at funny angles and looking a bit like someone playing the game Twister. "I'm ready. Take us in."

I nodded and took the plane down, slowly bringing us up behind Will's mocha SUV.

"If they didn't notice us before, they sure will now," I thought.

"Bring us up within a couple hundred feet," Charlie yelled over the sound of the wind. "And a hundred feet back on their left. Then try to hold that position."

Keeping level and even with the truck as it wound along the twisting path of the mountain road was incredibly difficult and took a bit of practice. The road had hardly any straightaway sections, so I was constantly banking left and right to follow the road and stay with them.

"That's the best I can do," I yelled to Charlie. "You'd better take your best shot the next chance you get."

Charlie nodded and turned to take aim, closing one eye and sighting down the scope of his rifle. I tried to hold the plane as steady as I could while he was aiming, but seconds passed, and I wondered if he would ever pull the trigger. Soon I would have to make another turn to stay with the road.

Just then he fired, and the deafening report of the rifle hammered the cockpit. The sound echoed through the cabin, making me nearly jump out of my seat and jerking the steering column as I went. The plane wobbled as I regained control and banked into a turn to keep following the road.

"Dammit!" Charlie swore as he cycled the bolt on the rifle and reloaded to take another shot. As I continued into the turn, I saw that Charlie had missed the tires and shot out the back window of the SUV instead.

"Will's not going to like that," I thought as I leveled out so Charlie could take another shot.

With the plane holding as steady and evenly as possible with the moving vehicle below us, Charlie took aim, and once again the cockpit reverberated thickly as he fired a second shot.

"You've got to be kidding!" Charlie bellowed as he ejected the spent cartridge and reloaded for yet another try, and I banked around yet another curve.

In fairness to Charlie, who I am sure was an excellent shot, the conditions were extremely difficult for him to hit anything. It was not only the winding road and having to shoot from a plane; he also was forced to bend himself into an awkward position in the seat next to me to shoot out the door.

Leveling out after the turn, I looked down to see Crazy Jack hanging out of the passenger side of the truck with what looked like a shotgun in his hands. At that same moment there was a loud plink of metal to my left, and I felt the plane shudder slightly.

My heart jumped into my throat. "What the hell was that?" I yelled, even as I figured out exactly what it was.

Charlie looked at me. "He's shooting at us," he yelled back.

"No kidding," I thought, and I immediately banked the plane sharply off to the left and pulled up to take evasive action. There was another plink of metal and a shudder as the plane was hit a second time.

I continued left, gaining altitude until I was satisfied that there was a safe distance between us and the truck. I checked the instruments and as much of the body and wings of the aircraft as possible to see if there was any serious damage. There were some small holes punched in the underside of the left wing, but as far as I could see, everything otherwise seemed okay.

"What now?" I thought, my mind racing. "How are we going to do this?"

"You are crazy," the little voice in my head was telling me. "What are you doing here? Get out of here as fast as you can before you get hurt or killed! You're not some Indiana Jones character from a movie! This isn't a movie, and you're just a normal girl!"

"Not today, I'm not," I said, clenching my teeth in anger. How dare they steal that gold from Charlie's family and shoot at me!

I turned to Charlie and swatted him on the arm to get his attention. "Here's what we're gonna do," I shouted. "I am going to come up from underneath them so they can't take a shot at us. Then I'll pop up right behind them, and you blow those stupid tires out."

Charlie nodded, his face grim and serious. "Got it," he said.

"And don't miss," I added as I put the plane into a dive.

Charlie braced himself against the chair again as I swooped down out of the sky and circled back to come up behind them once more. This time I stuck close to the mountain slopes underneath the level of the road, flying so low off the ground that I am pretty sure the wheels were hitting the tall grasses at some points. Occasionally, I had to pull up to duck over some tree tops, and when I did, I caught a glimpse of the mocha SUV on the road up ahead of us. They were driving fast, fishtailing back and forth like maniacs all over the dirt road.

"Drive as fast as you want," I thought, addressing Edward in my imagination. "The faster the better. It keeps the relative speed between us and you much lower, and it'll be easier to hit you. Too bad you studied journalism instead of physics, or else you'd know this."

"Here we go, Charlie," I shouted as the truck reached a short straightaway and I pulled back on the controls. "Daa da duh daa, daa da daa!"

"Daa da duh daa, daa da da daa daa," Charlie sang along with me as I pulled up abruptly and popped low over the side of the road, right behind them in the truck's left blind spot. I grinned broadly in extreme satisfaction, because I had positioned us perfectly. Not only wouldn't Jack be able to shoot at us from this angle, but they might not even notice we were there until it was too late.

"Do it, Charlie!" I screamed at the top of my lungs. "Pull the trigger!"

High Noon At The Top Of The World

Charlie's shoulder kicked backward as he pulled the trigger, and the cabin exploded again with a thunderclap of noise and vibration. The back left tire of the SUV burst violently, and the slack rubber fluttered around the wheel rim as they kept driving. The truck fishtailed back and forth out of control across the road, while Charlie pulled back the rifle bolt and quickly reloaded. He fired again, and this time the front left tire burst apart. The truck pulled hard to the left, and the brake lights lit up as the truck skidded to a halt.

I didn't want them getting out of the truck and shooting at me, so I put the plane into another steep turn and peeled off to the left, gaining altitude as I went and putting some distance between us and them.

Charlie pulled his rifle back inside and closed the door, leaning back over his shoulder to watch what the guys in the truck would do next.

"Look at that," Charlie said and whistled.

I looked back and saw Jack jump from the truck to the side of the road. He ran cross-country like a crazy man. In his hands he held his shotgun, and slung over his shoulder was a dirty leather bag that bounced against him as he ran.

"What in the world is he doing?" I asked. I reversed my turn so we could circle around for a better look while still keeping our distance.

"I have no idea," Charlie replied as we watched Crazy Jack scampering across the bare landscape and down the side of the mountain.

"Is he running away?" I asked, turning to Charlie. "Is that possible."

"I don't know," Charlie replied slowly. "I really have no idea."

We continued watching as Crazy Jack ran farther and farther downhill and away from the disabled SUV, where Edward was still sitting in the driver's seat. In the distance we could see Will and Jay quickly approaching in the borrowed pick-up truck. They would catch up with Edward in no time.

"I'd better call Will and Jay," Charlie said, reaching into his jacket pocket for his phone. "To tell them what's going on and to warn them that Edward is still inside the SUV."

I thought about this for a second. Something didn't seem quite right. Didn't Charlie say there were no phones in Chicken, Alaska? And if there were no phones there, would his cell phone work here?

"Is there cell phone coverage all the way up here?" I asked.

Charlie looked at me with an anxious expression on his face, and he quickly pulled his phone out of his pocket. I watched as he checked for a signal, but the expression on his face said it all. There was nothing.

"Dammit," he cursed. "I didn't even think of that!"

"Don't worry, darlin'," I said. "I have an idea."

Turning the control wheel, I quickly brought the plane around and headed for Will and Jay, who were still coming up the road fast. Making a close pass over them to get their attention, I made another quick turn and circled around behind them, coming in low and fast.

"What are you doing?" Charlie asked, sounding a bit nervous.

I brought the plane lower and lower, coming in directly over the heads of Will and Jay. As we approached, I could see Jay leaning out of the passenger-side window, looking back at us with a combination of confusion and fear.

"We have wheels now," I told Charlie as we thundered over Will and Jay's truck, barely missing it. "We might as well use them."

And with that, I brought us in for a landing on the road right in front of the borrowed truck. There wasn't much room up here for a landing, but I had enough of a straightaway to make it. I throttled back and brought the wheels down with a bump that shook the entire plane.

"Not my best landing ever," I thought as the tail wheel touched down and I slowly brought the plane to a stop. "But it will do."

Locking the wheels and shutting the engine down, I quickly pulled off my restraining harness and pulled open the door. Charlie was already outside, flagging his brothers down, who were just pulling up in the truck. I jumped out of the plane, and Charlie and I vaulted into the bed of the truck.

"Go, go, go!" Charlie shouted, slapping the roof of the truck with his palm. Will hit the gas, and within seconds we were careening down the highway toward the mocha SUV.

Charlie was standing and hanging on for dear life while he surveyed the scene in front of us. Crazy Jack was nowhere to be seen. The last time we had seen him, he was running like a lunatic down the mountain, already hundreds of meters away.

Charlie let us get a little bit closer to the SUV, then pounded on the roof for Will to stop. "Eddie's still inside," Charlie shouted as he jumped off the truck and raised his rifle. Will and Jay jumped out right after him and spread out across the road as they approached the SUV.

"Stay near the truck," Will told me, gesturing for me to keep my head down.

The three of them walked slowly up the road like they were in a cowboy movie, heading for a showdown at high noon.

"Don't be an idiot, Eddie," Charlie yelled to the SUV. He raised his arm in a signal for the others to stop, and there they stood, rifles to their shoulders and waiting.

I pulled myself up a little bit to watch over the roof of the truck. I looked around, up, down, and off to the side of the road. I was a bit nervous that Crazy Jack might show up again, but he was nowhere in sight.

"C'mon, Eddie, this is ridiculous," Charlie yelled. "You messed up, but don't make it worse by doing something stupid."

Still they waited, standing like surreal statues in the middle of the road. Edward didn't respond, and the only sound was the cold wind blowing over the barren landscape.

Charlie took another couple of steps toward the SUV.

"Last chance, Eddie," he said, using a tone I hadn't heard from him since that first night when he grabbed me out in the woods and dragged me over to their little campfire. It was a cold tone that sent shivers down my spine. It was a tone that meant he wasn't screwing around.

That finally got through to Edward, and the driver-side door opened a crack.

"Good job, Eddie," Charlie said, his tone warm and safe again. "Now empty the pistol and throw it to the ground."

Edward did as he was told and slowly emerged from the SUV with his hands over his head.

Will ran over and quickly checked him for any other weapons tucked in his pants or boots.

"He's clean," Will said and grabbed the revolver off the ground.

Charlie walked over and grabbed Edward's hands, jerking them down to his side again. "Put those down," he said. "This isn't an arrest."

"I'm really sorry, Charlie," Edward started to say but stopped cold in mid-sentence when he saw the furious expression on Charlie's face.

Charlie raised his palm. "Don't," he said simply, obviously struggling to contain his anger. "Don't you dare say another word."

Charlie shoved Edward over toward Jay and pulled open the rear hatch of the SUV. Inside, everything was packed and organized almost as we'd left it the other night, before Jack and Edward showed up. But the lid on the beer cooler was open, and the contents were in disarray.

"Jack took some when he made a run for it," Edward stammered, looking frightened and nervous. "And he took the photo too."

Charlie smiled and chuckled for a second. "How much?" he asked Edward.

"What?" Edward asked.

"How much did he take?" Charlie repeated.

"I don't know," Edward responded hesitantly. "Two packages?"

Charlie winced. "Twenty kilos," he said to Will, who had just come around the truck after checking the front seats.

"So what?" Will said. "Let him have it."

Charlie walked over to the edge of the road and looked down the slope of the mountain, probably hoping to catch a glimpse of Crazy Alaska Jack running for his life, but he was nowhere to be seen.

"What do you think, sweetheart?" Charlie asked, turning his head toward me.

"About what?" I stuttered. "About the gold?"

"Yeah," Charlie said, turning to walk toward me. "About the gold."

I wrinkled my nose and forehead and gave this some thought. I thought about the men and women getting off the boats in Skagway or Dyea and crawling their way up and down the mountain passes. I thought about the tent cities on Lake Lindeman and the treacherous whitewater rapids on the Yukon River. I thought about the thousands of stampeders landing in their boats at Dawson City and discovering the truth. That there weren't gold nuggets lying around on the ground waiting to be picked up. That all the rich claims had been staked long before they even took a single step toward the Yukon. And how thousands of them just turned around and went back home.

I wanted to go back home too, I decided. And I was suddenly overcome with an incredible feeling of sadness and pity for all those people who had risked so much for this stupid yellow metal.

"Just forget about it," I finally said. "Let him keep it."

"Don't you even want to know how much money twenty kilos of gold is worth?" Charlie asked.

I shook my head. "I know exactly how much it's worth," I replied, jumping down off the back of the truck. "It's worthless."

CHAPTER THIRTY-ONE

A Sacred Spot On Bonanza Creek

harlie drove the borrowed truck back to get new tires for Will's SUV, and he took Edward with him. Will and Jay stayed behind to guard the gold, so I was left to fly back to Dawson City on my own. But I didn't mind because it gave me some time to myself for the first time in days.

After landing back at the Dawson City airport, I pulled my borrowed plane back to where we'd found it parked earlier that morning. Buck was waiting there for me with Charlie's friend, the other Charlie.

"Nice shirt," I said to Buck as I shut down the engine and climbed out of the cockpit.

He was wearing a pink "I ♥ Dawson City" t-shirt.

"Ha-ha, so funny," Buck replied. "I finally get to take a shower, but the only shirt you guys left me was this ridiculous thing."

Buck had already spoken with his brothers about the stand-off at the Top of the World and while I was on my way back he'd arranged with the other Charlie to get my plane repaired so it would be ready to fly the next morning. It was no big deal, the other Charlie said, taking a couple of fifty-dollar bills from Buck to cover the cost. Crazy Jack had only cut a few of the spark plug leads.

The shotgun damage to Harrison Ford's plane, however, was a different story. "Keep going," the other Charlie said as Buck counted off a stack of fifties to cover the damage. "Keep going. A few more."

We said goodbye to the other Charlie, and because we had some time to kill before the others could make it back into town, Buck borrowed a car from a friend of his to take me on a tour of Bonanza Creek to see their family's claim.

Driving back toward town and up Bonanza Creek Road, we drove through the same dredge tailings that I'd seen earlier in the day from the air. At ground level they simply looked like a random mess of rock and gravel, but now that I knew better I looked closer and could see the almost rhythmic pattern they made as they snaked across the landscape.

The forest was making a comeback, however, closing in around the tailing piles, even growing straight out of them in places. Even the creek itself had found a way to make its peace with all the human interference, winding around the obstacles down into the Yukon River, as it had done for thousands of years before the gold miners came.

The road was full of bumps and gravel, and every time another car passed us it threw up a shower of rocks. I had already noticed that chipped windshields on the cars in the Yukon were just a fact of life.

On the way out to their property we passed an absolutely huge machine that looked like some strange awkward mechanical bird with wires and pulleys and all sorts of appendages coming out of it. It was a gold dredge, Buck explained. One of many that had worked their way up and down the creeks in this area for more than fifty years, ending only in the 1960s.

I stared at the ugly monstrous thing as we drove past. It looked more like a building than a machine that was capable of moving and clawing its way through the landscape to leave behind the traces that we'd seen. I shuddered to think what kind of noise such a machine would make. It hurt my teeth just to think of the iron claws and buckets chewing their way through the rock and earth twenty four hours a day.

A bit further along the road we stopped the car at the so-called Discovery Claim, which had a plaque marking the spot where George Carmack had staked the first claim on Bonanza Creek and had started the Yukon Gold Rush. Buck and I wandered down the path to the edge of the creek and looked around. The trees and forest had returned there, so it wasn't difficult to imagine it as it was on the day when gold was first discovered. I looked down into the water and simply couldn't imagine that fortunes in gold could be found in such a place, mixed in with the rocks and dirt of a small creek as peaceful as this.

We walked a bit farther and found an information sign showing a picture of how it had looked there at the height of the gold rush. It was incredible. The entire creek area and the sides of the valley were completely stripped clear of trees, and men had built log cabins and other wooden constructions and basic machines to assist them in their mining operations. Looking at the picture and up at the forest around me, it was difficult to believe that the forest had *ever* returned after such carnage.

Looking closer at the valley, however, I realized that the days of tearing up the landscape were not yet over. Lining the entire length of the valley were signs of ongoing mining operations—although now run by families and individuals as the claims on this valley once had been, instead of by huge corporations and dredges.

We returned to the car and continued our drive up the road we passed a spot along the creek that Buck called 'Number Six Above'. It was one of the earliest claims made after the initial discovery of gold, he said, six claims 'above' the original claim made by George Carmack. The claim had been worked by a variety of different people and companies over the years but was now owned by the local tourist association who allowed anyone who was interested to come and pan for gold along its banks and keep whatever gold they found. Which wasn't much, Buck added. Maybe a few flakes.

A bit further along Buck stopped the car and pointed out a fork in the stream where the flowing waters from two separate creeks joined together. Up to the left continued Bonanza Creek and up to the right was Eldorado Creek, the creek that had been even richer in gold than Bonanza. It was here at this fork in the river, Buck told me, that a young woman named Belinda Mulrooney had built a two-storey roadhouse and restaurant. She had come to the Yukon to make her fortune and on arriving in Dawson she had symbolically thrown her last quarter into the river so she could start fresh. Working hard and applying her considerable business know-how in what was truly a man's world she built up a small empire in Dawson City consisting of restaurants and hotels, including the one all the way up here at the confluence of the two creeks.

The men had laughed at her, Buck said, when she decided to build a roadhouse all the way out here. But she got the last laugh when she rightly assumed the miners would prefer having a place to eat and drink and sleep out here closer to their mines, rather than all the way down in the town itself.

Buck put the car in gear again and drove on a bit further Finally, we arrived at the Lewis family claim. Getting out of the car, I felt like we had reached a sacred spot that I had only heard of in legends. There was the mobile home off to the right, with signs of a digging underneath. That was where the gold had remained hidden for decades before Crazy Jack had found it. To the left were two ramshackle, old cabins, reminders of another era out here on the creeks.

"Which one belonged to your great-grandfather?" I whispered.

Buck looked at me strangely. "You don't have to whisper," he whispered back. "It's the one on the left." He pointed toward it.

I walked reverently to the cabin to peek my head inside. My eyes adjusted to the dim light as I examined the rundown interior and tried to imagine the scene there a hundred years earlier. This was the place where their great-grandfather, Captain Lewis, had finally found peace from the ghosts that had haunted him. And where Paddy MacDonald had shown up one day in the dead of winter and told his story of the curse before he died.

I went to look inside the other cabin as well while Buck waited patiently and stood nearby in case I had any questions. The other cabin was much the same, but what I was interested in seeing was the place where the stove had once been and where they had thought the gold had been hidden. The logs throughout the entire interior of the cabin were cut open and gutted from the family's fruitless search for MacDonald's share of the gold.

Buck and I walked back to the car together in silence. It still felt like this was a hallowed place—like visiting some important ancient historic site. There was so much history here, in this valley, at this place. But only a handful of people knew the story that gave this particular sacred spot its life.

This Harsh And Wild Land Had Infected My Soul

Driving back into town, Buck and I returned to the hotel and went to our separate rooms. We planned to all meet later for dinner once the others got back, but until then I had some time to take a much-needed bath and let it take away some of the aches and pains and bruises that I'd acquired over the course of the adventure.

After a bath, I wrapped myself in a towel and sat down to check the messages on my phone again. There were so many of them. Edward writing to me days ago to say he'd returned early from fishing and asking if I wanted to get lunch again. Frantic messages from my parents and Uncle Joe and Aunt Jenny around the time that I disappeared off the face of the Earth. It was too much for me to deal with, so I just hit "Delete all.'

With that problem solved, I went to the address book of my phone and called my parents. Our conversation was very emotional, and my mother and I both cried several times as I told them the story of the past few days (of course leaving out some of the more private details that belonged only to Charlie and his family). My mother insisted on catching the first plane up to see me, but I talked her out of it. I was perfectly fine, I told her, there was no need for her to do it. There was nothing to worry about anymore, and I would be home in a few days. I think my father, always the practical one, was relieved about this because the "next plane out to see me" meant his since there weren't any other flights that my mother could have got on such short notice.

After a very long talk, I said goodbye to my parents and called Uncle Joe and Aunt Jenny to repeat the whole story all over again for them as well. There was more crying, particularly by Aunt Jenny, who was delighted that I was alive and well, and I promised I would see them soon on my way home to Tofino.

I wanted to call Skeena next, but at that point the prospect of repeating the whole story for a third time with even more crying was too much for me, so I simply sent her a long text message saying that I was all right after a crazy few days and that I would be home soon. She would understand.

After all that, I just flopped down on my back on the bed. I was utterly exhausted—both physically and mentally—and I was looking forward to being at the controls of my own plane once again, up in the sky all alone with my thoughts and music. For me, flying was always a kind of high-speed meditation. Only up high with the clouds could I really find myself and get some perspective on the world.

I was about to let myself drop off to sleep when I heard a knock at the door.

I jumped up off the bed and ran over to look through the peephole. It was Will. They were apparently back from Top Of The World highway with the SUV and the gold.

"Who is it?" I asked out of habit, since I already knew it was Will.

"It's Will," I heard his voice through the door. "I just wanted to see if you're up for getting something to eat."

"Absolutely," I replied. "I'll be out in two minutes."

I quickly pulled on my clothes and brushed my hair, then met the rest of them out in the hallway. Edward was with them, but he was keeping his head down and looking ashamed. He looked and walked like some penitent criminal being led away in handcuffs, but of course Charlie and the others didn't have him tied up. I didn't know what their family punishment would be for him, but I also didn't care. I was just glad that he didn't try to talk to me, because I wasn't sure I wanted to say hello to him.

"Everyone feels like Sourdough Joe's," Charlie said. "But I told them we already were there for lunch."

"Doesn't matter," I replied, shrugging. "I'm up for that. Besides, we didn't finish lunch anyway."

With that decided, we left the hotel and walked through town down toward the river. It was a lovely evening. Surprisingly warm for a place so far north and so late in the year. But even in the warmth there was still a chill and a smell and a feeling in the air that reminded you that winter was coming fast and hard.

We pulled together some tables at the back of Sourdough Joe's to make room for all of us, and we ordered drinks and food. Beers all around for the others and a tea for me, plus another bowl of the delicious chowder and some fish and chips (Charlie's fish and chips from earlier in the day had looked pretty good, I decided).

"Cheers," Charlie said, raising a glass once the drinks arrived. "To Kitty, who did one hell of a job flying today."

"To Kitty," they echoed in reply (except Edward), and we clinked our glasses together while I blushed.

The food arrived shortly afterward and soon our table was alive with conversation and laughter. Even Edward managed loosen up a little bit and chuckled occasionally as the people around him made jokes at his expense. More beers were ordered and our little dinner party got even more rowdy.

By the end of the evening everyone (except me) was a little bit tipsy and had to stumble and lean on each other all the way back to the hotel through the dark and deserted streets. I said goodnight, and we arranged to meet the next morning at a bakery down on Front Street, close to where my plane was parked.

Closing my hotel room door behind me, I leaned back against the wall for a moment to catch my breath and collect my thoughts. Everything felt so normal now. It was now a world of restaurants and laughter and hotel rooms and hot baths and teeth brushing. The world of the Chilkoot Trail was already a million miles away.

But even though I was glad to be back in such a normal world and glad to be going home, a part of me still longed to be out there on the Chilkoot Trail, pulling myself to the summit, one boulder at a time. Sleeping in tents, riding the rivers, seeing the mountains and lakes and valleys by day, and looking at the skies full of stars and the northern lights by night. All of these things pulled at something inside my heart as I slowly readjusted myself to the real world. This harsh and wild land of the north and all its adventure had infected my soul, and I would never be the same again.

CHAPTER THIRTY-TWO

Don't Worry, Darlin'—We'll See Each Other Again

I woke up early the next morning, and after taking a shower I grabbed my backpack and went for a long walk through the town. The streets were nearly deserted, and the town still slumbered in the early-morning light. I walked up to Eighth Avenue again and stopped for a moment in front of each of the writers' homes that were located there. Continuing on, I wandered down along the banks of the Klondike and Yukon Rivers, taking the long way to the bakery, where we had planned to meet for breakfast.

Charlie was already there when I arrived, sitting in a corner booth drinking coffee and reading the newspaper. I took a seat across from him and ordered some coffee and a danish for myself.

"Good morning, sweetheart," he said, looking up from his newspaper.

He folded up his newspaper and put it off to the side. "What is your plan for getting back home?" he asked, taking a sip of his coffee.

"Whitehorse first," I said. "I figure that as long as I am up here I should do some sightseeing there and stay overnight. Then tomorrow back to Juneau and back home to Tofino the day after."

Charlie took a pen out of his pocket and scribbled down a telephone number on a napkin. "This is the number of my buddy Chet, who lives in Whitehorse," Charlie said, sliding the napkin across the table to me. "If you need anything, just give him a call, okay?"

I nodded and smiled. "Always have friends and outstanding favors in every port," I thought as I took the napkin, folded it and put it in my pocket.

"What about you guys?" I asked. "What will you do now?"

Charlie took a thoughtful breath. "First we'll go to the police here in Canada with Eddie," he said. "He will explain to them what happened, and we'll see what they think about that. And then, depending on how things work out, we drive back down to Skagway and do the whole thing all over again with the American authorities. And after that, I hope eventually we'll get back to fishing. We've already lost the entire summer fishing season, and I don't want to lose any more."

"And the gold?" I asked. "What will you do with that?"

"Like you said," Charlie replied. "We're going to cash it in and get what we can for it, then give the money to charity. Humpback whales and cancer research. Buck and Will have some other ideas too."

I smiled. "Good," I said. "I think that is definitely the thing to do."

Just then the bell hanging over the entrance to the bakery clanged loudly, and the door opened. Both Charlie and I looked at the sound and saw Will stepping through the door with Buck and Jay not far behind. Eddie was nowhere in sight, and somehow I was glad. He might be their half-brother, but he wasn't one of us. Somehow in my mind Charlie, Will, Buck, Jay, and I were "us."

Will slid into the booth next to Charlie and Jay, and Buck slid in next to me. The booth wasn't made for three people, but they shoved me over and slid in anyway.

"Move your butt," Buck said as he squished the two of us over and tore a piece off of my danish.

"Hey!" I said, swatting his hand away but not really meaning it. "Get your hands off!"

"What?" Buck replied, his mouth full of danish. I was going to miss the four of them so much. They were like the brothers I never had.

The other guys weren't hungry enough to order something, so I quickly finished the rest of my coffee and danish before Buck could grab it, and we slid back out of the booths again to leave. Charlie paid the bill while the rest of us stepped outside and walked slowly across the street to my plane.

"I guess this is goodbye," Will said. "For the second time."

I felt a knot growing in my throat and nodded. "But we'll stay in touch, right?" I asked.

"Of course," said Buck. "You have our e-mail addresses and phone numbers."

"Right here," I answered, patting my backpack where my laptop and phone were.

"And you'll come to visit us in Juneau sometime too, right?" Jay asked.

"Definitely," I replied, wanting to say more, but the knot in my throat was growing bigger by the second and making it difficult to talk without bursting into tears.

We headed down the dock and walked to where my plane was waiting for me. Charlie came jogging up behind us with a large gift-wrapped package under his arm.

"Surprise," Jay said, smiling.

I blushed as Charlie handed me a flat rectangular package.

"You shouldn't have..." I said, but I couldn't finish the sentence without crying.

"Open it," Charlie said. "We all picked it together."

I looked at each of them for a moment with tears slowly creeping into my eyes before I reached down and tore off the wrapping paper. Inside was a beautiful, colorful oil painting stretched over a wooden frame. It was a scene of a lone tent in the wilderness, surrounded by trees. In the distance were mountains and a lake, and in the sky above there were stars and the moon and the Northern Lights dancing. It was beautiful. It was perfect.

I looked up at each of them again, but I couldn't hold it in anymore and burst completely into tears.

Will was the first to reach over and hug me. I wrapped my arms around him and sobbed into his jacket. Then Buck joined the hug. Then Jay and Charlie, until the four of them were standing there on the dock in a big group hug around me at the center, bawling my eyes out.

"Take care of yourself, Kitty," Will said, patting me on the shoulder and giving me some room to breathe as I got my tears under control again.

"Yeah," Jay said, giving me another quick squeeze before stepping back as well. "Take care of yourself."

"I said it before, but I'll say it again," Buck said, leaning in to give me a last hug. "You're a hell of a pilot."

I wiped the tears off of my cheeks as Charlie came over and pulled me in for a big final hug. "These goodbyes are terrible, aren't they?" he said, welling up a bit in his eyes as well.

I nodded. "It's even worse the second time," I said.

"You'd better get going," Charlie said, reaching over to open the cockpit door for me. "You've got some sightseeing to do in Whitehorse. And we have to get back and untie Eddie."

"Untie him?" I asked in surprise.

"Buck's got him tied to a chair back in the hotel," Charlie replied. "You didn't think we'd trust him with the gold again, do you?"

"But the SUV is right across the street where we can see it," I said. "Isn't the gold in there?"

Buck smiled. "Of course it is," he said. "But we still didn't trust him."

I laughed and stepped up onto the pontoon by the cockpit door.

"Okay," I said, slowly climbing up into the pilot's seat and stalling for time. "This is it. This is goodbye."

"Kitty!" Charlie said, stepping up onto the pontoon. He put his hand on my shoulder and looked me straight in the eyes with a smile on his face. "Don't worry, darlin'," he said. "We'll see each other again."

I gave Charlie one last hug and climbed into the plane. Buck untied my forward mooring line and secured it before stepping back while I started the engine. I let it warm up and did my final checks to make sure I was ready to go, then signaled to Will to untie the rear mooring lines and push me out a bit from the dock.

They stayed on the dock waving as I taxied out into the river, but the current caught me quickly, and there was no time for long goodbyes once it did. I gave them one last wave as I powered up and then, wiping the last tears from my eyes, I was soon racing across the water, and my trusty De Havilland Beaver leapt up into the air.

And with that my adventure with the four brothers from Alaska to the Yukon came to an end.

There's Something You Have To See

The flight to Whitehorse wasn't a very long one, but I was glad to have whatever time I could to think and reflect on everything that I'd been through. The past week and the months of summer before that all seemed like a blur, and in that short time I'd experienced more adventure than some people do in an entire lifetime. But now it was time to relax a little bit and catch my breath. And what better place to do that than back in the air in my own airplane. Up in the sky I was in my element, with beautiful scenery below and nothing but my thoughts and me up above.

After reaching Whitehorse, I landed at the nearby seaplane base just outside the city and caught a taxi into town. My first sightseeing stop was the S.S. Klondike—a national historic site consisting of an old paddle-wheel riverboat from the gold-rush era that was permanently parked on the banks of the Yukon River. Visitors to the site walked through the boat from stem to stern (as they say) to learn all about the gold rush and the part played by the riverboats of the Yukon River.

Stepping onboard was like entering a time machine that carried me back to a different era. The cargo holds were filled with all sorts of familiar products bound for the Yukon. The tables in the dining room were carefully set as though they might be serving afternoon tea at any moment. Inside the cabins, the passengers had unpacked, and their clothes for the day were neatly laid out on the beds. And back behind the galley, in the pantry, a half-peeled bowl of onions sat waiting for the cook to return, as though he'd just stepped outside to smoke a cigarette.

As I wandered from place to place, it occurred to me that this riverboat was probably a lot like the one that Charlie's great-grandfather, Captain Lewis, had operated from the other end of the Yukon River. I tried to imagine what it must have been like for him, trapped on the river and frozen out in the wilderness for the entire winter.

Standing in the wheelhouse of the S.S. Klondike I had a reassuring view of downtown Whitehorse and the Yukon River, but from the wheelhouse of his own boat Captain Lewis would have had a completely different view. I shivered at the thought of those visions of the dead coming to him, walking across the frozen wastes and pointing their fingers in accusation. Or their faces pressed against the frozen window panes of his cabin when he awoke screaming from the nightmares that haunted him. You killed us, they had taunted. Your greed killed us.

Leaving the S.S. Klondike behind me, I wandered through the city for a little while, window-shopping and stopping for a coffee at Starbucks. I bought a postcard showing the Northern Lights over the Yukon and sat down to write while I sipped my coffee.

I was thinking about the man who had made this entire summer adventure of mine possible: Alex Tilley. He was the one who had provided me with the money to make my summer project a reality. He had even given me "*a little extra for some postcards and a good meal,*" as he had put it in his letter to me. I'd already had my good meal the night before, but now, at the end of the whole adventure, it was time to send him a postcard.

Of course, there isn't enough space on a postcard to tell the entire story of my summer adventures, but I promised I would write again later with all the details as soon as I got back to Tofino. And then, finishing my coffee, I mailed the postcard on the way to my next stop, the MacBride Museum of Yukon History.

After reaching the museum and stepping inside, I was greeted by the cashier, Haley, who explained the various programs they had running that day. "We have gold panning at 1:00," she informed me. "And The Real Sam McGee presentation at two and gold panning again at three."

It was nearly one o'clock already, so I paid my admission and walked through the museum a bit on my way out to the main yard, where the gold-panning demonstration would be.

When I got there I was surprised to see Haley with a stack of pans filled with dirt and rocks, waiting to start the presentation. She was not only the cashier but apparently also the gold-panning instructor as well.

It was fascinating to finally try gold panning for myself. It was tricky, but following Haley's instructions I slowly got the hang of it.

"Fill your pan with water," she said. "And tip it at an angle as you jiggle it back and forth so the gold flakes make their way to the bottom and into the corner of the pan. Then rinse it with water and let the water carry the top layer of sand and stones away."

I did this, over and over, carefully reducing the amount of sand and stones in my pan until there was almost nothing left. Rinsing was the worst part because I was scared to wash out the gold along with everything else.

"Don't be scared," Haley told me, showing me how to do it and scaring me again with how much dirt and rock she was washing out of the pan. "See how it's washing away only the top layer? Jiggling the pan makes the gold settle to the bottom, so it's safe to wash away the top layer because when you rinse it the gold is left behind."

In the end I reduced my pan of dirt down as much as I could and let Haley perform the final wash so we could check for gold. She was much better at it than I was, and after pouring the last rinse of water out, she expertly swirled the remaining dirt across the flat bottom of the pan and spread it out.

"You see?" Haley said, handing me the pan. "Gold."

I took the pan and was amazed to see a few tiny flecks of gold mixed in among the other small rocks and sand. It sparkled beautifully in the sun, and it was easy to see how people could become so hypnotized by the sight of even a few tiny flakes of gold.

Haley picked out the flakes of gold for me and put them into a small vial of water for me to take home. Holding it up to the sunlight, I watched the tiny flakes sparkle and glitter.

"You'd better be careful," I thought. "Or soon you'll have a bit of gold fever yourself."

Sticking the vial in my pocket, I made my way through the rest of the museum, looking at the different displays showing the history of the city of Whitehorse and the natural history of the Yukon. I timed it perfectly and made my way to a different outdoor yard of the museum and took a seat to see the presentation about the Real Sam McGee.

At 2:00 p.m., Haley joined us, dressed in a man's costume from the gold-rush era, complete with a top hat and fake moustache. Haley was apparently not just the cashier and the gold-panning instructor, but also the actress and poetry reader as well.

She read a the poem titled, "The Cremation of Sam McGee" by Robert W. Service. but first she took time to explain the details of Service's life and background. At the time of the gold rush he had lived in Whitehorse and worked as a bank clerk by day and was trying to make a living writing poetry by night. Then one day he saw the name 'Sam McGee' in one of the bank ledgers and he liked the name so much that he immortalized it in his most famous poem.

"*There are strange things done in the midnight sun,*" Haley intoned dramatically. "*By the men who moil for gold. The Arctic trails have their secret tales that would make your blood run cold...*"

Haley read us the entire poem and following a spattering of applause from me and a handful of other museum visitors, she said that the real Sam McGee had lived in Whitehorse and was a customer at Robert Service's bank. Sam McGee was from Ontario, Canada, not Tennessee as the poem states, and he was never a grizzled old prospector—he actually built roads for a living. But perhaps most important of all, the real Sam McGee didn't freeze to death in midwinter way out in the Yukon, nor was he cremated by the "marge of Lake Labarge" as the poem tells us. All of that was woven together by Robert Service from various experiences into the final poem, using Sam McGee's name.

"And if you need any further proof that Sam McGee made it out of the Yukon alive and well," Haley said, gesturing to a log cabin standing behind her, "here stands the actual cabin in which he lived between the years of 1899 and 1909, after which he left the Yukon to pursue his road-building career in warmer climates. He finally ended his days living on his daughter's farm in Beiseker, Alberta, where he died in 1940."

The audience gave Haley a final spattering of applause and then broke up to check out the real Sam McGee's cabin and look through the doorway. It was a pretty standard gold-rush kind of cabin with some moose antlers mounted over the door, and the interior looked like it was filled with all sorts of interesting stuff, so I waited my turn to poke my head in the door to take a look inside. While I was waiting, I looked down to read a panel giving information about the cabin, and I had the biggest shock of my entire life. I had to look two or three times before my brain could process it fully, and once it did, I frantically dug around in my backpack to grab my iPhone.

"Charlie?" I said after dialing his number and hearing him answer. "Can you drive down to Whitehorse tomorrow morning? There's something you have to see."

CHAPTER THIRTY-THREE

I Know Exactly What It's Worth

"I'll be damned, " Charlie said the next morning after he'd driven down from Dawson and met me at the MacBride Museum right after its doors opened. "I can't believe it."

"I know," I replied, not knowing what else to say.

We were both standing in the yard of the museum in front of the real Sam McGee's cabin, staring down at the information panel mounted just outside the front door. On the panel was some brief text explaining the history of the cabin and a photograph of a man wearing a clean suit and a bowler hat, sitting contentedly in front of the cabin.

SAM McGEE "AT HOME", WHITEHORSE, YUKON

The man in the photograph was older, but the smile and the content expression on his face was unmistakable—it was the same man in the photograph that Seamus MacDonald had given to Charlie's great-grandfather just before he died, the one with the handwritten message on the back. Charlie had shown it to me up on the Top of the World highway after the stand-off with Edward had ended.

"*I hid the gold in the secret hollowed-out logs behind the stove in my cabin*," the note had read. "*You have been a good friend, S. M.*"

"S. M." wasn't Seamus MacDonald, and the photograph that MacDonald had given Charlie's great-grandfather wasn't a photograph of himself. It was a photograph of Sam McGee. "S. M." was Sam McGee.

"And this is the original cabin?" Charlie asked.

"Yes it is," I said. I had done a bit of research overnight and had found out a few more details about the history of Sam McGee and his cabin. "It was originally located a few blocks from here, but it was eventually donated to the local historical society, and they moved it here to the museum in 1961."

Looking up from the panel, Charlie walked to the door of the cabin and did exactly the same thing I had done the day before—he looked in through the door to see where the stove was.

The inside of the cabin was dark and dusty and filled with a clutter of various historical artifacts and furniture from the gold-rush era. And along the wall at the left side there was a big iron stove.

"Do you think it's possible that this is the right cabin?" I asked.

"There's only one way to find out," Charlie replied, walking over to the left side. He took a quick look around the yard to make sure we were the only ones there, then he slipped into the narrow space between the wall of the cabin and the museum building.

Bracing himself, he leaned over and used the knuckle of his index finger to tap along the length of a log behind the stove.

Tap, tap, tap, tap, thwock.

Charlie froze in his tracks when he heard the sound of this final tap. On the first four, his knuckle had hit nothing but solid wood, but the fifth tap resonated differently. It was a sound that could not be confused with anything else—the log underneath his knuckle was hollow.

"Keep a lookout for anyone coming this way," Charlie said. "Cough if someone comes over."

I nodded, and Charlie continued tapping, back and forth, surveying to find the hollowed-out logs that made up the side wall of the cabin. From the number of empty taps I was hearing, there must have been quite a number of hollowed-out logs in that wall, and the available space inside them was quite large.

After he was satisfied that he'd mapped out the extent of the cabin's hidden spaces, Charlie slipped out again and joined me in front. He took a deep breath and looked at me uncertainly.

"Is it possible that the gold is still in there?" I whispered, even though there was no one around.

Charlie stroked his chin and stared off in the distance while he thought this over.

"I don't know," he said. "Is it possible that McGee would have left it there?"

"Surely he knew that his friend MacDonald had died," I replied. "Would he have still left the gold in there if he knew?"

Charlie shook his head. "You would assume not," he said. "But I don't know..."

I was growing more agitated by the second, trying to figure out the solution to the mystery. Was the gold inside the cabin or not? And if it was, what should we do about it? And if wasn't, then where was it? What had happened to it?

"We have to find out!" I said in excitement. "We have to check on the internet or historical records or whatever. We have to find out what happened to Sam McGee and what kind of life he led..."

"Kitty," Charlie said, calmly.

"Did he mysteriously have more money than he should have had?" I said, growing more and more animated as I spoke. "Or did any mysterious tragedies occur to him or his family because the curse was passed on to him, and..."

"Kitty," Charlie repeated, raising his voice slightly.

"Or did he just lead a perfectly normal existence?" I said, ignoring Charlie. "And the gold is still inside the cabin walls, or is it..."

"Kitty!" Charlie said again, grabbing me by the shoulders to look me straight in the eye. I stopped mid-sentence and allowed Charlie's calmness to bring me back to my senses. "Kit," he said quietly, using the familiar shortened form of my name for the first time. "It doesn't matter."

"But Charlie, the gold might still be inside the walls of that cabin," I replied. "Don't you know how much that gold might be worth?"

"I know exactly what it's worth," he replied softly, smiling his clever little Charlie smile. "It's worthless."

The End Of The Adventure

Charlie was right, of course. The gold was worthless. Somehow seeing the glitter of those gold flakes in the bottom of my gold pan had sparked something inside of me. It was like the gold was calling to me and pulling on my soul somehow. Telling me that I needed to have it, that I had to have more gold. And the thought that I could possess so much more of it—that it might be right there inside the walls of that cabin—possessed me.

It seemed that even I was not immune to catching gold fever, and I felt ashamed. But it made me realize what a powerful thing greed can be.

And so Charlie and I just let it be. We walked out of the museum together and left the mystery unsolved. It didn't matter, after all. Whether the gold was still there in the walls of the cabin, hidden away somewhere else, or long since spent by Sam McGee and his family. Whatever it was, it didn't matter anymore. What mattered was that the curse that had hung over Charlie's family for so long would be forever lifted, and there would be no more secrets to hide away and jealously guard for all eternity.

Charlie drove me back out to the seaplane base outside of Whitehorse, and after we said goodbye for the third time, I was soon airborne and heading for Juneau.

The flight south was quiet and easy and exactly what I needed after so much excitement. Uncle Joe and Aunt Jenny picked me up at the dock when I arrived, and we all went out for dinner at a place called the Twisted Fish Company. I figured I'd better have something Alaskan on my last day there, so I had clam chowder and Alaskan king crab legs. Needless to say, both were delicious, and it was a perfect evening to cap off my perfect summer in Juneau.

Early the next morning, both Uncle Joe and Aunt Jenny drove me back down to the dock and helped me load my bags inside my plane. It was a sad farewell, with plenty of tears from both me and Aunt Jenny. I couldn't believe the summer was over. It had gone by so fast. I hugged both of them one final time and pulled myself into the cockpit to start my journey home.

A few last waves goodbye, and soon I was airborne and heading south for Prince Rupert, British Columbia, which was my first refueling stop on the way home. From there I leapfrogged down to Port Hardy, on the northern tip of Vancouver Island, and started the final leg of my journey across the island back to Tofino.

It seemed like only yesterday that I'd flown this same route in the opposite direction on my way to my amazing Alaskan whale adventure. "And don't forget the Yukon," I reminded myself. "You found adventure in the Yukon as well. And made some amazing new friends along the way."

But even though the beginning of the summer seemed like only yesterday, it also felt like something out of ancient history. That summer had changed me somehow. I felt like I had grown up and lived ten years in the space of just a few months. I couldn't explain it to anyone if they asked, but I knew that I was returning to Tofino as a different version of myself than the one who had left not even three months earlier. The thought of this made me feel very proud, but it also scared me a little bit.

Nearing the end of my journey, I flew over familiar mountain peaks and islands, and I felt the past come rushing back to embrace me. I was almost home, and suddenly I couldn't wait to be on the ground again, back in good old Tofino, eating snacks from my own kitchen, sitting and watching television on my own sofa, and of course sleeping in my own bed.

As I swooped down over Meares Island, I knew I was really almost home. It was all like a dream somehow. But I knew it must be real because of all the familiar names that were appearing on my GPS as I gentled circled to line up myself up for a landing. Stone Island, Morpheus Island, Strawberry Island—all names that I'd seen on my GPS a thousand times before as I had come in for landings.

I finished my turn and started to bring my plane down. I could see my parents and Skeena waiting for me up ahead on the main pier in downtown Tofino. As I lined up my final approach, my mom and Skeena jumped up and down and waved excitedly. Some other locals were also nearby loading their boat with groceries from the Co-Op, and they joined in the welcoming party as well. As I continued down, they stretched out a huge banner that read "Welcome Home, Kitty!"

My mom was jumping so much that she almost dropped the box that she was holding. Even from a distance I could tell what it was—a Dairy Queen ice cream cake from the nearest Dairy Queen, all the way over in Port Alberni. And I knew what flavor it was too. My favorite. Oreo cookie.

"Are they crazy?" I thought, wiping tears from my eyes and laughing at the same time. "How do they expect me to land when I am so emotional and distracted?"

I was almost down, when suddenly from underneath the pier I saw the nose of a sea kayak emerge. "You have got to be kidding me," I thought. "If that is Amanda Phillpott, I am going to scream."

It *was* Amanda. She paddled out into the inlet right in front of me, and following proper protocol, I dutifully aborted my landing and pulled up to circle around again. I was swearing as I did it, but what else could I do?

"I know what I'd like to do," I told myself. "Show her a bit of the new Kitty Hawk."

The Kitty Hawk who got herself kidnapped trying to chase down gold-stealing criminals and spent days and nights painfully tied up as their prisoner. The Kitty Hawk who had climbed to the summit of the Chilkoot Pass. The Kitty Hawk who survived running out of fuel in midair and safely landed her plane on a fast moving and powerful river. And the Kitty Hawk who had chased down the armed and dangerous (and crazy) Alaska Jack, dodging shotgun blasts, flying like a stunt pilot over the tree tops and mountain slopes and bringing her plane in for a landing on a narrow highway at the Top of the World.

Sorry, correction on the last point. It was Harrison Ford's plane, not mine.

That was the new Kitty Hawk. But even she had to follow some of the rules of aviation, so I climbed back up again for another try. Over on the dock I could see my parents and Skeena and the small crowd of locals yelling and waving their fists at Amanda. I couldn't hear what they were saying, but I hoped it was something nasty.

My phone chimed from the passenger seat next to me. It was a text message from Amanda.

oops sorry kitty. didn't see you there

Yeah right. I shook my head at her stupidity and continued my long circle around for another attempt.

Why are you bothering? I asked myself. You know she's just going to turn around again and cut you off again as soon as you're lined up and ready to land again. Your phone will chime again and she'll say, oops, sorry Kitty, I forgot my.... whatever back at the dock.

But what else can you do? The little voice in my head said. Except circle around until she gets bored and leaves. At least this time she's being an irresponsible pain in the butt in front of witnesses who will hopefully give her hell about it.

Who am I kidding? I thought. She doesn't care.

So I just continued my turn back to line up for another landing. Out in the inlet, Amanda was sitting in her kayak, pretending to be adjusting something, but I knew she was waiting for just the right moment to turn around and paddle back in front of my flight path.

"Let's just hope she gets bored fast," I thought and started down again. Up ahead, whatever it was that Amanda was pretending to adjust was miraculously fixed just in time for her to grab her paddle again and start turning, of course ignoring all the people on the pier yelling and screaming at her.

Just then, I noticed a flicker of movement under the surface of the water, and to my absolute, utter amazement I watched as a humpback whale breached just to the left of Amanda's kayak. The whale's jump was so sudden and unexpected that it must have scared the crap out of Amanda, not to mention everyone back on the dock and me. The enormous wet black body of the whale glinted brightly in the sunlight as it leapt high out of the water and crashed down again with a huge smack on the surface, sending a minor tidal wave straight at Amanda in her tiny kayak. The tidal wave washed over the kayak and sent Amanda spilling out into the water. I wondered for a moment if she was okay, but then I saw her head bob to the surface, sputtering and gasping for air as her lifejacket held her safely afloat.

"She probably lost her cell phone in that wave," I thought. But otherwise she was fine, and so was I because now she wasn't going to mess up my landing attempt any more. I continued down, keeping an eye out for another glimpse of the whale that had just saved me a lot of trouble, but I didn't see anything.

"That was Walter," the little voice in my head told me. "Don't you think it just had to be?"

I nodded. "It was. I am sure of it," I thought. But I never found out, because I few moments later I landed safely to the cheers and applause of my personal little fan club up on the pier.

I taxied my plane into an empty space at the dock. I would later refuel it before taxiing it back to the dock farther down the inlet, where my father and I both kept our planes. Shutting down the engine, I took off my headset and unbuckled myself while my father quickly tied me up to the dock. Nearby my mother and Skeena and some of her cousins were cheering and clapping like maniacs as I opened the cockpit door.

"Yaaayyyyyy!" they screamed and whooped as I jumped out of the plane and down onto the dock to wrap my arms around everyone. I was crying full on by this point, and I didn't bother to even try to hold back the tears. There was no point. I was too emotional and happy and sad and crazy all at the same time. I just hugged my mother and father and best friend as tightly as I could, and I never wanted to let them go.

"This is it," I thought. "This is my home."

My summer of adventure was over.

EPILOGUE - PART ONE

Jump For Joy Or Cringe Painfully?

tried to sleep in the next morning, but I guess my body was too used to waking up early. I had imagined sleeping until past noon, but instead before the sun had even risen, I found myself lying awake and staring at the ceiling as I thought about all the things that I needed to do.

My mental to-do list felt like it had a million different things on it. I had to write a nice letter to Alex Tilley to thank him for his sponsorship of my research project and to tell him about my summer. I wanted to put in some pictures from the project, such as some of the amazing photos showing the humpback whales' cooperative bubble-net feeding techniques that I had witnessed. Next on the list was organizing all the data I'd accumulated over the course of the entire summer. I didn't look forward to sorting through thousands of photos and hours of video to separate what was useful from what was not, but it had to be done. Then there was the cross-referencing of all that information by locations, dates, times of day, and identified whales. Then cross-referencing all of that against the data from other researchers who had also made humpback whale observations over that summer and previous summers. All that combined information would be invaluable to researchers and students at the University of Alaska or Washington State.

"Oh God," I thought. "I'll never get all of that done. Shouldn't I take at least one day to just rest before I start dealing with everything else? My first day back shouldn't be about doing all the things that I need to do, right? It should be about doing some things that I *want* to do."

Right?

"That's right," I thought, and I got out of bed to walk downstairs to the kitchen to make myself some coffee using the Nespresso machine in the kitchen.

"Look at me!" I thought. I'm having coffee in the kitchen in my PJs! I don't have to fly anywhere today! I don't have to climb any mountain passes! I don't have anywhere to go except back to bed later on to have a nap!

It was glorious.

I pulled up a chair to the kitchen table and just sat there lazily drinking my coffee and surfing the internet on my laptop. By the time my mother came downstairs to get ready for work, I was already on my third cup of coffee and busy dreaming of the future.

"It's good to have you back, Kit," she said as she made herself a cup of coffee and sat down with me at the kitchen table to check her e-mail on her own laptop.

"Hey, kiddo," my dad said when he came down a few minutes later to join us for breakfast. He threw some toast in the toaster and went to the fridge to get some chocolate milk.

"I've been thinking about my future," I said. My parents immediately stopped what they were doing and looked at me suspiciously. Usually when a young person just out of high school says something like this, it either will make her parents jump with joy or cringe painfully. And judging by their reaction, I am assuming my parents were thinking the latter.

"Is that so?" my mother asked warily.

"Yes," I replied. "I've been doing some research this morning and making a few calculations."

"And let me guess," my mother said. "It probably had nothing to do with going to university next year?"

My parents and I had agreed that after high school I would take a year off and use it to make some decisions about what I wanted to do with my life. No one knows what they want to do with their life just out of high school, my father had said, and there was no point spending money on a university if it was just going to go to waste. But it was assumed that after this year off I would go to university.

My father thought I should do some flying during my year off to prepare for a commercial pilot's license. My mother was more in favor of me taking time to travel and see the world. But the idea that I had come up with that morning would combine both of these things, and I expected them to be thrilled.

"I want to fly around the world," I announced. "Just like Amelia Earhart."

My mother looked skeptical.

"*Just* like Amelia Earhart?" my father asked. "You do realize that she disappeared without a trace somewhere over the Pacific Ocean, right?"

"Not *just* like her," I replied, frowning. "I mean just like she had *planned* to do. I will even leave next year on the same day that she started her around-the-world flight."

My father thought about this seriously. "You'll need to put in some hours flying some larger twin-engine aircraft with longer range," he said after a moment. "But maybe I can call in some favors, and we can arrange it."

I shook my head. "No larger airplanes," I said. "In the Beaver."

Now it was my father's turn to look skeptical.

"In the Beaver?" he asked, shaking his head doubtfully. "I don't think it can be done. It doesn't have the range."

"Au contraire," I replied, spinning my laptop around to reveal a Google Earth presentation that I had prepared while waiting for my parents to wake up. "Of course I would need to get some auxiliary fuel tanks to extend the range, including a custom-made one that I found on the internet that can be fitted into the passenger cabin, but if I fly this route, making refueling stops at these locations on the way, I can easily make it."

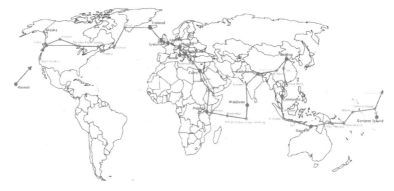

My parents both leaned over my laptop to examine the route I had laid out. My father was immediately intrigued and grabbed a pencil off of the table to use as a pointer while he went through the entire route from one stop to the next.

"And see?" I continued. "I made a list of all the places in the world that I wanted to see and calculated my route so I could visit all of them."

The mention of the possibility of travel and site-seeing got my mother intrigued, and she leaned forward to examine the route more closely.

"Iceland, Ireland, England, Austria, Italy, the Balkans, Greece, Egypt," I recited, naming off some of the major stops on the route I had envisioned. "Nairobi, the Maldives, India, Nepal, China, Cambodia, Indonesia, Australia, Hawaii..."

"You have a problem between Hawaii and the mainland," my father said. Of course my father would notice that. He didn't miss a thing.

I nodded. "That one I haven't figured out yet," I admitted. "But I've only had the idea for three hours now, so I am sure something will come to me."

"You could double back through China, maybe," my father said, thinking aloud, tracing the route across the screen with the pencil.

"Wait a minute," my mother said, pushing herself back and looking at me intently. "Are you serious about this, Kitty?"

I looked at her with surprise. "Of course I am," I replied.

My mother looked at me, then looked back at my planned route more closely, her eyes darting across the screen as she thought my crazy idea through. I could see her becoming convinced as she went from one stop to the next and realized all the amazing places I would see along the way.

My father took a sip of his chocolate milk. "Well, Kit," he said. "You know we'll support you whatever you want to do, but..."

"But what?" I thought. Here comes the "but."

"But something like this requires more than good planning," he said. "And don't get me wrong, for you to even *think* about doing this you're going to have to plan *everything* down to the tiniest detail, but..."

"Here we go again," I thought. Another "but," and he didn't even say what the last one was yet.

"But it's going to cost a fortune," my mother finished his sentence for him and turned to face me. "Kit, I can see you are serious, and I would love for you to do this, but where do you expect to get that much money?"

"I already thought of that," I said. "And I think I know where I am going to get it."

EPILOGUE - PART TWO

I Want To Fly Around The World

Ms. Kitty A. Hawk
P.O. Box 1971
RR1, Tofino, British Columbia
Canada V0R 2Z0

Dear Mr. Charles S. Lewis,

I am writing to you today to ask for your assistance with a project that I hope to undertake some time next year. I want to fly around the world.

I believe you will find that my financial needs are quite minimal. A detailed proposal and information on the modest funding requirements is attached to this letter. Thank you for your time, and I hope to hear from you soon.

Most sincerely and gratefully, your friend,
Kitty Hawk

Some Further Reading (if you're interested)

The Tilley Endurables Adventure Clothing Company: The Tilley company is a real company from Canada that produces the world's best adventure clothing - from hats to jackets, pants, socks, underwear, everything. Check out their website at www.tilley.com.

The Blundstone Boot Company: The Blundstone Boot Company of Australia is also a real company who have made amazing (and much copied) boots since 1870. These are Kitty's favourite type of shoes. Check out their website at www.blundstone.com.

The De Havilland Beaver: This amazing aircraft is one of the most remarkable planes that has ever been built. It was manufactured by the De Havilland Canada company between the years of 1948 and 1967 with a total of 1650 to 1700 aircraft ultimately being built (depending on who you ask). But despite being out of production for more than forty years the Beaver is such an amazing and well-loved aircraft that there are hundreds of them still flying. In addition to being tough they are also very versatile and can be outfitted with wheels or skis (for snow) or pontoon floats (for water). Kitty's trusty De Havilland Beaver is, of course, outfitted with pontoons for take-off and landing on water. Just Google "De Havilland Beaver" if you're interested in finding out more about this amazing little airplane. You can also check out jimthepilot.com and his YouTube videos if you want to see a De Havilland Beaver up close and in action.

Humpback Whale Bubble Net Feeding: The cooperative system of feeding used by humpback whales that is described in this book is a real phenomenon that actually occurs in nature. Visitors to the humpback whale feeding grounds in and around Juneau, Alaska regularly observe this amazing behaviour from organised whale watching tours. Try Googling "Humpback Whale Bubble Net Feeding" to find out more information and to find pictures or video. You can also try searching on YouTube for the IMAX films "Alaska" or "Whales" which also contain video footage of this remarkable system of feeding as well as of humpback whales and Alaska in general.

The Yukon Gold Rush: Obviously, the Yukon Gold Rush (aka Klondike Gold Rush) was a real historical occurrence that came about in pretty much exactly the way that it is described throughout this book. However, for anyone who is interested in learning more about this fascinating era in history there are many great books. My top three are: Klondike: The Last Great Gold Rush, 1896-1899 by Pierre Berton; Gold Diggers: Striking It

Rich in the Klondike by Charlotte Gray; and, The Floor of Heaven: A True Tale of the Last Frontier and the Yukon Gold Rush by Howard Blum.

The Haines Hammer Museum: This is a real place. Check it out at www.hammermuseum.org.

The Fjordland Express: Alaska Fjordlines is a real company based in Haines, Alaska that operates a custom-built high-speed catamaran that allows visitors to make a day-trip from Skagway or Haines to Juneau with whale and wildlife watching along the way. Check out their website at www.alaskafjordlines.com.

Clara Nevada: As many natives of south-east Alaska know, the Clara Nevada was a real ship and met it's end very much as described in this book. However, no one really knows whether or not there was actually any gold on board her when she went to the bottom. Nor does anyone even know how many passengers were on board at the time and were therefore lost. Record-keeping at that time in that part of the world and under the conditions that existed is difficult to come by. However, for anyone who might be further interested in learning about this ship and the mysteries surrounding it I can suggest a short but excellent book by Steven C. Levi entitled "The Clara Nevada: Gold, Greed, Murder and Alaska's Inside Passage". In this book the author recounts the facts of the case as well as the results of his meticulous research to dig deeper into its mysteries. The author even puts forth his own theory about what happened to the ship and where the gold might ultimately be found. I personally don't know whether or not there actually was a fortune in gold aboard the Clara Nevada (I often tend to think not, to be honest) but there's no doubt that the story is itself a gold mine for speculation and late-night campfire ghost stories.

Dyea (or what's left of it): The town of Dyea is a real place that was once a bustling gold rush town of over 8000 people that rivalled nearby Skagway as an entry-point to the passes leading to the Yukon. However, with the opening of the White Pass Railroad out of Skagway Dyea quickly died out and disappeared. All that is left of the town is very much as it is described in this book. A rotting wooden pier, a giant tidal flat overgrown with forest and grass where once there were streets and cross-streets, scattered lumber and building foundations, a false-front of what used to be a real estate office, and a gold rush cemetery containing (mostly) the victim's of what is called the Palm Sunday Avalanche. The area of the town is just a short drive from Skagway and a great place to spend an afternoon sort of reliving history. You can find plenty of information on the internet by simply Googling "Dyea" but also check out the United States National Park Service website for the Klondike Gold Rush National Historical park at www.nps.gov/klgo/index.htm for lots of additional information, including a leaflet for a self-guided walking tour of the townsite of the ghost town of Dyea.

The Chilkoot Trail: The Chilkoot Trail is a real hiking trail leading from the townsite of Dyea up along the Taiya River, over the Chilkoot Pass into Canada, and down from the summit to Lake Lindeman and the town of Bennett. The trail is based on one of the actual routes that stampeders heading for the Klondike would follow to get up into Canada (with their ton of goods - that part is true too) and into the headland lakes of the Yukon River which they would then ride all the way down to Dawson City. The 53 kilometre long trail passes through two separate National Parks on either side of the US-Canada border: The Klondike Gold Rush National Historical in the United States (www.nps.gov/klgo/index.htm) and the Chilkoot Trail National Historic Site of Canada (www.pc.gc.ca/eng/lhn-nhs/yt/chilkoot/index.aspx). The trail is just as it is described in this book and is hiked by hundreds of hikers every year (although the number of hikers allowed on the trail per day is limited). Try Googling "Chilkoot Trail" for a variety of pictures from both the past and present of this fascinating trail through history. Also try Googling "Chilkoot Trail Golden Staircase" for photographs both past and present of the challenging and steep final ascent to the top of the Chilkoot Pass. The photographs from the gold rush era of seemingly endless lines of men climbing to the summit are absolutely iconic images from the history of the Klondike Gold Rush. For a particularly good series of photographs from along the entire trail try Googling "Flickr CAZASCO Benoît Ferradini" who has a very nice photoset and links to video from the CBC of their hike over the Chilkoot Pass.

The Alaskan License Plate: Try Googling "Alaska Centennial License Plates" to see the design of men climbing the Chilkoot Pass that is pictured there.

Fireweed: Fireweed is a wild flower that grows in the northern parts of the world. Its name is a bit misleading not only because it's a flower, not really a weed, and it general evokes images of a blazing red or orange colour covering fields like a wildfire. The flower is actually bright purple and is usually the first plant to start growing again after a forest fire has devastated a region of forest, not to mention that it is found virtually everywhere - hence the name Just like described in the book the blossoms on the fireweed progressively work their way up the stem of the plant as summer progresses, reaching the top at the onset of autumn and winter. Try Googling "fireweed" to see what this distinctive flower looks like.

Grizzly Bear Tracks Versus Black Bear Tracks: Try Googling "Grizzly and Black Bear Tracks" to see the subtle difference between these two types of bear prints. Grizzlies have much longer claws on their front feet and this difference is very obvious in the footprints they leave behind. You can also Google "Bear Marking Tree Claw Marks" to see the kinds of markings that both of these bears leave on trees to mark them.

Standing Your Ground In The Face Of A Grizzly Bear Charge: Try searching for "Grizzly Bear Charge" on YouTube to see some examples of people standing their ground in the face of a charging bear. Despite their undeserved reputation a charging grizzly bear is almost certainly just trying to scare someone off rather than actually attack them.

Viking Wear Apparel: Viking Wear Apparel (or more properly Alliance Mercantile Inc.) is a company based in Vancouver that make fabulous outdoor clothing. "Brave The Elements" is their slogan and they aren't messing around. Whether it's for work or play, you'll never be drier and warmer out in the nasty weather than you will be wearing some of their gear (including jackets, rubber boots, etc). They also make cleaning supplies, oddly enough, which I am sure are just as good as their clothing is. Check out their website at www.alliancemercantile.com.

Lakes Lindeman and Bennett: These two lakes (and others) are real places that form an integral part of the history of the Klondike Gold Rush. As described in the book it was here that the Yukon River begins and where thousands of gold rush stampeders stopped to build boats for the voyage downstream. Try Googling "Lake Lindeman" and "Lake Bennett" to find all sorts of photographs, including some from the gold rush era showing the enormous tent cities lining the shores of these two beautiful lakes.

Aurora Borealis / Northern Lights: I probably don't have to mention that by simply Googling "Northern Lights" you will find all sorts of information and spectacular photos of this amazing phenomenon. Alaska and the Yukon are obviously among two of the best places in the world to view the Northern Lights, not to mention Iceland, Norway, Sweden and Finland as well. But what some people don't know is that the Northern Lights are by no means something that can only be see in the far north. In my experience I have frequently seen the Northern Lights even as far south as the US-Canada border, or further. And not just in winter, quite regularly even in mid-summer. The trick is to get away from city lights and out into the darkness.

<u>Harrison Ford's De Havilland Beaver</u>: Harrison Ford is a pilot and does, in reality, own a De Havilland Beaver just as described in this book. Try Googling "Harrison Ford De Havilland Beaver" to see some pictures of it or check on YouTube for videos from Harrison Ford himself discussing his fondness for this particular aircraft and for flying in general.

<u>Placer Mining</u>: The process of mining for gold that is generally associated with the gold rushes of the 1800s is known as "placer mining". This refers to the type of gold found in places like creek beds or soil that the prospectors used various techniques to extract. Placer mining is very much alive and well in the Yukon and Alaska to this day. Check out some information from the Government of the Yukon website (including the proper procedures on how to stake a claim) at:
www.emr.gov.yk.ca/mining/placermining.html
or www.emr.gov.yk.ca/mining/modern_day_placer_mining.html.

<u>Gold Dredges</u>: The massive gold dredges are real machines that are an unforgettable part of the history of gold mining in the Yukon and Alaska. Try Googling "Gold Dredge" to see some pictures of not only the massive machines operated by mining companies, but also some smaller-scale modern machines operating on the same principle. Also try Googling "Gold Dredge #4" which is a dredge just outside of Dawson City that is open to tourists and maintained by the Canadian government. And of course, try Googling "Gold Dredge Tailings" to see some of the ugly scars left behind on the landscape by these massive machines.

<u>Jack London</u>: Jack London is, of course, a real person whose name will forever be linked to the Klondike Gold Rush. He published several classic books and stories drawn from his experiences in the Yukon including "The Call Of The Wild" and "White Fang". His novel that is given to Kitty in this book is "A Daughter Of The Snows" which tells the story (in part) of a young woman's climb up and over the Chilkoot Pass. You can visit Jack London's cabin (half of it being authentic, the other authentic half being in California) in Dawson City, Yukon. Also try Googling "Jack London" for free online texts of many of his works.

<u>Pierre Berton</u>: Pierre Berton is a well-known Canadian author and Journalist whose name is also associated with the gold rush by virtue of the fact that he grew up in the Yukon, both in Whitehorse and Dawson City, and later wrote one of the definitive books about the era. The Pierre Berton House writer's retreat described in this book is a real home in Dawson City where Berton grew up and you can get more information

about it at its website at www.bertonhouse.ca. Try Googling "Pierre Berton House" to see what the real house looks like.

Robert W. Service: Robert W. Service is another writer whose name will forever be associated with the Klondike Gold Rush. While working as a bank clerk in Whitehorse he wrote a number of classic poems about life and death in the Klondike, the two most famous being "The Shooting of Dan McGrew" and "The Cremation of Sam McGee". He later was transferred to Dawson City where he eventually resigned from the bank clerk business and became a full-time author. You can visit Service's cabin in Dawson City as well. Try Googling "Robert Service Cabin" to see what it looks like.

Sam McGee and his Cabin: As detailed in this book both Sam McGee and his cabin are real. Sam McGee was a road builder whose name inspired Robert W. Service to immortalise him in a poem. He later left the Yukon and went south to continue his road building career and eventually died in rural Alberta, Canada. His cabin was moved from its original location in Whitehorse to its new home a few blocks away on the grounds of the MacBride Museum of Yukon History. You can visit the museum's website for more information at www.macbridemuseum.com. Or try Googling "Sam McGee Cabin" for pictures of the cabin itself.

The S.S. Klondike: The S.S. Klondike is a real ship on the banks of the Yukon River in Whitehorse that is open to visitors as a museum. For anyone interested in learning a bit of the history of the riverboats of the gold rush era this is a perfect place to go. Check out its website at www.pc.gc.ca/lhn-nhs/yt/ssklondike/natcul/natcul3.aspx. You can also Google "SS Klondike" to see what a typical paddlewheel riverboat of that era looked like.

Ted Harrison: Although his name is not explicitly stated in this book, the painting given to Kitty near the end of her adventures is a work by Ted Harrison. Ted Harrison is a well-known painter who has painted many scenes of life in the Yukon during the time that he lived there. Try Googling "Ted Harrison" to see what his colourful paintings are like or visit his website at www.tedharrison.com.

Did you enjoy this book? Personally, I thought it was pretty good, but then again, I am the author, so what do I know? But if you *did* enjoy it then read just a little bit further because what follows is a sample from Kitty's continuing adventures in:

Kitty Hawk And The Icelandic Intrigue

Book Three of the Kitty Hawk Flying Detective Agency Series

PROLOGUE
Peace Towers and Northern Lights

For the second time in less than a year, I found myself taken hostage. My lips and cheek ached from being hit in the face, and my arms were bound tightly together and twisted painfully behind my back. The sensation of the rope cutting into my bare wrists brought back unpleasant memories from the previous summer, when I'd been taken captive out in the woods near Dyea, Alaska, only this time around, my captors weren't going to turn out to be a group of benevolent outdoorsmen like Charlie and his brothers had been. These guys wore business suits and were frighteningly serious looking. Unlike Charlie, I had to believe that when they talked about killing me, they might actually do it.

"Oh God, how did I get into this mess?" I asked myself over and over again.

"I won't say, 'I told you so,'" the little voice in my head advised me.

"You do realize," I interrupted, "that whenever people say this, it is always followed by actually saying, 'I told you so.'"

"You're right," the little voice agreed. "But I did tell you so."

"Shut up," I said. "You're not helping."

Although I am not sure what exactly would help me in my current situation. I needed to think of something fast.

I was tied up and sitting in the back of some kind of military transport truck. You know the kind; you see them in movies all the time, with canvas sides and a bench on either side of the truck bed

311

for people (soldiers) to sit. It was on one of those benches that I found myself tied up with my arms twisted around behind me.

Outside it was pitch dark, and through the open canvas door flaps at the back of the truck, I could hear my captors talking nearby in some foreign language, presumably Icelandic (and I can tell you from experience that Icelandic is a language that is very strange and almost impossible to make any sense of, if you're a native English speaker). It was late, well past sunset judging from the darkness outside, and considering how far they'd driven since first grabbing me, I was sure that we were far outside of Reykjavik and nowhere near anyone who could possibly give me any assistance. I was on my own out here with a group of dangerous people, and I knew I had to get away from them as soon as possible, or my epic around-the-world flight (not to mention my young life) would be cut short barely after it had just started.

I didn't panic. I'd been on my own before. And if my experiences the previous summer had taught me anything, they'd taught me how to stay cool in frightening situations.

I slid carefully and quietly down along the bench toward the open canvas door. I wanted to see if I could make out anything in the darkness outside that might assist me in my escape plan. There was nothing. It was so completely dark outside that I couldn't see a thing. I don't think I'd ever seen such complete blackness before.

"Or wait," I thought. "Is it so black after all?"

I saw a hint of light from the corner of my eye. I leaned quietly forward to peek up into the sky beyond the edge of the truck door, and I smiled when I saw what had caught my attention.

I saw a bright spot in the clouds, off in the remote distance, that was illuminated by a narrow beam of light shining up from earth below. It was faint and very far away, but unmistakable. It was the Imagine Peace Tower back in Reykjavik—a memorial to John Lennon from his wife, Yoko Ono. It was an enormous column of light that shines up into the night sky.

I wrinkled my nose and forehead and thought this over. They usually only switched on the tower of light between October 9 (John Lennon's birthday) and December 8 (the day he was killed), and then again over Christmas and New Year, as well as for other special occasions.

"Tonight must be one of those special occasions," I thought. Or maybe they were just testing it. Either way, I didn't care. Thanks to its unmistakable tower of light blazing up into the heavens, I now knew which way it was back to Reykjavik.

"And if Reykjavik is in that direction," I thought, leaning farther down to look out of the truck at the night sky. "And there's nothing west of Reykjavik but ocean, then this way must be north."

I lowered my head even farther to see some constellations or the polar star so I could orient myself, and I gasped when I saw some other lights up in the sky to the north. It was the Aurora Borealis—the Northern Lights. The heavens outside, just past the corner of the truck's roof, were filled with faint wisps of ghostly green flickering across the night sky.

"That brings back memories," I thought, flashing back to the previous summer and the night on the shores of Lake Tagish, when Charlie had told the story of his family and the curse of the Yukon gold.

I smiled at the memory, but my smile quickly faded as I remembered the situation that I was currently in, which was kidnapped with my hands bound painfully behind my back, suffering from bruised and rope-burned wrists. The pain also brought back memories from the previous summer as well— memories from my trek up the Chilkoot Pass and the various twisting and wiggling of my arms that I'd tried in an effort to get free and escape.

Leaning back against one of the support poles lining the canvas sides of the truck, I slowly and powerfully twisted my wrists back and forth, over and over again in an attempt to work the bindings loose. It hurt like hell, but it was going to hurt a lot less than what the guys outside were going to do me when they came back from their little conference in the darkness nearby. My bottom lip and left cheek were still throbbing and swollen from where the fat one had punched me back in Reykjavik.

"These guys aren't Charlie and his brothers," the little voice in my head reminded me. "They aren't going to turn out to be a bunch of nice guys in the end. They are deadly serious, and they very well might kill you if you don't get out of here."

"Trust me, I know," I replied, gritting my teeth and continuing to work my wrists back and forth. The knots in the rope were slowly but surely getting tighter and leaving a bit of slack in the loops that were wrapped around my wrists. Just a couple more twists, and I would slip my right wrist completely out of the ropes.

"I know full well that these guys aren't Charlie and his brothers," I told the little voice in my head with a grin as I strained and finally pulled my hands free. "Charlie would have tied my wrists much better than that."

Stay tuned for more...

ABOUT THE AUTHOR
(a.k.a. I Like Root Beer)

I like Root Beer.

For me there is no other beverage that is quite as magical and mysterious and inexplicably smooth as a cold mug of Root Beer. From the very first sip this enchanting brew tingles your palette with a plethora of blissful sensations and slides slippery cool down into your stomach as it warms your heart. And don't even get me started talking about that sublime frothy icy mess that we call a Root Beer Float.

When I was younger I fancied myself a bit of a Root Beer connoisseur, drinking my favourite brand A&W from tall, narrow champagne flûtes where the ice clinking against the side of the thin glass created a magical tinkling ambiance as I looked down my nose at all the other inferior Root Beer vintages. As I grew older and began to travel across the globe I naturally was inclined to seek out the very best Root Beers that the world had to offer. Surely somewhere deep in some ancient temple in the heart of the Mongolian desert there was a hitherto unknown type of Root Beer brewed by a secretive order of monks using ancient methods passed down through generations.

Sadly, as I was to discover, Root Beer is very much a North-American thing and you can't really find it anywhere else in the world. The closest I ever got was in the jungles of Sierra Leone which smell a bit like Root Beer and diesel oil. (In fact, most non-North-American people to whom I have introduced this magical elixir have first cautiously taken a small sip then made a sour face, stating that "it tastes like medicine". Perhaps this is because the sarsaparilla root that gives Root Beer its name was originally used for medicinal purposes - typical for North-Americans to turn medicine into soft drinks, right?)

I was crushed. If there was no Root Beer out there in the whole wide world, then what was the point of leaving my house in the first place? No one really needs to leave the house, after all. Everything you could ever need can be delivered right to your front door, including pizza and Root Beer and books and everything else you can find on amazon.com. But as it turns out the world is a pretty great place even without Root Beer. There are a million amazing things to see out there and as many more ways for all of us to see them, as our heroine and friend Kitty Hawk finds out in this book and the ones that will follow.

Whatever you want to call it, "holidays" or "vacations" (I prefer to call them "adventures" and thus lift them out from the realm of the mundane because I believe that it's always an adventure any time one of us dares to go out and see just a little bit more of this world we inhabit), I always like to try and live life with what I call a "Hemingway Complex". I even once wrote a travel book using this as a title.

And what exactly is a "Hemingway Complex", you ask?

Well, some people might describe Ernest Hemingway as being "larger than life". But to say that is not entirely accurate. He was merely larger than other people's lives. He was certainly larger than my life, for example, but he fit quite comfortably into his own. My life isn't extraordinary like that of the great Ernest Hemingway. I've never run with the bulls or told people that I fought in wars or hunted German U-Boats in the Caribbean while drinking cocktails on a yacht. But to me living life with a Hemingway Complex means living in pursuit of the impossible. And it's the only way that I ever seem to do anything interesting. Like writing the very book that you now hold in your hands.

Thank you very much for taking the time to read my book. Don't forget to check out the latest happenings in the world of Kitty Hawk at www.kittyhawkworld.com and it you're interested also head over to www.secretworldonline.com and check out some of the songs that I write and record in my spare time in an effort to try and convince people that I am much busier than I actually am.

Talk to you again soon... in the next adventure.

Made in the USA
Lexington, KY
19 July 2014